The
Restless
Wave

The Restless Wave

A NOVEL *of the*
UNITED STATES NAVY

~

Admiral James Stavridis,
USN (Ret.)

PENGUIN PRESS   *New York*   2024

PENGUIN PRESS
An imprint of Penguin Random House LLC
penguinrandomhouse.com

LIBRARY OF CONGRESS CATALOGING-IN-PUBLICATION DATA
Names: Stavridis, James, author.
Title: The restless wave: a novel of the United Sates Navy / Admiral
James Stavridis, USN (Ret.).
Description: New York: Penguin Press, 2024.
Identifiers: LCCN 2023018475 (print) | LCCN 2023018476 (ebook) |
ISBN 9780593494073 (hardcover) | ISBN 9780593494080 (ebook)
Subjects: LCSH: United States. Navy—Officers—Fiction. |
World War,1939–1945—Naval operations, American—Fiction. |
LCGFT: Historical fiction. | War fiction.
Classification: LCC PS3619.T387 R47 2024 (print) | LCC PS3619.T387 (ebook) |
DDC 813/.6—dc23/eng/20230510
LC record available at https://lccn.loc.gov/2023018475
LC ebook record available at https://lccn.loc.gov/2023018476

Printed in the United States of America
1st Printing

Designed by Cassandra Garruzzo Mueller

TO THE FINEST SEA WRITERS:

James Hornfischer, historian
Patrick O'Brian, novelist
"Il Miglior Fabbro"
The Greater Maker
Dante Alighieri
Purgatorio, canto 26

Eternal Father, strong to save,
Whose arm hath bound the restless wave
Who bidd'st the mighty ocean deep
Its own appointed limits keep,
O hear us when we cry to Thee
For those in peril on the sea!

WILLIAM WHITING, NAVY HYMN, 1860

Midway upon the journey of our life I found myself within a forest dark, for the straightforward pathway had been lost.

DANTE ALIGHIERI, *INFERNO*, CANTO 1

CONTENTS

The
Restless
Wave

What's That Buzz?

Oahu, Hawaii

In his uneasy sleep, he heard a distant, steady hum. Bees.

He often dreamed of the bees, buzzing out behind the small cottage in the Florida Keys where he'd grown up. His mother, Bella, was a fanatic for fresh honey, a staple of her native Italy, where beehives were part of her family's country villa. Bella loved spreading the honey over fresh-baked bread or drizzling it over yogurt. She was born in Florence, of a prosperous family whose leather-tanning business failed, leading them to emigrate through Ellis Island early in the century. On the weekends in Italy, the family would go to a rustic cabin in the Tuscan hills for long, lazy dinners. The table was covered with bowls of fresh berries, cream in beautiful clay pitchers, bowls of yogurt, grilled lamb and rosemary-scented sausages, strong Chianti in green glass pitchers. For dessert there were beautiful sugar-dusted pastries, which the family drizzled with local honey. Bella had learned to gather fresh honey as a child, and in the hills around their rustic country home the family kept beehives. Each weekend night, the trees over the big table on the swept gravel behind the villa swayed in the summer breeze, leaning approvingly down toward the happy diners.

The love of sweetness came with her to America, and in Florida she devotedly tended a half dozen hives behind their home in the Keys. From his tiny bedroom at the back of the house, Scott Bradley James would often hear them droning on hot afternoons while he tried to focus on his schoolwork.

Long after Scott left Florida in 1937 to attend the U.S. Naval Academy in Annapolis, he would hear the bees in his dreams. The buzz would start softly, then grow louder and more insistent as the bees traversed the short distance from the tropical foliage on the fringe of the property to the hives. The bees loved the purple wild orchids, white and green honeysuckle, and bright-pink bougainvillea, returning again and again from their white wooden homes.

He'd been stung plenty but had learned to appreciate the bees' single-minded focus on the mission at hand: creating their tiny kingdom and fighting to build its waxy walls, guarding a queen at its buzzing heart. And the honey was good, raw, and sweet.

As he slept in Hawaii on this Sunday morning in late 1941, the hum began so distantly and softly that Scott was puzzled, even in his dreams, at the bees' lethargy. But then the droning became more insistent, at a pitch he recognized, and in his mind's eye he pictured his mother walking out the back door and heading toward the hives, her smoke pot in hand. He smiled in his sleep.

Then the buzzing changed pitch again, and Scott stirred, half waking. Something did not fit into the normal pattern of his dream. He opened his eyes. Kai, the young woman sleeping by his side, seemed to sense his unease and cried out softly in her sleep. She turned her head slightly, and in the dim first light shining around the edges of the khaki window blind, he could see the small gold cross dangling from her neck.

As he stirred, Scott remembered with pleasure that Kai's parents were away on the Big Island visiting relatives of her mother, a native Hawaiian. He knew they weren't entirely comfortable that their daughter had been dating an officer lately. He'd told them that he had duty aboard his battleship, USS *West Virginia*, that weekend and wouldn't be spending time with their only daughter. Changing a duty section sign-in sheet was easy. He had quietly slipped down the ship's after brow and jumped on his 1938 Indian Sport Scout motorcycle.

As he felt her next to him, all the images of the night before came alive in his mind. They had slept together for the first time, and Kai had fallen asleep well after midnight. He had stayed up another hour, smoking and looking at her. God, it was so good being here next to her. He wondered where all of this would lead.

Suddenly the lovely dreams and memories vanished. The buzzing climbed to a crescendo, and instantly he was fully awake. That sound was not made by South Florida honeybees.

Aircraft were passing overhead, many aircraft, flying in close formation above the dark green hills in the Lualualei Valley, where the small bungalow stood. They were not American planes. Scott loved the beautiful view out over the Waianae Mountains from the lanai in the back, where he had spent many evenings alongside Kai. Now all that was changing.

As the insistent buzz rose and rose, the full impact of his situation landed: absent without leave from his assigned duty, in bed with a chief petty officer's daughter, and uncertain why waves of planes were flying overhead. His stomach clenched, and he realized he was scared.

He reached for his watch on the nightstand. It was 7:30 a.m.

The buzzing grew even louder.

He stepped outside the bungalow and looked to the east for confirmation. Long lines of Japanese Zeros were overhead. Jesus, he thought, where are our fighters? He scanned the horizon, searching for U.S. aircraft and seeing none. All he registered besides the Zeros were the high, heavy rain clouds in the distance above the mountain range, which seemed gravid, with dark gray underbellies, serving as a cold, uncaring backdrop to the enemy aircraft whose engines whined louder and louder as they passed by.

He walked back into the bedroom and shook Kai awake. He leaned over her and kissed her. She murmured something he couldn't understand. "Those are Japanese aircraft, and they are headed toward Pearl," he said. "Do you have an air raid shelter on this compound?"

Confused, she shook her head. "I don't know."

Scott hugged her quickly. "Stay inside. Wait for the shore patrol. I have to get back to my ship." He walked outside, kick-started his motorcycle, and roared off.

2

Reef Points

FLORIDA KEYS

One day when he was eleven years old, his mother asked him what his first memory was. He told her it was of being in a car in a thunderstorm, sitting in the front seat between his mother and father, watching the windshield wipers go back and forth. She laughed and said, yes, she remembered that day—they were driving east and north on the road between their cottage in Key West and his father's fishing camp on Dark Forest Key. "Lord, that was a storm," she said.

What Scott didn't say was that above all, he remembered his mother's fear. She'd been afraid that his father would drive their dilapidated Model A jalopy into a watery ditch. Somehow, he sensed her fear that day, even as a tiny child. And he could recall her relief when they pulled safely up to the two-room cinder-block structure with a small dock out back on the island. The storm was passing over as they unloaded the car, and the last drizzle of the lingering squalls spat on the corrugated tin roof of the tiny dwelling. For the rest of his life, Scott would remember talking to his mother about the storm of his earliest memories. He'd see plenty of big Florida storms as he grew older, of course, but that sense of worry about seeing one brewing on the horizon, followed by a sense of relief and release when it ended, stayed with him over the years. He gained a faith in good outcomes but retained a healthy respect for how badly events could turn in an instant.

His mother was the reader in the family. Her family had once been rich, well educated, with an expansive home in Florence itself and a weekend cottage on half a dozen hectares in the Tuscan hills. The leather business had been good to her father, and his two daughters were educated young ladies. Bella had been taught both French and English as a girl, and she often thought back to those days when the family could afford fine clothes and beautiful books. She was proud to be from such an intellectual city and to have grown up with books around her.

When the business collapsed and the family emigrated with the last of their savings, they eventually came to Florida, seeking a fresh start in the agrarian center of the long peninsula, which her father joked reminded him of Italy—just hotter, flatter, and with no decent wine. Bella's father managed to rebuild his leather business, and while never as wealthy again, the family settled into a comfortable life in their new land.

When she met and married Scott's father, Robert James, a Navy sailor from the Florida Keys, she insisted on taking a small trunk of books to their new home on Key West. All were classics, including Homer's *Iliad* and *Odyssey*, the *Aeneid* by Virgil, and Dante's *Divine Comedy* with the Gustave Doré illustrations that terrified and fascinated Scott as a child. The prize at the heart of the tiny library was a leather-bound set of the Harvard Classics, a fifty-volume set that she turned to almost every night and from which she gradually educated her son. He loved hearing her read to him, the Italian accent softened by a decade in Florida, but still a lovely, lyrical voice that floated above and around his head as he would drift to sleep. Scott especially loved the seagoing memoir *Two Years before the Mast* by Richard Henry Dana Jr., about a young man's adventures under sail in the nineteenth century.

Bella and her new husband often went up to their modest place on Dark Forest Key. At first Bella hated going up there, far from her friends and books. And she hated the random violence of the Florida weather: the truly dangerous hurricanes, the sudden, blinding squalls and thunderstorms, the unpredictable flooding of hardscrabble roads. But over time, she came to realize that even the worst of storms would break. That sense of life as a series of passages through storms, holding to faith in coming through them, was the essence of Bella, and it was passed along to her only child.

Scott's father frequently wanted a midweek break from his daily work on Key West, where he captained a small recreational fishing boat. The weekends were spent taking rich northern men out to drink moonshine and beer despite the ineffective national prohibition. They smoked big Cuban cigars and went after the big marlins of the Gulf Stream. The clients were largely inept tuna fishermen, and the lunches Scott's mother packed for the customers would end up feeding the fish more often than not—thrown over the transom one way or another. But the excursions paid the bills, paid off the small cottage just off Duval Street, and kept Scott's father on the water, where he felt most at home.

Robert James hated being called Bob. He had been in the Navy during the Great War, a quartermaster on a little destroyer, where he learned celestial navigation, shot the stars with an old sextant, rode the huge blue and black waves of the North Atlantic, and bound himself to the saltwater life. When his ship sailed south from the high Atlantic toward its home port of Norfolk, he'd stand on the fantail of the destroyer as it shuddered through the gray-green swells, the afterdecks of the ship rising and falling. Robert's eyes would be drawn to the distant line of the horizon, where the sea met the sky, and in those moments, he felt a peace he'd not known growing up in central Florida on a midsize cattle ranch. He was looking at something far bigger than his own small life: God lives in those big rollers, Robert would think, and I'm looking at eternity.

After the war, Robert James came back to Florida, but he knew he wanted a life by the sea, not on an inland farm. Robert said goodbye to his parents and hitched a ride to the bottom of Florida, to the small village of Key West, and hooked on with a couple of fishing captains, bouncing back and forth between commercial fishing and charter work with tourists. He met Bella in 1920 in Tarpon Springs, and their only child was born late that year, at a time when the recovery from the Spanish flu and a high-flying postwar economy combined to bring tourists to the salt air and honky-tonk world of the Keys.

Robert James thought hard about a name for his son. Bella was happy to let him choose, and so Scott Bradley James was named after two naval officers. Robert James had two nautical heroes, and he thought about both of them as he held his newborn son. The first was the dashing British explorer Robert Falcon Scott, whose quest in *Terra Nova* to cross the Antarctic on foot ended in his death in 1913. Scott's courageous exploits had captured the imagination of the world, especially those who knew the sea and its challenges. To Robert he represented determination and a willingness to fight whatever the world put in front of him.

Robert also thought from time to time about a quiet American rear admiral who had embarked briefly aboard his destroyer during the Great War: Bradley Fiske. Robert admired Fiske's magnificent walrus mustache and heard from the lieutenant who was the navigator in command of the quartermaster's division that Rear Admiral Fiske was worshipped in much of the new American steel Navy. Robert could remember the lieutenant saying that Fiske was a brilliant inventor and the best ship handler anyone had ever seen. After Fiske retired, Robert read an article by him in a naval journal, laying out the case for a war between the U.S. and Japan in the Pacific. Robert didn't have an opinion about that one way or the other, but he figured anyone who could invent things, drive a ship, and write articles about big world issues was someone to admire.

When Rear Admiral Fiske walked onto the bridge of the destroyer, the destroyer's captain bragged to Rear Admiral Fiske about his young quartermaster, Robert James. He said no one had

Robert's skill with a stadimeter, the handheld device used to accurately measure the distance between ships. Fiske had invented it. Fiske looked thoughtfully at Robert James, unblinkingly examining the young sailor, and asked him a few questions about himself. The official party then moved on to tour the engine room; quartermaster Robert James stood at attention as the admiral departed the bridge.

At the end of the ship visit an hour later, Fiske asked to see the quartermaster again, and handed him a small book, *Reef Points*, about the Naval Academy. He told him to study it hard and think about becoming an officer someday. The young quartermaster took the book, black bound like a Bible, and saluted the admiral as he walked down the brow.

For the rest of his life, Robert wondered what might have happened had he followed the course suggested by Fiske. But the pull of his native Florida won out, and he fell in love with a beautiful Italian girl from Florence who sailed into his life with a trunk of books. In the end, he ended up a fisherman in the Keys, and a very happy one, who spent as much time on the ocean as any Navy officer.

So when it came time to name a son, Robert told his wife he admired the grit of Scott and the vision of Fiske. "I just hope the boy learns something more profitable than fishing," she said, and laughed.

The Jameses were never wealthy, but business was good enough that Robert bought the cottage in town and then a small plot of land on what many Floridians thought was the most beautiful of all the Keys in the chain of islands connecting southern Miami to Key West: Dark Forest Key, where the miniature deer unique to the Keys were abundant. Robert built the small fishing camp, and when time permitted during the week, the trio would make their way by car and ferry to be by the ocean, fish for red drum and bonefish on the flats, and unwind from the red-faced clients and the bar scene of Key West.

Scott grew up on boats and learned from his father every aspect of the water world that surrounded them in Key West and Dark Forest Key. Up at Dark Forest, Scott's dad kept a small sailboat, a couple of kayaks, and a putt-putt flats boat with a simple gas engine. They spent most weekends fishing, feeding the miniature deer, tending his mother's beehives, and enjoying the immense quiet of the sea around them. Often squalls and thunderstorms would blow through the Keys, and Bella would soothe the little boy, telling him that after the storm the sun comes out, and the sea gets calm again, and we can go and see the bees.

By the time Scott turned ten, in 1930, the Great Depression had South Florida in a stranglehold, along with the rest of the nation. Even as a boy, Scott could feel his parents' tension and unease. But his mother would say that all storms pass, and Robert could always turn to commercial fishing to help make ends meet. Scott too: he had become a saltwater cowboy who could fish and hunt anything in southern Florida.

By the time he was sixteen, Scott had added gambling and drinking to his repertoire and discovered he had a talent for both. His father had a relaxed attitude toward such things, so long as nothing got out of hand and the local authorities were not involved. His mother worried more, but Scott knew roughly where the boundaries were and sailed along smoothly enough. His father looked at him one day and said, "I'll be damned, but I think you're taller than your dad." Robert punched Scott on his shoulder and said, "You're going to be a middleweight or even more." Scott laughed and said, "As long as the girls like me well enough, Dad."

Around the time Scott turned seventeen, his father began to take an active role in teaching him the finer points of cards, especially five- and seven-card stud. "Especially if you end up in the Navy, it's a required skill on a ship, whether you're belowdecks or in the wardroom," he said. Robert coached Scott through plenty of practice hands and taught him how to count cards, when to bluff, how to hold his cards, and when to take a sip or two of whiskey while looking over the rim of the glass at an opponent. Robert also encouraged Scott to learn bridge: "There's more of that topside than belowdecks, and if you go the officer route, that might come in handy too." Scott liked gambling, the small victories and risks. He used it to his advantage on the docks, and his school friends learned not to play with him.

When his father would talk about his days in the Navy, Scott would ask, again and again, for more stories, greater details about ports visited and storms at sea and, increasingly, when he could enlist. On his sixteenth birthday, his father handed him the small black book he had received from Rear Admiral Fiske, the words *Reef Points* emblazoned across the front. The book was the primer for a midshipman, first published in 1903 by a Navy chaplain, and was required study for those headed to the U.S. Naval Academy.

"This might come in handy," his father said, secretly hoping his boy might steer a course that he had let pass by. "Maybe get you ahead of some of the others if you sail that way." His father held the book hard in his hand, and Scott almost had to tug it away from him. For Scott Bradley James, it felt like the key to Poseidon's kingdom, and he set out to memorize it.

The first thing he learned was the answer to the question "How long have you been in the Navy?" The reply was a response every midshipman had to spout from memory when challenged by an upperclassman:

All me bloomin' life, sir! Me mother was a mermaid, me father was King Neptune. I was born on the crest of a wave and rocked in the cradle of the deep. Seaweed and barnacles are me clothes. Every tooth in me head is a marlinspike; the hair on me head is hemp. Every bone in me body is a spar, and when I spits, I spits tar! I'se hard, I is, I am, I are!

That night he fell asleep saying the words to himself, over and over.

And he loved to fight. He learned from the local Navy recruiter that midshipmen at the academy had to take boxing classes, and he went looking for a coach. He learned to box early and well, taught by both his father and a local trainer who put on exhibitions and was known to have gone six rounds with Ernest Hemingway, despite giving away twenty pounds to the author. Scott often would go to the small wooden gym after school, just a boxing ring, some heavy bags, and a row of light leather speed bags by the doorway. He'd loosen up with light weights, then spend an hour or two sparring, hitting the bags, anything to burn the energy that was surging through his growing frame. As he hit the bags, he'd think to himself, Sooner or later I will be someone who can punch my way through anything—from a drunk in the bar to a roaring squall at sea. And I will get to the other side, where the sea is calm again.

Bella, Not *Pilar*

GULF STREAM, KEY WEST, FLORIDA

E rnest Hemingway lived in Key West, he loved fishing, and he could box. Scott knew these three things. He would hear about him at the gym, where his coach talked about the big man's right hand with near awe. The writer was a presence around town, from the docks to Sloppy Joe's bar. Robert James was often moored near *Pilar*, Hemingway's fishing boat. Hemingway ran the board hard and banged it alongside the pier often enough that other boats tried to avoid being tied up alongside her. In the spring of 1937, he ran *Pilar* aground on the flats off the mouth of Key West hard enough to crack the propeller, crush the rudder, and bend the shaft. *Pilar* had to be ignominiously towed back into harbor, and its famous owner slunk off to Sloppy Joe's, loudly blaming his long-suffering deckhand for not warning him of the approaching shallows.

When he heard *Pilar* had to be pulled out of the water to be repaired, Scott's father let Hemingway's deckhand know that his boat was available for a reasonable charter. Robert heard from the bartender at Sloppy Joe's that a group of men in Papa's gang were down from New York for a week of fishing and drinking, followed by more fishing and even more drinking. Robert knew they would need a boat of reasonable size, along the lines of *Pilar*, that could accommodate a few day trips out deep on the Gulf Stream. Scott was pressed into service with his dad and one other sailor who normally ran the family boat with the senior James.

On a bright, hot Tuesday around noon, a hungover-looking Hemingway led his crew of four friends up the small gangplank onto *Bella*, the James family boat. Hemingway asked about the origin of the name, and laughed when Robert told him the boat was named after his wife. "Maybe I should try that. Pauline isn't too happy about how much time I spend on a boat named after a heroine in one of my books. I keep telling her it's actually a nice nickname for her, but she always says, 'Why not Pauline?'" Robert laughed, the cronies all chuckled, and Scott let out a breath.

"Where's the beer?" the writer barked. Scott popped open the big ice chest, which he'd filled with Hatuey, a local Cuban beer that Hemingway liked. "Hey, youngster, good choice," he barked again. "This is named after an Indian the Spanish burned at the stake. When they were about to light him up, he was given a choice of heaven if he converted on the stake, or hell if he didn't." Hemingway took a swig of beer. "Damn if he didn't ask the priest where all the Christians went, and when they told him heaven, he said, 'I'd rather go to hell.' True story. Early fifteen hundreds. A toast, gentlemen, to Chief Hatuey, who ended up getting toasted himself, come to think of it." More laughter from the gang, and a polite smile from Scott.

After everyone had an ice-cold beer in hand, Hemingway got down to business, addressing Scott's father. "Cap'n Robert, I'm sure you know these waters as well as I do, and we're happy to be in your hands, at least to start. Let's get underway for the best fishing spot you know for big-game fish. How's the bait situation?" Scott opened another big ice chest, this one full of a choice of bait from small gulf shrimp to bigger bait fish glistening in the afternoon sun. Hemingway nodded his approval and held out his empty bottle of Hatuey. "And I'll take another one of these. What's your name, youngster?"

Scott neatly popped the cap on another beer and handed it across. "Scott, Mr. Hemingway."

Hemingway sized Scott up—strong and husky, almost as tall as Hemingway, with an open, smiling face. "Call me Papa," said Hemingway. "Everyone else does. As long as your actual dad over there doesn't mind." Scott smiled, nodded, and handed around another round of beers to the gang. "Grab one for yourself, youngster," said Hemingway, and ambled toward the flying bridge to confer with Scott's dad. It was clear Hemingway saw everyone on board as a drinking partner and a member of the audience.

They stayed on the water through a blistering afternoon, and the fishing was exceptional. After Hemingway landed the first big tuna, he spent most of the time coaching his New York friends, trying to duplicate his success for each of them. As the afternoon wore on, one by one, they all managed to bring something up and over the rail. Scott kept moving between them, backing up

Hemingway's coaching with fresh bait, repair of the fishing lines, and cold beer. By the time the New Yorkers had each landed something respectable, they were deep on the Gulf Stream, and cracking open the big bottles of Bacardi Carta de Oro rum Scott had brought out. Scott looked out at the turquoise-blue waters, seeing them merging with the darker waters just at the western edge of the stream. There was a small pod of dolphins playing right on the edge of the warmer Gulf Stream and the cooler Atlantic waters. Whenever Scott saw dolphins, he knew the fishing would be good. And their playful, athletic jumps, sleek and wet, made his own heart jump pleasurably in time with their leaps. God, he thought, I love being at sea. I could live forever out here.

It was a nearly religious experience for Scott being on the deep ocean, far out of sight of land, the sea and sky everywhere around him. He stood on the flying bridge with his dad, neither speaking. The sounds of the fishing party faded from Scott's hearing, and all he felt and sensed and heard was the rush of the blue ocean running under the keel, the steady hum of the diesel engine, and the humid, tropical air going by. His father had a hand loosely on the wheel, steering by sight on the sun's position and the color of the Gulf Stream. He looked over at Scott, their eyes met, and both smiled.

"Hey, youngster, look alive," shouted Ernest Hemingway from the bottom of the ladder headed up to the open bridge. He asked if Scott had any limes on board, and when Scott showed him a large basket full of limes and lemons, the big man's eyes lit up. "Now, for extra credit, youngster, any sugar?" Scott nodded and pulled a paper bag of sugar out of the cupboard in the tiny galley.

With ingredients in hand, Hemingway started chopping and squeezing limes by the handful, pulsing the fresh juice into a couple of big pitchers Scott filled with chipped ice. Then a big handful of sugar and a bottle or so of rum in each of the pitchers. Hemingway grabbed the handle of a gaff hook and stirred the daiquiris vigorously, creating a light froth on the top. Then he took one of the pitchers by the handle and raised it to his lips, drinking deeply. "One for me and one for the rest of you," he said, wiping the foam out of his beard. Scott handed around coffee mugs and soon both pitchers were emptied. As *Bella* turned west into a setting sun, the gang settled into a couple of deck chairs, the two fishing chairs, and impromptu seating along the rails of the small fantail.

The talk was mostly about the fishing, and the fresh daiquiris, and what they would do that night. Hemingway had asked Pauline to find some friends of hers to join his running mates on an excursion to Sloppy Joe's down near Duval Street, over on Greene. In a lull in the conversation, Hemingway looked over at Scott, nursing one of the last beers from the ice chest. "Hey, youngster, ever done any boxing?"

Scott nodded. "Sure, my dad taught me some when I was first starting, and I've been working a bit with Spider Lockheart, an old prizefighter and now a coach who runs a little gym down here. I like it pretty well. I'm thinking about trying to get into Annapolis, and they teach it there too."

Hemingway smiled. "Hey, that's great, youngster. I know Spider, and he's a good coach for a lefty. You're a southpaw, right? Been watching the way you handle the rods and the beers. Spider teaches everyone the same, whether they are heavyweights like me, middleweights like you, or flyweights like Bill here." He nodded over at one of the New York guys, who might have weighed 125 pounds soaking wet. "It's a sweet science, youngster. Come on down to Sloppy Joe's tonight and I'll show you a couple of things I've picked up along the way."

He turned back to his mates, and soon they were discussing the war in Spain. Hemingway looked out to sea, to the east, and said, "Spain's out there, few thousand miles. The Spanish ruled these waters for hundreds of years, and fought wars with the Portuguese, the Dutch, the English, then with us. Galleons sailed, full of silver. It fueled the Hapsburg empire. But now war has come home to them, and the civil war there is getting worse and worse. Anybody can see it's just a warm-up for a bigger one coming. I'm going to go and cover it in person soon." He idly threw an empty bottle of Hatuey over the transom and watched it float for a moment before sinking in the blue-green water. He turned and faced his gang. "The Spanish Republicans are holding their own, but the Germans and Italian Fascists are flying in to help Franco and the bastard Nationalists. Good people all around the world are heading over to help in the fight against the Fascists. I want to go and see it and bring it home to people here—maybe it can help stir up some support." Scott had no interest in the war talk and couldn't really follow the conversation about Republicans and Nationalists. I wonder if their Republicans are like ours here, he thought, and who the hell are Nationalists?

He went up to the flying bridge and asked his father about going to Sloppy Joe's. "For a boxing lesson with Papa Hemingway?

Hard to turn that one down, I guess. But watch yourself—the drinking he's been doing out here is just a warm-up for him, and believe it or not, he takes the fishing seriously enough to stay more or less sober on the water. But ashore, I've seen him in the bars when he's tanked up, and it's not always a calm stretch of water. Maybe go early, before he's head down and fired up on drink, Scott."

At eight o'clock, Scott walked into Sloppy Joe's and saw the large gaggle of family, friends, and fans that always surrounded Hemingway in Key West. As he approached, Scott noticed a tall, striking woman with platinum-blond hair standing at one end of the group nearest the bar, who was better dressed by a damn sight than the rest of the Key West crowd. She was dressed in a tight pair of slacks that emphasized the length of her legs. A martini in a cocktail goblet was perched on the bar in front of her. I wonder where a dump like Sloppy Joe's got a glass like that, he thought. She leaned against the bar and swept the crowd with a bored and mildly disdainful gaze. Scott saw that Hemingway was playing to her, smiling and nodding at his own witticisms and looking for her reaction. A small woman with dark hair stood next to Papa. Scott guessed she might be Mrs. Hemingway, based on descriptions he'd heard of her as kind of mousy. He'd also heard she was where the bucks came from to finance Hemingway's big lifestyle in Key West. She was turned away from the blond woman, standing close to the author. Maybe those two can have the boxing match, thought Scott. I'd put my money on the tall one.

One of the New York crew saw Scott and sang out to Hemingway, "Hey, look, Papa, the kid from *Bella* is here. By himself and looking like he needs a beer." Hemingway swung around, and even from twenty feet away, Scott saw he was well into a big night on the town. Scott began to wonder if coming to Sloppy Joe's had really been such a good idea. But before he could change his mind, the author pushed through his crowd and approached him, throwing a big arm around his shoulder. "Come on over and meet Pauline and the crowd," he said, slurring his words slightly but moving lightly on his feet. "And I'll get you a drink, a real drink."

In a moment Scott was swept into the melee at the bar, and found himself introduced to Pauline Hemingway, who looked at him with a skeptical eye. "Where did Papa find you, Scott? Is that your name?" Scott started to explain, but she quickly lost interest, her gaze drifting back to Hemingway, who was recounting a story from his days as an ambulance driver in the Great War. No one bought Scott a drink, and that was fine with him. The conversation rose in volume, and eventually Hemingway turned back to Scott.

"Hey, youngster, want to meet another author? A real war correspondent, with a press card and everything?" He reached out a long arm and pulled the blond woman to his side. "Meet Martha Gellhorn. She's got bigger balls than a lot of the guys I know."

The woman grimaced, adjusted her face into the semblance of a smile, and shook hands with Scott. "I'm a local, ma'am," he said. "Scott Bradley James. I met Mr. Hemingway on my father's boat today, and he asked me to stop by." She nodded and bit off one of the olives speared on a toothpick in her glass. Hemingway pulled Scott alongside him and said quietly, "You should talk to her about the Spanish Civil War. She knows more about it than anyone, and it's just starting. She'll be heading over before too long, and I just might go with her." He released Scott, who approached Gellhorn again but couldn't think how to start such a conversation. It occurred to him that she was not just out of his league but out of his universe.

"Can I get you another drink?" he said. Martha Gellhorn took another long look at him, in a way that didn't make him feel very confident. "Why not?" she said. Scott signaled the bartender and pointed at her empty glass. "Are you going to Europe, to Spain?" he asked her. "Probably, soon. The war there is just the edge of what's coming, and if the Fascists can eventually crush the republic, they won't stop there. I want to cover it, and I'll bet Hem will too." She looked at the author and nodded as he turned to her. Scott was thinking, How does a woman get into a war zone? But she looked like she could handle anything that came along. Her drink arrived and he handed it to her. She smiled slightly, nodded a thanks to Scott, got gracefully off the bar seat, and edged toward Hemingway.

That is a serious woman, Scott thought to himself.

Hemingway laughed. "I guess you didn't make the cut for small talk, kid. Maybe she'll interview you if you volunteer to go fight in Spain. Don't worry about it." He downed his drink and spun Scott around so the two of them were facing the ragged crowd. "Ready to go for a round or two?" he said. "And I don't mean a round of drinks." Everyone laughed nervously.

Scott smiled thinly and said, "Whatever you want, sir."

Hemingway frowned. "I told you to call me Papa." He again sized up Scott, who was several inches shorter and at least twenty pounds lighter. They looked directly at each other, both of them half smiling. Conversation slowed, then stopped. Pauline reached out and put a warning hand on Hemingway's forearm, which he brushed off. Gellhorn looked bored and took another sip of her martini. Scott wondered what was going to happen next. He couldn't quite believe this was actually happening. Hemingway carefully put his empty mason jar on the bar. Five seconds passed.

Then, like a small sailing boat suddenly coming out of a squall, leaving a storm behind, it was over, the danger fading rapidly in the wake of the tiny vessel. Hemingway laughed and said, "Let's stick with a round of drinks, kid. A beer okay for you?" To the bar owner he shouted: "Josie Russell, give the youngster a bottle of your finest ale." Everyone laughed again as the tension ebbed.

Scott exhaled. "Sure, Papa, a beer would be great." The conversation started up again, and when the bottle of Hatuey was placed on the bar, Hemingway reached for it and handed it to Scott. They clinked glasses as the conversation surged again around them, then Scott floated out to the edge of Papa's party, finished his beer, and slipped out of Sloppy Joe's.

For the rest of his life, Scott would remember that moment. Staring at Hemingway's face was like looking into a furnace with a swinging door. There was a bright, angry, flickering light in the author's eyes. He was clearly very intoxicated, but Scott had no illusions about how an actual fight would have gone. Everyone who had seen Hemingway fight, even with a belly full of alcohol, said the man had exceptional boxing skills, often practiced the sweet science with enthusiasm, and was a determined attacker with the reach and raw power to quickly hurt an opponent. But it was that look in the author's eyes that had caught Scott's attention, though the swinging door to the furnace had slammed shut as quickly as it had opened.

Scott asked his boxing coach about it a couple of days later.

"You dodged a bullet there, Scotty," Spider said. "You might have got a punch or two in—in fact, I'd bet on you to do it—but it only would have pissed him off even more. It would have been a rocket ride straight to hell for you. He's got twenty pounds on you and a ton of experience in bar fighting, which ain't exactly what I'm teaching you here. Plus, the cops or his associates would have broken things up, and it could have been a real mess. Not good on the record for trying to go to Annapolis."

Scott shrugged and walked over to the speed bag. He began hammering it hard, thinking about hitting Ernest Hemingway in the side of his head, once, twice, before the older and slower man could counter, then jabbing him hard with a right straight to his nose. It looked like it had been broken a couple of times at least. Those eyes, thought Scott, they were like looking into hell, just for a second. It was a look that he carried in his mind for years to come. It reminded him that a seemingly benign moment could fall apart in a second, especially in the face of a dangerous opponent you didn't really understand.

4

Plebe Summer

Scott knew he had obtained his appointment the old-fashioned way, South Florida style—by impressing the local congressman with his fishing, shooting, and boxing exploits. A few shots of whiskey in a Key West bar had also been involved. The congressman had also heard about Scott's skill around a poker table, and approved of that as well. When the letter with the appointment arrived at the James house, Robert took his son out fishing, just the two of them. He told him to be good to his shipmates, listen to the officers, but know that the chief petty officers were the backbone of the Navy. "Oh, and don't knock up any of those Maryland city girls," Robert said. "A lot of them run pretty fast." Scott knew his father's destroyer had been in and out of Baltimore Harbor a couple of decades earlier.

The new midshipmen fourth class of the class of 1941 had been ordered to arrive in groups of about forty. Many were dropped by their parents at the gate, handed over with extravagant hugs and tears. Scott was alone: he had taken two slow trains to Baltimore and hitchhiked the thirty miles from there. The last ride was from a truck full of produce, strawberries mostly. The trucker smiled when Scott told him his destination. "I hear you won't be needing them civilian clothes overly much," he said, pointing to the cardboard suitcase clutched between Scott's knees.

Scott hopped out of the truck near the front gate of the United States Naval Academy. He was about a hundred yards up the street where the farmer had to turn off and head to the market down near the docks. Picking up his bag, he started walking toward the black iron gate ahead. It was hot and humid, not unlike South Florida, but he could smell something distinct hanging in the July summer heat: it was crabs boiling, and the sharp smell of vinegar and Old Bay seasoning floated up from the docks off to his right as he walked toward his new home. He knew Annapolis was a long way from the sea, parked up the vast Chesapeake Bay, and he already missed the fresh sea air of the Keys, where the ocean was never more than a few blocks away. The cobblestones were unfamiliar under his feet, and he stumbled once or twice.

There were about a hundred midshipmen standing around the gates as he approached, mostly sizing each other up. Height was most important, and the taller ones tended to gravitate together. Scott felt pretty good in that regard, having grown another inch over the previous summer and now on the edge of six feet tall. Their clothes provided another clue, and here Scott was more unsure. He was dressed in a cheap suit and had a cloth necktie. Even he could tell the difference between what he was wearing and the tailored slim suits and silk ties of many of his classmates. Most of them had fresh haircuts and smelled vaguely of aftershave. Everyone looked fit, ready to run a marathon or sail a dinghy around Hospital Point at the Academy into the Chesapeake Bay. It was a moment for first impressions, and Scott was unsure how he would come across.

He looked over his classmates while they all looked at him. The biggest was a sizable Irishman, judging by his accent, a few inches over six feet. He was declaiming to a couple of smaller fellows in a brogue about how he was born in Ireland but was now from outside of Boston, down toward the Cape, whatever that was, and he didn't much like the heat in Maryland. "Could about swim through this," he said, and smiled at Scott, who smiled back. They shook hands and the Irishman said his name was Sean Kelley.

"Scott Bradley James is mine," Scott replied.

"So, you're a man with three first names? What, in case you lose one?" They both laughed.

The moments dragged on. Nothing seemed to be stirring within the gates of the Academy, although in the distance, toward the Severn River and the Chesapeake Bay, you could glimpse the tops of white sailing masts gliding by. Scott and Kelley looked at each other. "So, how does an Irishman decide to join the Navy?" asked Scott, a smile on his face.

"Ah, we're an island, an emerald island, to be exact, and we grow up with salt water in our veins. Especially me, Scott Bradley James, and don't you forget it." They were both smiling, but they were glancing at each other appraisingly.

He's got me by a few inches, thought Scott, but I bet I could wipe the smile off his face in a boxing ring. Out loud he simply said, "I've never been to Ireland, but my father sailed those waters in the Great War. He did say it was a beautiful place to see through a pair of binoculars."

Kelley's smile seemed more genuine. "Let's hope we can go there together on a midshipman cruise, Scott Bradley James. Where are you from in these fine United States?"

"Oh, our finest state, longest coastline in the union, Florida. I'm from the bottom, a place called Key West. Ever heard of it?"

Kelley looked perplexed. "Can't say I have. Why 'Key West' if the whole peninsula runs south?"

"It comes from an old Spanish name, Cayo Hueso, meaning roughly 'island of bones.' The Indians buried their dead, and the Spanish took it first. One of these days I'll show it to you."

Kelley thought for a moment. "Well, Ireland is nothing but hill after hill of bones, mostly Irish but plenty of the English bastards. You and I may get along, Scott Bradley James."

They continued to chat amiably, and introduced themselves to a couple of other classmates. Both Scott and Kelley knew they weren't part of the higher social classes, nor the sons of naval commanders, captains, or admirals. They stood close together and nodded at each other's remarks. Everyone looked like they were trying not to look nervous, and kept looking toward the big black gates. Scott looked up the road toward the intersection where the truck had dropped him off, then down a side street toward the docks. He caught a whiff again of crabs boiling and wondered when they would be fed, and what the noon meal would be.

He started to say something to Kelley about the crabs, but

before he got the sentence out, out of the iron gate came half a dozen upperclassmen, their faces contorted in performative anger. They were all in perfectly pressed tropical white uniforms, with gold stripes gleaming on their shoulders. The visors of their dress caps were polished and bright, as were their black shoes. "Fall in, toes on this line, eyes in the boat, goddamn it!" they screamed. "And don't goddamn speak unless someone senior to you is speaking to you, goddamn it!"

Somewhere in the distance, Scott could hear the tolling of a channel buoy in the Chesapeake Bay, just on the other side of the black gates. They were grouped into squads of a dozen, arranged by height with the tallest at the front of a file, and marched through the gates. Welcome to the Navy, thought Scott. In the back of his mind was a line from his mother's English translation of Dante's *Inferno*, which kept banging around in his head as they passed through the gates to Annapolis: "Abandon all hope, ye who enter here." In Dante's poem, the warning was literally carved into the gates of hell.

He thought back to his mother reading the first two lines of the famous stanza:

Through me you pass into the city of woe:
Through me you pass into eternal pain

I know I can take a lot of pain, thought Scott. I guess I'm about to find out exactly how much.

By the end of the first day, the 560 midshipmen had been grouped into companies of around 40 young men each. Like his classmates, Scott's hair was clipped short in an industrial process of initiation, and he was fitted with the white sailor dungarees called white works, issued a seabag full of uniforms and gear, assigned a room, and taught to march with some semblance of order. When he looked back on it decades later, he remembered induction day as a long, exhausting, timeless sequence punctuated by pushes, slaps, screams of derision, mistakes and harsh corrections, and an unending procession of the swearing, angry faces of the first-class midshipmen, the seniors, whose duty it was to mold the class of 1941 into something resembling a military formation. Several times Scott fell asleep while standing in formation, awakening only when he sagged onto the man next to him, who grasped him and tried to keep him upright. "Hang in there, shipmate," whispered a patrician voice. "It's just the first day."

At the end of that first day, the class of 1941 was assembled into a crowded, shuffling mass in front of huge Tecumseh Court, itself a kind of open space in front of Bancroft Hall, the massive stone dormitory that housed the entire two-thousand-man Regiment of Midshipmen. The first-class midshipmen pushed them into a semblance of military formation, lining them up into rows in their fresh uniforms. The smell was a mixture of sweat, starch from the new uniforms, and the faint salt tang of the Chesapeake Bay, which surrounded the Academy on three sides. Scott stared up at the commandant of midshipmen, a captain named Forde Anderson Todd, who administered the oath of office. With their right hands raised, they swore to support and defend the Constitution of the United States against all enemies, foreign and domestic, and above all to obey orders. Scott thought to himself that it would be a while before he was defending anything beyond his dignity and place in ranks, but the words still moved him.

Early the next morning, plebe summer began in earnest. Midshipmen James and Kelley, roommates by virtue of the proximity of their names, rolled out of bed well before dawn. They looked at each other for a moment, then sprinted to the single sink in the small dormitory room, jockeying for position to shave in front of the small mirror. Then they jumped into their gym gear for physical training on the broad fields of the Academy, surrounded by the seawall and the moaning buoys of the bay.

Scott and Kelley knew that the day would include plenty of hazing, both physical and mental. It was hard to eat anything in the cavernous mess hall with the upperclassmen constantly screaming, slapping food out of their hands, and forcing them to recite endless rounds of nonsense from *Reef Points*. Thank God I had that book early on, thought Scott. The first handful of midshipmen who decided not to be midshipmen anymore simply abandoned ship, walking out of formation to the office of the commandant and quitting. Scott's company of forty lost three on that second day. Scott and Kelley looked at each other with satisfaction each time someone walked out of formation.

The upperclassmen spent a lot of time talking about the honor code, which was simple, severe, and uncompromising: a midshipman will not lie, cheat, or steal. Scott wondered if having a personal copy of *Reef Points* before anyone else was a form of cheating. At this point, he wasn't sharing the fact that he'd been given a copy before arriving, and from a rear admiral's hand no less. The old copy he'd been given by his father from Rear Admiral Fiske was tucked away under the small pile of black socks in the locker in his room. His civilian clothes, as the trucker predicted, had been mailed home on the first day. His upper-class squad leader actually told him they were burned, and Scott was surprised to hear from his mother a month later that they had arrived safely in Florida. He couldn't imagine when he'd need them again.

They learned sailing, which was second nature to Scott; rifle and pistol, also a strength; and boxing—he was a natural middle-weight and left-handed and overmatched several of his classmates. Between these skills and the advantage of having studied the advance copy of *Reef Points*, he quickly emerged as one of the stars of the company.

That is, until they started close-order drill. If there was anything Scott Bradley James hated, it was executing regimented movements by following the shouted orders from the Marine sergeants assigned to drill the plebes. He just couldn't get motivated to learn how to march in a group on a parade field. "When the hell are we ever going to march on a destroyer at sea?" he asked Kelley, who planned on being a Marine infantry officer and liked it just fine. "Shut up and march, ya meathead," said Kelley. "You never know."

The two months of plebe summer passed in a blur. By the end of it Scott had staked out a respectable place in the hierarchy of his plebe company, now down to fewer than twenty-five of the original forty men. He knew his nautical terminology cold, had one of the highest aggregate ratings on physical training, and was well liked by his classmates, as was Kelley.

With the coming of Labor Day, the rest of the regiment would return from summer cruise, effectively tripling the number of screaming upperclassmen bearing down on the plebes.

In Bancroft Hall, the new midshipmen did not see newspapers. They were not allowed to switch on the heavy radio sets in their rooms. Yet they discussed the coming of war in the excited ways young men have always found to imagine what it might be like. One afternoon, Scott turned to Kelley during a rare break in their daily training and said, "So how does Ireland see the war? It's coming, and Germany is going to attack England."

Kelley looked pensive. "We don't love the limeys, but I guess we like the Germans less. Everyone is coming out of the Depression, and starvation is what drove my family to Boston, Scott. The short answer is I couldn't care less about England, but if the Germans get across the Channel, they aren't going to stop at the Irish Sea."

Scott thought about his roommate's view. He really didn't understand either the idea of a war or America's role. So all he said was "Well, you're an American now, like it or not. It's not our fight. At least not yet."

5

Parade Rest

U.S. Naval Academy, Annapolis, Maryland

dress parade at the U.S. Naval Academy is a powerful
facade.

From the outside, it is an extraordinary and extravagant display of precision, elegance, and military prowess: over two thousand midshipmen, all in their dress blues, with tightly fit double-breasted dark tunics, spit-shined black shoes, crisply creased trousers, polished rifles, and gleaming swords, moving as one. The music is stirring and martial; the parade begins with the heaviest bass drums thumping out the marching pace, taking control of the midshipmen, hammering the air like their own collective heartbeats, filling their chests with thunder as the bugles join in. Next come the snare drums and the brass, and finally the cymbals start to crash, accentuating the power of the massive formation of young men. It looks to be as perfect as the sun rising over a flat sea, as unstoppable as the most powerful waves crashing ashore, one after another, the companies of the Regiment of Midshipmen marching across the yard at the Academy.

Inside the formation, it is a very different experience. As a fairly tall plebe, Scott was positioned on the right side of his company's formation, but his view was obstructed by a taller classmate's shaved head and, in front of that one, the head of his roommate, Sean Kelley, the tallest man in the company. From behind him he smelled the mixed odor of sweat, shoe polish, and the vague alcoholic fumes of several upperclassmen still trying to sober up. The spectacle was a tale of two cities: the watching crowd applauded wildly, filled with patriotic zeal and admiration; and the midshipmen, knowing they were providing the entertainment, were just trying to go through their paces and get back to Bancroft Hall, away from the tourists. This is what it must feel like to be an animal in a zoo, Scott thought, and shifted the heavy rifle he was carrying to ease the pain on his shoulder blade.

As the Regiment of Midshipmen halted their march to raise their rifles as one to "present arms" and honor the reviewing officer on Worden Field, the regiment was ordered to "pass in review." Cannons fired and the crisp commands of the midshipmen officers were snapped. As the command "Pass in review" was shouted across the field, the regiment, almost as one, muttered their own derisive version: "Piss in your shoes." Scott wondered where that one came from but knew better than to ask anyone senior to him. He would have gladly pissed in his shoes to get out of marching in a parade.

Unfortunately for Midshipman James, life at Annapolis was full of parades, typically a half dozen in the fall and more in the spring. The midshipmen prayed for a rainstorm hard enough to force a cancellation, and the superintendent prayed equally hard for the events to go forward as a vehicle to impress senior officers and politicians and secure more support for the Academy. The parades were just a part of what Scott disliked about Annapolis— they seemed to him a mindless act of dumb repetition, in which anything creative was both symbolically and practically an enormous negative, like an elaborate Potemkin village, a kind of hollow shell of military precision within which many rebellious hearts muttered their quiet protests. Scott knew one fellow plebe who had submitted a poem to *The LOG Magazine*, the literary publication of the regiment. He was one of the few midshipmen who smoked a pipe, and the poem was only two lines long:

Poems and pipes are all of me,
That still remembers to be free

Scott wasn't ready to write a poem, but he understood what his classmate meant. The parade felt to Scott like being one of his mother's bees, droning along on their endless loop to fulfill an unquenchable thirst for duty. And it wasn't just the parades—they were simply a symbol of all Scott had surrendered to walk through the gates of Annapolis. He desperately missed the sea, and fishing, and the easy evenings watching the sun go down in Key West. Scott struggled to give himself over to the routines of the Academy, and to pay obeisance to the demigods of the upper class, so unformed themselves but willing to deal out corporal punishment at the least infraction. The classes seemed to him to be taught by rote, with much dependent on memorization and little chance to select courses or a major field of study. The lack of simple liberty hurt, especially without the comfort of girls or the chance to have a cold beer. The worst moment of the week was Sunday night, after he had finished shining his shoes, polishing his brass belt buckles, and ironing his neckties: as the moment came to simply close his eyes and go to sleep, his last thought was: Goddamn, I've got another full week of this ahead of me. As he drifted to sleep, he'd grimace and feel sorry for himself.

He hated the restrictions on his personal life. Midshipmen Fourth Class were only allowed off the Academy grounds for a few hours of liberty on Saturday afternoons and were required to be back in Bancroft Hall by sunset. Chapel was mandatory on Sundays, and occasionally liberty was allowed for a few more hours afterward, just enough time to go out in town for a sandwich or a cup of joe, a name some wags said referred to the decision of Navy secretary Josephus Daniels during Prohibition to cut off liquor on U.S. Navy ships. Scott would look longingly at the upper-class midshipmen swinging their dates through the few restaurants and bars of Crab Town.

Every Sunday evening Scott would sit with Kelley in their austere two-man room, spit-polishing his shoes, trying to study, but really thinking about whether he had found the right course to sail in his life. And Kelley was no help—he was utterly devoted to the idea of becoming a combat Marine officer, something so foreign to Scott that he might as well have been rooming with a Tibetan monk or a French winemaker. As he mentally summed up his week each Sunday evening, Florida and the sea seemed to beckon more and more. What am I doing here? he thought to himself, staring at his blurry reflection in his freshly shined boondockers. If he quit, he could pass directly to the fleet as an enlisted man, probably become a quartermaster and navigator like his father.

In his daydreams about chucking the Academy, he always made his break on a parade day. He threw down his rifle and ran up and down behind the files of midshipmen standing stiffly at attention and knocked their perfect hats to the ground. Scott wondered how many he could de-hat before the Marine guards tackled him. A couple of dozen for sure. At least. Maybe more.

But there were times he felt quite at home in Annapolis—aboard one of the small sailboats, in the boxing ring, or when arguing with Kelley about the relative merits of Florida and Massachusetts. But at other moments he simply felt adrift. There are ten times more people in my dorm than there are on Dark Forest Key, he mused. And to add to the surreal feeling of life at the Academy, shortly after the academic year started, a crew from Hollywood showed up to start filming a motion picture called *Navy Blue and Gold* starring Jimmy Stewart and Robert Young. The movie's subtitle was "The Love Story of Annapolis." Some love story, Scott thought. Maybe a love of pain.

And the pain of plebe year was very real. Every morning started with a screaming fit by the upper class, a number of whom were detailed to yell, punch, slap, and drag the fourth-class midshipmen out of their bunks. Every night as Scott laid his head on the flat, formless Navy-issue pillow, he had a sick feeling in the pit of his stomach knowing that he'd be in front of a verbal firing squad in a few short hours. Like most of his classmates, he found that sleeping was hard when you dreaded the coming morning.

After reveille, plebes had to perform the mindless "chow call," bellowing the movies playing in every theater in Annapolis, the menu for breakfast, the officer of the watch patrolling the long corridors of Bancroft Hall. They then sprinted to a formation outside, no matter the weather, where every aspect of their appearance—the dimple in their necktie, the polish of their shoes and belt buckle and cap visor, the closeness of their shave—would be inspected by scowling upperclassmen. Any slight infraction would be noted and demerits awarded, which accumulated as the week went on, leading to "punishment tours" marching back and forth during the weekend over the stones of the outdoor passages around Bancroft Hall.

This was followed by a similar chow call and formation at noon meal, more classes in the afternoon, a mandatory sports period, then a third round before the evening meal. By the time Scott finished gagging down an unsatisfying dinner—all the while being browbeaten by a squad of upperclassmen—he literally staggered back to his room for a mandatory three-hour study period. Each day blurred into the next, broken only by sports and being able to listen to the radio on the desk between him and Kelley. It was a horrible existence, and Scott asked himself every night why he was doing it.

The classes were demanding, and the sports—Scott, of course, had chosen Regiment Boxing—were fulfilling; but every other minute of every hour of every day was a black box of anger and fear. He wrote his parents bland letters, simply saying it was hard but he was determined to get through it, and got bland letters in return. He had deliberately cut ties with the girls he'd dated in

Key West, thinking it was better simply to focus on what was ahead of him. But he hadn't reckoned on the sheer, bleak pain of that first year.

And so he passed, unsettled and unsure, through his first year at Annapolis. He knew at least that in the summer after plebe year he'd embark on a training cruise with the fleet, on a commissioned warship, and get away from all the nonsense and regimentation. He couldn't wait.

Youngster Cruise

SAN DIEGO, CALIFORNIA

After Scott walked aboard the old cruiser in San Diego at the start of his youngster cruise, the first thing he did was check the watch bill. He had the first turn at the wheel on the second dog watch after the ship got underway. That meant taking the helm of a light cruiser, sailing a massive ten-thousand-ton warship into the setting summer sun. If Scott's faith in Annapolis had been tested during the past year, that Friday evening out of San Diego made him Saint Paul on the road to Damascus. The scales of doubt dropped from his eyes. As the sun settled in front of him on a dead-flat sea, the fading rays illuminated a path across the calm water stretching west.

He and his classmates were now midshipmen third class, having risen to that exalted status after the class of 1938 graduated in June. He wondered if he was the only midshipman aboard the cruiser who saw his destiny in the Navy's surface line—the battleships, cruisers, and destroyers of the fleet. Others still thought about the Marines, or naval aviation, or submarines. But for Scott, the surface line beckoned, even given the long "midwatches" from midnight to 4 a.m., the early-dawn navigation drills to determine the exact position of the ship using a sextant, and the deep study of the boilers and turbines that drove the steel vessel through the pulsing sea.

Scott and Kelley convened the next morning for breakfast wearing the dungarees of ordinary sailors. The Navy's theory was that this first cruise for a young midshipman should take him far from the starched linens and served dinners of the officers' wardroom. The midshipmen were outfitted like the petty officers of the warship, assigned a "running mate," and fed on the mess decks like any other seaman. "Who are you lined up with, Kelley?" asked Scott.

"My running mate works in the engineering spaces, and it is so goddamn hot down there I don't know if I can stand it. I feel like I'm headed into hell every time we go belowdecks, steam and hot air blowing, a hundred fifteen fucking degrees. I'm going to try and get assigned to the Marine detachment. At least that would be useful. Anyway. You?"

"Other end of the warship, Kelley," Scott said. "I'm with a petty officer in the signal bridge, up behind the navigating bridge. We put up the flag hoists, do the flashing light. I forgot most of the Morse code from plebe summer, but it's coming back fast."

They sat down, each with a metal tray loaded with runny scrambled eggs, limp bacon, and a slice of bread covered with creamy meat gravy. "Shit on a shingle," said Kelley, looking at the bread and ground beef under a sheen of creamy fat.

Another midshipman approached, Joe Taussig, son of a rear admiral and known in the class as a good guy for an admiral's kid. "Join you two?"

"Sure, Joe. Who're you running with?"

Joe sook a sip of coffee and made a face. "Boy that's been around since the midwatch last night. I'm up in radio, pretty good spot to see the intelligence. They let me print out the intel book for the CO last night, and I got to proofread it."

Kelley and Scott looked at Joe intently. "So what's the skinny, kid?" said Kelley.

"The first dispatches were about Europe, just background stuff. That war in Spain is going terribly for the Republicans, and the Nazis have a ton of troops there. Hitler is making noises about more conquests in Eastern Europe, and so far the Brits and French aren't really doing much. But the real stuff is about the Pacific and the Japs. They are on the move, and what they are doing is impressive. Then there was another section just talking about the Jap shipbuilding programs. Man, they are cranking out the ships, and some of the intel is pretty impressive."

Kelley scoffed. "Those little bastards? Half of them are under five feet tall from what I hear, and don't most of 'em wear glasses?"

Scott had nothing to say—his knowledge of Europe was very sketchy, other than hearing his mother talk about the rise of Mussolini and how he was bringing the country closer and closer to Hitler. He thought Kelley sounded ignorant, but he didn't have anything factual to offer.

Joe Taussig did, however. He said mildly, "My father knows many of the Japanese admirals, including some who speak perfect

English and went to Harvard or the Naval War College in New-port. He says sooner or later we are going to have to fight them or just give them all of Asia. And they will force the British out and make the western Pacific a big Japanese lake.

Scott remembered his father telling him that Rear Admiral Fiske had written an article about exactly that years ago, around the time Scott was born. He described it for Taussig, who nodded vigorously. "Exactly. The U.S. and Japan are like two warships at sea, sailing slowly toward each other almost without the other knowing, like two magnets gradually heading toward a collision."

The three midshipmen had run out of conversation and got up to dump the contents of their breakfast trays in the big trash can near the starboard door of the messdecks. "See you guys at lunch," said Scott, and headed up toward the signal bridge.

The conversation unsettled Scott. He realized how little he understood the big chess board of the world that Joe Taussig was describing, and he wondered if Joe even really did. I need to read more, get more out of the newspapers, he thought to himself. But what really bothered him was the sense of looming threat he heard in Taussig's voice, a sense of inevitable collision. For the first part of the morning watch, he couldn't quite put his finger on what had hit him about it, then suddenly, as he was pulling down a hoist of signal flags, their bright colors flashing against the dark blue of the Pacific Ocean, it hit him: it was a poem. Scott liked memorizing poems from time to time, especially ones about the sea. Back home, his mother would challenge him to recite them, everything from Shakespeare's sonnets to contemporary poets like Ezra Pound, William Carlos Williams, and Robert Frost. On the signal bridge that day, thinking back to conversations about the way the war felt like it was creeping toward them, one sea poem hit him like a rogue wave washing over the forecastle.

It was Thomas Hardy's elegiac poem "The Convergence of the Twain," which Scott had read in his Literature of the Sea class. Scott remembered the story of the doomed ship *Titanic* and the vast iceberg, one built in a shipyard and the other in the North Atlantic. That night Scott went to the small ship's library, found the poem in a battered anthology, and read it with fresh eyes again and again, committing it to memory. It was the final verses that he couldn't get out of his head:

VIII
And as the smart ship grew
In stature, grace, and hue,
In shadowy silent distance grew the Iceberg too.
IX
Alien they seemed to be;
No mortal eye could see
The intimate welding of their later history,
X
Or sign that they were bent
By paths coincident
On being anon twin halves of one august event,
XI
Till the Spinner of the Years
Said "Now!" And each one hears,
And consummation comes, and jars two hemispheres.

As he read the poem in the cramped space, the ship rolling a bit in a southwestern swell, Scott wondered to himself about the U.S. and Japan: Who was the iceberg and who was the *Titanic?* It would come down to ships, he thought, and his destiny would be found in that collision. He knew that the world of destroyers, cruisers, and battleships—the high temples of naval service—was for him. While many of his classmates wanted to serve in the surface Navy, more and more were talking about the new submarine force, or naval aviation, or even the Marine Corps like Kelley. But that isn't for me, Scott thought. I want to drive a ship, a warship, from the bridge, conning it right into the heart of the sea. He copied down the poem, dated it, folded it carefully, and placed it in his shirt pocket. When he got down to the big bunk room where the midshipmen were berthed, he opened his locker and put the slip of paper inside his copy of *Reef Points.*

Navigating Rocks and Shoals

Youngster year was a summer's day sail with a steady light breeze after the harsh and unpredictable squalls of the endless plebe-year experience—the screaming faces of the upperclassmen, the totally restricted liberty, the casual corporal punishment, the awful collapsed look of the plebes who chose to quit. It had been a brutal experience, and over a third of the class had simply walked out the door. He'd had no chance to see his parents, his Key West friends, or even a girl for nearly a year. But if the pressures of that terrible first-year regime were gone, other, more subtle strains replaced them. Academics grew much harder, as if the plebe courses had been designed to simply warm up the midshipmen's minds. Physics, advanced calculus, principles of engineering, and differential equations emerged as demanding challenges. For Scott, plebe year had been easy in one respect: given no options for doing anything but studying, he had managed to do pretty well academically.

But now, other activities beckoned. He'd met a girl, Caroline, at a tea dance late in the spring of 1938, toward the end of plebe year. Tea dances commenced with the herding of the plebe class into half of a cavernous hall, a floor-to-ceiling curtain hemming them in their half of the building. On the other side of the curtain were a like number of girls, students from nearby colleges and high schools. At the far end of the curtain, the Academy's social director, the wife of a long-retired captain, simply pointed to a midshipman and a girl who was of an appropriate height, a bit shorter than the mid. Scott couldn't imagine what would possess a self-respecting girl to subject herself to such a process, but he didn't care so long as he could talk to a female, smell her perfume, and do some chaste dancing in the hall once the selections were complete and the band started up.

Once a mid and girl were matched up, they remained a pair for the duration of the dance. Scott's draw was Caroline Sheehan, a sophomore at Goucher College, a girls' college of under a thousand students in nearby Baltimore. Her father was a Navy officer assigned to a destroyer out of Norfolk, so at least Scott didn't have to explain what a ship was to her. A willowy blond, she seemed to enjoy chattering away with him over poorly made nonalcoholic punch, swaying around the dance floor, and he ended up inviting her back for June Week, the graduation celebration for the class of 1939. Even lowly plebes could bring a drag, Academy slang for a date, to June Week.

When she returned for the festivities the first week in June, they went arm in arm for a walk around the Academy and later a visit to her room at the nearby bed-and-breakfast that catered to young ladies visiting midshipmen. It was a warm afternoon, and to his delight, the boardinghouse was empty of other couples at the moment. It turned out she was unusually advanced in her view of modern courtship, and they spent a quite enjoyable hour in the narrow bed of her third-floor room. He slipped out when he heard voices downstairs, but before going, he jotted down her telephone number at her dorm and her address at Goucher. Scott promised to call and make the arrangements for her to stay again at another of the many boardinghouses just outside the gates of the Academy that catered to such visits. That fall, she visited a number of times. Afterward, he would go off whistling to class, the single anchor of a third-class midshipman freshly polished on his collar.

He was especially happy when he was heading to his favorite class, Navigation. For nearly as long as he could remember, he'd loved the craft of navigating, however small the vessel. His father started teaching him basic visual navigation when he was eight or nine, drilling him on the height of the sun, the cardinal directions, lining up on landmarks, looking at current and tidal motions—all the clues to fix the location of a sailboat on the vast Florida coastline. They would sail, just the two of them, from Dark Forest Key down to Key West. Scott learned young how to figure progress in nautical miles and find his way home. Over time, more lessons taught the use of charts and dividers and compasses and other tools to take the real world and pin it down on a piece of paper, marking the small boat's location, course and speed, and speed of advance across the sea. By the time he was ready to go to Annapolis, he'd graduated to the use of a sextant.

At the end of the second semester of his youngster year, Scott faced what ought to have been the easiest examination of his entire four years: celestial navigation. He'd been doing such work since he was thirteen. His father, the old Navy quartermaster, had taught him every aspect of the art and craft of finding position by the stars. He had sailed through the first semester of Navigation, which had been a refresher on things Robert had taught him before he was ten years old. When Scott first gripped a Naval Academy sextant in the early spring of 1939, it had felt like gripping his own wrist to steady his other hand—natural and comfortable. He was routinely the first of his classmates done with the intricate calculations of navigation position, including the use of the thick nautical almanac and the other printed aids to navigation. As his entire five-hundred-midshipmen class approached this same exam, he felt supremely confident.

So it was an unpleasant surprise to him when he walked into his two-man room and his roommate announced, "Hey, we've gotten a copy of the final exam. How's that for finding the gouge?" Of all the expressions at Annapolis, one of the most sacred insider terms was *the gouge*. It meant, simply, knowing what was going to come in the next big event, generally the questions on the exam. Sometimes it was innocuous, an instructor's encouragement to study certain things from the syllabus. Other times it had a harder edge—a midshipman might have developed a close relationship with a professor, say, and some aspects of the exam had leaked. In

Scott's experience, there was a lot of soft gouge but very little of the hard variety, something that came with real certainty.

Scott bent to look over the jotted notes on Kelley's desk. It looked like very hard gouge indeed: specific questions, annotated correct answers, detailed navigational problems. Scott leaned back sharply. "Where the hell did you get this?"

"It is sailing around the hall. Someone wanted us to have a bit of advance warning."

Scott shook his head and said: "Someone is going to have hell to pay if this gets out, Kelley. Throw that away."

"Sure, I've already read it over," said Kelley cheerfully. "Forewarned is forearmed."

Scott thought for a minute. This was a path to getting kicked out of this place. But then he heard Kelley saying again that it was flying around Bancroft Hall, and he figured, What the hell? Everyone is doing it. They can't kick us all out. He absorbed most of the questions, jotted a few notes on a scrap of paper, and retreated to his side of the room to memorize them. "Don't even think about taking anything written down into the exam, Kelley," he said to his roommate.

Kelley snorted. "I'm not that stupid, shipmate. But this is the real gouge."

They went to sleep that night fortified with an insurance policy, but Scott passed an uneasy night thinking to himself, What am I doing here? I know this stuff cold—why take a chance? But by the time he drifted off to sleep he'd convinced himself it would be all right.

The next day was the navigational exam for the class of 1941.

They trooped into the examination hall, hundreds strong. Because it was a navigation exam, they were allowed to bring in their copies of the nautical almanac. After they were settled in their desks, about to receive the exam, a senior lieutenant commander—a British exchange officer—suddenly stood up at the front of the room and faced the hundreds of midshipmen. He had a displeased expression on his face. He swept his eyes around the class, shook his head, snorted in disgust, and announced in a crisp Oxford accent: "All of you . . . stand up and step two paces away from your desks. Do it now."

At that moment, dozens of fleet lieutenants, their instructors, walked into the room and posted behind the four hundred or so midshipmen, a lieutenant behind each group of about forty midshipmen. They immediately began to go from desk to desk, examining the materials the midshipmen had brought into the room, going page by page through the nautical almanacs. Soon about one in ten of the midshipmen were led, shamefaced, away from their desks and told to brace up against the wall in the adjoining passageway. It was obvious to Scott that these poor souls had jotted down the gouge in a corner of some page in the nautical almanac—the answers to the multiple-choice questions and, even more damning, the positional information that would provide a perfect score on the exam. Somehow the Academy had learned of the security breach, and now there would be hell to pay. Scott looked around the room at Kelley. Surely he had not been stupid enough to actually jot down answers in the margins of his nautical almanac, Scott thought.

Kelley's instructor was flipping slowly and deliberately through his copy of the nautical almanac. After a long, long moment, the instructor dropped it on the desk and moved on to the next midshipman. When it was Scott's turn, his instructor barely opened his book, knowing how skilled Scott was in navigation. But I saw the exam answers like everyone else, screamed Midshipman Scott Bradley James in his head. I wrote them down. I studied them and memorized some of them. I didn't walk in here with a copy of them written down, but I sure as hell cheated. His eyes clouded, and he looked down while his navigation instructor moved on to the next midshipman in the file of desks. He knew he'd skated on the very thin edge of guilt, then had sailed across the line. He had taken the information, rationalizing it as gouge that everyone was seeing, but in that moment, watching classmates pulled out of their seats, he knew, with every shred of his sense of right and wrong, that he was just as guilty as any of them. He just hadn't been foolish enough to walk into the exam room with the answers written down in the margin of one of his textbooks. It hit him hard, and he swallowed, gagging on the sour phlegm at the back of his throat that had welled up from a churning stomach. In that moment, Scott thought wildly about pulling at the lieutenant's sleeve and saying: "I am as guilty as anyone."

But he didn't. He folded his hands, put them on the desk ahead of him, put his eyes in the boat straight ahead, and waited to be dismissed.

8

A Code of Honor

T he investigation of the cheating scandal of the class of 1941 was brutally thorough. The potential for dozens of midshipmen, perhaps hundreds, to be expelled hung in the air like spume over waves crashing one behind the other on a lonely beach. And everyone, both midshipmen and administrators, knew that mass expulsions would be an extraordinary decision, considering the gathering clouds of war.

The probe began with interviews of everyone in the class by the Academy's master-at-arms force, augmented by members of the faculty. The questions were simple enough: Did you have advance access to the test? If so, what did you do with the information you obtained in that manner? Do you know of anyone in your class that had advance knowledge of the exam? Did you hear any rumors of the gouge being available? If so, did you apprise the commandant's office or at least your company officer of such rumors, and if not, why not? Many, perhaps most, of the midshipmen simply lied, because essentially everyone in the class had had at least some level of knowledge of the gouge being available, including Midshipmen James and Kelley. In whispered conversations, they debated the right course of action, whether they should inform on other classmates, perhaps try to cut a deal with the investigators. They heard rumors that some of their classmates were bilging their fellows, naming names, and therefore would get probation and hundreds of demerits but still be allowed to continue with their class. "You know the honor code as well as I do, Kelley," said Scott in a whisper in their Bancroft Hall room. "Pretty damn simple: a midshipman will not lie, cheat, or steal, nor tolerate those who do. We are down for three out of four. At least we didn't steal the exam. Right?" He looked sidelong at Kelley. "Nope, not me," replied the Irishman, looking incongruously hurt. "We were just part of three quarters of the class, at least, that got a sneak peek. But we better come up with a strategy here, and quick."

They decided they would tough it out, simply deny everything. Kelley told Scott he wasn't even sure which classmate had provided him a copy of the exam, something Scott didn't believe but chose to view as noble amnesia. Scott realized that if he were to simply tell the truth and take responsibility—that he'd been offered the gouge—the next question would be why he hadn't turned in the classmate who offered it to him. He didn't have any answer to that other than that Kelley was his roommate and best friend, and he had made a choice that put his relationship with a classmate and friend above the harsh honor code of the Academy. They were both notified they were to be interviewed on the same morning.

A couple of days before their interviews, they sat at the desk in the center of their small room, each on one side facing the other. Their radio, a small wooden one, was playing show tunes that neither of them liked, and Kelley irritably turned it off and sighed. Scott looked at him with half-closed eyes, his glance drifting over the Irishman's shoulder toward the gray rocks of the seawall. It was a foggy morning, and through the half-open window Scott could hear the fog signals from a tug out on the Severn River. I never really liked this place, he thought to himself. Maybe this is a ticket out of hell. Kelley cleared his throat and said, "Okay, we've been over this already, but I don't see any way we get hit for this unless one of us breaks. I know it's not gonna be me, classmate. How are you feeling this fine morning?" He smiled wanly.

Scott sighed and turned his head toward the closed door, as if reassuring himself they were alone. "About like I have all along, Kelley. I feel shitty about it, from top to bottom. We should never have brought that gouge into this room, goddamn it. And we should never have looked it over and memorized it." They both looked down at the desktop. Scott looked up first and simply said, "But we can't unring the bell. And there's a war coming, and we both know we want to be in it, and goddamn if I'm gonna walk out now. So yes, goddamn it, I'm good. I never got the gouge, never saw it." Kelley lifted his head and Scott saw the relief in his eyes.

Again and again, over the course of days, they pledged to each other that neither of them would crack. No matter how relentless the questioning, they would simply deny it all.

The morning came. A few hours before their interviews, they convened one final time in their room. Kelley said, "I just don't give a fuck, Scott. They are a bunch of bastards, and if they couldn't keep the exam secure, and it leaked out, what the fuck? They always tell us that you've got to 'cooperate to graduate,' right? Then this gouge is released into the wild. Come on, this isn't our fault, it's theirs."

Scott shook his head. "You know the honor code as well as I do, Kelley. A midshipman will not lie, cheat, or steal. We are down for cheating, and if we deny this, we are lying as well. Goddamn, how do we live with that?"

Kelley snorted again. "Spare me the big honor bullshit, okay? I was raised by nuns and all they told me was 'If you lie, I'll rip your knuckles with this ruler until you bleed out, you big Irish bastard.' Don't you see it's all a game?"

Scott looked out the window of their room on the fourth floor of Bancroft Hall, an open vista across the Chesapeake Bay. He wished he were out there, sailing a dinghy or helping crew one of the big sailing boats of the Academy or, best of all, back in the Gulf Stream with his dad. The thought of his father made him stop and gather himself. "No easy way out here, Kelley. Jesus, I want to graduate, and I know I know navigation better than most of the instructors, let alone our classmates. Okay, I get it, let's tough it out. No cracks, deny it all, lie our way to graduation. But I hate it."

For Kelley, it didn't seem like a big deal. He went to the interview later that day and came back and told Scott exactly that: they don't have anything on us. Kelley had clearly had plenty of experience lying to authority, Scott figured. Growing up Irish in Boston will do that to you. But Scott had a twinge of disappointment in Kelley—it just seemed *too* easy in a way that didn't do him much credit. It made Scott wonder just how much he could trust his best friend in the clutch. He set that aside as a topic for another day, and tried to focus on what was immediately in front of him.

So Scott Bradley James went into the small interrogation room, its walls painted a pale shade of green, feeling sick to his stomach, with his heart pounding in his chest. One of the interrogators was his navigation instructor, who refused to look Scott in the eye when he came into the room. Scott stood at attention until ordered to stand at ease and take a seat. He took off his hat and placed it on the table between them.

The master-at-arms, a grizzled old chief petty officer, looked down at a sheet and began to read his rote list of questions, and Scott answered in terse phrases, looking down at his polished shoes and hoping he wouldn't throw up. He realized he'd never been scared, truly scared, in his life. Now he was, and it was terrible. It was the slow pace of it that was the worst, a feeling of being on a small boat at sea, with water coming over the side and even bubbling up from below. Scott felt like he was bailing with all his might, but the boat kept sliding a few more inches into a dark pool of languidly moving sea. In his dreams, night after night, he wound up in the water, flailing in the gloom, awakening with all his muscles tensed up, startled by his own hands moving under the sheets.

All his ambitions, his hopes and those of his father, the opportunities he'd more or less taken for granted, hung in the balance. "Mr. James, one of your classmates has testified that you and Midshipman Kelley were given access to the exam by his roommate. It's a sworn statement." The investigator slipped a single sheet of paper across the table, with the signature block hidden behind masking tape. Scott had no way of knowing if this was a technique to entrap him or a legitimate statement. What flashed through his mind was a moment from his Sea Power class, when the instructor was quoting an ancient Chinese warrior-philosopher, Sun Tzu. The instructor had said that Sun Tzu advises us to dissemble, to lie, to twist away from the main attack of an enemy. And there are times when that is the right course of action. But Sun Tzu also says, "When on death ground, fight."

Scott Bradley James was on death ground. "That's bullshit," he said. The investigator stared at him. Scott looked him in the eye. "It's total bullshit," he repeated.

His navigation instructor looked at Scott, meeting his eye for the first time. He nodded once, very slightly, almost imperceptibly, and the investigator pulled the paper statement back. They stared at each other for a long time, Scott refusing to turn away from the chief's gaze. Finally the chief looked down, picked up the paper, and snorted in disgust. All he said was "You are dismissed, Midshipman James. Do not discuss this interview with *anyone*, especially members of your class." Scott picked up his cover off the table between them, fitted it to his head, and strode out as stiffly as if he were on parade. He could feel the stares of the investigator and his instructor on his back.

The next three weeks were agony for Scott and Kelley. Other classmates were run in and out of the interrogation rooms, and rumors were wild: the whole class would be expelled, or half of the class, or there would be a general amnesty given the size and scale of the scandal, or the Academy would try to hush everything up. And the background drumbeat of a coming war was sounding louder by the minute.

Throughout the investigation through the spring of 1939, Scott, Kelley, and Joe Taussig discussed world events. Scott was working harder to understand Europe and Asia, and the role the U.S. might play in a conflict. "I can't believe the Nazis invaded Poland. That's the start of the war in Europe, right?" he said to Taussig. Kelley was polishing the barrel of his parade field rifle, not contributing to the conversation.

Taussig said, "It's simple. This guy Hitler is going to take as much as anyone will give him. If the Brits and the French don't stand up to him, he'll be in Paris by 1940 and London by 1941."

Kelley lifted his head. "The limeys deserve it."

Scott shook his head. "Grow up, you stupid Mick. The Brits are on the front lines for us now. The Nazis aren't going to stop anytime soon. And the Japs are right behind them. And one good thing is that if this cheating scandal goes much further, they aren't going to want to get rid of all of us."

Scott figured the likelihood of throwing out an entire Annapolis class was low, given the very real possibility of combat operations that would inevitably involve the U.S. Navy. But the chances of a few dozen being sent home seemed high. For the thousandth time he wondered whether or not there was a real statement implicating him and Kelley.

Some midshipmen, like Kelley, were able to tough it out and go about their business, heading toward the celebrations of June Week. Others found themselves unable to focus on the simplest tasks. One member of the class, a midshipman named Robb Potts, who lived across the hall and had been part of Scott's sailing team, seemed increasingly distracted, detached, and scared. Scott tried to talk to him several times, but Robb kept pushing him off, saying they could talk on the weekend.

Two days before June Week, there came an announcement about Midshipman Robb Potts. He had committed suicide. He had hanged himself in the tiny shower in his room in Bancroft Hall while his roommate was at lacrosse practice. Scott wondered if perhaps he was the one who first supplied the gouge that now threatened to sink the class.

The entire regiment raised their voices in song that Sunday in the massive Chapel of the Academy, the stained-glass windows alight with the spring sun, depicting naval heroes alongside religious scenes. They sang the Navy Hymn, "Eternal Father, Strong to Save," their two thousand voices mourning a classmate, shipmate, and friend:

> *Eternal Father, strong to save,*
> *Whose arm hath bound the restless wave,*

Who bidd'st the mighty ocean deep
Its own appointed limits keep
O hear us when we cry to thee
For those in peril on the sea!

Well, Scott thought, Robb Potts never got his commission, but wherever he is sailing today, I hope he and God can both hear us.

9

The Fallen Angel

U.S. Naval Academy, Annapolis, Maryland

The investigation surrounding the navigation exam was finally over in early May. The results were not released immediately, keeping the entire class of 1941 twisting slowly in the wind. In the normal course of business, the investigation would be turned over to the commandant, who would then decide to refer individual cases, or entire groups of midshipmen, to the Regiment Honor Committee, the group of midshipmen, selected for their integrity and judgment, who formed an honor court to conduct trials and adjudicate accusations and investigations involving honor violations—lying, cheating, or stealing. Scott, guilty on two of the three, having at least glanced over and absorbed some of the material, felt the walls closing in. He dearly hoped that the "statement" waved in front of him had been a ploy.

But Scott had another worry. Caroline had sent word through a friend of hers who was dating a classmate: she thought she might be pregnant. The news hit Scott hard, like a straight shot to his gut in the boxing ring. For a moment, he couldn't breathe, and he dropped to one knee. Everything in his life suddenly seemed on the line in a way he couldn't have imagined a few months earlier. He was swept by a wave of self-pity: How unfair it was to have all this coming at him! How would he tell his parents, especially his mother? He shook his head hard to clear it. Goddamn it, he thought, I've got two death blows right in front of me: cheating and knocking up a girl. When will something actually go my way?

He walked back to his room, dragging one foot after the other, and collapsed onto his bunk. Kelley was sitting at his desk, and Scott rolled over to face him. "Jesus Christ," he said. "She thinks she might be pregnant. Shit. Don't girls *know* one way or another? We only did it a few times over the course of this whole year. Maybe four and a half times. And I've been trying to sort of cool that one down. I asked her to June Week again because it's fun to have a date for the events, but I want to keep my decks clear for the summer cruise. Now this." He shook his head slowly.

Kelley stared at him, mouth agape. "I don't even want to know what you mean by half a time, Scotty, but what are you going to do? You need to call her and find out what the hell is going on. And if you have to marry her, you'll have to quit the Academy— no married midshipmen allowed, boyo."

That weekend, Scott went to find a phone at the Maryland Inn, a rooming house in the old part of Annapolis. The only phones the midshipmen could use were a bank of pay phones with no dividers between them in Dahlgren Hall. Because there were no phones at the Academy where he could get any privacy, he didn't trust himself within the confines of the Yard, to be honest. The entire event just weighed on him too much. He needed to be outside the physical walls of the Academy as he dealt with all of this. As he dialed Caroline's number, his fingers felt numb. Someone answered on the fourth ring, a girl's high and breathy voice, not Caroline. He could hear other voices in the background. A radio playing "If I Didn't Care" by the Ink Spots. He asked for Caroline in a quiet voice. "Sure," the girl said, "just a minute." The phone banged against the wall where she had let it slip and dangle.

He hung on the line, his breathing shallow, until she came on, her voice subdued and low. "Hello, Scott." She didn't directly mention the possibility of a pregnancy, but said she had some big things to figure out and had no idea what to do next. "My parents can't hear about this," she whispered into the phone. "They'll kill me. And you." Her father was a full commander, and Scott's mind was filled with fear of what a senior naval officer could do to him, reaching a long arm through the Navy to Bancroft Hall. It didn't cross his mind to ask how she felt or inquire about what her plan would be. His mind was churning with thoughts of all the terrible possibilities ahead for him.

For a while, he didn't know what to say. Behind him he could hear sounds from the bar at the Maryland Inn, a woman laughing too hard and a jazz combo playing softly. After a long pause, he asked, "What do we do now?"

"We better figure out a way to take care of it," Caroline said. "I'll need some money, okay? There's a girl here who had something like this and took care of it, but it cost a couple of hundred dollars." There was a long pause. For Scott, this was an astronomical sum. She repeated, "I can't tell my parents, they'd kill me. And you."

After another long pause, Scott said, "I will figure something out to get the money, and I'll call you back in a couple of days."

"I'm so sorry," she said. "I thought it was a good time of the month the last time."

When he got back to the Academy just before the expiration of liberty, Kelley was waiting up for him. "What did she say?" he asked, his thick black eyebrows raised and his face set in sympathy.

"She said she needed a couple of hundred bucks to take care of it," Scott said. "And that she thought it was a good time of the month. I guess it wasn't."

"Ah, fair enough," said Kelley. "At least she isn't trying to drag you to the altar. Yet."

As Scott and Kelley polished their shoes the next morning, they planned their campaign to find the money. Neither of them had much in the way of funds, and neither's parents would likely contribute to what Kelley had dubbed Scott's "Fallen Angel Fund." He knew in his heart it was his fault, his own callow set of values, such as they were. But the more Scott reflected on those afternoons in bed during her visits, the more he felt she was the more experienced of the pair. If anyone got seduced, he told himself, it was me. When he laid that theory out to Kelley, the Irishman said simply, "That's bullshit, Scotty. Takes two to tango. Somehow I doubt you were exactly a pure angel when you tumbled into bed with her. Wake up, boyo, and figure out how to solve the problem. And you better hope she stays willing to go through with it. Believe me, they can go very, very wrong. I've seen it. And then you are done here—off you go to the fleet as a petty officer, if you're lucky. The good news is that isn't exactly what she is hoping for either: to be married to an enlisted man."

There was only one moneymaking skill in which Scott was at all adept: gambling. Growing up in the bars and on the boats of Key West, he'd learned early how to wager and was an accomplished stud poker player. His nerves were good, and his memory in a single-deck poker game was nearly perfect. His father had always been a good card player and reckoned it was a skill he should pass along to his son.

He and Kelley managed to scrape up a small stake by taking loans from several wealthier classmates, and the two of them headed out that Saturday night to the Mandris Restaurant, a red-brick tavern on the corner of the seafood market in downtown Annapolis, right on the edge of the city docks. The Mandris was the current incarnation of the historic Middleton Tavern, which dated to the late 1700s. George Washington, Thomas Jefferson, Benjamin Franklin, and members of the Continental Congress had dined there, and in modern times it was frequented by legislators from the nearby Maryland State House. Off and on throughout its long history, it had also served as a center for gambling, as well as housing the Maryland Jockey Club. A Greek couple, Cleo and Mary Apostol, had bought it in 1932 and changed the name to Mandris.

There was a poker game on Saturday nights in the tavern's back room in which midshipmen were allowed to participate. Scott did not know the owner, but one of his classmates, Niko Stavros, a Greek American from Tarpon Springs, Florida, had met Cleo

Apostol through the Annapolis Greek Orthodox prayer society, essentially an excuse for members to drink ouzo and speak Greek on the weekends.

With the advocacy of his Greek American classmate, and with Kelley as a bodyguard, Scott showed up on Saturday night with sixty-five dollars in his pocket and his good-luck charm, a bullet pried out of the first deer he'd shot and dressed with his dad on Dark Forest Key. He rubbed the well-worn cartridge as he settled in at the table. Kelley sat behind him, a mug of beer in his hands, a looming presence like a lighthouse above the marine-layer cloud of cigar smoke that filled the room. Cleo Apostol moved around the table, sizing up the first set of hands and parking himself across the room with a skeptical eye on the midshipmen.

The first couple of hands went well for Scott, and the half dozen players in the game began to look at him a little differently, less like a rube ripe for fleecing and more like a serious player. In seven-card stud poker, Scott had committed to memory a series of short rules his father had taught him: start very slowly and conserve your money while you size up the table; memorize the cards already played in earlier hands; when you get a big hand, hit it hard as hell; and don't be afraid to bluff within reason. Following those maxims usually resulted in a good return over the course of an evening. While Scott lost a bit more than he won for the first hour, he was still solvent, and the others, unlike him, were steadily drinking highballs. In the second hour, the mix of cards began to turn in Scott's direction, and he found himself again and again still in the game after the river. The Annapolis crowd called it the 7th Street card. As betting went into a third hour, Scott was winning every third or fourth hand, and his opponents were losing enthusiasm for his presence.

One of the players across the table, a heavyset man with a grim face who owned a pair of crabbing boats, started carping about having a midshipman in the game. "Aren't you supposed to be back for a bed check or something, middie?" It was nearing ten o'clock and Scott had liberty time to burn until curfew at 1 a.m., and he was up well over a hundred bucks. But he caught something in the man's tone he didn't like. He folded early on the next couple of hands, and he and Kelley excused themselves. "I don't need that dumb fuck dropping a dime on me to the commandant's office," he growled to Kelley as they sauntered back to the gates of the Academy under a winter moon.

"Oh, he'll not be too worried about that tonight," said Kelley. "While you were laying down on those last couple of hands, I went around back and flattened all four of the tires on his Studebaker. The best defense is a good offense."

With $145 in hand after paying off their investors, Scott called Caroline and told her where he stood. "I'm doing the best I can, Caroline. Look, this isn't exactly my fault. You started it, you came at me. You know that, right?" Even as he said it aloud, he knew how terrible it sounded, how it wasn't right.

She didn't speak for a long minute. Finally she said, "Scott, we both wanted it, and I think it was you who said 'Let's go upstairs' the first time. And I'm the one who has to go through this. All you have to do is come up with the money, and you won't even be there with me. And it's dangerous, and not in a hospital, and I'm scared." The frightened tone in her voice was real.

Scott registered how unfair he was being, and thought to himself, Let's just get through this, and we can start over. I can be better than this. But all he said was that the $145 was the best he could do on short notice, and he knew the clock was ticking. He asked if she could find the additional $50 or so. He felt lousy about it, but it was the reality of the situation.

She said she'd try, and asked him to call her back in a couple of days.

Scott walked through his classes in a fog of uncertainty. The silence on the investigation front didn't bolster his mood. He couldn't focus in the boxing ring; his coach commented on his lack of punch. Christ, thought Scott, it's all I can do to get my hands up in front of my face, but the punches keep coming through. When he tried to outline how he felt to Kelley, what he got in reply was "Quit feeling so fucking sorry for yourself. No news is good news from the cheating scandal, and Caroline is the one doing all the work on that front. So stop with the whining already." Scott felt worse than ever.

Two days later he was back in the lobby of the Maryland Inn and dialing her number at the Goucher dorm. When he got her on the line, she sounded tired. But the news was good enough: she had been able to scrounge up the remaining money somewhere and said she would make the necessary arrangements. Scott couldn't help but think that she sounded pretty experienced in what was needed, although understandably not enthusiastic. He kept his comments brief and noncommittal, and they hung up after a few minutes.

When he got back to Bancroft Hall and told Kelley the news, the Irishman's reaction was direct: "Not her first trip on the good ship *Lollipop*, I suspect," he said. "Next time you see her, be a damn sight more careful. Wear a rubber, boyo."

"She keeps telling me her parents are going to kill her if they find out," said Scott, "but I'll be damned if I'm going to drop out of Annapolis and marry her." Kelley nodded vigorously. "And her dad is a commander, I think the executive officer of a destroyer down in Norfolk. She'd never want to marry me if I was just a Florida flats fisherman anyway, or an enlisted sailor." Scott rationalized: "This way we both get what we want, and June Week is still on course—it's only a month out." He slept better than he had in weeks.

Escape and Evasion

T he next morning, at the first formation of the day, an announcement was made that the cheating investigation
was about to conclude and there was a final two-day
window in which any midshipman who had information concern-
ing the theft of the navigation exam must come forward. Doing so
would provide a limited level of "consideration" for midshipmen
who decided to belatedly come clean. Scott and Kelley held another caucus of war and decided to stay the course, hunkering
down behind the wall of lies they had built. "In for a penny, in for
a pound" was Kelley's succinct assessment. Scott's conscience
continued to assault him, making every waking minute a struggle
to focus on the tasks at hand. It was a hard, miserable time, only
made worse by the fact that Kelley seemed to be able to simply
ignore it. Scott wondered to himself if Kelley was really so unaf-
fected, and tried several times to engage him on the subject. But

he could tell such conversations simply caused his classmate to shut down and walk away. "Too late for thinking about our 'honor,' whatever that means," said Kelley. "Don't go soft on me now, classmate" was a frequent conversation ender.

Scott's only escape valve was the boxing ring. Selected to compete for the regiment boxing championships, he was training daily for a couple of hours after classes concluded. The physical act of dressing for a fight—his wrists and ankles taped, gloves laced, headgear fitted, mouthpiece inserted by the midshipmen managers—calmed his mind. He would warm up on the speed bag, thrumming its light form in a smooth and mindless rhythm. He'd then turn his attention to the heavy sawdust-stuffed bag, its oily, dark, and creased brown surface a target to be beaten in a jab-jab-cross pattern with a manager holding it firm against his blows.

The boxing coach, a portly former Marine gunny sergeant, stopped to watch Scott. "Something bothering you, James? You're off your game, middie. But I bet it's nothing a few more rounds with the Beater wouldn't fix?" Bob "the Beater" Beatson, the best boxer in the gym, outweighed Scott's middleweight 155-pound frame by a solid 10 pounds of muscle. Scott shrugged, and a few minutes later, the two midshipmen were hammering each other in the center ring. Scott found his rhythm quickly and used speed and footwork to move around the heavier Beatson, landing a series of light jabs. That worked fine until suddenly it didn't, and a heavy cross smashed the side of his head, showing him lightning bolts when he blinked his eyes. The gunny stepped between them, took a look in Scott's eyes, and said, "Enough for the day, James. Hit the shower." He and Beatson touched gloves and Scott slid between the ropes and headed to the locker room. When he turned on the taps, hearing the rusty scrape of the old copper piping, he realized he hadn't thought about either Caroline or the investigation for almost an hour. It was the best hour of his day, even if the side of his face felt like a gravel road.

When he got back to his room, Kelley was sitting on the bed on his side of the room holding a sheet of paper with a mimeographed message. He looked up at Scott and grinned widely. "We're all clear, Scotty. They announced the list of expelled midshipmen— thirty-two in all, mostly on the other side of the regiment. Nobody in our company, even, not a single one. We got nothing but clear and open water up ahead, shipmate."

Scott's legs felt elastic, like they did in the last round of a long fight, slightly numb, tingly, and uncertain in their support. "God, I cannot believe it's over," he said, sinking down on his bunk. Even as the words came out of his mouth, he knew for him it would never be over: in his mind he had cheated, plain and simple. Sure, he hadn't brought notes into the classroom with the answers—but he had looked closely at the gouge, had memorized some of the key questions and prepped for them in advance, and was more than aware that some classmates had cheated. And he had lied about it again and again. What did the honor code mean for him? Would he do it again when it mattered even more? He glanced across at his roommate, who was grinning stupidly like he had won the Irish Sweepstakes or a blue ribbon at the County Cork Fair. He knows and doesn't care, Scott thought. Why can't I be like him? For the millionth time since he had glanced at the gouge before the exam, he wished he could undo that moment. But he'd crossed his Rubicon of lies once and forever, and he'd carry those actions on his heart wherever the voyage took him.

"I'm going for a run," he said to Kelley. Scott put on his PT gear and was out the door without another word. He went straight to the seawall of the Academy, a couple of miles of jagged granite boulders that separated the grounds of Annapolis from the Severn River and the wide reaches of the Chesapeake Bay beyond. Scott leaped on the first rock and began to jump from boulder to boulder in the dimming twilight, risking a bone-breaking miss with every stride. As he found his pace, he began to jog, then run, and finally to sprint from rock to rock to rock. It took every ounce of his concentration to pick the next landing spot for his flying feet, his breath burning harshly, the cold late-winter air scorching his lungs. "I lied and I cheated, and I got away with it," he kept saying over and over to himself, an endless loop of guilt, each word punctuated by a footfall on a granite rock. To his right, the river moaned, the lights of Annapolis harbor came up over the dark band of the Severn River, and in the distance he heard a foghorn tolling out on the bay. Scott Bradley James ran and ran, each stride a risk surmounted, each stride taking him further away from all that he thought he'd known about himself. The honesty and honor he had thought were at his core had deserted him in a moment of weakness. Life, he thought. You can't get away from the moments where you screw up what you want to be. Like these rocks under my feet, each one a slab of stone that could make me slip again. A pile of rocks shaped into a trap.

But so far he'd escaped, and would sail on.

Perilous Path

Scott read it in a newspaper, *The Baltimore Sun*, in the daily events column toward the end of the second section of the paper. It was a single line, buried in a series of happenings in the city: "Miss Caroline Sheehan of Baltimore, Maryland, a student at Goucher College, the daughter of Commander and Mrs. Gerald Sheehan of Norfolk, Va., died of sepsis in the city hospital on May 15, 1939." Monday. Two days earlier. When he read the line on a Wednesday afternoon, he was sitting on one of the green benches on Stribling Walk, a few yards from the statue of the Delaware Indian chief Tecumseh.

It was a fine afternoon, with a bright sun sparkling through the new leaves in the emerging green canopy above him. Scott looked up and directly in his line of sight was the massive copper dome of the Academy chapel. Every Sunday he and two thousand other midshipmen packed the pews to attend mandatory chapel. Scott had at best an ambivalent relationship with God and didn't much like going to church ashore. For him, just looking at the ocean, focusing his eyes on a distant point where the sea and sky came together, filled him with a sense of calm akin to prayer. But that Wednesday afternoon he unfolded himself from the bench and started walking woodenly toward the huge bronze doors of the chapel. On the way, he discarded the newspaper in one of the green wire trash cans along the walking path. The paper felt hot and sticky in his hand, although the day was cool. Inside the chapel, he saw one other midshipman seated near the altar at the front, and so Scott sat on the opposite side near the very back. He put his hands on the back of the pew in front of him and leaned forward so his head was touching the back of his hands, which felt hot and dry on his forehead.

He had no way of knowing exactly what had happened, but he could take a pretty good guess. With the cash, she'd moved forward and must have "taken care of the situation." But something had gone wrong, and she had ended up with an infection bad enough to land her in the city hospital. Her parents, far away in Norfolk, might not have known anything was amiss until it was too late. Would she have tried to contact him? God, he hoped her friends had helped her, tried to get in touch with her parents above all. It didn't seem possible that she was gone; but in some way to Scott, it felt like it was the logical conclusion of the bad choices they had both made. He clenched the pew harder and tried to sort through what he was feeling. Memory flooded him. Scott remembered her sly smile as she tugged at his hand, leading him upstairs to her bed at the small inn on the edge of Annapolis Harbor. When they made love the first time, he could hear the seagulls outside, cawing as they circled over the small sailing boats in the harbor. Caroline had always been an optimist, hungry for whatever life had to offer. They'd enjoyed each other enormously, both physically, when they could, and always in the snappy conversations about everything from whether the best cocktails had bourbon or rye to whether a war was coming in Europe. Or her wise observations on the Navy and the fleet, honed by years of growing up the daughter of a naval officer, living on bases, going to Sunday brunches at the officers' clubs in Norfolk or Pearl Harbor or Charleston, comparing them in detail. He rubbed his head on the back of his hands on the pew. He couldn't believe it. She was gone.

Scott thought back to their second date, when they couldn't find time to be alone but ended up in a crowd of his classmates, all dragging dates around the small downtown. It had been Caroline who became the ringleader of the party, finding a tavern off of Maryland Avenue where she mysteriously knew the bartender, and ordering Manhattans for the gang. She was the center of the group, a cocktail in hand, describing how she and her girlfriends at Goucher would dodge the chaperones and make it out of the dormitories without signing out. Scott had laughed and said, "We have a name for that here at the Academy: 'going over the wall.' Not sure you could make it up and over twelve feet of concrete wall wearing that skirt." She took a sip of the rye Manhattan, threw back her mane of blond hair, and said, "Oh, we have a saying at Goucher too, Scott: 'Where there's a *wall*, there's a way.' Sometimes you have to walk around a wall, sweetie, not just try to climb it." Everyone laughed. And she could be so sweet and gentle in bed, teasing him in the moment, leading him along, and pulling him toward her and urging him on. Or walking along the seawall wrapped in his school sweater, or cheering the midshipmen at the football game. All of it flooded into his mind and he gently tapped his head again and again on his hands in the narrow pew.

Now, through the shock, he felt a deep sense of guilt. Not only had he been with her in that narrow bed those times, without any precautions, but he was the one who had found the money that sent her to have an illegal abortion that ended up killing her. Killing her. A vibrant and adventurous girl. Even if he knew in his heart that he was not in love with her, nor would have married her, he could feel the trajectory of her life, all her aspirations, the potential he had sensed in her that had made her attractive to him. But Caroline was dead. Gone. Sailed on across some distant sea. Jesus, it just didn't seem real to him. He sat alone in the chapel for another long hour, lost in his memories.

Perhaps worst of all was the kernel of feeling inside him that he realized was relief. The situation was resolved in the cleanest way possible for him. He wasn't going to have to deal with her pursuing him, staking a claim on him after what she had sacrificed for him. Scott mourned the death of Caroline, he felt real guilt and regret, he knew he was in the wrong in so many ways; and at the same time, he reached toward that sense of relief inside himself and touched it and thought, I shouldn't feel that way. It's not right. It sickened him to realize the nature of his reaction. Finally, he raised his head from his hands, stood and put on his cover, squaring it on the center of his head, and walked back through the bronze doors into the late-afternoon light.

12

Setting a Course

The next two years passed like the wake of a destroyer stretching out behind it as it clipped along fast and true. With the navigation exam cheating scandal behind them, the class of 1941 focused on getting to graduation, and on war's lengthening shadows. Sometimes, at night, they would sneak out of Mother B and sit on the granite rocks of the seawall, smoking cigarettes and arguing about when or where or how the United States could be dragged into a European war. Like the rest of their class, Scott now kept up with events as if his life depended on it, as well it might. One night he said to Joe Taussig, "The Germans are going to cut through Poland like a knife through butter, but my French professor thinks the Grand Armée will slow them down. And the British have a big army in France. What does your dad think?"

Joe took a long drag on his Camel. "The first thing he would tell you is that the British still control the seas, so they have options. But he doesn't think much of the French navy, and not their army either. He visited Germany a couple of years ago and came home just shaking his head at how the Nazis are cranking out aircraft, good ones. The second thing he would say is that for us, Europe is a sideshow compared to the Pacific. The Japanese fleet is huge, and their armies are running the table all around the southeast and western Pacific. We're just sitting in the Philippines, on Midway, back at Pearl. Japan is on the march."

At the mention of the Philippines, Kelley's head came up. "We got no business being in the colony business to begin with. It's not like the Brits are getting much out of their 'empire' now, and it's going to cost them to try and defend it."

Scott nodded. He ground out his cigarette. "Let's get back to our rooms before the bed check, guys. All I know for sure is that if we go up against the Japs, I want to be part of it. No Atlantic convoys, thank you very much. I want a battleship and plenty of sea room. I'm betting the class of 1941 may very well get an early graduation and maybe a date, maybe with the Japs or the Germans."

The prospect was very appealing to Scott. His second class year, in the wake of Caroline's death in the spring of 1939, had an air of bitterness about it, like drinking the last cold cup of coffee out of the bottom of the pot on some benighted midwatch at sea. In his darkest moments, he thought again about quitting Annapolis and reverting to being an enlisted sailor, the penalty for departing after the start of the junior year of classes. But abandoning his chance at obtaining a commission would be a terrible blow to his parents, especially his father. So he slogged through his classes, he kept coming back to the boxing ring, and on the weekends he would check out a small sailing dinghy and sail up and down the Chesapeake Bay alone. Caught up in the rhythm of the Academy, time moved fast.

He also found in himself something he would not have bet on: ambition. He had come to Annapolis with a sense that not paying tuition was a good deal financially. And it would let him get out on the water and allow him to simply enjoy the next step in the life of a Florida boy who loved the ocean. Above all, it would make his father proud. Scott never saw himself as someone who would get caught up in the trappings of rank or would push himself to be part of the striper system, the ranks of first-class midshipmen who ran the regiment under the watchful eyes of the officer cadre at Annapolis. But as his junior year came to an end in the spring of 1940, he went to his company officer, a lieutenant commander who had served on destroyers in the Great War, and said simply: "I'd like to get as high a rank as I can next year, sir." His company officer was pleasantly surprised and said he would see what he could do. Scott had fairly high grades and excellent physical scores, including being a runner-up for the regiment boxing championship as a middleweight, and was well liked by his peers and seniors. The company nominated him for battalion command, one of the top positions at the Academy, and after a series of interviews with senior officers including the commandant himself, Scott was selected for four stripes and the command. As he put on the four bars of a midshipman commander for the first time, he glanced in the mirror and realized this was a big deal. Scott would be one of the top ten leaders in the two-thousand-man Regiment of Midshipmen and would march at the front of a battalion of hundreds when the midshipmen went on parade. He liked it, the feeling that he was in charge and mattered. Kelley, who was unlikely to be appointed to anything much above a sergeant at arms, the lowest rung on the leadership ladder, simply said: "I told you the marching might come in handy."

When the regiment re-formed in the fall of 1940 after summer cruise, Scott looked in the mirror at himself wearing the four stripes again and smiled. It felt good. But it also felt like he was still an impostor, participating in a charade like the parades. And being in charge of a battalion meant not only leading on the parade field but also dealing with leadership in ways he'd never had to do before. The company commanders, his classmates, reported to him and brought their troubles his way: plebes who were not succeeding and would need to be provided special attention; upperclassmen who were headed into academic problems and needed tutoring; varsity athletes who had let the stars on their letter sweaters—one awarded each time a team beat West Point—go to their heads; disciplinary action for everything from drinking to fighting to gambling. Scott began in that fall of 1940 to hammer out his own nascent philosophy of leadership and practice it with the midshipmen under his command.

He started with something he had learned from his father: Stay calm. When he was out with his dad, hunting or fishing or building something, no matter how bad a situation seemed to be, he'd look at his father and see a steady man calculating the odds and doing everything he could to resolve a dangerous situation, from a summer squall to a wounded wild pig. The job of an officer is to bring order out of chaos, one of his company officers had said, and Scott figured losing his temper and screaming, something a lot of Academy graduates seemed to think a useful form of leadership, would only lead to more chaos and bad decisions.

Second, Scott did everything he could to communicate clearly and cleanly. He used a variety of ways to get the word out but consistently focused on keeping the message simple and aligned with the mission. Whether that meant providing mimeographed notices under the door of every room in Bancroft Hall or ensuring his company commanders rehearsed their oral communications to the regiment in front of him, Scott kept himself on top of the message daily. "Here's the thing, Scott," the lieutenant commander said over a cup of coffee in the battalion wardroom. "A leader has to communicate consistently and honestly, whether you're talking to a few seamen on the deck plates or to a wardroom of junior officers or to the whole fleet if you make admiral. I've seen it again and again, especially in junior officers—making the mistake of trying to shade something for the sailors, either good or bad. Believe me, they have the best bullshit detectors in the military. But if you shoot straight with them, tell them what's going on and how it's going to be—good or bad or terrible or whatever—they will sign on and sail with you wherever you point the ship." The ability to communicate was intrinsically linked with leadership. The advice stuck.

Third, he began to think hard about new ideas and how important they would be. It was dawning on him that leaders were often critical to the formation and execution of big and new ideas. Plenty of good ones welled up from the lower decks or laboratories ashore, or from the civilian world, but without leaders willing to seize them and energize them and drive them forward, they didn't go anywhere. He saw that in history and the study of sea power, and admired the big thinkers like Alfred Thayer Mahan and Stephen Luce and Fiske and others. He said to Kelley one day that if the nation did end up in a war, there was going to be an almost endless appetite for new technology, strategy, and tactics. Even Kelley agreed with him. "Yeah, what the Marines are doing now with new amphibious tactics is incredible for such a traditional force. My weapons instructor just got here from the Fleet Marine Force, and he spends more time talking about that than anything."

Scott was a long way yet from the fleet, but he reckoned he would begin with the small day-to-day activities of the regiment and figure out new ways to do business. Scott knew that none of what he was in charge of in commanding a battalion was all that critical to the Academy or, ultimately, the nation—in fact, he had taped a small note to himself in the top drawer of his desk that simply said, "Remember, nothing important happens here." But at the same time, he felt his time as a striper at Annapolis was a beginning. When he would gather the six company commanders in the battalion together for a conference, he'd sit down at the head of the small table in the wardroom and think, Yes, this is what it's all about. In the fall of his first-class year, he was selected to orchestrate the movement of the entire regiment to Philadelphia for the Army-Navy game. It seemed daunting, requiring Scott to organize the endless trains and buses, figure out which of the senior midshipmen would be in the lead and who would bring up the rear, where would the officers go, how to brief the superintendent about the overall operation, a thousand details. He spent weeks on it, meeting with everyone from the commandant to the regiment's marine operations officer to the midshipmen in charge of bringing up the venerable Navy goat.

Kelley, watching Scott burn the midnight oil, gave him some grudging respect: "I gotta hand it to you, roomie. Two thousand swinging dicks all needing guidance and discipline and a *plan*. Man, I watch the rest of the senior stripers, most of whom are butt-kissing knuckleheads, look at you, and they are all dying to know what to do next. You've got this whole regiment turning on a dime. Not bad for a Florida bait shop owner's son."

Scott knew it wasn't like commanding a destroyer squadron in combat, or even organizing a big military exercise at sea. But it was a real chance to practice *leading*. When he went to the striper meetings to represent his battalion as a commander, he felt like he mattered. Around the table, each of the battalion commanders was expected to give a short synopsis of how training was going for the hundreds of midshipmen under his leadership. He watched several classmates stumble through their presentations, saw the commissioned officers in the room rolling their eyes or exchanging grimaces. When it was his turn, he spoke crisply and in short, direct sentences, used real facts and numbers, and included a couple of quick anecdotes about several of the individuals he was grooming to take on additional duties. When he finished, he looked at the full commander who was charged with overseeing

Scott's battalion, and caught an approving nod of the head from the officer, himself a former destroyer officer in the convoys of the Great War. Scott nodded back.

Something unfamiliar was beginning to burn in the heart of Scott Bradley James: being in charge. He liked it.

13

Underway Early

K elley was the first to know. He walked into their room and closed the door. "We are shipping out early, boyo. The whole class, graduating early. Holy shit, we're getting commissioned early, classmate."

Scott looked up from his copy of Mahan, took in the wide grin on Kelley's face, and said one word: "When?"

Kelley put a finger to his nose. "Them that knows, they say we'll be gone early in the year. I think they want us to actually graduate in the year of our class—would be hard to spend my whole career explaining that the class of 1941 actually graduated in 1940 or whatever. But fuck it, Scott, we are going to get out of here. And soon."

They discussed all the implications of an early departure. Most midshipmen would be cheered at the prospect of getting out of Annapolis and into the fleet faster. Scott said, "Blue water, lots of it, is the path to promotion, Kelley, even for a jarhead like you. Got to get some glory at sea, and service to the country."

Kelley nodded and with a wry smile said, "There are gonna be a few of our classmates who won't think like that. Some of those really smart engineering ones are doing research that won't get wrapped up in time. And some of our classmates in true love have fiancées ready for a big June Week wedding that now is gonna either be a rushed ceremony or postponed in the face of departure to fleet assignments. Boo-hoo. But for us? This is pure gold."

Indeed, Scott was not alone in finding it hard to concentrate on studies or even sports. Joe Taussig, whose father was the highest-ranking naval officer any of them had even the most tenuous connection with, had an inside line on a series of bleak events in both Asia and Europe. "My dad says we better be ready to go, and he thinks we're gonna be in this thing before 1941 is over. With the Germans looking unstoppable and the Japs kicking the Brits out of Asia, we have to think of combat, combat, and combat." Joe set up a daily "briefing" in the wardroom for the first-class stripers, who were supposed to take the "war gouge" and get it out to the entire class of 1941. He used a combination of newspaper reports, radio broadcasts, and some special intel from his father.

As the Nazis swept over the center of Europe, Winston Churchill spoke in his maiden speech in the House of Commons in May of blood, toil, tears, and sweat. Joe choked up reporting it, and the faces in the wardroom were somber. The Royal Navy had seemed invulnerable, the standard against which they measured themselves. Kelley's reaction was the most visceral: "Blood, toil, tears, and sweat. All he left out was shit," he observed. "And I'm thinking the Brits are going to be eating a lot of that if they can't figure out a way to get us into this war on their team."

One of the most haunting details in Joe Taussig's briefings was the way city after city was being terror-bombed by Hermann Göring's air corps in Europe and put to the sword in Asia by the Imperial Japanese Army. The midshipmen focused on the capability of the Royal Navy, the final dark-blue line between the home islands and the fate of Belgium, the Netherlands, and France. "Jesus," said Scott after one more depressing briefing, "when you think how hard we've studied the Napoleonic Wars, and Lord Nelson saving England at Trafalgar, and the 'wooden walls of England' and all of that, now it's playing out in front of us." Watching the evacuation of Dunkirk and the improbable salvation of the three hundred thousand troops at the core of the British Army was heartening, a small flicker of light in an increasingly dark tableau. Those limeys got lucky, Scott thought. As a small-boat sailor, he knew how dangerous the unstable waters of the English Channel could be. He pictured himself in a small fishing boat overloaded with British troopers and all their gear, and shook his head at the image, trying to clear his mind to study a calculus problem. The day-to-day regime of uniform inspections, dull classes, and tepid sports encounters felt increasingly silly and irrelevant.

Joe Taussig wrapped up the briefing on Italy entering the war against France by saying, "Screw them. I never liked spaghetti anyway." Taussig, like Scott, was a four-striper, a midshipman lieutenant commander with senior command responsibilities in the two-thousand-man Regiment of Midshipmen. Unlike Scott, he came from naval royalty, was the grandson of a rear admiral and the son of a rear admiral, but despite almost constant ribbing from his classmates for his exalted place in the naval aristocracy, he was well liked. He and Scott often discussed the war. They agreed the right place to focus would end up being the Pacific. As much as they admired Winston Churchill when he said in June that "the battle of France is over. The Battle of Britain is about to begin," it was clear that the heavy punch of the U.S. Navy was going to be the endless expanse of the Pacific. Surely for the foreseeable future, the European theater was going to be convoy action—countless boring hours punctuated by U-boat attacks—important work, but not the glory of battleships going hull to hull and gun to gun with the Imperial Japanese Navy. They considered trying for naval aviation, but both midshipmen knew that battleships would dominate the Pacific war, and the high science of the battleship world would be gunnery. Naval Weapons was the only class that either of them spent any serious time studying for.

By the fall of 1940, the official announcement of early graduation had been made. On the maps in the company wardroom, Joe Taussig annotated the Japanese successes daily. They had swept down through China and into Indochina to the south. They were clearly pointing toward Singapore, the City of Lions. One of the British naval exchange officers spent an hour in one of their naval history classes talking about the impregnable city, how the British fleet would be able to hold off the Japanese from the sea. Scott didn't believe a word of it. In September, Japan, Italy, and Germany signed the Tripartite Pact, which would force the British fleet to stretch itself even more thinly across the world.

When the pro-interventionist President Franklin Delano Roosevelt was elected to his unprecedented third term, most midshipmen were jubilant. "America First is a dumbass crock of isolationist shit," summarized Kelley. "We've got to get out there, and I mean both us middies and the country. Otherwise, we'll end up like the limeys, fighting them on the beaches or whatever."

The last weeks at Annapolis were a hazy mix of quick trips home over the Christmas holidays, packing professional seabags, and the mindless grind of administration—getting seven copies of official orders printed, having fittings for seagoing uniforms, undergoing medical exams for commissioning, on and on. Scott managed to get south over Christmas week, which was unseasonably cool, but not cold enough to prevent him and his father from going up to Dark Forest Key for some deer hunting.

On the drive up, Scott's father seemed to be struggling with something he wanted to say. He started to talk about the Great War and the North Atlantic, where he had served, but the conversation petered out quickly. When they put the car on a small ferry to cross over to Dark Forest Key, he seemed to take confidence from being on the water, and turned to Scott. "So here's what I want to tell you. Being at sea on a Navy warship isn't easy, son. I know you've done a month or so on those middie cruises, but let me tell you, when you take in the lines and come off a pier and you don't have the damnedest idea when you'll come back, it can take it out of a man. You think you're ready for whatever comes, and I bet you are. But when you've been out of sight of land for months, six months or more, and every couple of days there's a

U-boat popping up and sinking one of the convoy ships, and the captain's so tired he can't think straight, and the XO is down in sick bay with shrapnel in his legs from a shell that blew up on deck, and your chief ain't the best, well, it just gets hard." He looked out at the sea again, and the small ferry shuddered, passing over an unseen wake. "You don't know how you'll do until you're out there doing it is all I'm saying, son. But however it comes at you, whatever happens, your mom and I are always going to be so proud of you, because we know you'll always do the right thing. You may not know what that right thing is this minute, but it's often a very hard thing to do, that can cost you a lot. Be the kind of man who does the hard right thing over the easy wrong one."

Scott stood next to his father, looking at the sandy shore of Dark Forest Key ahead as the ferry closed in on the rickety dock. "Dad, I will try. I will try. And I hope to God I have what it takes out there." His eyes welled up and he turned so his father wouldn't see. Scott paused for a long moment and thought about telling his father about the mistakes and missteps he'd already made, but he did not. They looked at each other in silence. The ferry made a grinding sound as it lay against the dock.

The hunting was good, and over a couple of days they packed out three of the small key deer to smoke back on Key West. On their last night, over a couple of cans of Schlitz followed up by a shot of Old Grand-Dad, Scott told his father the good news he'd been saving. "Dad, I grabbed the brass ring on service-selection night. I'm going to a battleship, the USS *West Virginia* out of Pearl. And no absolute promises, but my company officer knows the weapons officer there and said he would put in a word for me to be in the gunnery division, with the big guns." It was a prime as-signment, the absolute best a midshipman could get.

Robert pushed the coals of the fire as they sipped another shot of the fiery bourbon. He got up, tossed three big logs on the fire, and gave it a big squirt of kerosene from a can. The fire spurted up, and all three logs instantly caught fire. The heat came off in waves, with crackling sounds like gunfire in front of them. His father smiled widely for the first time on the trip. He handed his son another cold beer from the cooler. "A battleship. Gunnery. Proud of you, son. Now let's get these bucks down home, and we'll catch up with your mom. She was hoping you'd be on the East Coast like I was in the last war, maybe just up in Charleston, but she'll come around. This is the right thing for you, however all this war talk turns out. I know it."

When Scott and Kelley returned in January, the reality of their impending graduation really sank in. "Goddamn," said Kelley as they trudged off to sailing class, which he hated as much as Scott hated marching. "Are we lucky or what? We get to bail out of this fancy afloat zoo and get to the fleet almost six months early. And the Japs haven't come at us yet. I'm hoping to get to one of the forward garrisons, either on Corregidor or Wake or at least Mid-way." Kelley was headed to Quantico, Virginia, for a truncated ver-sion of the Marine Corps' Basic School, which put the brand-new second lieutenants through their paces in small arms, orienteering, squad-level tactics, gunnery spotting, and the other skills of a basic Marine grunt junior officer starting out in the Corps. "Hope we can still do some marching," said Kelley, winking at Scott.

"I just hope they send your ass to a real warship, and you don't end up with a platoon of grunts guarding the gates of Philadelphia Naval Station," Scott said.

The final assignments for the Marine second lieutenants wouldn't be announced until they were close to finishing the Basic School. Scott hoped Kelley would end up with him and Joe Taussig in the Pacific Fleet. Scott and Taussig had decided to throw in together on a bachelor pad—a snake ranch, as Kelley called it—when they got to Pearl Harbor. Taussig was headed to a gunnery assignment on another Pacific battleship, USS *Nevada*. They would take a train together to San Diego and catch a destroyer ride over to Pearl Harbor.

Scott spent a contemplative few days looking back on his time at the Academy. One evening after a last dinner in Bancroft Hall, he took out the old, battered copy of *Reef Points* his dad had given him and rubbed its black cover once again. As a result of nearly four years of handling, the gilt of the title had almost been rubbed away. He'd carried the book with him every day of plebe summer and often in the years since. It had initially been a talisman that pointed to his future; then a guide stone through wrenchingly difficult days; and finally perhaps the lucky talisman that allowed him to cheat fate in the case of a cheating scandal and a pregnant girlfriend. He took no joy in either of his escapes, both unfair twists of life that had spun in his favor but would remain with him forever, hovering like twin patches of haze in a distant sky. He looked down again at *Reef Points*. The object in his hand felt now like just a little black book, an emblem of the past at the Academy and nothing more. He took the single sheet of paper with the poem he'd copied out on youngster cruise, "The Convergence of the Twain," and put it in his shirt pocket. For good luck and good hunting, he thought. The United States Naval Academy was just a place he'd gone to college. Now it was time to go to sea.

Carrying the small book in his left hand, he walked out of Bancroft Hall toward Hospital Point, one of the spits of land at the Academy that protruded into the Severn River. It was where the Academy situated its infamous obstacle course, which Scott had painfully completed hundreds of times in his nearly four years "by the bay, where Severn joins the tide" in the words of the vaguely annoying Annapolis alma mater song, "Navy Blue and Gold." Standing at the edge of the dark river that flowed through the Chesapeake Bay and out to the great world ocean, he stopped for a moment and pulled out the copy of *Reef Points* a final time. After a moment, he threw the book as far and as hard as he could, far out into the murky waters of the cold river, reflecting the dim winter's twilight in its slow-flowing waters. The small book floated briefly, bobbed on a small wave, then sank into the river.

Pearl

The 2,300-ton destroyer USS *Helm* pulled into the pier at Pearl Harbor in early March. The hull number on her gray side was 388, but the pounding on the voyage over from San Diego had made both of the eights look like blurry threes, and the sleek hull was showing running rust in spots. Ensign Scott James had the conn, and he landed the ship neatly without a tug for assistance. "Nice job, James," said the commanding officer. "Sure you don't want to stay in the destroyer Navy?" Scott laughed and the captain smiled broadly. They both knew that his assignment in the gunnery division on board the battleship *West Virginia* was a much better posting, and more in line with what an Annapolis graduate who had been a striper in the Regiment of Midshipmen would expect. Scott said his goodbyes to the skipper and the navigator on the bridge and went below to grab his seabag.

Taussig was waiting for him on the pier. Smart in their fresh kha-kis, they went swaggering down the pier and headed to the offi-cers' club to grab a beer and plan their next move.

With a few days of postgraduation leave left to them, they headed down to the Waikiki Beach area downtown to begin to get a sense of the island's charms. Joe's father had been in and out of Pearl on ships over the years. He'd helped put down the Boxer Rebellion in China, published articles in the professional naval journal *Proceedings*, and been reprimanded publicly by the presi-dent for his blunt predictions of a coming war with Japan in 1940. Both midshipmen held Rear Admiral Taussig in awe. He had rat-tled off some advice for the ensigns over a neat glass of scotch in front of the fireplace at the Army Navy Club in downtown Wash-ington before they headed west.

"Stay out of the sailor bars—you don't want to be mixing so-cially with your men. Or maybe just go for one beer very early in the evening. If you do go, make sure you buy your leading chief a drink. Never go to a strip club. Never. You can meet some nice girls in the hotel bars, especially at the Royal Hawaiian Hotel. It's the big pink one. Try one of their daiquiris, but not too many—they can really sneak up on you and they're pretty damn expen-sive. That's a drink that started down in Cuba, but it's big in the islands now. They serve them here in the Army Navy Club, but this doesn't seem like the place to drink 'em.

"If you want to get a place off the ship, stay out of the down-town, and get something close enough to the base that you can always get to your ship on foot if you really have to. And you've heard me say this before, but there's a real war brewing out there with the Japs. Don't underestimate the chances of seeing combat unexpectedly at some point, maybe something that starts while you're at sea. If that happens, you could be gone from Pearl for a long, long time—so make sure you have a full seabag of uniforms on your battleship." He paused and drained his scotch, signaling the bartender for a refill. "Damn, I'd like to be out there with you." The wistfulness was not just that of an old sailor envying the young. The admiral had gotten cross-threaded with President Roosevelt for having testified in April 1940 before the Senate Naval Affairs Committee that he thought a war with Japan was almost inevitable. The United States needed to build more battleships—and do it now, he said. Roosevelt thought otherwise and caused a reprimand to be placed in his file, and he was forced to retire.

At Naval Station Pearl Harbor, "happy hour," a practice invented by the Navy during the Great War, was just ending. The two ensigns changed into their tropical whites in the head at the club. They combed their hair and applied some Old Spice cologne, dropped their seabags behind the front desk of the officers' club, and grabbed a taxi from the stand near the main gate to the base. The sun had set early in the mild late-March evening, and the trade winds had kicked up a bit. "Downtown," said Scott. "The Royal Hawaiian Hotel."

"You got it, boss," said the driver, putting the cab in gear and heading into the soft Hawaiian night.

15

The Pink Palace of the Pacific

ROYAL HAWAIIAN HOTEL, OAHU, HAWAII

The two ensigns surveyed the bar scene at the baroque Royal Hawaiian Hotel. An impressive edifice of pink-painted limestone and coral built just before the Crash of 1929, it had quickly become the top spot in Waikiki for the mon-eyed crowd. The ensigns settled on a table across the room from the local band playing hapa haole music, an adaption of Hawaiian-style island tunes run through a big-band filter with mostly English lyrics. It was not a successful synthesis, nor did Scott and Joe like the astronomical price of the daiquiris they ordered: one dollar, before tip. Plus, the clientele looked too old to be of much interest, mostly senior Navy and Army officers, some in uniform and others in their civvies, sitting with their wives. Even the waiters looked old.

Scott felt a big physical presence behind him, and a meaty hand dropped on his shoulder and spun him around. "Well, I'll be goddamned, Martha. Look who's in the fleet." It was Ernest Hemingway, a big drink in his hand, and Martha Gellhorn next to him with a flute of champagne. Scott's first thought was, How the hell did he recognize me after this many years? His second thought was that Martha looked tired, out of sorts, and like she could use a martini instead of a little glass of bubbly. "Goddamn, youngster, you look pretty good in those whites. Who's your shipmate?" Scott introduced Joe and gave Hemingway a quick sketch of his new duties on a battleship. Hemingway nodded vigorously.

Gellhorn was looking around the crowd. Her bedside manner certainly hasn't improved, Scott thought to himself. Hopefully, she's better actually in one. He recalled hearing that she had become the third Mrs. Hemingway around 1940. "Congratulations on your wedding," he said to her.

She looked at him with red-rimmed eyes and an expression somewhere between mild annoyance and boredom. "Thanks. But I'm not exactly using that on my business cards. I've still got my own reporting and writing going on. In fact," she said, "we're just back from China. Not exactly a honeymoon, but I filed more stories than Hem from over there."

Now it was Hemingway's turn to look annoyed. He said, "Hell, in the end there just isn't much to write about. Bunch of coolies trying to play soldier, and the Japanese are going to scoop it all up in the end. Best part was flying over on the Pan Am Clipper service. Now that is traveling in style." He launched into a long, disjointed description of what he referred to as a "flying presidential suite," describing how it would stop for fuel every day—at Pearl, Midway, Wake Island, Guam, and Manila—and let the guests rest overnight in five-star hotels with the best chefs on the various islands and access to the most beautiful beaches. Then back in the air again, with a "damn good barman," just reading, drinking, napping, and "maybe a little wrestling with Mrs. Hemingway here." He shot her a look and she rolled her eyes and walked off—to get a real drink, Scott guessed.

Hemingway rambled on: "We spent a few months stomping around China, and it's a shithole, boys. Believe me, you made a smart move going to the Navy. The Army and their Air Corps are going to find playing war with the Japs in China is going to be hell in a big place. A land war in Asia is not exactly going to be a picnic." He paused for another swig of his big tropical cocktail. "When do you figure the Japs are going to attack one of the U.S. bases? Where's it going to be? Wake, maybe? Or strike us in the Philippines? Confidentially, I was on a mission from the U.S. government that I can't really talk about—intelligence stuff, that kind of thing. That's why Martha filed more stories than I did. I was too busy on, let's say, 'other things.'"

Scott and Joe glanced at each other with a look of bemused curiosity. Before Scott could ask a question, Hemingway had drained his drink, suddenly seeming bored with the two ensigns. "Well, youngsters, I'm off to a luau with the king and queen of Hawaii. Hope they have a good fat pig for us. Tell your dad I remember him and his boat pretty well. The *Bella*, right? After the war, I'll come back to Key West for old times' sake. We can have a race between *Pilar* and *Bella*. And you can make me one of those daiquiris, youngster." He softened. "You two be safe out there. War's a funny thing and you never know how it bounces. But be

brave, because there is no other way a man can be and be a man."
He chuckled softly. "And don't be afraid of the water. You're in
the Navy, but if you can avoid it, don't even go near the goddamn
water." He laughed and turned away, headed toward Martha's tall
form at the bar.

Scott thought about his mother Bella's two-word assessment of
Martha Gellhorn: "bottle blond." He didn't envy Hemingway his
travels. She was obviously a fine reporter, and as brave as any man
out there, but there was something about her that intimidated
Scott, and probably Hemingway too. The mysteries of marriage,
thought Scott, especially on round three. Kind of the triumph of
optimism over experience.

Over one more expensive daiquiri, Scott and Taussig compared
notes. Neither had been overly impressed with either Hemingway
or Gellhorn. "But he does write some good books," said Joe. "Big-
time bestsellers. I wish we could have gotten a photo with him."

With a shrug, they returned to discussing the idea of getting
out of the Pink Palace and heading to Hotel Street. Joe said his
dad would kill him, but Scott insisted. "No one is going to know
us there. Unless Hemingway gets bored at the king's luau." He
punched Taussig on the shoulder and saw that Joe was not overly
comforted by his classmate's analysis. But the night was before
them, they still had dollars to burn, and Scott kept pulling Taussig
toward the door, looking for a cab.

They walked out of the most expensive hotel on Oahu and
headed toward the cheap and crowded sailor bars on Hotel Street.
"Jeez, I hope my dad doesn't hear about this," Joe fretted.

Scott couldn't be sure if his friend was kidding about Rear

Admiral Taussig, five thousand miles away, keeping tabs on their barhopping. "Never fear," he said, "we'll keep it low-key. After all, what's gonna happen to a couple of junior officers just looking around on their first night in town?" One look convinced Scott that Joe had been serious. "Like I keep telling you, nobody knows who we are. And nobody cares."

On Hotel Street, they joined the masses of sailors, a few Army troops sprinkled in, and the occasional member of the shore patrol, the fleet's own "good order and discipline" unit. Typically led by a junior officer or chief petty officer, the small shore patrol groups sported black armbands with the letters *SP* and had billy clubs swinging from well-worn leather belts. But the crowd was almost entirely a swimming sea of enlisted white jumpers, sailors in their liberty uniforms, their jaunty caps jammed on the backs of their heads, bobbing up and down as they strode from bar to bar. The narrow sidewalks of Hotel Street allowed passage for only three sailors or so at a time, and there was plenty of pushing and good-natured cursing. Signs in the windows advertised beer for a nickel a mug, Vat 69 scotch for a dime, and a photo with a real "hula girl" for twenty cents.

It was still early in the night, and most of the sailors were sober enough to know they were supposed to salute the two ensigns. Scott reflected that just a month or so ago, he had received his first salute as an ensign on graduation day at Annapolis. Tradition demanded that on that milestone day you must hand the first enlisted man who saluted you a shiny silver dollar, which Scott had duly done. As he and Joe navigated the crowded street, the constant need to return salutes started to tire them out. *I never* thought I'd get tired of getting saluted, Scott said to himself, but at least I don't have to pay a buck apiece for the privilege.

Joe nudged Scott and pointed to a run-down building across the street. "That's the cathouse," he said, pointing to the line of sailors out the door. "It's actually run by the government, and all the girls get medical inspections every week, so it's pretty safe." Scott wondered how his friend knew this. He contemplated the arrangement for a moment. He'd never paid for sex and didn't intend to start doing so, but his curiosity got the better of him and he walked across the street. "Hey, Petty Officer," he said to a callow-looking sailor toward the back of the line, "how does this work?" The sailor turned to face Scott with an uncertain look on his face, wondering if he was being set up for something. Assessing that he was just being quizzed by a very green ensign, he said, "I don't think it's for officers, sir, but basically you go in and the girls pick out the guy they want. Then you go upstairs. You get ten minutes, and then one of the mamas comes by and knocks on the door. Oh, and you leave two bucks on the nightstand before you start, and when the ten minutes is up, you're all done, even if you're not all done, if you know what I mean, sir."

Scott nodded, amazed at how organized it all seemed. They moved on, turning across the street into the Black Cat bar, near the YMCA at the end of Hotel Street. They received a series of surprised and appraising looks from various tables filled with sailors in various stages of inebriation, but no one appeared to be overtly hostile. "We are a long way from Annapolis," said Joe. Bellying up to the bar, they ordered scotch on the rocks and took their drinks to a table toward the front of the joint. It was an open-air establishment, taking advantage of the tropical breezes to keep the smell of cheap whiskey, beer, young men, and cologne moving. They settled into their flimsy folding chairs and toasted each other on their audacity in drinking in a real-life sailor bar while other junior officers were making nice with senior officers' wives at the stodgy officers' club on base.

As they sipped their watered-down scotch, they heard raised voices a couple of tables away. Then a slap, hard and sharp. The two ensigns turned and saw a couple of sailors holding back one of their shipmates, who was struggling to get his hands on a young Hawaiian waitress. She was of medium height and slender, with a soft golden complexion and jet-back hair falling just below her shoulders. She wore a golden cross hanging from a gold chain around her neck, and a printed skirt designed to look like part of a hula outfit. She was lovely, and there was a fire in her eyes.

"Keep your hands off me," she hissed at the drunk sailor.

"I'll grab you anytime I want to, you dumb bitch," he yelled, "and if you try slapping me again, I'm going to bend you over this table and show you who's the boss." He was a big, florid sailor, a second-class petty officer with a machinist mate's symbol on the rating badge on his arm, meaning he likely worked in a ship's engine room as a snipe.

Joe turned to Scott. "Hey, aren't we the senior Navy people in here? Kind of Senior Officer Present Ashore—SOPA? Shouldn't we do something?" For the past three and a half years they had had it drilled into their heads that the senior officer present must take charge in a moment of crisis. The sailor broke free from his companions, grabbed the much smaller girl by her arms, and started to shake her hard. She bounced off another passing waitress whose tray, with glasses full of beer, crashed to the floor. The sailor kept his grip on the girl.

Scott stood up and quickly made his way to the scene. Adopting what he hoped was his most authoritative voice, he tapped the sailor on the back and said, "Hey, Petty Officer, let her go. You're way out of line. Let go." The sailor spun around and saw the single gold bars on the ensign's collar and wasn't impressed. Joe Taussig walked up next to Scott to add authority and backup.

With a sneer so direct it almost seemed to hang in the air between them, the sailor said, "Get your goddamn butter bars out of here, *sir*, before you get your pretty little ninety-day wonder's face all messed up."

"One more time, Petty Officer," Scott said evenly. "Grab your hat and your ass and you can still walk out of here." The drunk sailor looked at Scott and sized him up. He had at least twenty pounds on the ensign, most of it topside in his shoulders. He had an ugly leer on his face and seemed to be coming to a decision. He released the girl, and as she stepped back, the sailor sagged slightly and then popped back up with a right-hand haymaker, the classic feint-and-attempted-sucker-punch combination. Scott's long hours in the boxing rings of Annapolis kicked in, and he smoothly ducked the right hand, hit the sailor hard three times in the center of his face with a tight left jab, then came in on the body with a hard right to the ribs. The sailor went down like an anchor being dropped into deep water.

The sailor's friends stared down at him with their mouths agape. "Let me introduce you to one of the finest boxers from the

United States Naval Academy, class of forty-one," Joe said, gesturing to his friend. "Ninety-day wonder, my ass." It was clear Joe was almost as offended by being accused of being an Officer Candidate School product as he was by the fact that the sailor had taken a swing at his classmate.

Moments later, a shore patrol group arrived, consisting of a slim chief petty officer in his thirties and a couple of beefy, baton-carrying seamen backing him up. The shore patrol chief saw a sailor on the deck slowly gaining consciousness and two ensigns standing over him. He walked up to Scott and asked: "Mind telling me what happened here, sir?" It flashed through Scott's mind that it might not be the best introduction to his new ship—one he had not even reported aboard yet—for them to find out that he had been in a fight in a seedy sailor bar. He looked at Joe and sensed that his worst fears that his dad might learn about his liberty choice were floating before his eyes.

"Chief, it appears there was some beer on the deck and this sailor slipped and fell. I believe his shipmates were about to pick him up and get him back to his bunk."

The sailor's buddies nodded enthusiastically. "Yeah, that's it. He slipped." They began helping him get to his feet.

As the now-upright sailor began to moan a bit, Joe whispered to Scott, "Well, at least you didn't kill him. That's good."

It was clear to the chief that no one had slipped, but he had respect for the young officer who did not seem anxious to subject the sailor to the punishment that might be meted out at Captain's Mast, the Navy's nonjudicial forum for discipline, which would normally result from a sailor taking a swing at an officer. The chief probably figured that the petty officer had suffered enough between Scott's fists and the humiliation, Scott thought.

By this point, the bar had cleared, and only the participants in the small drama remained. The chief walked over to the young woman, whom he appeared to know. "Kai, what the hell are you doing here? Do your folks know you're down here? What the hell happened?"

She looked down at the beer-soaked floor, then up at the chief defiantly. "I was picking up some spending money waitressing and doing a few of the hula photos, Chief Finn. My mom knows I come down here sometimes, but no, probably she hasn't told my dad. And I don't want you to tell him either. All that happened is that snipe tried to grab me while we were taking a picture, and I slapped him. Then he went crazy and was screaming at me, awful things, and he was shaking me and then he"—indicating Scott—"made him stop. He hit him hard three or four times and he went down. Nobody slipped on the floor."

The chief laughed. "I know, honey. But you don't want to be a witness if I write this sailor up, do you? Your dad the radio chief would probably find out." He nodded toward Scott. "I think this ensign did you and this drunk a favor."

Chief John Finn walked back to where Scott and Joe were standing. "What's your name, sir?" Scott shook his head. "I'm Ensign Scott Bradley James, Chief. This is Ensign Taussig." He slurred Taussig's name slightly, hoping to keep the admiral's name out of it. Chief Finn looked shrewdly at the ensigns. "Sir, I appreciate the way you handled this . . . this . . . umm . . . accident. And by the way, this young lady is the daughter of one of my fellow chiefs, Radioman Chief Petty Officer Mike Wallace. And her mom is a very nice island girl I've known for a long time. You might not think it looking at her here in this dive bar"—he looked searchingly at Kai, who blushed—"but she's a student at the University of Hawaii. She looks a little shaken up. Maybe you two could get her in a cab and home, which is over at the ammo base west of the naval station?" He turned to the four shipmates of the drunk, who was still struggling to stand up. "You guys, scram. Tell your buddy when he sobers up, if I ever hear of him disrespecting ladies I will personally keelhaul his dumb snipe ass."

As he herded the drunk out the door, the chief looked back over his shoulder. "By the way, I hear you've got a nice left, Ensign. Might want to get on the boxing team on your battlewagon. I do a little boxing myself, although I'm not down at Pearl, I'm the ordnance chief up at Kaneohe Bay. You're gonna fit right into the Pacific Fleet, Ensign." And he was gone into the soft, humid Hawaiian night, swallowed up by the white jumpers and sailor caps. Kai first looked uncertainly at the two ensigns, then raised her head sharply and walked out the door of the bar. They followed her to the cab stand by the YMCA.

A New Snake Ranch and an Old Motorcycle

PEARL CITY, OAHU, HAWAII

I t was well after the nominal 1 a.m. curfew for sailors by the time Scott and Joe got Kai back to her parents' home, a small bungalow in a group of senior enlisted houses near the Naval Magazine on the western side of the island. On the cab ride across Oahu, she expressed her appreciation to Scott for coming to her rescue, and in a way that might not get her in trouble with her father. Learning that Scott was new to the island, Kai promised him a surfing lesson on the following Saturday. They made whispered arrangements as he walked her to the door while Joe Taussig dozed in the front seat of the idling cab.

"I'll come get you at noon on Saturday, okay?" Scott said.

She smiled in the moonlight. "Way too late, you haole boy. We'll have to stake out a lane on the North Shore. Be here at six a.m."

Scott had no idea what she was talking about, but an early start was fine with him. He might have duty on the ship, but he could get out of it if he did. "Is a motorcycle okay?"

"My dad has one and will love it, not that he'll be awake. But when we come back, you can meet him and my mom and compare your motorcycle with his. And my mom will hate it, but that's okay. I've been riding behind my dad since I was a little girl." Scott didn't actually own a motorcycle at the moment, but he hoped to rectify that before Saturday. He walked her to the door, and she brushed his cheek with a chaste kiss, squeezing his left hand. No lights were on inside. She carefully opened the unlocked door, carrying her sandals, and slipped inside in her bare feet, disappearing into her parents' home.

The ensigns took the cab back to the bachelor officers' quarters and returned to their separate rooms. Scott smoked a final Camel cigarette in his room, thinking about Kai. She was a bad choice in many ways—the daughter of an enlisted man, an island girl working in a sailor bar. But his own father had been a sailor, and she was beautiful, with a spirit that stirred him, and something about her tugged at the untamed side he felt in himself. The Hawaiian Islands and the Florida Keys, he thought. A match made in heaven. A snippet of a memorized line from *Reef Points* floated to the top of his mind: "I was rocked in the cradle of the deep." He dozed a bit and thought, Maybe we both were.

Hey, it's only surfing, he thought as he fell asleep. Settle down.

Scott and Joe had agreed to meet in the morning and figure out a place to live, somewhere near the base. Scott was awakened by the sound of a fist pounding on the door of his small room. "Come on, haole boy," Joe cried. "We gotta get you a place of your own to entertain your new friends here in the islands." Scott stumbled out of bed and put on khaki pants and an Izod sport shirt, the latest thing at Murphy's, the clothing store in Annapolis that had outfitted decades of midshipmen becoming officers. He splashed on some Bay Rum cologne, tried to comb his tangled hair, and headed with Joe to the reception area of the sprawling single officers' housing complex. There they found plenty of business cards and flyers on the community bulletin board with rental agents' names, mostly Hawaiian or Asian. Picking one at random, they waited in line for a phone booth and set up an appointment with a woman named Mai Ling, a Chinese American who had the biggest flyer on the board, with a hand-drawn anchor.

They met her at noon. She'd told them to meet her at Pearl City Tavern, an open-air bar just outside the base. Mai Ling— short and thickset, with cropped black hair—was not much older than the two ensigns. They found her smoking a Marlboro in the parking lot. "This is a good place for boy officers," she said. "Not so much sailor bar. They have live monkeys behind the bar. Good whiskey, not so much water in it. Fun place, and close to the gate." The ensigns looked at Pearl City Tavern without much enthusiasm. Scott hoped her taste in bungalows would be better than her choice of bars.

Mai Ling was energetic and had an encyclopedic knowledge of the neighborhoods immediately around the gates of Pearl Harbor Naval Station. It was a series of rough neighborhoods, without much in the way of formal zoning—tattoo parlors and small "gentlemen's bars" stood next to two-story houses and tidy little island bungalows. Due to some financial support from Joe's family, the ensigns were able to expand their horizons beyond the normal means of a couple of very junior officers. Mai Ling was pleasantly surprised at their budget and quickly guided them into a two-bedroom bungalow with a decent lanai overlooking the base. It wasn't much over a mile to the main gate, and the ensigns were comfortable splitting the rent after the "Rear Admiral Taussig supplement" was applied. "You two did well here," said Mai. "I'll have papers for you Monday. Just make sure you have the deposit all set for me and I'll give you keys." She departed in a cloud of cigarette smoke.

Next stop was a used car lot close to the base. There was a tired assortment of beat-up 1930s sedans, mostly with peeling paint and tires so threadbare you could almost see your reflection in their shiny black surface. Scott walked by them to the half dozen motorcycles at the back of the lot, Joe trailing behind him. "I don't get it, Scott," said Joe a little primly. "A motorcycle? Aren't they for the chief's mess?"

Scott laughed. "Joe, I've been a biker since I was fourteen, and my dad was one too, after he got out of the Navy. I bought my first bike when I was fifteen, and part of the reason I played so much poker was to keep trading up until I could get a mint 1935 Indian Super Scout. I kept it under wraps at the home of one of my dad's old shipmates outside of Baltimore the whole time we were at the Academy."

"Good idea," said Joe. "Unauthorized use of a car or motorcycle would have gotten you enough demerits to rip those four stripes right off your shoulders."

"Well, they never caught me, and I gotta tell you, taking that thing out on the country roads over toward Chesapeake Bay kept me sane during a couple of those years."

The cash from the sale of that bike was now burning a hole in his pocket. He looked carefully over the offerings in the lot. "Ah, here's what I'm after." He stood in front of a 1938 Indian Sport Scout, a slightly newer and marginally lesser motorcycle, but it looked serviceable. Gesturing to the salesman, he said, "I'll take this one for a spin if that's okay?"

Fifteen minutes later he was back. "Needs a tune-up, and the front brakes are a little off, but if you can fix those and put a new pair of tires on, I could get close to your ask." He pointed at the sticker taped to the gas tank. The salesman nodded vigorously, and Scott said, "I want it by sixteen hundred, all right?" They went to a diner next to the Pearl City Tavern while the work was done and had decent shredded barbecued pork. They picked up the bike and headed back to the base to gas it up. Scott turned to Joe. "Not a bad day's work, Ensign Taussig. A pleasure sailing in your company here in the tropics." Joe smiled back, and the two ensigns headed to the officers' club to celebrate.

Scott now felt ready for Hawaii—he had a classmate as a wingman, a good motorcycle under him, a bungalow with a nice deck, and at least an idea about a girlfriend. Not bad for a weekend's work, he thought as he showered at the officers' club before hitting the rack. All he needed to do now was to check aboard his battleship. The thought made him nervous, but it was a good nervous. He recalled something else Rear Admiral Taussig had said to the ensigns: "Your first three months will be the most uncomfortable.

But the next six months will be the most dangerous—because that's when you start to think you know what you're doing, and no one ever really does learn the ropes that quickly." Monday couldn't come soon enough. Scott was more than ready to be uncomfortable, so long as he could have a ship's deck under his feet.

A Tale of Two Georges

ABOARD USS *WEST VIRGINIA* AND USS *NEVADA*

BATTLESHIP ROW, FORD ISLAND, PEARL HARBOR
NAVAL STATION, OAHU, HAWAII

E nsign Scott Bradley James stood at the foot of the officers'
brow and looked forward toward the raked bow of the
battleship. The Navy, being highly caste conscious, had
separate brows for officers and enlisted men. Scott swallowed
hard, lingering below the stairway and looking up to the narrow
wooden passage that separated the land from the sea. He could
feel the active bustle of a Monday morning. As he looked up at the
busy quarterdeck, he saw a lieutenant junior grade wearing gloves
and holding the traditional spyglass required by Navy regulation
to signify his authority. The "officer of the deck" presided over the
gateway to USS *West Virginia* with a solemn look on his face,
glancing toward his team, the petty officer of the watch, a couple

of very young-looking enlisted men who were the messengers of the watch, all under the gaze of a salty-looking chief petty officer, who also seemed to be supervising a small working party energetically chipping paint off the deck just aft of the quarterdeck. The racket made Scott wonder if any other organization in the world removed paint with hammers. His head throbbed slightly, but he couldn't tell if it was a mild hangover or nerves. Probably both, he thought to himself.

The lieutenant junior grade, just a couple of years older than Scott, glanced imperiously down to the pier and swept his eyes down him. His expression blank, he looked like a black-and-white photo taped up on a bulkhead. After a long moment, he looked away and said something to the petty officer of the watch, who moved toward the ship's announcing system to ring the ship's bells, marking the nine o'clock hour. Two bells rang out smartly.

It was the appointed hour for Scott to check aboard the ship, and still he lingered at the foot of the brow, his hand on the rail of the stairs. I've been waiting for this forever, Scott thought to himself. But now I'm nervous. Not afraid but nervous. He exhaled hard and adjusted his service dress white uniform. The single-breasted white jacket that buttoned from top to bottom was known in the fleet as "chokers," since the uniform's stiff standing collar generally had that effect. Scott hoped he would not have to wear the outfit much. Regulation required a dress uniform when reporting aboard a new command, and it was too damn hot to wear his dress blues.

He moved his hand to try to get some air down the neck of his chokers and then climbed the steps to the brow of USS *West*

Virginia. Just before stepping onto the quarterdeck, he pivoted to the ship's stern and snapped out the requisite salute to the forty-eight-star American flag that he could not quite see from his vantage point. He stepped onto the quarterdeck itself, turned to face the young officer of the deck, saluted again, and said, "Ensign Scott Bradley James reporting for duty, sir." The JG smiled thinly, shifted the spyglass to a position under his left arm, and reached out his right hand in welcome. "Welcome aboard, Ensign James. Good to have a new George in the wardroom." Scott grimaced inwardly. The junior ensign in a navy warship's wardroom is universally known as either the "boot ensign" or simply "George." It was going to be a pain, a bit of hazing not unlike going through plebe year at Annapolis. He knew he'd have to kowtow to the senior ensign, generally known as the "bull ensign." It's all so stupid, he thought to himself, but hopefully on a ship with a wardroom this size, some other poor bastard will show up pretty soon.

The officer of the deck turned to the petty officer of the watch. "Have the messenger take Ensign James down to the ship's office to get him checked in." Turning to Scott he said: "You've got your orders, right, James?" Scott nodded and held up the thick vanilla-colored folder that held his service and medical records and seven copies of his orders. Scott followed the seaman deuce down the steel passageway, lifting his legs over the eight-inch "knee knockers" that provided the foundation for the watertight doors but also slowed travel. Scott had never set foot on a battleship, and the buzz of male voices, the insistent sound of chipping hammers up on deck somewhere, and the smells of metal, paint, cigarette smoke, and coffee almost overwhelmed him.

They climbed a couple of "ladders," the steep stairs in the warship, and in a few minutes he was sitting at a green-gray desk with a chief petty officer yeoman on the other side of him. "I'm Chief Johnson, the ship's secretary," said the chief, a slender man in his late thirties with a pronounced southern accent. "We'll get you checked in right away, Mr. James, then up to see the executive officer." He turned to another seaman. "Paulsen, take Mr. James to the wardroom and he can have a cup of coffee while we process the orders and set a time to see the XO. Mr. James, you'll be assigned to the gunnery department working for Lieutenant Commander Wilson, the gun boss. He'll figure out where to assign you exactly. I suspect he'll have a division for you, maybe one of the sections assigned to the forward turret. We're short a couple of ensigns, so there's some luck for you. When we've got your call on the XO arranged, we'll come and get you."

Dropped off at the wardroom, Scott settled into one of the chairs in the sitting area and picked up a copy of the U.S. Naval Institute's *Proceedings*, the professional magazine of the sea services. Scott had only glanced at it during his years at the Academy but knew vaguely that it was headquartered there. He started reading an article in the February issue about the Continental Navy sloop *Hornet*, which had been rigged with ten nine-pound guns at a shipyard in Baltimore in 1775. Man, things sure have changed, he thought, reflecting on the *West Virginia*'s guns, which fired 2,700-pound shells. Scott found the article surprisingly interesting. And he figured it wouldn't hurt if people saw him reading *Proceedings* rather than the copy of *Life* magazine also in the sitting area. I guess I've got to start taking this seriously, he thought to himself. His attention started to drift. Coffee, he thought.

As though reading his mind, a large Black mess attendant stepped out the swinging door of the pantry, where the officers' food was prepared. He was a big man, almost six foot four, and had to be carrying over 230 pounds on a generous frame. He said, "Welcome aboard, Ensign. Are you joining the wardroom, sir?" He had an engaging grin and a Texas twang, which seemed incongruous on someone who looked like a prize fighter he'd seen on newsreels in Madison Square Garden.

"I'd love a cup of coffee," said Scott. "Black is fine. I'm Ensign Scott James. What's your name, sailor?"

Another grin, "I'm Petty Officer Miller, sir. People call me Dorie. Coffee coming right up. You want a doughnut with that, Mr. James? We've got a damn good bakery on board."

Scott smiled broadly back. "You bet. That would be swell."

Later in life Scott would wonder how he could have given so little thought to the racial segregation of the U.S. armed forces. Black sailors were relegated to noncombat roles, with the vast majority serving as mess attendants or stewards, like Dorie Miller, trapped in the role of cooking and cleaning. Some stewards essentially served as valets to the officers. Scott had first seen the system on his midshipman cruises and found it foolish. He'd grown up in the Keys with many highly capable Black fishermen, flats fishing guides, and small-craft handlers. He'd fished and sailed with many Black men and found them his equal in all the things that mattered in his eyes. But there were no Blacks at Annapolis as midshipmen, only as cooks and cleaners alongside Filipino sail-ors, another group held down by the system. Scott didn't particu-larly like the system, but he didn't spend a lot of time pondering it either. It was just part of the Navy. At the moment, he was thinking mostly about his pending appointment with the execu-tive officer.

As if in tune with Scott's thoughts, a very young yeoman popped into the wardroom and said, "Mr. James, the XO says he's got too much to do today to meet with you, and for you to check in with your department head. You'll be bunking in the JO junk room—excuse me, sir, the junior officer joint stateroom. Miller here will show you where that is, and if you go back to the quar-terdeck at fifteen hundred, they can get you connected with the gun boss around then. And Chief said to check in to sick bay to have them review your medical record, which we sent down there." The yeoman withdrew.

Scott turned to Dorie Miller with a sour grin. "Looks like I have plenty of free time. Where's this junior officer bunk room?"

Miller barely hid a sympathetic grin and said quietly, "I'm happy to show you, Mr. James. Where's your seabag?"

"Down on the pier, and I'll go bring it up."

Miller looked surprised. "You sit right here, Mr. James, I'll go fetch it, and then maybe we'll go for a walk around the ship if the ensign would like that? I've got spare time until boxing practice at noon."

Scott looked up sharply. "Boxing practice?" His first impres-sion of Miller had been right. "What's that all about?"

Miller grinned. "Oh, we got the best boxing team on Battleship

Row, Mr. James. I'm the heavyweight, and I'm feeling good about our team's chances in the big tournament later this spring. You box?"

Scott grinned back. "Regiment boxing champ, middleweight division, class of 1941. Wouldn't mind trying out for your outfit, Petty Officer Miller."

Miller raised his eyes. "Oh, it ain't my outfit, that's for sure, but we got a chief that was a prize fighter up in Chicago and coaches us. I heard that *Nevada* got one of them Academy types, a hard hitter but a little fella. What's your boxing weight, Mr. James? Where in middleweight?"

"I'm right at one sixty normally, Dorie."

Miller nodded. "And you a leftie, right? Saw you reach for that coffee mug and doughnut southpaw." Scott nodded. "You gonna fit right in, Mr. James. I'm gonna get your seabag, and we'll take a walk around. Then let me introduce you to the boxing team on the fantail."

Scott was beginning to feel more comfortable aboard his new home. "How'd you get the name Dorie, anyway?" he asked.

"Well, sir, my real first name is Doris," Miller said. "It's a lady's name, one of my mom's friends. So I was a Doris, which folks in Texas thought was kind of funny. Growing up as a boy named Doris, that's how I first learned how to fight." They both smiled.

Over on USS *Nevada*, just a few football field lengths down the pier on Battleship Row, Ensign Joe Taussig was having a very different introduction to his new home. After saluting the flag and the officer of the deck on the quarterdeck, he identified himself to the officer of the deck, a full lieutenant whose eyes widened at the name Taussig. The lieutenant spun around to Joe and pumped his hand enthusiastically. "Terrific to meet you, Ensign Taussig. Heard a lot about your family. The captain told us you'd be checking in today, and he's asked for you to be escorted to his cabin immediately upon arrival. Where's your seabag? We'll have the messenger of the watch deliver it to your stateroom, which is all reserved for you and ready to go. Do you want to go through the wardroom first, or right up to the captain's day cabin?"

Joe felt the long reach of his father's gilt-covered sleeves stretching across the miles from Annapolis to Pearl Harbor. The naval aristocracy takes care of its own. Even though his father had been forced to retire, his outspoken stance for building more battleships and preparing for a possible war with Japan had made him an icon within the fleet.

Joe shrugged inwardly. He certainly was not looking for special treatment but figured there was nothing he could do about it. He smiled. "Thanks, sir. I'm so glad to be joining the best battleship in the fleet. Ready to go up and see the captain right away, of course, and if someone could get my seabag to my stateroom, that would be outstanding."

"You bet, Mr. Taussig—mind if I call you Joe?—and after you're done with the captain, the XO will be waiting outside the CO's cabin to personally escort you down to the ship's office, get you checked in, and I'll see you at lunch. By the way, I'm your official sponsor, Lieutenant Tommy Broadcross, but my friends call me Cross."

Joe smiled again and followed the messenger of the watch to the CO's cabin. After a friendly chat with the august four-striper, who mostly wanted to pump the ensign about Rear Admiral

Taussig and his views on the war and shipbuilding, Joe was warmly welcomed by the ship's executive officer. "Good to meet you, Ensign Taussig—mind if I call you Joe?—we've got you all set in a stateroom just aft of the wardroom and near the head. You'll like it—same location of my stateroom when I was a lieutenant JG on *Arizona*. But that's going back a ways."

As he unpacked his seabag in the commodious stateroom designed for two lieutenants, Joe reflected that it was good to be part of the Navy family. He hoped Scott James was doing well next door.

Surf's Up

NORTH SHORE, OAHU, HAWAII

That Saturday, just before sunrise, Ensign Scott James kick-started his Indian Sport Scout motorcycle and headed out to collect Kai. It was breezy even by tropical-island standards as he piloted his motorcycle into the narrow gate to the Naval Magazine toward the small cluster of bungalows where the chiefs had their quarters. Scott noticed a slight smell of barbecue in the air, maybe left over from a luau behind someone's small house from the night before. It smelled good. Roast pig, he guessed. He was hungry.

Out of respect for the neighbors, given the early hour, he killed the engine and walked his motorcycle the last fifty yards leading up to Kai's house. The sun had just risen on the far side of the island, and in the long shadows cast by the mountains he could barely see a small figure standing in front of the house. It was Kai, dressed in a flowered sundress, carrying a small satchel. On the grass next to her was a cup of coffee and rolls of some kind arranged on a paper napkin. "Black coffee okay?" she asked.

"Yup, I'm in the Navy, missy," he replied, a slightly mocking tone in his voice. He drank the coffee gratefully and attacked the pastries, which were sweet buns like he'd seen locals eating down at Waikiki. They were fruity and full of sugar, with a flavor he couldn't quite place. "Boy, that's good," he said.

"It's a malassada," she replied. "Sometimes we call them Portuguese doughnuts. Those have papaya in them. Glad you like them, 'cause you're not getting anything else to eat until we have Spam and rice for lunch. Let's get this show on the road. We're headed to the North Shore, to a beach I know where we can borrow a board for you. Turtle Beach. Mine is up there already. Time to go, haole boy." Scott jumped on the bike. He wondered what Spam was but didn't feel it would be smart to ask.

They headed north on a two-lane road that took them by the Army's Schofield Barracks. Scott was enjoying the warm feeling of Kai hugging him tightly from her seat behind him and occasionally whispering a comment in his ear. She narrated the journey, pointing out the expansive pineapple fields on both sides of the road, a big part of the economy of the islands, farmed by the Dole family for decades. She talked about the soldiers from the division at the barracks, who had a lightning bolt symbol on their shoulder patch. "They don't get into Honolulu as much as they like, and when they do, they like to fight with the sailors," she said. "Mostly the sailors get beat up pretty bad." When they had been touring Hotel Street the week before, Scott and Joe had quite literally bumped into a few Army lieutenants as they strolled by the sailor bar. Like Scott and Joe, they had looked a little out of place in their dress khaki uniforms. If there was going to be a fight with the Japs, Scott thought to himself, these boys from the famous "Tropical Lightning" division headquartered at Schofield Barracks at the top of the island of Oahu had better have some lightning in their veins. They looked skinny and kind of nervous to him.

After an hour or so they arrived at a turnoff to a dirt road marked by a small, hand-painted sign reading "Turtle Beach." Scott parked his Indian Sport Scout on a small bluff and looked down at the waves rolling in. It was a bit after 7 a.m., and there were already a couple of dozen surfers attacking the waves on their big wooden boards. "Man, those things look like boats," said Scott.

Kai laughed. "They are actually mostly hollow, with holes drilled into them to cut the weight down, then covered up on the top and bottom with really thin plywood. They call them Blake boards after the guy who came up with the idea first, and they can cost a lot of money—some of them could cost an ensign a month's pay. And most of them now have little fins on them, which helps when you are trying for a hot curl." Scott looked dubious, and she laughed again. "Don't worry, you won't be doing that anytime soon. We're going to start with just getting you wet." She stepped out of her sundress, revealing a very tanned body in a one-piece suit that did little to help Scott keep his mind on surfing. "Let's grab some boards."

As they walked to a small surf shack by the beach, Kai chatted about her surfing life. "My mom taught me to surf when I was about ten, and I wasn't really big enough for a real board, so they bought me a little version. But I'm hearing there is this new stuff called fiberglass that will make all the boards lighter and make it more even between girls and boys on the waves. "She knocked on the screen door of the surf shop and called out, "Uncle Duke, you home?"

A tall Hawaiian man who looked to be in his late forties came around the counter and hugged her while picking her up. "Beatrice, so nice to see you."

Kai looked uncomfortable for a second. "Uncle Duke, this haole boy is an ensign in the Navy, and he did me a favor on Hotel Street last week. Scott, this is Duke Kahanamoku, the sheriff of Honolulu, but apparently there is no crime there because he spends most of his time up here surfing." Scott and Duke shook hands. "He's not really my uncle, but his family and my mom are really close."

Duke smiled and looked at Scott appraisingly. "So, you're going to be a surfer? I'll believe it when I see it, but you've certainly got the cutest teacher on the beach." He rummaged through the stack of boards leaning against the back wall of his small store and handed one to Scott. "Here's a good starter board for you, Ensign. Try not to bang it up too much. Oh, and stay off the rocks, big guy. Mahalo."

As they put their boards under their arms and walked the short distance to the surf, Scott asked, "Did he call you Beatrice?"

Kai looked annoyed. "Yeah. My father insisted I be named Beatrice after his mother. My mother wanted to call me Kailani or just Kai, which means 'ocean' and 'sky,' which is my middle name. I much prefer to be called Kai—but some people insist on Beatrice."

Scott nodded and grinned. "Yeah, I'd go with Kai if I were you too."

Happy to change the subject, Kai filled Scott in on her "uncle." "He won three golds and two silver medals swimming in the Olympics from 1912 to 1924." At first Scott assumed she was kidding, but it quickly dawned on him that she was not. "He only ran for sheriff 'cause it leaves him plenty of time to surf, run his little shop, and work on guiding the outrigger teams."

"What's an outrigger team?" Scott asked.

She laughed again, something she did frequently in response to Scott's questions, he had noticed. "I thought you were a Navy man, haole boy. Outriggers have been on this ocean for, maybe, three or four thousand years. My mom's ancestors came here in them, and now there are teams all around the islands. Uncle Duke is the best steersman ever, and I bet he'll win the championship every year until he dies. Which will be a long time, 'cause he's almost like Superman. And his wife, Nadine, is gorgeous, by the way, a high-society dancer and piano player who is the headliner at the Royal Hawaiian, which even you must have heard about." Scott nodded and tried to say something, but she was on a roll. "Nadine loves Uncle Duke, but he doesn't make any money, so she keeps performing."

Scott kept his voice casual, as though he went to the Pink Palace of the Pacific nightly. "Oh, Joe and I dropped in there last weekend. Nice place, but a little dead. Really older crowd. We had drinks but left to find some action. Caught up with Ernest Hemingway too, he's a friend from Key West. Didn't see anyone named Nadine performing. But we wanted something a little live-lier, which is how we met you, by the way."

She laughed again and said simply, "Now we surf."

With that, she grabbed her board, said "Watch me a few times," and splashed into the waves. Scott tried to focus on her request to observe her technique, but mostly he enjoyed watching her body slide around in the black swimsuit. Surfing looked like a combination of a bunch of different physical skills, he thought: the paddling looked pretty easy, but then she was positioning herself on the edges of the swells. He watched her crash through a couple of big ones, diving like a duck to get by them. Kai then turned the board and seemed to effortlessly pop back up on it, looking quite tiny on the big surfboard. Her balance seemed steady, and she rode the wave to the shallow water. Scott started to walk forward toward the waves a little uncertainly, but Kai stopped him. "Let's start on the beach, Scott." It was the first time she had called him something besides haole boy, which felt like progress.

For the next half hour, they practiced "surfing" on the beach. First she had him stretch thoroughly, something he hated doing and often neglected, even when warming up for boxing. His inclination was always to simply jump in and warm up as he went along. But on her beach, it was her rules, he figured, so he stretched as she directed. Next she had him practice throwing the board down, kneeling on it, then popping up. Finally, she gestured to him to pick up his board and come down to the water.

This surfing thing is a lot like life, Scott thought to himself. You spend too much time warming up, your equipment isn't exactly what you want, someone better at it is always judging you, and you're pretty sure you're going to fall on your ass a bunch of times. And that was exactly what happened, over and over again. When he did manage to stand up, he immediately fell off the board. A couple of times the board veered into the lane of two well-built Hawaiian teenagers, who waggled their hands good-naturedly, their little fingers and thumbs sticking out from their fists, saying something that sounded like "snack" or maybe "shack." Back on the beach, Scott asked Kai, "Hey, what are those guys saying to me?"

She laughed. "Don't worry, it's friendly. They are saying 'shaka,' which means 'take it easy' or 'things are great.' They think it's funny an old haole boy like you is trying to surf. They all started learning around the time they started walking. I was actually late starting, 'cause my dad said I had to learn how to swim first." She shook her wet mane of black hair, squeezed the water out of it, and threw it over her shoulder. The little gold cross around her neck was swinging back and forth, glinting in the late-morning sun. "Let's get some lunch."

As they walked away from the surf, Scott pointed to the cross around her neck. "Do you always wear that? Even when you're surfing?"

She touched it. "It never comes off, ever. There's no clasp. My parents put it on me when I turned twelve and said it would protect me, and the jeweler soldered it in place."

Scott raised his eyebrows. "Well, that's one way to avoid losing your jewelry." They both laughed and she touched the cross again.

They walked back to the shack, where Duke was serving up fist-sized helpings of Spam—pink pressed pork loaf—and big hunks of rice. He was grilling hot dogs out back. Dessert was chopped-up pineapple and coconuts from a cooler. Everything cost a quarter. Another cooler was filled with Primo beer, Cokes, and some kind of Hawaiian soda called Kist Kola. Kai insisted on paying. She ate a hot dog and a big chunk of Spam, and downed two beers, which was more than Scott managed. "Got to keep your calories up for surfing," she said.

For most of an hour, they sat in the shade of a couple of scraggly bushes and talked about their families, Navy connections from having fathers who had been enlisted sailors, the differences between Florida and Hawaii. Scott said, "Back in Florida, we worry a lot about hurricanes. You call them tsunamis here, right?"

She nodded. "We get them once in a while, but we're really just a handful of little dots in a huge ocean. Not like Florida, just hanging down from the U.S. like a big target. Have you gone through one?"

Scott nodded. "Too many times. Key West seems to attract them even more than other parts. And they can cause tornadoes, winds over a hundred knots, and flooding. The sky turns black, and you think there is no way it'll ever go away. But after they blow through, you clean up and rebuild and the air gets so calm and clear."

Kai cocked her head. "Sometimes you have to go through the storm to get to the safe water," she said. "I'm studying history at the University of Hawaii, and focusing on the Pacific and the big migrations from east Asia. You see it again and again in world history: the storms and then the clear water."

Scott didn't know much about the history of the Pacific, but what she said made sense. There's more to this girl than surfing and Spam, he thought.

After an hour, Kai stood up. "Okay, haole boy, now you are going to have to ride at least one wave in, or my reputation on this beach is finished. Don't get nervous just 'cause everyone is watching you." Two hours later, after dozens of attempts, Scott managed to ride three waves by his score, or, as Kai put it, "one and a half okay, and another one that maybe wasn't terrible." He was exhausted, sweating under the late-afternoon tropical sun, and wondering what came next. "Shave ice," said Kai. "Time for shave ice at Waiola down near Waikiki. It just opened last year. I've been having shave ice since I was a baby—it is big with the Japanese families." Scott did not look enthusiastic. "You'll like it, haole boy. Just fluffy ice shaved into a bowl with lots of yummy toppings. I like mango, but you can mix them up. And on the very bottom is a kind of paste made out of sweet red beans. You can even have a little vanilla ice cream on top. Perfect end to the day, 'cause I told my mom and dad I'd be home for dinner."

Scott had been hoping to take her somewhere for dinner. He felt a little let down but sensed it better not to press his luck. "Okay, *Beatrice*, if you insist," he said in a mock-dejected tone.

She swatted his arm. "I'm going to make you buy me one with pomegranate seeds on it. My favorite, and not cheap, haole boy."

They packed up, dropped off their boards, and said goodbye to Uncle Duke. Soon they were on Scott's motorcycle and headed south to the Waiola grocery store. As they rode, Scott called back to her, "I'd like to do that again. Surfing. I could get better, I bet. You don't want people on that beach to think you failed at your mission." He paused. "And maybe we could go fishing sometime, 'cause I think I could show you a few things about that." She hugged him hard and kissed his ear, her lips warm and slightly damp. "I *bet* you could, Ensign Scott James. That's a deal."

Half a Year

PEARL HARBOR, OAHU, HAWAII

When Scott looked back on this time decades later, he thought of Kai and the long, lazy days learning to surf and eventually achieving a modest level of adequacy. He thought of finding his way around the island's surfing beaches and small local restaurants under her guidance; slowly becoming closer to her physically, with brief kisses turning into longer and longer embraces, his hands roving a bit, although always kept in check.

Roaring around Oahu every weekend on his motorcycle, he loved the feeling of her soft frame wrapped around his back and her lips whispering local lore into his ear. They spent every weekend together, at the beach or on the road somewhere around Oahu. Kai learned—and later told Scott—that her parents were a bit nervous about the level of attention paid to their daughter by the young officer, but they both knew Kai well enough to realize that any attempt to limit her exposure to Ensign Scott Bradley James would only push her in his direction. Kai's mom told her that her father rationalized: "Well, for an Annapolis graduate, he isn't as stuck up as most. And his dad was a quartermaster. Plus, he's got a good motorcycle."

Kai continued to surprise Scott with the scope of her studies at the University of Hawaii. "Jeez, who knew they had a big Department of Pacific History over there?" he said to Joe Taussig. "She is deep into Chinese and Japanese history, going back a couple of thousand years."

Joe nodded. "My dad spent some time over there when he was stationed at Pearl. Told me they have some of the top people in the U.S., especially on Japan."

When Scott pressed Kai on why she was studying Japanese history, she said simply, "They are a big part of these islands, haole boy. In case you don't know, there are big Japanese communities all over Oahu, and they run lots of the important small businesses. They came here in successive waves, and they are a big part of the melting pot of these islands. It would be terrible if we were to get into a war with Japan, and I bet it would go very hard on them. There is a lot of stupid prejudice against them, but I have a lot of friends and plenty of classmates at UH who are Japanese but proud to be part of America."

Well, Scott thought to himself, if we end up fighting them, someone is going to have to figure out what to do with the thousands of Japanese Americans here. He vowed to learn more about their history. He discovered that Joe Taussig was already studying Japanese.

Scott and Joe's snake ranch had become a destination for junior officers on Battleship Row, but it was Joe, not Scott, who had the "hot and cold running dames," as Second Lieutenant Kelley observed upon his arrival. Kelley was one of a trio of junior Marine Corps officers in the hundred-man Marine detachment aboard USS *Arizona*. "I asked for the Philippines or even Wake Island, but some bastards in the class pulled strings and got the forward billets," he said. The irrepressible Marine had arrived in Pearl in the midsummer, fresh out of the Marine Corps' mandatory course for fresh-caught second lieutenants, the Basic School at Quantico, Virginia. "Never forget they capitalize the *T* in 'The Basic School,' God knows why," Kelley said, draining a can of Hawaiian Primo beer, which he dismissed as flavored horse piss. "But at least it's cold. Horse piss is pretty warm, I hear."

Their three battleships—*West Virginia*, *Arizona*, and *Nevada*—competed in every dimension alongside the rest of the eight warships on Battleship Row, and the young officers were soon caught up in it. Kelley and Scott were on their ships' boxing teams, and Taussig had signed up for the Battleship Row golf tournament. He was a near-scratch golfer, known for a conservative but steady approach to the game that eventually wore down and defeated his opponents. "He bores them to death out there," said Kelley. After winning a round, Taussig was known for pulling out of his pocket an expensive Danish harmonica he'd purchased on youngster cruise while at Annapolis and serenading his defeated opponents with "Auld Lang Syne." No one was exactly sure why he chose that song, but it annoyed the hell out of the losing teams.

"It's probably the only song he knows," Scott told Kelley, "outside of 'Navy Blue and Gold' and the Navy Hymn."

"He better learn 'The Marines' Hymn' if this war starts," Kelley said. "And he better quit playing that thing on the golf course, or sooner or later someone is going to stick a putter up his ass."

Beyond Kai and his Academy classmates, what mattered to Scott James was excelling on his ship. He was regarded as a bit of a halfway character, not a "real" officer with an upper-class pedigree and certainly not a card-carrying member of the naval aristocracy like Joe Taussig; but he was also an Annapolis graduate, and the fact of his time as a four-striper at the Academy, one of the top leadership spots in the Regiment of Midshipmen, had become known. The wardroom could not quite figure him out: he was a Naval Academy graduate but spent a lot of time hanging out with an island girl and drove a motorcycle like a sailor. He seemed to pal around with an admiral's son but was the offspring of an enlisted sailor from the swampy Florida Keys. He was a top-notch boxer but spent a bit too much time talking to the Black sailors on the team. To many of his shipmates, he was an enigma, and that was fine with Scott.

He continued to carry deep inside himself a feeling of guilt and inadequacy that he doubted he'd ever entirely resolve. Partly it was his blue-collar background, partly it was his guilt over cheating on the navigation test, partly it was his own uncertainty as to whether he belonged in the highest levels of the Navy. He confided some of his doubts to Kai one night. "You know, we are both children of enlisted men, of sailors. Maybe that's why we belong together?"

To his surprise, she grew angry. "Maybe that's how you think about it, Scott, but I don't. I'm a college student, and someday I'm going to be a historian and a professor, and teach people about the Pacific. And you are an Annapolis graduate and supposedly on a top ship and, according to you when you talk to your friends, doing really well. And you're my boyfriend, which is about the best thing I can think of about you. So stop feeling sorry for yourself." She got up from the couch and walked out onto the lanai, wrapping herself in a silk kimono.

Scott walked out, put his arms around her, and kissed the back of her neck. She settled back into his arms and they looked across the mountains and didn't say anything else.

But something else was harder to shake. At odd moments, Caroline came back to haunt him. She had died alone and afraid, and his imagination tortured him with visions of her final hours. She sometimes appeared in his dreams waving at him languidly from across the brow of a ship. Worst of all, he felt the guilt of knowing that her ending had been his beginning. He'd not lived up to his ideals, and certainly not to the Navy's.

Scott told Kelley about his nightmares one night when the two of them were alone at the house, drinking the Jameson Irish whiskey that one of Kelley's uncles had shipped out to them. Kelley took a sip of the warm amber liquid and rolled it around in his mouth before answering. "All I know, Scott, is that you did what you could. Maybe you didn't think enough about her and what she was going through. And maybe you weren't ready to quit the

Academy and have a kid and go back to the Keys and be a fisherman, but somehow I doubt that was a future Caroline was very interested in either. Sometimes life just has its way with us, and things don't turn out fair or right all the way around. Back in Ireland, we say to travelers, 'May the road rise up to meet you,' but sometimes when it rises up, it smacks you square in the face, and knocks you down to boot."

Scott nodded, but he was unconvinced. There was a block of sadness inside him, mixed with a sense that he had failed at something important, that had formed into a stone lodged at his core.

Some mornings, Scott literally ran up the officer's brow, throwing himself into the endless routines of a junior officer on a battleship, as if trying to outrun all of his doubts. He quickly mastered his duties as a division officer in the vaunted gunnery division, assigned with his battle station to a forward turret. He had gotten to know the twenty-five sailors under his direct command, and could call them by first name, aware of who was excelling and who was having trouble. He liked and respected his chief gunner's mate and had learned a lot from him about how to keep his distance from the men without seeming too aloof or uncaring. He sensed his chief liked him as well. "Hey, Chief, how are we doing?" he asked Chief Pontius one day, as he often did. "Should I be pushing the weapons officer for more training time? More live gun shoots? What could we be doing better?" They were sitting in a corner of the chief's mess, where Chief Pontius had invited Scott for a midmorning cup of coffee.

Pontius picked up a doughnut from the platter on the table

between them. "We're doing okay, Mr. James. You let me worry about the men and the training for now, and you concentrate on the paperwork and impressing the department head. Tell him about some of the good sailors we got, figure out how to get them advanced in rate. In this here division, we got to keep our division of labor, sir." He took a huge bite of the frosted doughnut and nodded vigorously.

Scott nodded. "Makes sense, but I have a couple ideas on the training side, Chief. I jotted a few of them down here." He pushed a couple of sheets of yellow legal-pad paper toward Pontius. "We could rotate the men into different roles, make sure if someone was hit in action, someone else could step in. Kind of cross-training. I'd like to think about that. Take these and let's talk in a couple more days. And thanks for the coffee." He stood up.

The chief nodded amiably, watched Scott depart the wardroom, and finished his doughnut. On the way out, he threw the papers into a trash can and brushed the crumbs off his uniform before heading up to the forward turret.

While the ship was in port, Scott spent extra time qualifying belowdecks as an engineer, learning the intricate piping of the steam propulsion system, regarding the huge pipes and valves as the blood vessels of his own future. "Are you trying to be a snipe, James?" asked the main propulsion assistant, a pudgy thirty-five-year-old non–Annapolis graduate. "You're way too topside for that, Ensign. I thought you were in the kiss-ass gunnery division."

Scott smiled politely. He liked the engineering spaces, their own sweaty kingdom, a dimly lit, stygian set of caverns belowdecks, with the engineers flitting over and around the massive boilers, the main reduction gears that drove the huge propellers, and the huge gray distillers, arrayed like boulders in an iron desert, that created the water that was boiled into steam to drive the shafts.

When he told Joe Taussig he was tracing engineering systems, Joe told him he was crazy. "For an ensign, it's all about the gunnery and the ship handling. Everyone knows that."

Scott rolled his eyes. "Hey, you're studying Japanese, for Chrissakes. Knowing what goes on belowdecks is at least as important, at least for a JO." Scott regarded each piece of gear in the system as a key to a door he wanted desperately to open: a door to advancement, to command, to winning the race against his contemporaries.

He qualified as an engineering officer of the watch in his spare time over the course of five months, something nearly unheard of for a topside officer. The executive officer, an ambitious commander himself, took notice and commended Scott with a terse note: "I hear a Bravo Zulu is in order, Ensign James. Not many deck watch officers get their engineering qualifications done so quickly." Scott cherished that single "BZ" above any grade he'd ever gotten at Annapolis.

He also made rapid progress on the bridge, qualifying as junior officer of the deck within a few weeks. He was chosen to conn the ship back into Pearl Harbor from a week at sea in only the second month he was aboard. The captain, famously aloof, feigned not to notice the skill of his junior officer's rudder commands, but the pilot, a retired Navy captain, said, "You've a nice touch with the conn, Ensign. Been at sea before the Navy?" When Scott quietly told him he was the son of a Navy quartermaster, the old pilot's eyes lifted up, the crow's-feet at the corners flaring. "Ah, good, where is he now?"

Scott said simply, "My father's a charter skipper in South Florida, Cap'n."

Nodding, the pilot said: "That's a fine spot for an old quartermaster, Ensign. You tell him Captain Bob Natter said that his son's a good ship handler."

Scott wrote his father a letter, passing along the name and compliments of the retired captain, and a month later got a short note from his father: "He wouldn't remember me, but Commodore Robert Natter led my old destroyer squadron. He's a good one." Scott tucked the letter into a battered cigar box in which he kept mementos and letters that were especially meaningful. Alongside it were his father's chief petty officer anchors, his own four-striper midshipman lieutenant commander insignia, and a couple of short, sweet, and still-scented notes from Caroline that he couldn't bear to throw away.

The best part of each week was the weekend with Kai. But the best part of every weekday was boxing practice on the fantail of the battleship. The gear was simple—four heavy bags suspended from the overhead, a ring for sparring, a half dozen speed bags mounted on the forward bulkhead. Working out in tropical heat, on a steel deck, took a huge physical toll on the twenty-man team. They had a lead boxer in each weight class, and Scott quickly nailed down the middleweight slot. He became good friends with Petty Officer Dorie Miller and often sparred with him. The big man's weight and reach made it a battleship-versus-cruiser kind of fight, but Scott used his slightly better speed and much better technique to get in enough punches to keep it interesting. He suspected that Dorie could drop him with three or four punches in a real fight, but the experience of dancing around the heavyweight kept Scott in the best shape of his life. "You were on fire today, Mr. James," said Dorie in his Texas twang after an exhausting five-round sparring session.

Scott, trying to get his wind back, simply nodded. When he got his breath, he said, "Just trying to work off those doughnuts you're always feeding me, Dorie. Just think what I could do if you weren't weighing me down."

Miller feinted with his left and came up fast with a right hook, pulling it at the last second. "You're plenty fast, Mr. James. I'm gonna make sure you get double ice cream tonight after dinner."

Occasionally they would conduct practice matches with one or another of the battleships. Kelley had become the captain of the USS *Nevada* team. He and Miller were a good match, although if forced to bet, Scott would have put his money on the big Texan mess attendant. The battleship tournament, which led into the wider Pacific Fleet competition, was scheduled for late in the fall. "We're gonna clean your clock," said Kelley to Scott while they sprayed a mixture of vinegar and spices on a pig shoulder roasting on the charcoal grill behind the lanai.

"Nope," Scott said. "You know I can take your middleweight, that gunner's mate, and my money is on Dorie at heavyweight, not you."

Kelley took a long swig of beer. "You're dreaming, Scottie, my boy. You better come up with a better battle plan."

They looked down at the sizzling pork just as Joe Taussig appeared in his golf regalia. "Are you two arguing over boxing again? Why don't you take up golf? That's the officer's sport, you know."

Kelley looked Joe up and down. "Not gonna be a lot of golf when the war starts, laddie. And for some of us, I'd say boxing is going to come in a lot handier."

Kelley had decided to save his money and live on his battleship in a small stateroom, but he spent so much time at Scott and Joe's bungalow that they joked about charging him rent. Kelley made up for it by bringing beer and scotch and sharing his Irish whiskey shipments, and by tending the bar and bouncing the occasional drunk junior officer. Soon the snake ranch by the Pearl City Tavern acquired a name for itself, and plenty of local girls found their way to the Friday- and Saturday-night parties. Scott kept Kai close, often with an arm draped over her shoulder. They were a striking couple, she with an orchid in her onyx hair, he with an easy Florida grin, light freckles, and sandy hair, often in need of a regulation cut. He picked up that some of the junior officers wondered what he was doing with a "native girl," but his reputation for boxing and hard work on the ship silenced the negative commentary, at least in his presence.

Unlike Scott, Joe Taussig was always the perfect Navy junior officer, his hair cut weekly by a local barber recommended by his father and pomaded brilliantly, flashing under the tiki torches they lit at sunset on party nights. The local girls, mostly daughters of Navy captains and rear admirals, knew all about the Taussig family and competed for Joe's attention. "My dad's really not liking his 'retirement,'" Joe said to Scott one evening. "He's taking it pretty hard being kind of shut down by the White House. All he did was tell the truth—that he thinks we are heading for a war with Japan."

"Ah, it only adds to your reputation as the admiral's kid, Joe," said Kelley. "Most of our dads wouldn't know a damn thing about it. Hell, Kai knows more than most of the bozos in my family." He winked at Kai, who rolled her eyes at him and punched him on the arm. Joe went back to working the crowd, effortlessly flipping the records between big-band and Hawaiian ukulele music. The bar on the folding table always had rum, whiskey, and plenty of ice. The beer was in a big washtub alongside the folding-table bar, with a church key dangling from one of the legs to open the beer bottles. Kai loved to mix rum with fruit juices, and her favorite was pomegranate, especially with a few of the tiny seeds on top of the tropical daiquiri. The events lasted until well after midnight, usually with plenty of dancing and some quiet departures of couples for either the bungalow's bedrooms or other destinations.

As the night grew late, Scott would maneuver Kai toward one of the three small bedrooms. They felt the physical side of their relationship moving forward slowly, like a deep ocean swell. They shared long kisses, hugging fully clothed on Scott's lumpy bed, with Scott's hands moving gently over her body, urging but not demanding. Kai was only nineteen and not ready for much more, and Scott sensed her hesitation alongside a hunger to go forward. Gently, gently, he thought to himself. Work the reel gently, haole boy. The time was coming, he thought, as the summer slowly turned to fall.

War remained a kind of steady background noise. It was the buzz on radio programs about another city falling to the Japanese, the newspaper headlines about Nazi advances, the worried looks on people's faces and the flat tone in their voices when they talked at the officers' club on the base. Everyone could hear it, but almost everyone tried to ignore it and pretend they couldn't quite make out what it was.

But what *does* a war sound like, Scott asked himself, when it is coming toward you? He pondered the question on a long night on the midwatch in *West Virginia*, steaming smoothly off the west coast of Oahu for gunnery exercises. It was the sound of marching soldiers, for sure, a steady, rhythmic drumbeat of boots hitting ground. War was also the sound of airplanes buzzing through a night sky, like wasps or bees. And war was the sound of huge steel ships firing their enormous guns, hurling tons of explosives with every massive broadside. The sound of death. Part of him wanted it to come, and come fast, so he could be part of that war and fire those big guns at distant, unseen enemy ships. He knew it was wrong to wish for war, and part of him did not, but what he deeply wished for, what he wanted above all, was to be promoted fast and to show that he mattered, that he could be a part, maybe one day a big and important part, of the U.S. Navy.

One night when he got off the midwatch on the battleship, he walked aft toward his rack in the junior officer bunk room, past the radio shack. Coming from inside he heard the click and clack of the teletype keys hitting the perforated rolls of paper, a thousand times a minute between all the machines hurling knowledge and intelligence and orders to the battleship. He paused and looked into the radio room, at the radiomen moving between the terminals and a chief in rumpled khakis sipping coffee at a table near the door. The chief looked up at Scott with a blank expression, got up, and shut the door to the passageway. Classified, I guess, Scott thought. As he ambled back to the wardroom for midrats, he thought about that sound, the clickety-clack of those keys. That too was the sound of a war coming. Scott reflected that those daily messages were the keys to his own fate, the future of his battleship, and the destiny of the Navy in a coming war. "Look, Scott," Joe had said to him earlier in the week, "Japan is on the move. U.S. intelligence is gathering more and more indications and warnings of a coming storm, classmate. It's still a distant squall, still deep in the Pacific, but it's coming. You don't have to be an admiral to figure that one out."

Scott, Kelley, and Joe discussed it all endlessly. Kai listened, and often added a thought that hadn't occurred to any of them, a piece of history or the meaning of a word in Japanese or something about the Chinese coastline. "You know, Churchill said to Roosevelt, 'Give us the tools and we will finish the job.' Boy, that's some balls," Kelley said, then looked at Kai and said, "Excuse my French." Everyone knew that Lend-Lease was all that was keeping the British afloat. All of them except Kai had nothing but scorn for the America First crowd, who sought to keep the U.S. out of the war. "Hell, we can fight them over there—an away game—or sooner or later they will come here, and we'll have to fight them on the home court. No thanks. I'm ready to go," said Kelley.

"My dad thinks we won't have to wait much longer," said Joe. He pointed out that the Japanese were crushing the Chinese on every front through the long summer of 1941. "And with the Russians being invaded by Hitler, they won't have any competition in the North Pacific."

Kai looked thoughtful. "But no one's attacking us here. Why should we go and fight for them, the British or the Chinese? Those are big oceans."

The three young officers all twisted their lips in disgust. "Come on, Kai," Scott said. "Your dad's a Navy man. You know better. We can't let the Japs just roll across Asia. Look at that idiot Charles Lindbergh, some hero. He said the other day that the British, the Jewish, and the Roosevelt administration are trying to get us into a war. He's a Nazi-loving bastard."

Kai just shook her head and took another sip of her pomegranate daiquiri. "It won't be all glory and medals, you know. Look at the Great War. Twenty million dead, and that's just in Europe."

The argument continued, and Scott found it hard to tune out Kai's quiet logic. But Kelley said, "Look, I hate those limey bastards, but they are in the shit and fighting hard. I'll give them that, and I'm for what Roosevelt is doing. And yeah, we should keep talking to the Japs, maybe we can work something out, but my guess is Joe's dad is more right than not, and our job is to be ready."

Scott sensed something changing in Kai as the war talk increased through the summer and fall. She was both more intimate physically and less emotionally involved. After months of calling him Scott, she had reverted to mostly referring to him as haole boy, and often in the third person: "Would haole boy like to come by on Friday night?" He couldn't figure it out, because despite her slightly mocking manner, she clung to him fiercely, grappling with him on his single bed, offering more liberties than ever. It confused him, and excited him. He thought maybe she knew this could all end at any minute. "If a war breaks out, I'm gone on that battlewagon for a year or more," he had told her. The thought of losing her either way—through the harsh discipline of separation engineered by a war and his service to the Navy or through her own fear of committing to someone who might be gone in a moment—was deeply unsettling.

When an opportunity came to spend a night with her, a real night without a curfew imposed by her parents, he seized it. In late November, she mentioned that her parents would be going to see one of her mom's relatives on the Big Island over the first weekend in December. As the weekend approached, he asked, "Are you staying home alone, all by yourself at your house?" Kai looked at him with wide eyes and nodded. "Let's go out to dinner on Saturday," he said.

Pausing a second, she replied, "Why don't you just come over early, and leave your motorcycle outside the base? Walk to the house after dark, and I'll make us dinner, something good." Scott was in the duty section Saturday night, required to be on the ship. But with no quarterdeck watch scheduled, he figured he could arrange for someone to sign his name on the duty roster.

They looked at each other and smiled. For Scott, in that moment, all that was before him was a beautiful island girl and all the time in the world. It was December 6, 1941.

Love and War

K ai made him a light dinner of steamed shrimp and coconut rice, with a side salad of papaya and shredded peppers, served on her mother's hand-polished teak flat plates. She looked lovely in a colorful sundress with a halter top, her hair loose and falling to her shoulders. Scott brought a bottle of white wine he'd bought at the Pearl City Tavern. They had a long, lazy dinner as the sun set and the smell of woodsmoke rose in the breezy night air from the Saturday-night barbecues around the western side of the island. She spun a few records on her parents' turntable, mostly big-band and jazz groups and songs like Glenn Miller's "In the Mood." Before dinner, she had a daiquiri, and he drank a whiskey on the rocks. They didn't talk a lot, but after she'd had a second glass of wine over the food, she reached across the table and simply squeezed his hand, looking down at the table. Scott got up, pushing his chair back, and pulled her up and into his arms. Together they walked down the hallway in the center of the bungalow and kissed at the entrance to her bedroom. "Are you sure this is what you want?" he whispered into her ear.

"Yes, now, I want you now," she said, her head on his chest. They moved into the tiny bedroom and fell together onto the narrow bed.

Scott had been with other girls, first in his midteens in the freewheeling world of Key West, then on cruise while at the Academy, and with Caroline. But never, as far as he knew, with a virgin. He wanted it to be a voyage of gentle discovery for Kai. He knew enough to take it slow and sweet. Afterward, as they lay together, he asked her how she was doing. "I love you, Scott," she said.

"I love you too."

They began again, this time longer and more certainly, and when they finished, she kissed his chest and moved to lie on her side and wrap herself around him, possessing him more confidently than he'd ever been held before. They fell asleep sometime before midnight and awoke a few hours later when the moon rose, reaching for each other once again.

Afterward, Kai fell asleep first and Scott smoked a final cigarette, looking at her chest rising and falling as she lay on the bed under a single sheet in the light of the tropical moon. The cross had gotten tangled in her hair and turned around, displayed on the back of her slender neck. He ground out his smoke, yawned, stretched, and finally dozed off, awakened sometime after dawn by the soothing buzz of bees that changed into the sound of Japanese fighters droning in the air overhead. For the rest of his life,

Scott couldn't hear a bee without feeling afresh the horrible realization that the United States was under attack.

One thought dominated all the others in that terrible moment on Sunday morning: Ensign Scott Bradley James was absent without leave from his duty station in a time of war. With a sick, cold feeling in his gut, he kissed Kai hard once, opened the screen door to the bungalow, ran to where he had stashed his motorcycle, and violently kick-started it. As he sped away from the Naval Magazine, he knew his career hung in the balance that Sunday morning, to say nothing of his life. Gunning the motorcycle, he looked up at the lines of Japanese Zeros overhead—they were flying straight at the naval base, and Scott couldn't understand why there wasn't an opposing line of Navy and Army Air Corps fighters challenging them. Then he answered his own question: the fleet was waking up to holiday routine. Jesus, we will be sitting ducks. Just then the first explosions could be heard ahead, toward the naval station, deep booming sounds punctuated by shorter static bursts—anti-air guns firing, maybe some machine guns.

Scott frantically swerved the motorcycle into the lane of cars trying to get into the base—everyone was trying to get to their ships, even as the bombs were falling. He could see smoke rising over Battleship Row and heard the more distant thump of additional explosions over toward the flight line. He steered the motorcycle up the narrow shoulder of the road to the main gate, where the Marines were simply waving cars in, trying to get as many officers and sailors to their stations as possible, screaming in frustration at the confusion. Jesus, Scott thought, how am I going to get aboard in the middle of general quarters? It hit him that ironically the attack was perhaps the best-case scenario for a surreptitious return to the ship—no one was going to be focusing on a single ensign running up the officer's brow. And they'll probably just be trying to get the ship underway, he thought. Leaving his motorcycle by the side of the quay wall, he jumped into a liberty barge someone had commandeered and headed to Battleship Row on Ford Island, jumping across the bow of the small boat and sprinting toward his ship.

USS *West Virginia* was moored next to USS *Tennessee*. Scott eyed the Japanese planes flying back and forth over the harbor, concentrating their fire on the battleships. He glanced at his watch: a little after 0800. The gongs of general quarters were sounding again and again as he mounted the brow, tossed a salute at the flagstaff where the U.S. flag should have been flying, and headed to his battle station. At that moment, he felt a Japanese torpedo hit the port side of his ship, which shuddered violently, wrenching under his feet almost simultaneously with a big explosion toward the stern. The big ship shuddered again, and a shiver ran through Scott as the deck suddenly tilted. Over the next confused minutes, explosions seemed to be multiplying around the length and breadth of the ship. The acrid smell of smoke, fuel, and cordite filled the passageways. He tried to count the number of big explosions: at least six torpedo hits, and bombs at the level of the main deck. And now he began to hear the screams of the wounded, the shrieking of men in excruciating pain, and the hoarse shouts of the officers and chiefs trying to organize some kind of resistance. A lieutenant he knew slightly, the assistant fire-control officer, Claude Ricketts, swept by him trying to organize a damage-control effort back aft.

Scott pressed on to get to the forward gun turret, where his division was mustering.

As he hustled by the wardroom, he saw Petty Officer Dorie Miller looking up and down the corridor. "What are you doing, Dorie? Where's your battle station?" Miller looked sickened. "It's right here. I came here to the wardroom, Mr. James, to get further instructions, but no one is here. So I'm going to get topside. The captain must be up on the bridge right now, and he may need me up there. I want to go help Captain Bennion."

Scott didn't have the authority to order anyone from his battle station, but he knew Dorie—nothing would keep him from the fight topside. He simply said, "You got it right, Dorie. Go where you hear the guns firing and try to help. I'm going up to the forward turret with my division. Good luck." The ship shook again, hit somewhere forward and below the waterline by what Scott guessed was an air-launched torpedo. Almost immediately, he could sense the huge battleship beginning to settle into the water. So much for getting underway, Scott thought, as he pushed his way through the smoky passageways toward the bow.

He quickly saw that the expanding fires would cut him off from the forward gun mount. And anyway, Scott figured no one was going to be using a nine-inch gun against Japanese Zeros, so he returned aft toward the wardroom and almost ran into Dorie Miller's massive form. Scott grabbed his arm and said, "Let's go to Times Square and see what we can do." At the central crossing point in the passageways of the ship, they made their way through the smoke and haze, skirting parties of sailors fighting internal fires. At Times Square, a chief shouted at them to head up to the midships anti-air mounts where more men were needed. Before they could set out that way, the ship's communications officer, Lieutenant Commander Don Johnson, grabbed them by the arms and said, "Come with me to the bridge. The CO is hit, and we need to get him down to sick bay."

When they got to the conning tower, Scott saw his aloof commanding officer slumped over on the metal deck, dark blood oozing out of his stomach, where he was clutching a towel. Dorie reacted first, pulling a stretcher out of a nearby damage-control locker and putting it gently on the deck next to the CO. Their captain tried to wave them off, but Scott and Dorie rolled him sideways onto the stretcher, Dorie whispering to the CO. "Let's get him off the exposed part of the bridge wing," Scott said. The three of them got him under a steel bulkhead in a safer position. Fully conscious, the captain kept asking Scott for a damage-control report, although his voice was weakening.

Scott looked down at him. "We're taking on water fore and aft, sir, but the damage-control crews are in position and fighting the fires and the flooding." He had no idea if that was accurate but hoped it was what the captain would want to know. The captain nodded weakly, shivered, and closed his eyes.

Scott saw a corpsman coming around the corner and waved him over. Leaving him in charge of the captain, Scott went to the side of the ship and looked up and down Battleship Row. He saw nothing but fire, smoke, and sinking ships. Goddamn it, I want to shoot something, he thought to himself. The corpsman waved them off, and Scott and Dorie fell in with another lieutenant Scott knew slightly, Fred White.

Together they headed down a couple of decks and found two unmanned Browning .50-caliber antiaircraft machine guns just aft of the conning tower. "You ever shot one of these things, Lieutenant?" asked Dorie. Scott shook his head.

"I know how they work," barked White, giving them some basic instructions. They each manned a gun, with White directing. As Scott tried to get a feel for the heavy machine gun, he turned to look at the much larger and stronger Dorie Miller swinging his muzzle out in front of a Jap Zero. He pressed the firing key, and a line of tracers zipped out. The Zero exploded in flames. Scott lined up his muzzle ahead of another Zero and pressed his firing key, but the gun jammed. Lieutenant White stepped in and tried to clear the jam, while Scott shifted over to feeding another belt of ammo to Dorie, who again knocked a Zero out of the sky. There was no more ammo in the ready magazines, and as Dorie stepped away from the .50-caliber, Lieutenant Ricketts reappeared, shouting for help to move the captain again, this time up to the navigation bridge. Moving through the clouds of thick, oily smoke, Dorie and Scott helped manhandle the bleeding captain.

"Jesus, Mr. James, I don't think he's going to make it," Dorie whispered.

Scott figured his chances were better in sick bay, but the captain refused to leave the bridge. They deposited the captain on the slightly safer navigation bridge, then looked at each other. "Let's go down to the main deck and see if we can help anybody down there," Scott said.

When he thought about it later, all Scott could remember was the sound. More than anything else, it was the raw, unfiltered noise. The worst of it came when a bomb hit USS *Arizona*, moored just aft of the *West Virginia*. The weapon penetrated the battleship's armored deck near the ship's magazine. The resulting explosion showered debris all over the adjacent vessels and Ford Island. It was clear that *Arizona* was doomed. Scott watched as the massive sister ship went down and flipped over. This cannot be happening, he thought.

For the rest of his life, Scott would remember that day as a pivot point. Everything changed forever in a few moments. He had begun the morning with Kai in his arms, starting that Sunday dawn with her, dreaming of bees from his mother's hives in Key West and savoring the sweetest of memories. How could a day ever begin better? Within an hour, he was watching his shipmates exploding before him, their blood splattering the bulkheads of his warship. His captain had bled to death in front of him, barking orders to the end, even as the mighty *West Virginia* burned from stem to stern and settled into the jade-green waters of Pearl Harbor. Scott's mother's gentle voice, reading Dante's *Inferno*, came to him: "Thus he went in, and thus he made me enter the foremost circle that surrounds the abyss." God almighty, thought Scott, we are in the abyss now. And I don't see a Virgil anywhere around to guide us. Heaven help the U.S. Navy.

Scott would always think back ruefully to how his .50-caliber machine gun had jammed while Dorie Miller's barrel had swung so smoothly, leading the Zeros like a hunter's shotgun in the field. Several weeks later, Dorie's heroism was recognized: he was awarded the Navy Cross, pinned on by the new commander of the Pacific Fleet, Admiral Chester Nimitz. The surviving crew of the

West Virginia looked on, and Scott thought, Goddamn it, that could be my medal too, even as he congratulated Dorie after the ceremony. He tried not to reflect on the fact that he could easily have shared the fate of his one hundred shipmates who did not survive the attack. That old demon, ambition, flared inside him. He thought: It's like I wasn't even there.

On USS *Nevada*

Night fell on December 7, and Battleship Row was dark. Eight of the massive steel floating cities had been grievously wounded, some of them fatally. Scott was told that as many as two thousand sailors were missing and presumed entombed in USS *Arizona*, which had inverted and sunk at the pier before his eyes. In a stroke of luck, on Saturday morning Scott had told Sean Kelley that he had free run of the snake ranch on the night of December 6, so Scott presumed that his classmate Second Lieutenant Kelley had survived the attack. That Irish bastard will be pissed to have missed the show, he thought to himself. He will be killing himself not to have been in the thick of it.

Hundreds of sailors and Marines from other battleships had not been so lucky. He knew they had been killed in explosions or trapped to die agonizing deaths by drowning. The smell of death was everywhere, and confusion and rumor ruled the island. Scott wanted to talk to Joe Taussig, thinking he would have the best sense of what had happened. At least the carriers were at sea. Thank God for small gifts.

There was an enormous sense of anger building in Scott, but also of fear: The Japanese striking fleet was still at sea, presumably within range to launch another attack, many of the land-based American fighters had been destroyed, but other rich American targets—including the fuel depots, ammunition magazines, and carriers—had survived. Surely the Japanese would return to finish the job. Scott heard rumors from a Marine junior officer from Nevada about a Japanese amphibious assault on Oahu. The officer had heard that Japanese Americans were being isolated and rounded up.

Aboard USS *West Virginia*, the captain was dead, the executive officer wounded, and the officers, chiefs, and crew exhausted. Many of the officers and chiefs had homes on the beach, and they badly wanted to get ashore to check on the safety of their wives and children. Scott attached himself to the acting XO, who was organizing damage-control parties, trying to dewater many flooded compartments, ensuring that the ammunition was in a safe condition, and gaining an accounting of casualties. The junior officers who were not badly hurt were tasked with these missions, and the work continued for days.

For Scott, the hours flew by, filled with one grim task after another. He saw that his men were accounted for and that those in need had medical care. We can always repair the guns, refloat the damn ships, he thought, but finding trained sailors to replace those we have lost is going to be hard and even more time-consuming. Scott was amazed his division had lost only a handful of sailors; other divisions had been far less lucky. After three long days, Scott's department head told him to take a few hours off and go ashore to clear his head.

Instead, Scott went down Battleship Row to see Joe Taussig on USS *Nevada* and compare notes. On the way down the pier he literally bumped into Second Lieutenant Sean Kelley. He gave him a bear hug of relief. It turned out Kelley was on a similar mission to see if Scott was still in one piece. "I see you managed to get through Sunday duty, Ensign," he said in a flat voice. "How did things come out with Kai? Is she okay?" Scott nodded. "Fine," said Kelley. "Now let's go check on the king of the ensigns over on *Nevada*."

USS *Nevada* had the distinction of being the only battleship to have managed to get underway during the fighting, probably because she was alone at the end of the line of battleships and had room to maneuver denied the others. But like her sister ships, she had been hit below the waterline by a torpedo, and a half dozen bombs had hit her as well. The Japanese gave *Nevada* special attention when she got underway, hoping to sink her in the channel and block the escape of other ships. The word on the waterfront was that she had been forced to beach on a coral reef in the harbor and, after several hours of flooding, had settled to the floor of the harbor. The losses were light by the standards of the morning—under a hundred killed and about that many wounded. Scott and

Kelley figured that out of a crew of a couple of thousand, that gave Joe pretty good odds.

They arrived at the battleship's former position at the far end of Battleship Row. The quarterdeck had been set up on the pier—no one was going out to the beached ship other than repair personnel. They asked a duty officer about Ensign Joe Taussig and got a shrug. The man pointed them to a bulletin board. "What we know of casualties is posted over there. Can't remember seeing his name one way or another. He's the ensign with his own stateroom, right?" Scott and Sean moved to the corkboard and ran their fingers down the lists. They were relieved not to see his name. They turned back to the lieutenant to plead their way onto a boat making a run to the grounded ship. Just then a messenger of the watch in a grimy set of whites walked to the corkboard and pinned a new sheet to it. The name at the top of the list was Ensign Joseph Taussig Jr. Next to his name were the words "Tripler Army Hospital."

"Fuck," Kelley said. They looked at each other.

"Okay," said Scott. "Let's go find him. Can you come with me?"

"Nope," said Kelley. "I only got liberty for a few hours—they are mustering the surviving *Arizona* crew members later this morning to give us our follow-on orders. Can you go? Is that motor scooter of yours still running?"

Scott flipped him the bird and walked to the head of the pier to catch a boat over to the main gate. "Meet me at the snake ranch when you can," he shouted over his shoulder.

"Hey," said Kelley, "what about Kai? Where the fuck is she?"

Scott looked at his friend, pausing slightly. "Later, Kelley. I'm going to check on Joe. She's with her parents, I guess, or at least with her mom."

Scott got across to the main part of the base. Amazingly, his motorcycle was still where he'd dropped it. He had a half tank of gas. Good, he thought. There isn't going to be much of that going forward for a while. He kick-started and revved the motorcycle and headed to Tripler Hospital, dread in his heart. He turned off the main highway and pushed the motorcycle hard up the hill to the massive pink building. It loomed over the Oahu suburbs like a massive concrete flamingo. Scott had never been on its spacious grounds. As he parked under a gray banyan tree, it started to drizzle in the tropical manner, a little "liquid sunshine" as the Hawaiians say. He caught a glimpse of a rainbow over the base at Pearl. Hope that's a good sign for Joe, he thought.

He walked past a line of burnt corpses lying on the ground, partially covered with bedsheets. A few still had rings on their charred fingers, poking out from the edges of the white sheets. It was the worst thing he'd ever seen in his life. In some cases, a hand was raised as though to ward off an attack. All Scott could think of was pictures he'd seen of Pompeii, the Roman settlement destroyed by the sudden explosion of Mount Vesuvius. The lava and ash had simply frozen them all in place—their lavish decorations, public buildings, private homes, businesses. These bodies on Pearl were likewise blackened, snatched to death in the midst of life, their limbs askew, protesting this terrible and unfathomable turn of events. The dead of Pompeii had stayed in that killing field of fire and lava for more than a thousand years before excavators and looters finally found them and reopened the city. His shipmates and classmates and friends would at least be buried, although many would never be identified with real certainty.

At the hospital, there were no rainbows. It was worse—much worse—than he expected. Corpses were laid outside on the emerald-green lawn, and nurses flitted back and forth like pale spirits, clipping hospital wristbands off and pulling dog tags over heads, a welcoming committee for souls headed to another life. Scott had walked into hell. The sounds were awful: a continuous churning wave of moaning, occasional sharp screaming. Nurses and doctors moved with slack limbs and exhausted eyes through the chaos. Scott thought of something that had been said over and over again at Annapolis: the job of an officer is to bring order out of chaos. Good luck with that one today, he thought as he dodged a slender nurse pushing a cart of what looked like severed arms and legs. He retched and moved to the makeshift administration area past the entrance, guarded by two Marines with red-rimmed eyes in dirty uniforms.

He gently touched the shoulder of a nurse leaning on the wall smoking a cigarette. "I'm Ensign James from USS *Nevada*," he lied fluently, "here to check on a shipmate, Ensign Joe Taussig." The nurse turned and looked at him with dead eyes. "Okay, fine. Sit over there. Hey, have you given blood today?" Scott admitted he had not, and before he knew it, an orderly was plunging a needle into his arm and filling a bag with bright-red blood. By the time he was through, the nurse was back. "Your friend is in bad shape, but awake. I'll take you back for a minute. You should know he's lost a leg."

Scott looked up sharply. He was suddenly on the verge of tears. He walked behind the Army nurse, breathing in small breaths through his mouth, the odors of alcohol, death, defecation, and infection mixing like a spirit sent directly from the piping systems of hell. They walked by row after row of the wounded, and all Scott could think of was luck. How lucky he was to be walking down this row and not lying in it. How lucky Kelley had been to be ashore on the morning of December 7. And how unlucky Joe Taussig had been. Even as the thought crystallized, he rejected it and said to himself, Joe is going to be fine. Lots of wounded here. He's going to be fine. He repeated it to himself, like he was repeating memorized lines from *Reef Points* again and again as a young teenager trying to be ready for the Naval Academy. Joe's going to be fine.

And then he stood by the bed and looked down at his classmate and one of his closest friends. Joe, his normally perfectly coiffed hair askew, looked up through cloudy eyes. "Scott? Jesus, what are you doing here? Isn't *West Virginia* underway? We got underway, goddamn it. Why are you here?"

Scott looked down at the lower half of Joe's body, at the sheet given shape by only one leg. "We didn't get underway, Joe. You guys did. We're all proud of *Nevada*. You're the only battleship to get underway."

Joe looked off to one side. "But it didn't matter a fuck. We ran aground, and they blew off my leg, and I watched the Zeros come again and again for us, and all I remember is the ship settling into the water off the side of the channel." He started to sob gently.

Scott reached out and patted his shoulder. "It doesn't matter. You got underway. We are all proud of *Nevada*."

"Here's all I remember," Joe said. "A sailor waking me up around zero seven hundred. He said, 'Mr. Taussig, it's zero seven hundred. You have the forenoon watch, sir.' I remember getting to the deck right before a quarter to eight. I do know that the guy I relieved as officer of the deck was still on the quarterdeck at about five minutes to eight; maybe he was completing his log. There was a liberty party of about a dozen sailors, early birds, waiting for the zero-eight-hundred liberty launch. It's funny, Scott, all I could think of was whether the correct-sized national ensign had been ordered for the raising of colors at zero eight hundred on a Sunday morning. Jesus.

"And I remember sending a messenger forward to call from our bow to the stern of the *Arizona*, moored just ahead of the *Nevada*, and I was watching the sailor pass up the port side of the *Nevada* when I caught a glimpse of a torpedo plane flying from the east and very low over the water.

"Its bomb-bay doors were open, and out dropped a torpedo. My reaction was thinking, That's a funny move by one of our planes, but maybe it's a drill. It would be a break in the Sunday-morning slog, watching the salvage operation dig a torpedo out of the mud under forty feet of water. You know that's the controlling depth of Pearl Harbor, right, Scott? You have to know that to be the officer of the deck." His voice rose in agitation, and Scott knelt and patted his friend's shoulder again.

"About a minute later, a plume of water spouted from the side of a ship ahead of the *Nevada* in Battleship Row. I couldn't tell which one. *Arizona?* You guys on *West Virginia?* Then there was the noise of the explosion as the torpedo hit, and I realized that the bomber was a Japanese plane, the big red Rising Sun on its wings clear and visible. I almost fell down. I was looking around, wondering how to call the command duty officer, when I realized everyone was going to be hearing the explosions.

"So I hit the general quarters gong on my own, and the petty officer of the watch called it over the 1MC. So I left the quarter-deck and climbed the six ladders to my battle station in the star-board antiaircraft director. All I can remember now is that I was conscious of the fact that before I reached my battle station, the starboard antiaircraft battery was firing and someone had pulled the safety firing cutouts, which normally restricted the firing ele-vations of the guns to sixty-five degrees. As I climbed through the door of the director, I was conscious that the crosshairs on my check sight were on an airplane, and I saw that it was hit almost immediately and went down trailing smoke.

"The director was already slewing around for another target, Scott. Then . . ." He paused and his eyes rolled back and forth. "I was hit by a big piece of shrapnel, which passed completely through my thigh and through the case of the ballistic computer of the director, which was directly in front of me. It sounds crazy, but there was no pain, and because I was clutching the sides of the hatch as the director slewed around, I didn't even fall down. My left foot was somehow up and under my left armpit, but in the detachment of shock, I didn't even realize that this was particularly

ADMIRAL JAMES STAVRIDIS, USN (RET.)

bad. It looked funny and I was almost laughing at it. I'm thinking that I'm in combat for no more than five minutes and my leg is already gone. I guess that isn't that funny, but it was a strange minute, and then all I could think of was my dad. He knew. The war. God, I wish he was here." Joe sobbed softly for a minute. "I hope he knows I tried. I tried my best. But my leg didn't work right." He closed his eyes for a moment.

"Then they carried me into the sky-control structure between the two AA directors and laid me out on the deck. Eventually a hospital corpsman arrived with a basket stretcher, administered a shot of morphine, and got me into the stretcher. But they said it was too hard to move me. I spent the rest of the morning 'observing' the battle of Pearl Harbor through the eyes of the enlisted sailor who stayed with me. He kept telling me what was going on, and I felt the ship get underway, then more explosions, then we just stopped and the ship shuddered again and again. At some point, I passed out, and when I woke up I was here, in Tripler. Without one of my legs, in case you didn't notice."

Joe lapsed into silence. Scott held his shoulder and leaned down, touching his forehead to the crown of his friend's head, one hand on his shoulder and the other on the side of his face. "Jesus, Joe, I can't believe this. But we are going to get them back. And you are going to be part of it. I swear it." They looked at each other with uncomprehending eyes, two young officers, full of anger and fear and resignation about the long haul ahead, stunned that war could descend so suddenly and viciously, despite all the chatter. Now the first real test of their lives was unfolding before them.

For a long moment, neither spoke. Scott stood up by the bed and patted Joe's shoulder again.

Turning his face up toward Scott, Joe blinked and swallowed. "Hey, what's going on with Kai?"

"I don't know," Scott said. "Everyone keeps asking me that."

The Broken Ship

OAHU, HAWAII

After Scott roared off on his motorcycle in the early moments of the Japanese attack, Kai had lain in bed for over an hour. She listened to the Japanese planes passing overhead, agonizing about what the future held for her island, for her country, and for her and Scott. God, she thought, how can this be happening? For the first time in my life I'm in love, and with a man I want, and then the world blows up. What happens now? He'll be gone and I'll just be grinding away at school? Does anything matter?

After a while, she got up and scanned the smoke-filled horizon. Feeling helpless, she sought comfort by making a pot of tea, using a Hawaiian lychee black leaf from Maui her mother liked. As she spooned a little honey into the cup, she idly wondered when her parents would be getting home. It was going to be hard for them to get across from the Big Island, but her dad was a chief and would be desperate to get back to his duty station here at the Naval Magazine. Unable to process the attack's implications, Kai focused on what was close at hand. She thought again and again about the past night. It had been so easy and natural, even with the fumbling and inexperience. Her parents could not know. I've got to scrub it all down, she thought. The dishes have to be perfectly back in place. But God, I wish my mom was here, and my dad too.

Everything she heard on the radio was terrible news. Everything was bad, from a Japanese invasion force supposedly sighted off the North Shore of Oahu to constant reports on the status of the ships in Pearl Harbor. She could smell the oily black smoke drifting from the east, carried by the ubiquitous trade winds of the islands. Kai sat on her bed, put her face in her hands, and cried—tears for the sailors killed, the lives upended, the pain that was coming, and the awful irony of finding a man she loved just as the world was about to sail into a massive war. How in God's name will we get through this? She fingered the gold cross around her neck.

The next day, her parents made it back from the Big Island. The chief had cadged a ride on a patrol boat heading back to Pearl. They had been unable to get a call through and were immensely relieved to discover Kai unharmed. They took turns hugging her. "Jesus, I can't believe the Japs didn't come after the ammo," her father said. "And it looks like they missed the big fuel farm on the west side of Pearl. But they might be coming back. We've got to get you two out of here." The chief looked at the two women and his eyes narrowed. "I think it's going to be hard on all the Japanese living here, and maybe on Hawaiians too. The military and police are going to lump them together with each other, which is crazy. There couldn't be two more different lifestyles, languages, and cultures. But neither have white skin, and that's going to be a problem with people going nuts after the attack. You two lay low, stay here in the house until things calm down. I'm going to the magazine administration building and see what needs doing. We'll figure out where to get you two when I get back." With that, he walked out of the bungalow.

The two women looked at each other for several long, sad seconds before Kai's mom spoke. "Have you heard from your ensign, sweetie? Is he okay?"

Kai winced. "Nothing yet. From what I can hear on the radio, Scott's ship was hit pretty bad, but nothing like the *Arizona*. One of his best friends, a Marine, is over there on that ship. And his other best friend is on the *Nevada*. On the radio they said it got underway but then had to run up on the beach—what do you call it?—grounded. They're both nice boys, and they went to the Academy with Scott." Her voice caught, and tears drifted across her eyes, blurring her mom's face. She blinked hard several times in quick succession and looked away. Her mother wordlessly came over to her side and put her arms around her daughter. They both looked at the screen door the chief had stepped through, and at the lush green grass and bright-red flowers beyond, and at a sky still hazy with smoke.

Kai's mother hugged her hard and moved toward the kitchen. "I'll make some coffee. I brought a big bag of the Kona Gold from Hawaii that you love. I'll put some condensed milk in it to sweeten it up for you. Things will be okay soon." Kai nodded and hugged herself, shivering slightly. She thought of Scott learning to surf, falling off the board again and again.

The next week was a blur for Scott, crowded with report after report of ships crippled, fresh lists of casualties, destroyed shore-side facilities. "I am so fucking tired of this bullshit," said Kelley over a clandestine bottle of beer behind the fence of the officers' club. "But when I get pissed, I think of Joe and those Jap bastards and all we have to do. But just cleaning up the mess here isn't going to get anything done."

Scott took a sip of his beer. "I know you want to get into the fight, into the islands. And I want to get to sea on anything that will float. But first we are going to have to square this away, and get ready to rearm the carriers, and figure out which of these bat-tleships can be fixed. Step by step, Kelley." They tossed their empty beer bottles into a green wire trash can and headed back to the pier.

Like every officer and sailor in the Pacific Fleet, they worked to organize rescue efforts first, then formed working parties to clear debris, set up pumping stations to skim the oil and blood out of the harbor's waters, rig electrical cables around shattered switch-boards and generators, on and on. They gave blood whenever they could, visited their shipmates in makeshift clinics in the small breaks between larger tasks, and wondered where they would go, how they could get into the fight that was coming. Scott finally got a message through the chief's network to Kai, assuring her that he was fine. He relayed the good news that Kelley had not been aboard *Arizona*, and the bad news that Joe was badly wounded but expected to recover. He'd come visit as soon as he could. The message was necessarily antiseptic, since it was passed though Navy channels—and through his girlfriend's father.

Scott and Kelley got off the base together only once that first week to see Joe Taussig, Kelley's first visit. When they got to Tripler, they were told that Taussig had checked himself out and returned to duty. "He did what?" Scott exclaimed to the nurse.

"Yeah," she said, "he grabbed his crutches and said he was going to war. I hear he is manning a desk at CINCPAC headquarters, something in intelligence. He's a crazy one, that one. He better hope that stump doesn't get infected."

"Jesus, only Joe Taussig would have the balls to pull that move off," Scott said. He and Kelley mounted the motorcycle and reversed course back to Pearl, and sure enough, found Taussig back at work. His hair was back in place, and he looked very much his original self. "My dad called a couple of times. Looks like he may get recalled to active duty with all this. Or at least he thinks so." A devilish grin crept across Joe's face. "Remember that letter of reprimand Roosevelt gave my dad after he predicted all this? Ha." Scott and Kelley nodded. "The president has now ordered that it be removed from his file." The three classmates shared a grim laugh.

"Now my father is hoping he can get back in uniform and can get out here, of course. Jeez, you don't think my getting banged up had anything to do with Roosevelt pulling that letter? My dad said it was pulled the day after the attack, on the 8th."

Scott raised his eyebrows. "Somehow, I doubt the president has time to track every ensign that got shot up, Joe. More likely

Roosevelt realized that since your dad was right about how poorly prepared we were for a war that was obviously coming, it was gonna look pretty bad to have him sitting on the beach, fired for having gotten right the biggest thing that just about everyone else got wrong."

Kelley grunted his assent. "Who gives a fuck why he did it, Joe? If it gets your dad into the fight and helps us go after the Japs, it's a good thing."

Joe considered this. "You know, Dad is a three-star now. They had to give him a tombstone promotion when they retired him because of his service in the Boxer Rebellion. I wonder if he'll have to revert to two stars if he comes back."

Scott and Kelley looked at each other blankly. Decisions at that level were Olympian, and they were still on earth trying to put the pieces of the U.S. Pacific Fleet back together. And they all knew that Admiral Kimmel, the fleet commander, was probably going to be on the chopping block. Figuring out the flag moves was not a top priority for either man.

Kelley slapped Joe on the shoulder. "Hey, I heard you're gonna get some highfalutin medal. A Navy Cross? That is a big deal, classmate."

Joe rolled his eyes and patted what remained of his amputated leg. "I could care less. With this hit, I'm guessing I'm not going to be standing long bridge watches, so I'm working even harder at learning Japanese." He pointed at a primer of English and Japanese on his desk. "After they get done firing all the intelligence weenies who missed this one coming, I'm guessing there could be some openings."

Kelley laughed. "Still, a Navy Cross, wow, Taussig. Imagine what you would have gotten if you had gotten your dick blown off. It's still there, right? I know you've got to protect the line of future Taussig admirals."

Taussig shot him the bird. The three friends grinned at each other. Scott felt better than he had in a long time.

And yet he couldn't help but think that a friend and classmate was going to get a medal that would propel his career. When will I get my shot? Scott checked himself. It was uncertain if Joe could even remain on active duty, although the fleet surgeons assured him they would have him fitted with a prosthesis shortly and that, with training and practice, he could probably handle some kind of desk job long term. That wasn't exactly what Joe wanted to hear, but it was at least a start. Maybe he could get on his father's staff, if he did come back in a command role as a two- or three-star on active duty. Normally, working for your dad would not be allowed, but what the hell? After all there was a war on. For Scott and Kelley, the problems were far simpler: They urgently wanted to be reassigned to either a ship or a staff that would get into the fight. USS *West Virginia* might be repaired, but it was likely the ship would have to limp or be towed stateside to be put back together properly. And USS *Arizona*, along with most of Kelley's shipmates, rested at the bottom of Pearl Harbor.

After their visit, both Scott and Kelley began to campaign in earnest to get assigned elsewhere—to a fast carrier for Scott, a Marine unit headed into combat for Kelley. This meant drafting and sending formal letters requesting transfer through their thinned-out chains of command. Neither of their seniors was keen to lose a capable and determined junior officer. Both were frustrated, but the ambition that burned inside of Scott Bradley James was roaring, and the only thing that could quench it was a long dose of pure seawater. "God, Kelley, I got another form letter back from some weenie at the Bureau of Naval Personnel saying in effect to shut up and get used to being on a broken ship. I can't wait around for it to get fixed."

Kelley sighed. "Same here, classmate, except the Corps keeps telling me to sit tight, stay in shape, they are re-forming Marine units. So at least I've got some chance. You better hope they don't drag you back stateside with that battlewagon of yours."

A week after the attack, Scott convinced his acting department head to let him take an overnight off the ship. He used his last bit of gasoline to go to Kai's house as evening fell. It felt like going back in time to another world. When he knocked on the screen door, he saw the little bungalow was dark, but he heard the family out back. He could smell a pig roasting. He walked back to find Kai sitting on a lanai chair, reading. Her father stood at the grill. When the chief saw Scott, he let out a happy cry. "Well, what do ya know, it's Ensign Scott, all in one piece, Lord be praised. How about a beer?"

Kai jumped up, ran to Scott, and hugged him tightly. The chief and his wife looked away, and Scott turned, Kai still wrapped around him, toward the circular Skotch plaid cooler on the ground. He drew out a beer. The chief handed him a church key to open it and patted him on the back. "How's *West Virginia*?"

Scott took a long pull of the beer. "They are going to try and refloat her, Chief, but I'd say that's gonna take months. Then the scuttlebutt is she'll head back to the mainland for a big-time refit. Maybe get that new fire-control radar. But I'm working to get off and get to a carrier or even a flag staff. I can't sit around the first year or so of this war in a damn shipyard." Scott's eyes flashed.

"Makes sense," said the chief, nodding slowly. "Maybe you and Beatrice can go inside and set the table. This will be ready soon; can you stay for dinner?"

Scott and Kai walked hand in hand into the tiny bungalow. Scott kissed her deeply once they were out of sight. "Why are you trying to get a transfer, Scott?" she asked, her voice uncertain as she pulled back from his embrace. "Why can't you stay here with the ship and try to fix it up?"

Scott felt his throat tighten. "I. Am. Not. Going. To. Miss. This. War. Two of my friends already have Navy Crosses, and all I've done is rewire electricity to keep pumps working to refloat a broken ship. Fuck that. I'm going back to sea, and the sooner the better."

Kai looked shocked. She bit her lip and looked back toward her parents in the backyard. "Scott," she started to say, a hard look on her face.

At that moment her mother came bustling in through the back door. "I'm going to shred some peppers to go with the pig. Kai, time to put the rice on. Scott, you can go help the chief baste that pig, and set the table outside. Scott and Kai turned to their tasks, barely glancing at each other. "Let's have a nice meal before the ensign has to go back to his ship," Kai's mother cried.

My *broken* ship, Scott thought to himself. Kai doesn't get it. My broken fucking ship.

To Begin Again

PEARL HARBOR, OAHU, HAWAII

S cott was soon temporarily detached from his ship, part of a general draw for junior officer manpower. His interim assignment involved supervising a radar and communication relay station on top of a mountain near the North Shore of Oahu. One of the new fire-control radars, called CXAM, had been removed from the stricken USS *California* and set up on a little hilltop off the Koolau Range, behind Fort Shafter. It was operating alongside the Army's longer-range radars and was emplaced in a small campsite up a dirt road. Every morning he rode his motorcycle up to supervise the small team of radiomen and radar operators on the top of the range, where a primitive camp had been established.

Morale was low, although he enjoyed bantering with one of the radiomen from USS *California*, Ted Mason. The third-class petty officer, who had a literary streak—he had bemoaned losing his collection of Shakespeare's plays in the battle—had been assigned to the fire-control director of his ship, and he'd had a bird's-eye view as the fight ensued. "It was like a scene out of Dante's *Inferno*, Mr. James. I could see all the battleships on fire, and bodies everywhere. Only one that got underway was *Nevada*, and we were all cheering on *California*, but you could see she was taking on water, and it looked like the whole superstructure was on fire. The Japs started to really work her over, but all her topside guns were firing, and you could see the Stars and Stripes on her stern. We were crying and screaming, and all I knew for sure was that I'd remember everything. Everything. For the rest of my life. Not that I had any idea how long that was going to be. My best friend was killed, and my chief too." He drew a long breath.

Scott nodded and patted his shoulder. Mason continued, "Then we saw *Nevada* run herself aground so she wouldn't block the channel. But right after her came a destroyer, USS *Aylwin*. She had got underway too, and we were watching her with the big glasses in the director, and there was a motor launch chasing her. In the bow of the launch was an officer waving like crazy at the destroyer as she got steam up. We looked at the bridge, and there was some ensign up there driving—probably the duty officer. Got to have been the skipper in the little launch, but the JO just kept heading for sea. That was all right, but then the other two destroyers that were nested with her were hit, the *Cassin* and *Downes*. They burned to the gunwales, right in front of us. I looked around and everything seemed to be on fire, and those Jap planes kept going back and forth. Battle stations. Right. It was more like slaughter stations. Finally, they called 'abandon ship' as *California* started to tip over."

Scott knew all the feelings. It was the 17th of December, and they'd just heard that Admiral Kimmel had been relieved of command that day. There was martial law in the territory of Hawaii, run by the Army, which had taken over from the figurehead governor Joe Poindexter. *I wonder if Duke is still the sheriff,* Scott mused to himself. *Not much surfing going on, I guess.* He missed Kai, but with the war raging everywhere, getting away even for a few hours would be hard. He'd read of the attacks on Guam and Wake Island on the 7th and the Japanese invasions of Malaya and Thailand. When Scott had last gone by Battleship Row, it had still been like a shelf in Satan's playroom, with broken toys strewn carelessly in the once-light-aqua waters of Pearl Harbor: *California* heavily listing to port; *West Virginia*, his ship, still smoking ten days later and resting flat on the bottom, her main deck awash; *Oklahoma* fully capsized; and *Arizona* the worst of all, the forward part of the ship ripped open like a cardboard box full of random metal parts, the bridge and foremast toppled, and just three of her guns from the number-two turret poking up through the water's surface. Scott had heard the death total from the entire attack was going to be nearly three thousand or even more, and probably as many severely wounded. If anyone knew, they were not saying.

Kelley summed it up over another clandestine beer behind the closed officers' club. "Lemme get this straight: the Japs blew us apart here in Pearl, are on the march all over Asia, are knocking at the door of the Philippines, gonna take Guam, the Brits lost their capital ships, *Prince of Wales* and *Repulse*, and Singapore is up for grabs, and the only bright spot so far is our Marine garrison on Wake Island—which is gonna fall soon anyway, I figure. Gotta tell ya, Scottie, we are doing something really, really wrong. We haven't laid a glove on them so far. But a couple of months ago, everyone said, 'Oh, the Japanese, they don't really have the equipment, and they can't really fly airplanes, and hell, their eyesight isn't that good.' Jesus. We are getting our asses handed to us. What the fuck is wrong with us?"

Scott had heard from Joe Taussig that the Wake Island relief expedition, built around the carriers *Lexington* and *Saratoga*, was preparing to go to sea. How Joe knew that, Scott had no idea. "Maybe the carriers can get some licks in," Scott said. They tossed their beer bottles in the trash can behind the club and went their separate ways.

By late December, the hesitancy in the heart of the new acting commander of the Pacific Fleet, Vice Admiral Bill Pye, was showing. After organizing the relief expedition for Wake, Pye was having second thoughts. Ted Mason, who had known Pye as the embarked flag officer on *California*, said, "You know, Mr. James, sometimes the admirals you got in the peacetime Navy aren't the right admirals when the bullets start flying. I was in the CINCPAC HQ a couple days ago, on the 21st, and everyone was talking about the relief expedition. Those Marines on Wake have been holding on since the 7th, and they managed to sink two Jap destroyers, one with a shore battery, and an F-4 got the other one. But a buddy of mine in the flag radio shack says Pye is too scared of losing the carriers and pulled the expedition back. Jesus."

Scott said nothing—uncomfortable to be engaging in criticizing a senior officer with a junior enlisted man. But that night, he told Kelley what he'd heard, and Kelley confirmed it. "On the Marine circuit, everyone knows this is the Navy dicking over the jarheads. The Marine fliers are going crazy, talking about mutiny." On December 23, Wake fell, and all Scott and Kelley could do was drink a toast to the brave garrison behind the empty officers' club. "When the fuck is this place gonna open up?" said Kelley. "Jesus, we can't even get the booze supply right."

For Kai, the days crawled by. Beaches were closed to surfing, the bars on Hotel Street were lightly attended, most of her Japanese Americans friends were being rounded up or put under house arrest, and her dad was essentially living outside the house, working on repairs to ships' magazines, loading up ammo, and trying to help the families that had lost sailors in the battle. Kai's mom tried to keep her daughter focused on anything but the war and Scott. Scott made sporadic phone calls, but there were no parties at the snake ranch, and certainly no visits to the Naval Magazine.

In their short phone calls, Scott seemed distracted. "I don't get it, Mom," Kai said one morning. "What's wrong with him? Why can't he at least come by here?"

Her mother looked out the back window of the bungalow at the distant curve of the mountains, covered with a few sprinkles of clouds. "He's a wild one, that one. You have to give him some time to really come to the beach. It's like surfing, sweetie, sometimes you have to let the first wave go by, but the next time it curls, you can jump on it and ride it home. Don't be impatient, is all I'm saying."

Kai sighed and went back to her room, quietly closing the door and lying on the bed staring at the ceiling. Oh well, she thought, at least I'm not pregnant. She opened a textbook and tried to concentrate, but all she could think of was the war.

On New Year's Eve, 1941, Scott Bradley James arrived at Kai's bungalow at 7 p.m., riding his motorcycle right up to the sidewalk in front of the house. In a small satchel, he'd brought two small bottles of Five Islands whiskey, a harsh and undistinguished spirit for a harsh new year, but Kai's mom made a great show of concocting an improvised tropical sour with the whiskey, some cherry juice, and fresh-squeezed pineapple. Scott stood with Kai and her parents in a circle around the barbecue outside and toasted "all the sailors still at sea." It was a somber moment.

As they headed to the grill, Scott said lightly, "Well, I'm hoping to be one of those sailors at sea soon." Kai stared at him, eyes wide. "And I wanted to let all of you know I've got a line on a billet on USS *Enterprise*, the fast carrier. She's in Pearl right now refitting, and I think I may have cadged a spot as an assistant communications officer in the ship's company, and maybe I'll even end up on the flag staff. Not exactly a swanky job, but at least I can get into this fight." The chief nodded encouragement, but Kai looked stricken. "They've had me up working on communication and radar on this mountain behind Fort Shafter, and I think they figure I can handle whatever is on the Big E. That's the nickname of the ship. What I'm doing now is up on a ridgeline way above Pearl, kind of between the naval base and Honolulu. I can do it at sea, I guess they figure."

The chief punched Scott on the shoulder. "Go to it, Ensign James. You've got to get into this thing. It's killing me practically being a damn sand crab myself here at Pearl."

Kai's mom hugged Scott. "Let's eat. It smells like that chicken is burning."

Kai raked her eyes down Scott from his sandy hair to the bottoms of his shoes. "I thought you wanted to stay with *West Virginia* and the battleships. They are the future of this war, right?" She looked a little sad, a little angry.

"I've got to get in the fight, Kai. In case you hadn't noticed, the goddamn battleships are all on the bottom of Pearl Harbor. So yes, I'm going to sea." He turned to the chief and said, "That chicken is really cooking, Chief. Maybe better get it off the grill." By the time the chief pulled the quartered chicken pieces off the grill, they were blackened. In a horrible flash, Scott saw his shipmates at Tripler, burned to death, lying on the emerald green of the grass. He sighed heavily and walked out of the bungalow without a backward glance. He mounted his motorcycle with a jarring kick-start and roared off.

The Big E

PEARL HARBOR, OAHU, HAWAII,
AND THE SOUTH PACIFIC

Ensign Scott Bradley James walked up the officers' gang-plank on USS *Enterprise* on the 7th of January, 1942, a month to the day after the disaster of Pearl Harbor. He had thrown together a seabag full of working uniforms, parked his motorcycle inside the front door of the bungalow he shared with Joe Taussig, and dropped the keys to the snake ranch with Kelley. He wasn't proud of so abruptly parting company with Kai in front of her parents, but everything had built to a crescendo in his head—the death and mutilation of his friends, the broken hulks of Battleship Row, his sense that the war was somehow passing him by. All he could think about was getting to sea *now*, while it really counted.

The set of orders he carried in an oilskin pouch had been initiated within the Bureau of Naval Personnel by the assistant chief of staff to Vice Admiral Bill Halsey, a captain Joe Taussig's father knew well. Scott would be on the admiral's flag staff, working for the communications officer, mostly haunting the radio shack, ensuring the smooth flow of messages to Vice Admiral Halsey. It didn't feel as good as being a gunnery officer on a battleship, but at least he would be headed to sea now, not months in the future when the big guns returned to the fleet.

Scott saw that the ship was in a healthy state of turmoil—a huge quantity of supplies was being delivered, including fuel, huge pallets of canned supplies, and fresh fruits and vegetables. There was a smell of fuel oil in the air and a general sense of motion everywhere. We're all a hive of bees, he thought to himself, and I'm about to go to work for the queen herself. Cranes were swinging loads of bombs and ammo aboard. The Big E was done with fishing, waiting for a nibble of the Japanese fleet in Hawaiian waters—she was about to go hunting in the deep waters of the South Pacific.

Scott saluted the American flag on the fantail and then the officer of the deck. He was directed up to "flag country," where the staff of the admiral was berthed. The ship seemed enormous to him, even though *West Virginia* had been roughly the same tonnage. The carrier was longer and the vast scale of the hangar deck, located just below the flight deck, gave a sense of a real city at sea. There were many more officers and sailors aboard as well, and the presence of Vice Admiral Halsey gave the Big E a sense of real gravitas in the fleet. Scott knew that they would sail on the 11th with a capable task force: heavy cruisers *Chester, Northampton,* and *Salt Lake City*; a big fleet tanker, the *Platte*; and a brace of six destroyers to screen and scout ahead of the big guns of the cruisers and the planes of *Enterprise*. Scott tossed his seabag into the junior officer junk room he would be sharing with four other ensigns and lieutenant JGs on the flag staff and checked in with the assistant chief of staff for communications, Captain Bill Varley.

"Reporting for duty, sir," Scott said.

The older officer stood up and extended a hand across his battered steel desk. "Good to have you here, Scott. Heard good things about you from Admiral Taussig. How's his boy doing?"

Scott smiled. "Believe it or not, he's back on duty with some kind of . . . What do they call it? Prosthesis? I wouldn't want to call it a peg leg, but he does. He's working with the intelligence spooks in the dungeon ashore on Admiral Nimitz's staff. I've seen him a couple of times, and he looks like he's doing fine, just limping."

The captain nodded. "He's a good young man, and from what I've heard was right in the middle of it on *Nevada*." Varley picked up a piece of paper from the desk and handed it to Scott. "Here's the flag watch bill. We're going to start you in the radio shack under supervision for a couple of days, then you'll be the flag communicator on duty in the shack. They've got a good crew in there, and the admiral keeps them busy. You'll pick it up fine, and when you get set, we may move you over to the combat center in direct support of the boss. Keep your eyes open and your mouth shut, by the way. Everything flowing in and out from the admiral's inbox has to be kept totally close hold, no matter what the actual level of classification is. Loose lips and all that. No rumors.

You know the drill. Okay, get one of the yeomen to show you the radio shack, and start getting a feel for the ship. We'll be underway in a day or so."

Scott thanked him and headed to the chattering world of radios and teletypewriters, smelling of cigarette smoke and burnt coffee. It was a long way from the glamour job he'd had running a turret on a frontline battleship. Oh well, he thought, it's a start.

He walked down to the hangar deck and looked at the tightly packed rows of fighters and bombers, their wings bent for storage. Part of him idly wondered if he should have chosen naval aviation as a career path, but when he walked to the edge of the massive elevator that shuttled the aircraft up and down from the flight deck, he remembered that it was the sea that tugged at him. He moved to the edge of the railing and leaned out to watch the long wake of the ship cutting through the dark-blue waters. I'd never be happy just flying over the waves, he thought to himself. I've got to ride them, wherever they take me.

As he came to know the aviators in the air wing, he realized they had little interest in the sea. It was only a huge blank canvas to them, devoid of anything they cared about—until its pristine surface was broken by an enemy warship, and then, happy as little boys with something to break in front of them, they could swoop down upon their prey. But for Scott, the ocean was the heart of why he stood on the mildly rolling deck of a slightly pitching city at sea: it was a living organism, a watery universe into which he would pour the most precious moments of his life.

While Scott settled into the routine of shipboard life on the flag staff, Kai was struggling to reclaim her momentum as a college student at the University of Hawaii. An enthusiastic and thoughtful student in peacetime, she was finding it more than difficult to buckle down to study the fine points of nineteenth-century American history and its impact on the Pacific.

Studying felt pointless, but whining about it was also hopeless. She thought maybe if she called Kelley or Taussig they could give her an update on Scott. She tried the number of the snake ranch on a Friday night in late January and was surprised when Kelley answered on the second ring. He seemed surprised to hear that Scott had not been in touch at all. "Listen," he said, "you are welcome to come by tonight. We can catch up a bit if you want, and I'll tell you what I know about Scott's schedule—can't do it over a phone line. Joe Taussig will be here too—he got hit bad, I'm sure you know, but he's upright and we have a few of the old gang over on weekends."

A little after 7 p.m., she was walking through the screen door of the bungalow. A half dozen people were gathered in the backyard, where a small firepit was burning. The Andrews Sisters' "Boogie Woogie Bugle Boy" was spinning on the record player just inside the back porch. Someone had set up an impromptu bar on the folding card table, and she helped herself to a couple of fingers of local whiskey, pouring some pineapple juice out of a scratched-up pitcher and adding a couple of sad-looking ice cubes. Joe Taussig struggled to his feet, and she hugged him gently. She heard footsteps, and Sean Kelley loomed behind her, putting a friendly arm over her shoulder and plunking another bucket of fresh ice onto the bar. "Hi, Kelley," she said. "Not much of a party, but I guess that's the times we're in, right?"

He shrugged and poured himself a large whiskey, adding some ice and swigging half of it. "I'm not at my best, Kai, but I don't think many of us are these days. Hey, let's try to have some fun."

Kai looked up at him. "You told me you had some news about Scott?"

Kelley took another pull of his drink. "He's on the Big E, USS *Enterprise*, on the staff of the toughest admiral in the fleet, Bill Halsey. A three-star, bucking for a fourth—and the oldest officer to ever qualify as a Navy pilot. He said he couldn't really command aviators unless he was one. The air wing worships him. They pulled a ton of supplies, fuel, and ammo last week. New coat of paint and they are haze-gray and underway. Headed south and west, looking to sink some Japs. Also resupply Marines scattered around the Coral Sea."

He drained the rest of his drink and moved toward the bar for a refill. "You still like those pomegranate daiquiris, Kai?" She nodded slowly. After mixing her the drink, he said, "Halsey is a real hunter, and my guess is he'll be out for a while—weeks, maybe longer. He will want to put some trophies on the shelf. Got that ambition like young Scottie does. They are a pair of jacks. The only difference between them is the amount of mileage on them, and the number of gold stripes on their sleeves."

Kai nodded. "Do sailors on aircraft carriers get mail regularly?"

Kelley could see where this was going. "Yeah," he said. "That's one of the good things about flattops. Their mail service is better than most."

Kai looked around the lanai and into the bungalow. "He left his motorcycle here, huh? You got the key?" Kelley nodded. "We should go for a ride sometime," she said, a defiant look in her eyes. "You allowed to drive it?" He nodded again, and she said, "How about now?"

Kelley looked at her beautiful, slender form. He swallowed hard. "Sure, why not? Where to, Kai?"

She looked him in the eye and touched her gold cross. "Let's go up to the North Shore." When Joe Taussig looked up a moment later, they were gone.

The Big E was thousands of miles away, surrounded by her escorts and on a patrol line running east–west a hundred miles north of the Samoan Islands. Halsey drove the air wing hard, sending endless patrols to the northwest, hunting the enemy. The heat was nearly unbearable, even for the pilots flying with open canopies, driving their planes through the tropical rain showers on purpose for some relief. To Scott, it seemed the carrier strike group had sailed over the edge of an old map, with a smudgy margin and the words "Here be dragons." On the bridge, you could get a little breeze, but down in the un-air-conditioned staterooms and berthing compartments, nights were long and sweaty. The sailors woke up parched and groggy with nascent dehydration. Worst of all was duty belowdecks in the engineering spaces, a stygian world with pale, ghostly men in dirty white T-shirts and greasy dungarees flitting from station to station. By late January, they were well and truly gone from Pearl and untethered from any reliable supply chain. In war, Scott had heard his professors at Annapolis say, amateurs study strategy, but professionals study logistics. So it was for Bill Halsey, from what Scott could see: the admiral was obsessed with where his next fuel rendezvous would occur, how his ships would get stores, where ammunition would come if they went into action.

Scott went up on the bridge of *Enterprise* to watch a replenishment underway. It was a delicate dance between two enormous whales—a thirty-thousand-ton aircraft carrier and a slightly smaller refueling ship, the latter essentially a massive gas station at sea. The two ships had to sail on perfectly parallel course a mere fifty feet apart, a distance anyone could throw a biscuit across. For the gasoline ship, it was easy: their captain simply had to maintain course and speed. For the carrier, where the captain typically took the conn himself, the ship had to gradually ease itself into station, maintain a steady course and speed, and allow itself to be penetrated fore and aft by massive fuel hoses. Brutal sex at sea, was all Scott could think. Without the fuel, the warships would be nothing but listless hulks adrift between distant ports. The at-sea refueling was what gave real punch to the strike group. Scott watched the captain closely as he maneuvered alongside the oiler, imagining at some point doing the same. By the end of January, both *Enterprise* and *Yorktown*, sailing in parallel missions to the South Seas, were equally fueled. Both carriers were ready for battle under the watchful eyes of their captains. Scott sensed the professionalism of the crew on the Big E: This was no draftee or conscript force. These were volunteers to a man, most experienced sailors with a decade or more under their sailors' caps.

The air group was finely honed and brilliantly led. Scott had gotten to know Lieutenant Dick Best, the executive officer of one of the squadrons on board, through a mutual friend at Annapolis. He knew that Dick had lost his best friend and Annapolis roommate at Pearl Harbor, and they talked about Joe Taussig's wounds. Scott was gradually accepted in the wardroom of the squadron. It helped that they knew he had a handle on the gouge, the latest skinny from the flag communications shack. Scott kept a careful watch on what he said, but within reason, he was willing to let the aviators know what was going on.

He was amazed at how they were so fully committed to Halsey and his mission, and whatever his vision might be. In the end it was all about killing Japs. That worked for Scott. Whatever the complex equation he had to solve to ascertain what was legitimate to share with the frontline killers, the bottom line, he thought, was that the admiral would want these guys to know what was going on. Scott got to know pilots, just a few years older than him, who led men and machines into the killing fields of the Pacific. Men like Lieutenant Gene Lindsey, skipper of Torpedo Squadron Six, who greatly impressed Scott. He was fearless, able to take a punch, and utterly dedicated to the mission. Scott also came to worship from a distance the commander of the air group, Lieutenant Commander Wade McClusky. These aviators were a wild and untamed breed, and backed up by their three-star admiral, Bill Halsey, who roamed between his small flag cabin, the combat center, and the flag bridge drinking endless cups of bitter black coffee, swearing constantly, and smoking like a smoldering brushfire. Best, Lindsey, and McClusky were all mentors to young Ensign

James, whom they gently ribbed about his lack of aviator wings but respected for his clear ambition.

The fighting in the Coral Sea through the spring of 1942 was, in the end, not consequential. *Yorktown* scored some hits on Japanese ships, and a few morale-boosting medals were awarded. And yet when Bill Halsey and his strike group returned to port for a brief week, it was a balm to American spirits, and a ramp-up to the task of revenge on the Japanese for their attack on Wake Island. In early February, Scott had his feet firmly anchored in the mission: up at 3:30 a.m. for the 4–8 a.m. watch in the flag communications space; followed by breakfast with the flag staff— bacon and eggs—where Vice Admiral Halsey would hold forth on the day's events; an afternoon working on paperwork and spending time with his friends and mentors in the air wing; nonalcoholic cocktails with the admiral and the staff (Scott could have sworn the admiral's libation had a distinct smell of bourbon, but rank hath its privileges); and then back on watch. He was learning every day, and the admiral seemed to have a kind of curmudgeonly affection for the very young ensign.

Before and after every watch in the radio shack, Scott went to the ship's bridge, standing quietly in the back of the space, watching the officers and sailors navigate the ship through the Pacific. After a few days, one of the lieutenants asked him, in a friendly voice, what he was doing loitering up there. Scott said, "Just learning about the ship, sir. My normal watches are in radio, and I got my last ship, a battleship, shot out from under me. So I'm trying to get the hang of carriers."

"Well, if you are all that fascinated, I can get you on the bridge watch under instruction, if you want to stand a few real watches up here," said the lieutenant. "The coffee is bad, but it'll keep you awake." Turning to the boatswain mate of the watch, he said, "Boats, give the ensign a mug of your lousy joe."

"Thanks, sir," said Scott, taking the proffered white flat-bottomed mug full of dark liquid that looked like it had been brewing for a week. Scott blew on the hot surface of the coffee and said to the lieutenant, "This midwatch is usually free for me. I'll start coming up regularly." Scott realized he was sacrificing a chunk of his limited time for rest, but he couldn't resist the offer.

Within a couple of weeks, he was conning the ship, and by late February, Captain Murray, the CO, was commenting on his touch with the carrier and letting Scott take a turn at the most difficult maneuvers, including flight quarters and fuel replenishment at sea. Holding the carrier steady just fifty feet from the oiler required every bit of Scott's skill as a mariner, but he felt most alive doing it. When they would break away from the oiler, *Enterprise*'s tanks refilled to the brim, Scott would order a full rudder on the carrier, and as he looked out to sea from the bridge wing, he watched the nose of the ship swing across the ocean, smoothly gliding away from the gray bulk of the tanker, then jumping forward to find the wind and launch its planes.

But Scott knew that all was not good on the horizon. From what he could gather in the flag radio shack, the war was going badly. The strikes in the South Pacific felt like tiny pinpricks on the impenetrable skin of the Japanese war machine. Singapore was overrun on the 15th of February, and the ship kept losing aircraft and pilots to accidents and maintenance issues. One night during his communications watch, Scott learned that the Big E was getting a new mission, a strike on the Japanese occupiers of Wake Island, and they laid a course to the northeast. Over fifty planes would attack, backed up by the heavy guns of Halsey's cruisers. When the day of the attack arrived, Scott left the radio shack and watched the lines of bombers and fighters—Wildcats and Devastators—led by the air group commander, Wade McClusky.

He later learned that Lieutenant Dick Best, who had become a mentor, had dropped a couple of perfect strikes. By the time Scott was back on the bridge, the strikes were over—worthwhile, but insufficient to make a real difference. But it was enough to allow Vice Admiral Halsey and the group to head back to Pearl for a brief ceremony commending him and the strike group. Admiral Nimitz pinned a Distinguished Service Medal on the craggy flag officer in an afternoon ceremony as the ship refueled. After the ceremony, the traditional movie was about to start on the hangar deck, and Halsey walked to the front of the nearly one thousand members of the crew and stood impassively for a moment, looking at them. He ran his steady eyes over row after row of young men, four decades separating them in age. He touched the medal on his chest and with real emotion in his voice said simply, "Men, this medal belongs to you. I am honored to wear it for you. I am so damned proud of you I could cry." And then he almost did, eyes misting over like the bow of a destroyer coming through a drizzle. His boys, a thousand strong, stood and applauded, on and on and on. So many of them were literally boys, not yet twenty. They had already seen men die, their shipmates, and they were afraid, but they were willing, and they cheered their old admiral with long, thunderous applause. So did Scott, thinking, This is the man I want to be someday.

25

Mr. Doolittle Goes to Tokyo

NORTH PACIFIC

By April 1942, Scott had qualified both as a deck watch officer aboard the carrier and as a flag watch officer in the combat center. He still pulled a few watches in the radio shack, both to keep his strong relationships with the radiomen and their chief and to maintain his own sources of information and intelligence on the strike group's plans. It was a busy time, but every day he honed his craft as a surface warfare officer. Scott remembered something his dad had told him about being at sea in combat: "When you're out there, it is like you never want to come back to port, because doing so breaks up the rhythm of the mission. But when you're ashore, it's the other way around: you dread going back to sea."

On a brief port visit the carrier made in Pearl, Scott managed to get an overnight liberty. He called Kai and took her for a ride on his motorcycle, hoping to resume their lovemaking and bantering as though the months of sea duty had not mattered. But nothing was the same. She came to the snake ranch for an evening party but then insisted they go down to Waikiki to the Royal Hawaiian. The Pink Palace had essentially become an officers' club, requisitioned by the government, and was full of pilots drinking cheap whiskey and worse gin with gusto, their arms around the waists of their wives and sweethearts. May they never meet, Scott thought to himself, recalling a sailors' toast going back to the British Royal Navy and probably back to the Vikings. Scott and Kai had a cocktail, provided on the house by some kind of local "support the Navy" club. They found they had little to say to each other. He took her onto the dance floor, where she was stiff and unresponsive in his arms. I might as well be at sea, he thought. Somehow, he felt he had become the foe.

After a couple of drinks, he said: "Where to?" She sullenly said she had better be getting home. At the door of the bungalow, she gave him a quick, hard kiss on the lips and went inside. So much for liberty call, Scott thought to himself. He rode his Indian Sport Scout slowly through the dark streets of Honolulu and let himself into the snake ranch. Joe Taussig was fast asleep, and Sean Kelley was nowhere to be found. Scott wheeled the motorcycle into the living room for safekeeping. The next morning, they would be sailing again, this time to the North Pacific, mission unknown. Cold up there, he thought as he drifted off to sleep. Like Kai.

The Big E got underway with a new load of fighters, the F-4F, featuring folding wings. To Scott, walking on a quiet flight deck before dawn, they looked like idle birds of prey squatting on the hard steel decks. There were new anti-air guns, advanced radars, better communication gear. As Scott said to Dick Best, "We are getting the best stuff thrown at us. Now we just have to figure out how to use it and deliver the punches." That night on the evening watch on the bridge, Scott was looking out when he saw another American carrier break the horizon, like a mirror suddenly reflecting an image of the Big E herself. It was USS *Hornet*. As Scott watched through his binoculars, *Hornet*'s escorts popped into view. The cruisers *Vincennes* and *Nashville*, another oiler, the *Cimarron*, and the usual brace of destroyers swept into formation with the Big E and her escorts. Because he saw the message traffic, Scott knew that *Hornet* was under the command of a savvy and well-regarded captain, Marc Mitscher, who was viewed as a pure aviator captain, having been through flight school many years before. Scott looked closely at the flight deck of *Hornet* and saw what he was looking for: not Navy fighters and bombers but strange ungainly airplanes with twin rudders and engines. They were Army B-25s, Mitchell bombers, named after a pioneer of military aviation, Billy Mitchell. Scott knew *Enterprise* and *Hornet* were on some special mission, but even with his access in radio and around the flag spaces, it wasn't clear what that might be. Perhaps they were just ferrying the B-25s to reinforce a land base in the Aleutians?

When he got off watch, Scott was summoned by the staff communications officer to a meeting in the flag mess to serve as a notetaker. He was stunned to learn the mission: Vice Admiral Halsey was to take the powerful two-carrier force to within five hundred miles of Tokyo and launch an *Army* air strike—led by a man widely viewed as the best aviator in the U.S. Army, Lieutenant

Colonel Jimmy Doolittle. Sixteen Mitchell bombers would strike the Japanese capital and then, if they survived, continue for another 1,500 miles to bases in China. Scott at first wondered why the Army, then realized that no Navy bombers had the range. As he jotted notes, he saw that it was a plan of breathtaking audacity yet pure simplicity. The biggest challenge was going to be just getting the lumbering B-25 airframes safely off the pitching deck of a carrier and into the air in one piece. The bombers certainly weren't going to be coming back to the ship once they launched: not only were the Army pilots not trained to make a carrier-arrested landing, but the aircraft themselves had no tailhooks to catch the carrier's "wire" and be wrestled down to the deck. Doolittle and his men were on a one-way mission. No one had tried launching a B-25 from a ship before, although the Army had experimented ashore with a field marked out with a carrier's dimensions and deemed it possible to get off. And as if that weren't enough of a risk, the Army pilots were not experts in the art of navigating over a trackless ocean, with no landmarks or coastal features to guide them. "Brave, sure," said Dick Best to Scott when they discussed it in hushed tones up in the dirty-shirt wardroom, "but competent for this mission? Who the fuck knows?"

After the flag meeting broke up, Scott was told to get down to radio and, at the chief of staff's direction, send a single one-line message via secure means to each of the ships in the strike group: THIS FORCE IS BOUND FOR TOKYO. The reaction was electric throughout every ship. The Big E echoed loudly with the cheers and shouts of the crew. The admiral paced the flag bridge like a boxer confined in a too-small ring while Scott watched and waited for his next signal. He looks like a small version of Ernest Hemingway, minus the beard, bouncing off the ropes in a boxing gym, Scott thought. But I know he'll pull this off. We are going to kick the Japs in the balls, then sprint home. Then we'll go back and do it again. Halsey can pull this off if anyone can.

As the mission launch point came closer, the air grew heavier with the possibility of Japanese scouts discovering the carrier task force. "How long are we gonna head at the Jap home islands?" Scott asked the haggard-looking chief of staff, a rumpled aviator who had barely slept in a week.

"Dunno exactly, Scott, but every damn mile we steam will reduce the risk for the Army aviators—and increase the risk for us."

From his perch behind the admiral, Scott could almost hear the gears in Halsey's head whirling, calculating, guessing, and finally, deciding. The admiral suddenly turned to Scott. "Take a message, Mr. James: Launch planes. To Col. Doolittle and his gallant command, good luck and God bless you—Halsey."

Everyone on the Big E who could get to a porthole or up on deck fixed their eyes on the pitching deck of *Hornet*. Mitscher had brought her smartly into the wind within minutes of receiving Halsey's signal. Scott raced to the ship's bridge to watch. The sixteen lumbering Mitchells would go off one at a time. Scott—like every man fortunate enough to have a view—held his breath for each launch. He reached into the pocket of his khakis and rubbed the rifle shell he carried for good luck. His dad had given it to him, pulled from the first buck he'd shot and killed back in the Florida Keys when he was a small boy learning to hunt. As he rubbed it, Scott thought about Halsey's short, graceful message to

Doolittle and his fliers: "Good luck and God bless you." As each plane lumbered off the deck, Scott whispered a small addendum: "And good hunting."

After the launch, Scott figured the best place to be was radio, and he headed there, accepting a mug of lukewarm coffee from the chief radioman. "Did you see them get off the deck, Mr. James?"

Scott took a sip. "Yup, they look like a gaggle of old, fat turkeys trying to cross a ravine, but they got in the air all right. You got that Tokyo Rose bitch up tonight?"

The chief nodded. He said it was standard operating procedure to have the vicious propaganda broadcast tuned in so the intelligence officers could see what they might pick up from an oblique comment or two.

Scott felt the ship turn gracefully as the two carrier strike groups smoothly reversed course and headed due east at maximum speed. It was easy to pick up the dulcet tones of Tokyo Rose, delivered in perfect king's English. In the middle of a tirade about the uselessness of resisting the Imperial Japanese Army came a sudden burst of Japanese language, and with an abrupt click, the station went off the air. Scott and the chief looked at each other and smiled. "Looks like Colonel Jimmy is making a special delivery about now," Scott said. "That shut down the bitch. Hope one of those bombs lands on her head."

The radio gang felt the Big E straining to the east, moving at well over twenty-five knots, back to safer waters. As the cold northern sunset approached, lighting up the long wakes of the carriers and their escorts, Scott went back on deck. He could feel

the crew beginning to relax. In the flag mess, the admiral autho-
rized a shot of whiskey from his "medicinal stores," and they all
laughed at the thought of the outrage and confusion in Tokyo and
the speculation about where the raid had been launched that filtered in through the intelligence reports delivered to the admiral's hands. One of the admiral's assistant chiefs of staff called for
a moment of silence and read a portion of a "letter to Mr. Tojo of
Japan," penned by a creative sailor: "Dishonorable Sir, It gives me
great pleasure to inform you, in case it has not been brought to
your attention, that, in accordance with the terms of your contract, accepted by us on 7 December 1941, the first consignment
of scrap metal has been delivered to your city." The flag mess
roared, and another round of the admiral's bourbon was distrib-
uted. The letter concluded, "You entered into this contract of
your own volition and must pay the price of same in full. Further
details can be worked out to the satisfaction of my concern when
we meet in your city in the near future."

Vice Admiral Bill Halsey raised a glass, turned, and faced his
happy companions, his lined face cracked in a thin-lipped smile.
"To hell," he toasted, "where we will send you." As if it heard him,
at that moment the Big E dipped her bow into a huge green wave,
shuddered hard, and, putting her massive steel shoulders into the
race homeward, threw tens of thousands of gallons of heavy seawater out of the ship's path. The sun fell below the horizon, and
Halsey's strike force sped through the night toward home.

26

Meeting at Midway

CENTRAL PACIFIC

A fter launching the Doolittle raid, the Big E touched land briefly in Pearl before loading up again and heading southwest, toward the distant Coral Sea. Scott had no liberty but didn't know if he would be welcome at Kai's anyway. Pearl was a madhouse, with a pair of the Big E's sister ships, the carriers USS *Lexington* and USS *Yorktown*, already pulling stores to sail and oppose an expected Japanese thrust toward Australia. By the 30th of April, the combined *Enterprise-Hornet* strike group was straining across the calm seas of the central Pacific, headed to join up with the other two carriers. They were cracking on all speed, but to Scott's immense frustration, they were still days away from the action down south when it heated up.

The first strike in what became known as the Battle of the Coral Sea was a success for the American forces. Scott was in the radio room and got to pass a message personally to Halsey that brought a broad smile to the admiral's face. Planes from *Yorktown* and "Lady Lex" had caught and sunk a Japanese carrier, the *Shoho*. The lieutenant commander who reported the success was laconic: "Scratch one flattop" was the totality of his radio report, which quickly reverberated through the hangars, flight decks, and mess decks of all four of the carriers.

Scott was in the flag mess talking about it with the ship's pudgy assistant chief of staff. "The Navy is only a small family—it feels like everyone on all four of these carriers know each other—but it won't stay that way, Scott. These days, most of the pilots and other officers went to Annapolis, trained at Pensacola in flying or San Diego in ship handling, and have operated closely together for years. You can feel it here in the flag mess when we all sit down to dinner. Everyone just knows everyone."

It had been a good few days, and Scott was heartened. But before Halsey and his powerful force could arrive on the scene to follow up on the Japanese carrier kill, the tables were turned. To his horror, Scott saw the flash traffic on the 8th of May: planes from Japanese carriers *Shokaku* and *Zuikaku*, which had killed so many at Pearl, struck both *Lexington* and *Yorktown*. Fires swept both the carriers, and Lady Lex was also hit with a couple of torpedoes below the waterline. With the Big E still a day away, the superior Japanese forces managed to sink *Lexington*, with the loss of many hands. Scott saw the look in Halsey's eye when he handed him the message. He crumpled the paper and turned to Scott. "Get the staff together. Now. In the flag mess." As Scott turned to implement the order, he looked into the admiral's eyes, framed under bushy brows. It was like looking into a furnace. The anger that radiated from them was so intense that Scott instinctively raised his hands to shield his face as he backed out of the room.

The news stunned the crews of the Big E and *Hornet*, instantly erasing the joy of the Doolittle raid and the sinking of the Japanese carrier. Scott watched Halsey closely in the hours after he heard of the sinking of *Lexington*, a carrier that the admiral had landed upon as a flight trainee. The look on his face now was a combination of exhaustion, rage, and frustration that was frightening to behold. "Goddamn it," he hissed to the flag staff group, "we are a few hours out of range, and now she's gone. *Lexington* sunk, gone forever. Goddamn it. What's the condition of *Yorktown*? We've got to get her back to Pearl and back into the fight."

His chief of staff spoke up. "Admiral, with Lex gone, we're down to three flattops in the whole damn Pacific—*if* we can keep *Yorktown* afloat. *Saratoga* is back in the yards stateside, and that just leaves us, *Hornet*, and hopefully *Yorktown*. We got in some good licks here in the Coral Sea, and the Japs are withdrawing north, but Jesus, we have got to get these three big ladies back to Pearl in one piece."

Halsey looked at the chart spread out in front of the staff, paused, and then said simply, "Let's keep hunting. But we'll work our way north while we do it. Tell Nimitz." Scott saluted and headed to the radio shack.

So the Big E and *Hornet* headed north and ran up the 170th meridian, searching the trackless sea for any sign of an injured Japanese carrier they could strangle in its weakened state. Scott took to dropping by the flag plot and poring over the big chart where the radarmen were marking the position of the Big E, and intelligence reports from the other carriers and scout destroyers. They saw no Japanese ships. Halsey sat in his chair on the flag bridge and drank pot after pot of coffee, smoking his cigarettes endlessly and staring out to sea.

When Admiral Nimitz ordered them back on the 16th of May, he accompanied the order with two words: EXPEDITE RETURN. "That's a damn funny thing for one admiral to say to another in the middle of a war," Scott observed to Dick Best as they prepared to eat a couple sliders. Scott watched his double cheeseburgers sliding off the grill in the dirty-shirt wardroom where the aviators hung out.

"I'll bet Nimitz knows that Halsey will take his time and try to find something else to kill out here," said Best, "and I'm with him." But the seas continued to frustrate Halsey. No victim fell into the air wings' long-range search patterns, and after a few more days, Oahu loomed on the horizon again. Scott thought about trying to see Kai, but it was clear this was going to be the ultimate quick turnaround.

The Big E was in port only a single day and most of a night pulling stores, first under a tropical sun, then under huge search-lights illuminating the buzzing dock. Scott heard an announcement over the 1MC: "Pacific Fleet arriving," followed by bells. *Ding, ding,* pause. *Ding, ding.* The sequence was repeated until eight bells had been tolled. Then a pause and one final *ding,* signifying that the admiral had set an august foot on the quarterdeck. Nimitz had come aboard the ship to award medals for actions in and around the Coral Sea, including a Distinguished Flying Cross to Lieutenant Commander Wade McClusky. As he pinned on the prestigious medal, he spoke to the young aviator in a quiet voice. "My guess is you're going to have another crack at one of these in the next few days."

When Best relayed the remark to Scott, it all came together in the ensign's mind. He'd seen Taussig at the snake ranch while ashore, and Joe had asked Scott if he knew much about the atoll of Midway. "Not a damn thing," Scott said. "Why?"

Joe had shaken his head and put his weight on his good leg to settle into a chair. "Lot of fingers starting to point in that direction, Scott. Central Pacific, not so far from right here. Keep your admiral's head up."

But the next morning, Vice Admiral Bill Halsey was sent down the gangplank of the Big E, owing to the fact that much of his body was covered with severe dermatitis, an ugly and debilitating rash, probably stemming more from complete exhaustion (and a steady diet of caffeine and nicotine) than from any serious medical condition. When he went ashore, his dark-blue three-star flag was hauled down, and up went a two-star flag, indicating that the command had been assumed by someone new to the Big E—the quiet, thoughtful Rear Admiral Ray Spruance, neither an aviator nor a colorful character, but reportedly a cool hand on the tiller. Scott worried about losing Halsey and pondered whether Spruance was up to the task. "So what's the gouge on this new guy?" he whispered to the flag communicator, who had graduated a few years before Scott from Annapolis.

"Well, the book on Spruance is that he's smart as hell, doesn't ever blow his own horn, and never loses his temper."

Scott pondered that. "Sounds like the opposite of Halsey," he said.

"Yeah," said the lieutenant commander. "Kind of everyone is either on team Halsey or team Spruance, but all I know is they both want to kill Japs. I'm for the both of them on that one."

Scott and Joe pooled their intelligence the night before the Big E sailed. The Japanese, under the command of the formidable and dangerous Admiral Isoroku Yamamoto, were turning their focus away from the Coral Sea and threats to Australia, intending to thrust instead toward Midway and the Aleutian Islands. Yamamoto was hated but respected by the U.S. Navy flag officers: he had served in D.C. as an attaché following a couple of years of study at Harvard and spoke reasonably good English. Many of the U.S. admirals had met him. "My dad knows him and says he's the most dangerous of all the Jap admirals. He's a gambler, according to all the reports we have," Joe said. "He'll play anything and bet on it. He told one of the other attachés that his real passion would be to go to Monte Carlo and open a casino." He's placing quite a bet at Midway, Scott thought to himself. And so is Admiral Nimitz.

"I've got a seat alongside the real intelligence professionals," Joe said, "like Ed Layton, Nimitz's chief intel officer. He's only a commander, but he's the smartest bastard we've got. You ever seen a pachinko machine, Scott? Big in the casinos here in the Pacific. That guy can almost visualize the balls of the pachinko game of the Pacific war banging back and forth, spinning. You remember Brownian motion from physics at Annapolis? But Ed says that the real wizard in the intelligence dungeon is a lieutenant commander, a guy named Joe Rochefort. He's a quirky bastard who wears a bathrobe and bedroom slippers while on duty. Jesus. They've got me working directly for Joe Rochefort, and the balls of the world's biggest pachinko game are about to land in the central Pacific at Midway, Scott. It's going to be a battle of the gods, or the titans, a battle that is gonna echo forever. And that's where I think the Big E is headed, shipmate."

Joe told Scott that according to communications intercepts the Americans were reading—and the Americans were decoding about one third of the Japanese high command's traffic—the Japanese believed the Americans were down to only two carriers. They thought *Yorktown* had joined *Lexington* on the bottom of the South Pacific, and thought that they would be in the prime position, bringing four carriers against two. Thus, the Imperial Navy divided its forces and sailed in five major groups. Later Scott would say to Joe Taussig, when they compared notes after the battle and could figure out the Imperial Navy's plan in retrospect, "Sometimes when you try to attack everywhere, you end up attacking nowhere." But in the first days of June, it seemed the Japanese were effectively everywhere, a cloud of angry and energetic yellowjackets, about to start stinging in earnest. The Americans had three carriers, plus the unsinkable flight deck on Midway Island. The odds were even.

And so they sailed toward Midway. On the flag bridge, they got to know their new admiral. Rear Admiral Ray Spruance, a short and slender man, loved to walk while he thought. Scott watched him stride along the flight deck whenever flight operations were on hold, asking questions of the staff, getting to know them one by one. The admiral's energy and quiet intelligence pulsed from deep within him, and he was a listener. Scott thought he had a battery inside him that he charged up by interacting with others. After a couple of days of absorbing the quality and capability of his staff, he gathered them around the big chart table on the flag bridge and went around the room to each of his department heads to solicit their views. They were largely in consensus, and cautiously optimistic about the odds for the American side. *What else are we gonna say?* Scott thought. *But you might as well believe you're going to win. What's the point otherwise?*

After listening to each department head, Spruance summed it up. "So here's what I see. We've got the entire Jap navy headed toward Midway and maybe the Aleutians. All we have is three carriers—and one of them, *Yorktown*, ought to be in the yards having her guts replaced—and an air wing on *Hornet* that has never seen combat. We've got a bunch of cruisers and destroyers, but not a true big-gun battleship in sight." He paused and looked at his staff. "Well, we've got 'em right where we want 'em, I guess." He chuckled dryly. "But we've got two big things going for us: One, we will know where they are going, while they think they have surprise. It'll make them careless and overconfident. And two, Midway Island can't be sunk—it's like having another carrier that you know will be there for the entire battle. God bless those code breakers back at Makalapa, starting with that crazy commander in the bathrobe. I'm betting they are going to give us the location, timing, course, and speed of the Japs before this thing is over, and we are going to use it to concentrate our forces and pound the hell out of the Japanese. They just don't know it yet."

Spruance instructed the team to build a plan to get the maximum level of combat power available fitted against the assumptions coming from "Station Hypo," the intelligence wizards. Scott told Dick Best that everything was pointing to the 4th of June.

"We'll be ready," Best said. "God help us to get the drop on them this time, like they did to us at Pearl."

Scott got up at 3 a.m. on the 4th, and headed to the radio shack. When he arrived, the flag communications officer told him to head back to the flag combat center and just stay close to the admiral. By 7 a.m., a nervous Ray Spruance had moved to the flag bridge, accompanied by a few of his senior staff and Scott, his message drafter and runner. Scott glanced down at the chart spread over the navigation table on the flag bridge: The Big E was about three hundred miles east and north of Midway, the unsinkable aircraft carrier that was the big advantage for the Americans lying in wait for the ambush that could change the course of the war. A runner from radio entered the flag bridge and handed Scott a message, which he wordlessly passed to the admiral on the bridge wing. Spruance carefully put down his binoculars and read: ENEMY CARRIERS. It came from a single report by a Catalina PBY, a flying boat that doubled as a patrol bomber and was operating out of Midway. The note by itself wasn't much help. Scott ran a series of questions to radio for transmission to Midway, including disposition of enemy forces, aircraft numbers, and location of the Japanese carriers.

A little after 8 a.m., the positions were clarified, and they were in sync with the intelligence estimates. The trap was set and orders issued to the force, which Scott walked to radio: PROCEED

SOUTHWESTERLY AND ATTACK ENEMY CARRIERS WHEN DEFINITIVELY
LOCATED. Devastator torpedo bombers, Dauntless dive bombers,
and Wildcat fighters fired up their engines and were powered into
the air as the carriers sped up to generate sufficient winds for the
launches. Dick Best, Gene Lindsey, and Wade McClusky were
leading the flights from the Big E. Their contemporaries were
launching at roughly the same time from *Hornet*. Scott darted up
to the flag bridge and, from a vantage point just behind Rear Admiral Spruance, saw many of them launch. He noticed that Spruance's hands were steady on his binoculars, holding them to his
chest, although his lips were moving silently, perhaps wishing
them luck, perhaps praying. Scott's hand found the rifle shell and
he massaged its smooth-worn surface in his pocket, wishing them
good hunting.

The first wave was a disaster. Just after 11 a.m., reports began
to filter back to the flag staff—the American planes had spread
out and were headed toward the Japanese carriers when a cloud of
Zeros flitted down from above them, raining death on the lumbering American attack aircraft. The Wildcat fighters were no
match for the speedy Zeros, and U.S. planes began to fall from the
sky. Lindsey and his gunner died in the midst of the American attack, shot down either from above or by shipboard antiaircraft
fire, which was thick and effective. Of the fourteen Devastators,
only four made it back to the ship. There was not a single hit on a
Japanese ship. Scott's fingers were tight around the talisman in his
pocket, and Spruance's shoulders slumped as he watched what remained of his dive bombers limp back to the Big E. The flag staff
gathered protectively around their boss, but there was nothing to

say in that awful moment. Scott, like most of the officers, looked down at his black shoes, wishing he were anywhere else. But he knew there were other balls in the pachinko game.

Meanwhile, the Dauntless bombers were searching in another quadrant, with McClusky and Best leading their formations. After he returned to the Big E, coughing up blood from a failed oxygen distribution system in his aircraft, Dick Best described the run to Scott: "It was just before noon, and we were having trouble with oxygen—that's why I'm so chewed up—but I was also worrying about fuel. Then McClusky saw the wake from a small boy running like a dog with a bone in its teeth." Scott smiled at the description: *small boy* was the usual aviator derogatory term for a destroyer. "We figured he had to be sprinting to catch up with his main body. And we were right. It was right after noon, but the Wildcats were dry and had to bingo back to the base or run out of gas. And right then we saw those Jap bastards—four of them carriers as big as barns—same bastards that gave it to us at Pearl. Wade divided us up, and down we went. It was right out of a textbook from Pensacola: a dive bomber's wet dream. Big bombs everywhere, onto the flight decks, down the stacks, into the magazines. It was two minutes of pure hell and then everything on the surface of the sea was on fire." Best was vigorously illustrating the air action with his hands. Left hand for the Americans chasing the right hand, which represented the Japanese. Scott thought to himself, I finally know what the aviators mean when they call their stupid air-battle hand movements "shooting your watch off."

Wade McClusky chose that moment to walk into sick bay and check on Dick Best. "You telling war stories, Dick? You better save your breath, man. I'll pick it up." He turned to Scott. "We had a cloud of Zeros all around us, but you could almost see them getting distracted 'cause their home plates were all on fire. Kind of takes it out of a fighter pilot, knowing he isn't going to be able to land when the mission is over." He smiled wickedly. "We lost a lot of fine men out there. I think we only got eighteen of the SBDs back, out of thirty-two went up with us. But we'll pull some of them out of the drink, and every man on that flight would make the trade: our planes shot down or run out of gas, but we put three of their fleet carriers down, and down hard. Call it a down payment on Pearl, and there is plenty more to come. I know *York-town* got hit hard, and I hear she might not make it home this time. Sooner or later her luck was going to run out. But the trap worked, and we hit them a ton harder than we got hit.

"Plus," he went on, "around dusk, Earl Gallaher—you know him, right, Scott?—got off this deck with another twenty-four Dauntless bombers, most of them with thousand-pounders. Some of them were from *Yorktown*, the rest of what was left from our air wing. We got another carrier, the *Hiryu*, I think. Gallaher and his gang just got down; in fact, you can hear the last couple of traps overhead now." It was just after 8:30 p.m., the end of a day of flight operations that had begun at three thirty in the morning. The 4th of June was at an end. Scott, who had been awake for well over twenty-four hours, made his way back to the flag bridge, exhausted but exhilarated.

Spruance was getting the last of the battle damage assessments and issuing his final night orders, including keeping some of the Wildcats aloft as combat air patrol in case the Japanese tried anything else. The look on his face, calm but elated, was one of relief and pride. He chatted quietly with his intelligence team. The next decision was a hard one to Scott's mind. "We could linger here through the night and see what the dawn launch turns up. Or we could roll the dice and go right at them, head due west and keep pressing." Scott, listening from his usual position behind the admiral, had zero doubt what the impulsive and combative Halsey would have done. But he guessed Spruance would take a more prudent course. The admiral pivoted toward Scott. "Mr. James, draft me a message to get the force moving east. Still a lot of big Japanese guns out here, from their battleship forces to cruisers to plenty of torpedo destroyers. Let's take our winnings off the table tonight and head back toward Pearl."

Right call, Admiral, Scott thought. He drafted the message, sent it, and went to bed. He dreamed of a swarm of angry bees flying into a smoky wood fire.

On the morning of the 5th of June, two things were clear to Scott: the Japanese had been hit hard by the Americans; and there were still targets in the area. Scott was back on the flag bridge again, watching the patchwork air wings take off. Dick Best was down in sick bay, still coughing up blood, but the composite force went in search of *Hiryu* and the surface ships. That night, Scott went down to see Best and give him an update: "They searched all day, Dick, but didn't come up with anything worth attacking. The admiral knows there are at least some surface ships hanging around, and maybe one of the flattops we hit is still limping along."

Best nodded slowly. "Well, there's always tomorrow." Scott nodded and went to his stateroom to sleep deeply.

When he surfaced, like a swimmer coming up from the bottom of an ice-cold stream, it was the 6th of June, and he could hear thumps on the flight deck as yet another set of bombers was launched. By the time he got a shave and made it up to the flag bridge, the first scouting reports were coming in: not flattops but a pair of cruisers and a half dozen destroyers. This time there were no Zeros to oppose the Navy fliers—all the Japanese planes had gone to the bottom when their carrier homes were destroyed. So the Wildcats got in on the fun, strafing the surface ships while the Dauntless bombers rained thousand-pound bombs on the warships. Scott read a report to the admiral: "Both heavy cruisers hit and on fire, sir. Cruiser *Mikuma* assessed to be sinking, single destroyer escorting her and picking up survivors. Cruiser *Mogami* burning and losing fuel, two destroyers escorting her. No sign of battleships or troop transports."

The admiral sighed with pleasure and ordered a final photo reconnaissance. He sent a message, which Scott drafted, to Admiral Fletcher, the other senior U.S. commander at sea during the Battle of Midway, inquiring about *Yorktown*, which was still afloat, albeit barely by the end of the day on the 6th. "Jesus, I want to get her back to Pearl," said the admiral.

Scott knew that the captain of *Yorktown* was back aboard the ship with a damage-control party doing all they could to save the wounded ship. "She had her guts ripped out in the Coral Sea," Scott said to Dick Best, "and they just stuffed the pieces back inside her and sent her out here. I don't see how she can pull off another miracle."

Best sighed heavily but said, "I wouldn't count her out."

But on the 7th of June, the gallant ship listed, limped a few more sea miles, then capsized and hurtled down over two miles through the cold sea to the bottom of the Pacific. Scott was in the flag plot when the final report came in, and watched the radarman mark the spot carefully, lovingly, on the big chart. He put a small cross in black ink on the spot, and wrote "RIP Yorktown" on the chart. Scott felt tears and saw a chief turn away and put a rag to his eyes. Like too many of her pilots and aircrew, *Yorktown* had given her all. Scott James went down to the hangar deck and stood looking out to sea in the direction of *Yorktown*'s last stand. The exhaustion and emotion of the last four days hit him like a rogue wave. All he could think of were the hundreds of pilots and gunners lost, many of them good friends.

He looked down at the oily, dark water rushing by the hull of the Big E. It could as easily have been his ship as the *Yorktown*. Yet he knew that the winnings, the sunk and damaged Japanese carriers—four of them—were worth the brutal cost. The intelligence reports, many lifted from Japanese transmissions, were staggering. In addition to the four fleet carriers, the Japanese had lost a heavy cruiser and had another one badly damaged; around 250 aircraft and all their trained pilots were gone forever; and more than three thousand experienced officers and sailors in total had been killed—evening the score from Pearl Harbor. The U.S. had lost only the carrier *Yorktown* and a single destroyer. About 150 aircraft and around three hundred aviators and aircrew would never fly again, a grievous loss, certainly, but far less than the damage to the Imperial Japanese Navy. Scott knew as well that the victory had come not from the land-based air flying out of

Midway but rather from the carrier-based pilots on *Yorktown*, *Hornet*, and the Big E, so effectively led by Ray Spruance, a fighting surface admiral with a lion's heart and the calm demeanor of a college professor.

It was a moment of real victory, and Scott hoped it might end up being the turning point in the war; but as he reflected on his role, there was a nagging sense that he'd done nothing compared with the pilots and the gunners. Sure, he'd helped the flag staff support the admiral and make the smart decisions that led to a victory. But really, what was his role? And where was the opportunity for him to attain the recognition of a Dick Best or a Wade McClusky? As he stared moodily out to sea, he concluded that a flag staff was not where he wanted or needed to be. He was a surface warfare officer, and if the battleships were sidelined, he would goddamn well get to the destroyers, and to the front lines of the fight, and make his mark. He just didn't know how. Yet.

27

After Midway

A fter the Battle of Midway, the surviving victorious American carriers—the Big E and *Hornet*—headed for Pearl Harbor. Admiral Nimitz had effectively told them, like the ancient Spartans, to go into battle with their shields and come home either holding them as victors or lying on them in death. Three U.S. fast carriers went into battle, and only two came home. The sinking of USS *Yorktown* underlined the risks, but the extraordinary victory highlighted by the sinking of all four Japanese carriers changed the trajectory of the war. Scott felt the impact of the moment, watching the smooth water of Pearl Harbor surround the Big E as she returned home.

The crews of *Enterprise* and *Hornet* mourned the loss of *Yorktown* deeply but quickly got to work preparing to sortie again, pulling aboard supplies and repairing battle damage. Rear Admiral

Ray Spruance was feted by the commander of the Pacific Fleet, and there was talk of his being given a third star. Many among the victors were similarly rewarded. Among them was Scott Bradley James, meritoriously promoted to lieutenant. Scott spent ten minutes in front of the mirror in the officers' washroom on the Big E adjusting the shiny silver devices that Navy officers called railroad tracks on his collars until he had the angle just right. Then he jogged to the officers' brow, obtained permission from the officer of the deck to go ashore, and walked up and down the pier for half an hour, relishing the enthusiastic salutes he received from the enlisted men, and now from ensigns and JGs as well.

He walked to a liberty launch and headed over to the officers' club, where he met up with a couple dozen fellow junior officers who had likewise been advanced, joining them for what the Navy called a wetting-down party. This consisted of strenuous drinking underwritten by the newly promoted officers, culminating in the celebrants putting their new insignia at the bottom of a glass of bourbon and downing it—with luck, catching the device in their teeth, not swallowing it. This Scott did with aplomb. Swiveling around on his high stool in the darkened bar, he surveyed the happy crowd.

Everyone was grabbing their shipmates and retelling the stories of the most important parts of the battle. Soon Scott was in the middle of an excited group of midgrade officers holding bottles of beer and glasses of whiskey or, for the more adventurous, a powerful Hawaiian moonshine called Okolehao or oke for short. "I swear, Admiral Spruance was a cool one, start to finish. Damn, I was proud to be there next to him, even if all I did was run messages back and forth to radio," Scott said to an aviator, Tom Johnson, a classmate from Annapolis. "You guys were all heroes, Tom. The whole country knows about this now."

Johnson, a Wildcat pilot, smiled. "Yeah, in the air wing we were really worried when we lost Halsey, but I gotta admit that for a black shoe, that Spruance is a good one. Wonder if Halsey will come back soon."

Scott reflected for a second on the weird fact that naval aviators traditionally wore brown shoes with their khaki uniforms and surface warfare officers wore black. No one could explain why. He took a swig from the bottle of Primo beer. "Well, I'm not supposed to say, but the rumor around the flag staff is that he will come back, but that Nimitz may alternate him and Halsey on the cruises so neither one of them burns out again like Halsey did before."

The small circle of junior officers chewed on that for a minute, until one of them made the obvious comment: "But what about us? Who do we get to alternate with?" No one answered.

Scott shrugged. "Look, I've also heard that Nimitz may pull Spruance onto his staff as chief of staff or even deputy commander of the Pacific Fleet. The guy's got an electric brain, and Nimitz loves him." Scott put a couple of dollars on the bar to pay for his round and headed out to grab a taxi to the snake ranch. His plan was to show up at Kai's house to show off his new railroad tracks, and he needed to get to his motorcycle.

When Scott walked through the screen door of the snake ranch, he heard music coming from the backyard as he walked slowly through the house. He noticed his motorcycle had been moved slightly and was leaning up against the wall at a strange angle. As he walked into the backyard, he saw Kelley's back to him. The big Marine was raising a glass of what looked like rum and pineapple juice in a crowd of about twenty young people, men and women, all about to do the same. The men in the crowd were mostly in uniform, the women in luau garb. There was a barbecue smoking on the side of the yard and an impromptu bar with limes, pineapples, lemons, and a half dozen different bottles. The record player was spinning "Don't Sit Under the Apple Tree" by the Andrews Sisters.

Scott paused just inside the door on the edge of the lanai so he wouldn't interrupt the Marine's moment. "So, ladies and gentlemen, we kicked the damn Japs' asses at Midway, sank the same fucking carriers that attacked us here, and now it's time to head off and do the same with their army. But this wouldn't have happened, this big victory, I mean, without the intelligence boys in the dungeon over at fleet headquarters giving the gouge to our pilots and our admirals. And I think everyone knows that one of our own was right there in the middle of that, and his name is Joe Taussig."

Scott saw that Joe was seated in the center of the crowd, facing Kelley. No one could see Scott, still in the shadow of the porch's overhang. Kelley went on, "And, ladies and gentlemen, tonight I want to toast Joe, and especially congratulate him on his promotion to be the very first lieutenant commander in the proud class of 1941. Our first 0-4, if you can believe it. I give you *Lieutenant Commander* Joe Taussig, or as we call him from now on"—he paused—"sir! To our classmate, shipmate, and friend, congratulations, *sir!*" Everyone cheered and laughed, downed their drinks, and crowded around Joe, patting him on the back and mock-saluting him as he basked in their applause and good spirits.

In the shadow of the porch, Scott James reached up and touched his new lieutenant's bars, wishing he could muster the enthusiasm for them he had felt just an hour ago. Not for the first time, he thought, Good for Joe, but I'm just falling behind, following in the wake of a classmate and close friend who has been promoted to an even higher rank and probably given another medal. Joe was a good guy, and someone he respected, but it didn't make it any easier.

Scott put on a smile, gathered himself, and was prepared to emerge and join the crowd to congratulate Joe. Just before he did, his hand on the screen door, he saw a slim form detach from the crowd and walk over to Kelley. It was Kai. She had an orchid in her hair and was wearing a tight-fitting summer frock. In her hand was her traditional cocktail, a daiquiri made with pomegranate juice. Scott could see the dark-red color of the drink even across the expanse of lawn. She walked up to the tall Marine and put her hand around his waist, and as Scott watched, Kelley leaned down and whispered something in her ear. She smiled up at him in an animated response, laughed lightly, and hugged him.

Lieutenant Scott Bradley James turned on his heel, walked back into the living room, reached into the bowl where keys were always stashed, and wheeled his motorcycle out the door to the street.

He kick-started it, gunned it loudly, and swiftly departed the scene.

For the next hour, Scott drove his motorcycle hard over the

top of Oahu, heading to the beaches on the North Shore, where he'd spent so many hours with Kai. As he drove, he noticed the motorcycle seemed out of tune, occasionally even backfiring. The single headlight went in and out with every bump in the road. Like my career and my love life, thought Scott, going fast but so damn erratic.

And who has been riding my motorcycle? Scott knew damn well one-legged Joe Taussig wasn't riding it, so that left Kelley. Not much doubt he's riding Kai too, thought Scott bitterly as the miles passed under the racing wheels of the motorcycle. At least I don't have to be back at the carrier until Monday morning, he thought angrily. Great, a whole day to wallow in self-pity. He turned his head to the side and spat. Man, this isn't what making lieutenant and being part of the biggest naval battle in American history is supposed to feel like, on a beautiful Saturday night in the Hawaiian Islands.

Scott arrived at the beach, pulled the motorcycle down near the waves, and leaned it against a palm tree. It was after midnight, dark and balmy, a prevailing offshore breeze stirring the palm fronds above his head. He tried to figure out a plan that didn't involve punching Sean Kelley in his big fat Irish face, hard and fast, maybe two or three times before the Irishman got his guard up, but he couldn't come up with one. He dozed off and awoke to see the sun rising off to his right, a pink and hopeful tropical morning. Red sky at morning, sailor take warning, he said softly to himself. He contemplated the old saying for a long moment. Fuck it, he thought, I'm going to go see Kai and just ask her what is going on. That's all the plan I need.

Kai at Night

OAHU, HAWAII

E ven as he wheeled the motorcycle up to the bungalow of
Kai's parents, Scott felt he was making a mistake. In some
strange sense, he knew that his actions at this moment
would be a pivot point in his life, but reversing course felt impos-
sible. As with giving a rudder order on a ship close to the pier, the
sense of commitment to whatever was going to happen was
palpable. As he brought the motorcycle to the curb, he almost
backed it away and returned to Pearl Harbor. But something
pulled him forward. Jesus, he thought, I'm like Ulysses in that
narrow channel with the Sirens singing to me, but I forgot to put
the wax in my ears.

He didn't see any lights on in the house. Again he thought,
What the fuck am I doing here? He stood indecisively on the
pavement in front of the small bungalow. But he saw a light switch

on suddenly on the porch, and the door opened, and her small form emerged.

"Scott? Is that you?" Kai asked in a quiet near whisper, as if she had seen a ghost.

He looked steadily at her, the black hair framed by the yellow porch light, her body highlighted from behind her. "Are your parents at home?" he asked.

She looked up for an instant and said simply, "No."

He moved the motorcycle to the side of the screened porch, came around to the front door, and took her hand. "Can I come in?"

Without a word she pulled him through the entrance, and they looked at each other in the diffuse light from the porch, standing just inside the door. "My parents are in Honolulu seeing my relatives. They won't be back today."

Scott squeezed her hand. "Let's go sit in the back."

They settled in the chairs on the back lanai. "Just tell me, okay?" Scott asked. "What's going on with you and Kelley?"

She paused, looked up at the mountain range and the fat rain clouds settled on it, and then back at him. "I was spending all my time at the university. I kept going on the early Pacific voyages, the first of my people who sailed these waters, thousands of years before your Navy existed. It was lonely, and I couldn't get focused, and you were gone. You didn't call me or write me or even send me a telegram or whatever you call it from a ship. And you even worked right there with the ship's radios, I know that—you could have contacted me somehow. But you didn't. And Sean was nice to me. We got . . ." And she paused, and Scott's heart beat once, twice, three times, and she said, "We got close." He looked at her, and she looked away again. "But I waited for you in my heart, Scott. And I always will." She looked into his eyes and teared up.

"I don't want to know any more about all that," he said. "I was gone. But I'm here now, and I want to be with you again, like we were before. I did come back. I found my way to port, to you, to this moment now."

She stood up, still holding his hand, and led him back to her bedroom.

She stepped out of her dress and fumbled to undress him. In an instant they were on her bed. The shades were drawn, but the morning light filtered into the room like it had the first time they made love on the Sunday of the Pearl Harbor attack. She was more assertive than he remembered, taking charge and maneuvering herself on top of him. As she moved gently above him, he thought, All I want is this girl, nothing more. He pulled her face down to his and kissed her as she continued to move above him, exquisitely, as steady as the sea, as sweet as the honeybees buzzing in their distant hives. God, he thought, let everything end here and now, and I'll never want for anything else.

They lay together afterward and talked. He asked her more about the university. "Are any of the professors caught up in the war effort? Are all the classes just going on, or have the schedules changed?"

She got out of bed, laughing as she stepped into her shift. "Of course. Even though you and the carriers go out to sea, life is going on here. My dad says the Japs are already being pushed back. Were you at this Midway place? You won't have to go back to sea again soon, will you?"

"Let's have some coffee, okay? You still have some of that Kona your mom bought?" After they settled at the kitchen table with their coffees, Scott took a deep breath and said gently, "Kai, this is going to be a long war. Not a week, not a month, not even a year. I'm going to be gone for long stretches. Like your ancestors, sailing a huge sea. All the land in the world would fit inside the Pacific Ocean, and we are going to have to fight the Japanese in every part of it before this is over. They are good, but we are better, but the war will take time." He took another sip of the hot black coffee. "And I cannot abide just being on a staff on a carrier. I'm going to ask the admiral to help me get orders to a destroyer, and I want to go south to really help beat down the Japs. I don't know if he will let me, or how long I will be gone, but if I go forward, it is going to be for a long time, I'd say. I don't know what's between you and Kelley or anyone else, and I don't have the right to ask you to wait for me, but I'm going to ask anyway. But it is up to you."

He looked at her over the chipped rim of the white old-fashioned Navy coffee mug her dad had appropriated from a chief's mess on a warship. She stared back, a sad look in her deep black eyes. "Scott, I want to be with you, and I've done some things I probably shouldn't have, but now I'm here. And I will be here when you get back. But you can't just jump on a motorcycle and roar off into the next adventure. We don't have to get married, but I want to know that you will be here when this thing ends, whenever that is going to be. If you can't promise that, then maybe it's time for you to go, before my mom and dad get back, which they will soon."

She fingered the gold cross on her neck. "I want you to take this, haole boy. It will keep you safe." She opened the tool drawer in the kitchen and took out a small set of pliers. Before he could object, she cut the gold cord and pushed the gold cross into the shirt pocket of his khaki uniform. "It will keep you safe, I promise," she repeated.

Scott drained his coffee mug and gently set it down on the small kitchen table. "I will be here for you, Kai. There may be lots of sea duty and battles and worse things between now and then. You will always be in my heart, and God willing, I promise that I will come back to you. I promise. With your cross, on your cross, I swear it." He pulled her up and kissed her. Just then, her parents walked through the front door of the bungalow.

An Admiral's Gift

T he next morning, Lieutenant Scott Bradley James knocked on the door of the flag cabin and walked into the presence of Rear Admiral Ray Spruance. The admiral, a short, lean man with recently clipped gray hair, had a lively intelligence in his eyes. He looked at Scott with a slight smile. Admiral Spruance was not someone inclined to become overly involved in the personal lives of his staff, but he'd developed a mild interest in Lieutenant James during the Midway campaign and seemed reasonably focused on the visit. "What can I do for you, Mr. James? Oh, and I guess congratulations are in order. It took me a *long* time to make lieutenant, but war has *some* benefits." He smiled thinly at the new railroad tracks on Scott's collar.

Scott smiled in response and tried to look humble. "Sir, thanks for taking a minute with me. I wanted to talk about my job. You know I've enjoyed being on your staff, and especially being part of the flag staff during Midway. I have done my best to be part of your team, and I've learned a lot. But I want to get to the front of the surface Navy. Admiral, you are a destroyer, cruiser, and battleship man—I am proud to be a part of your staff, but I don't want to fight the war from the flag bridge of a carrier. I know you get that, sir. I want to be down on the surface of the sea, firing guns and striking the Japs myself. It may not be the way we beat them in the end, but I don't care. I want to be on the front line." He paused. "So, I'd like to get to a destroyer, sir. I know I'm hitting you cold, but I'm asking for your help . . . and advice." Scott added the last words in a small nod to the audacious nature of his request, and then looked down. Part of him thought that Spruance would simply nod and say, "Sure, Scott, let me see what I can do," and then forget all about it. He had low expectations.

But Raymond Spruance, an "admiral's admiral" who cared about his crews on destroyers and now about his flag wardroom, looked thoughtfully over the bridge wing of the Big E, where Scott had ambushed him, and said, "I guess I'd feel the same if I were you, son." A long pause. "Let me see if I can get you to destroyer duty. The best thing for your career would be to become the gunnery officer. You're young, but you're a lieutenant and you could figure it out. And the best thing would be to serve in a tin can heading deep into the South Pacific, because that's where the fighting is going to be, for months or longer." Spruance added a caveat: "Do well out there and someday, after we get more salt on you, I can pull you back to this flag staff." Scott's face lit up. But the admiral continued, "Let me talk to some people and see if I can pull this off. Don't tell your mom and dad—or your girlfriend, if you have one—that I pulled any strings for you, Scott. Where you may be going is the hottest action in the Pacific. If you end up spending the rest of eternity on the bottom of the South Pacific, I don't want them blaming me, no matter how all this comes out. It's a big war, whether you're an admiral or a lieutenant, but I understand what you want and I'm not going to stand in your way. Not for a minute. So let me see what I can do."

Scott snapped to attention as the admiral left the flag bridge. Spruance looked over his shoulder and said, "Godspeed, Mr. James. Sail proud."

Scott figured it would take weeks, maybe months, for the admiral to arrange a transfer, if it ever actually happened. But the next morning he was summoned to the admiral's cabin again. "Some people have all the luck," said Spruance as Scott entered.

Genuinely confused, Scott blurted out, "How's that, sir?"

Spruance looked thoughtful. "Well, not the gunnery officer of the USS *Fletcher*. The poor son of a bitch was swept overboard in heavy seas two days ago. Just declared lost." Scott began to sense where this was going. Spruance continued, "So the ship—the first of its class, by the way, the best we've got—is in desperate need of a replacement. And that would be you."

Scott stifled a smile, knowing his good fortune was thanks to the bad luck of a fellow officer. "I appreciate the opportunity more than you know, sir" was all he could muster.

"The other part of this is the ship needs you *now*. So you have to be out of here in the next thirty-six hours. So get out of here and get packing."

At that moment, the admiral's flag writer walked in and handed

Scott his written orders. "Hey, Mr. James. Good luck out there. Need another yeoman there, just let me know." The admiral shot the yeoman a dark look. Scott took the mimeographed packet of orders. Jesus, he thought to himself, that was fast. He walked down to his bunk room to pack his seabag. In about an hour he was walking across the brow of the Big E for what he hoped would be the last time. The carrier Navy had been good to him—better than the battleship Navy—but he realized that on a carrier he would always be a second-class citizen to the "sacred aviators" who constituted the main battery of the warship. He burned to command the long-range guns, close-in air defense fires, and deadly torpedoes of a destroyer, and in his hand was the writ—of the fleet's best admiral, no less—to do exactly that.

Scott had been avoiding Kelley since his latest tryst with Kai, and with these orders, everything had simplified in his mind. He sped to the Naval Magazine to break the news to Kai, but her mother explained that Kai was at school cramming for final exams. Scott was oddly relieved to not have to explain his sudden departure. A blessing, he thought. Let Mom do it. "I've got emergency orders to ship out by air to pick up my new destroyer," he told her. "They just came in. Leaving tomorrow. I don't know when I'll be back, but can you explain it to Kai? I need you to square it with her. Tell her I had no idea the orders would come in so quickly."

Her eyes wide, she said, "I'll do what I can, Scott, but you haven't been the best man, the most reliable man, in her life lately."

Scott didn't have time to parse that comment but wondered how much she knew. He said in a stutter, "It's the war. I'm doing the best I can, and I told her I am always here for her—well, in my heart, anyway. Tell her I will write . . . this time."

Kai's mom gave him a flat, noncommittal look. "Be safe out there, Ensign . . . I mean Lieutenant Scott," she said finally. He walked back to his motorcycle. They had nothing further to say to each other.

Less than an hour later, Scott was at the snake ranch. Kelley was at the Marine barracks, but Joe Taussig was there on a rare afternoon off. Scott grinned and threw him an offhand salute, which Joe brushed away. They hugged each other awkwardly. "Wow, you're a real telephone commander," Scott said. "Just keep saying 'commander' and everyone will snap to."

"Shut up," Joe said. "What's going on over on Spruance's staff? I hear we're going to pull him up to CINCPACFLT as the chief of staff, maybe as deputy. He's the smartest guy on the waterfront, according to Nimitz."

"Well, he's plenty smart," Scott said, "but all I can say is I love him, because he just finagled me orders to a destroyer in the South Pacific." He waved the orders in front of Taussig.

Joe's face clouded. "Scott, you remember when I told you the next hot spot was Midway, right? Well, the next thing, the next big one, is going to be a place called Guadalcanal, near the Solomon Islands. And I think Kelley is headed there with the Marines. It's going to be a big show, and if we knock the Japs back there, it could really be the turning point. A lot of people say Midway was that, and maybe it was in some ways, but my bet is you've got to beat the Jap army, and that isn't going to happen at sea. So be careful there, Scott. Lots of lead going to be flying. You remember your *Reef Points*, right? Son of Neptune and all of that? Well, this is gonna be Neptune's inferno. A fire at sea that never goes out, or at least doesn't go out until this war is over. Be careful out there, classmate."

Scott took all this in and said, "Yeah, that's why I'm going, Joe. When is Kelley shipping out?"

Taussig glanced at the lanai in the backyard. "He hasn't been here in a couple of days, since you took your motorcycle away. Why didn't you say hello, by the way?"

"It's complicated, Joe," Scott said simply. "Tell Kelley I said I'll see him in Guadalcanal. On the way to hell, or Neptune's inferno. I've got to go."

They hugged again, neither of them entirely comfortable. But for Scott Bradley James, it was the embrace of a classmate, a fellow officer, and a friend he treasured. I'm sailing to the South Pacific, he thought, and who knows when I'll have that again?

The First Circle

A long ten days later, Scott slung his seabag into a motor launch pulled up alongside the destroyer he'd hitched a ride on from Pearl to a lagoon off Tulagi, on the opposite side of the strait from Guadalcanal and Tassafaronga, two places he had never heard of before shipping out. It was a dead-flat calm day, not even a hint of breeze. He missed the trade winds around Pearl and the steady sea breeze on the open bridge of the destroyer. He could see all the way down to the coral reefs below the churn of the small boat. The small and slightly protected anchorage had become a place for destroyers and patrol craft to moor, avoiding Japanese aerial attacks. Scott noted with amusement that the anchorage was in the Florida Islands. Not exactly what my dad thinks of when he says "the Florida islands," he thought as the motor launch cut through the clear water. In the distance, across the strait, he heard a steady booming sound. Naval gunfire.

Scott's boat was headed ashore to Tulagi, at a very temporary forward base for the flotilla of surface ships. Initially the U.S. naval forces had based from Nouméa, New Caledonia, sometimes staging through Espiritu Santo, New Hebrides, traditionally called Vanuatu. Work on the port and airfield facilities at Espiritu Santo was well underway but only partly complete when the Guadalcanal operation began in late summer. Fortunately, where Scott had landed, there was also a good harbor at Tulagi, across Savo Sound and the strait from Guadalcanal, but it was vulnerable to air attack so was generally used in the early stages as a temporary overnight anchorage and a base for small craft and tugs, before being built up to a major PT boat base.

All of this was necessary, as Scott could see from studying the charts, because there was no adequate harbor on the island of Guadalcanal itself. There was still a shortage of amphibious ships, so the general concept of operations was for cargo ships to arrive off Lunga Point on Guadalcanal, near Henderson Field, which the Marines would defend to the death. They would come in at daybreak to off-load cargo to lighters to take the cargo ashore. If the ships weren't going to be done by sunset, they would head over to Tulagi to spend the night and resume the next morning. A Japanese air attack during the day was considered a somewhat lesser danger than Japanese destroyers at night. Tulagi would become a destroyer and cruiser base for the Solomons campaign.

As the motor launch headed toward the dock at Tulagi, Scott let his mind play back to the transit south on USS *Nicholas*

(DD-449). As a full lieutenant, he'd been quickly pressed into service on the watch bill, and he'd enjoyed driving the highly powered destroyer. It was a sister to the lead ship of the class, USS *Fletcher*, which he was about to join. The immense power of the engines applied to the relatively light hull of just over 2,100 tons made the quick ship superbly responsive. She literally quivered under the taut commands from the bridge, like a highly strung hunting dog held on a tight leash. When he barked out an order for full rudder during a man-overboard drill, the horizon of the sea spun around in front of him, and he had to throw the rudder hard in the other direction to steady up and pick up the life jacket the XO had tossed over the port side to kick off the drill. "Nice job, Mr. James," the captain murmured from the sanctity of his chair on the starboard side, taking his pipe out of the side of his mouth. "You've got a nice sense of this class of destroyer, especially considering you've never conned one. Course, we're all learning, given they are brand-new. Been a pleasure having you aboard, and I suspect we'll be operating alongside you over there on *Fletcher*. You are lucky to be on the lead ship in the class, by the way, and give my compliments to your new skipper. And the XO, Lieutenant Commander Wylie. He's a smart one."

Scott grinned and turned the conn and the deck over to the oncoming watch. He headed down to his tiny stateroom to pack his seabag. He reflected on just how small the prewar Navy had been, and how a service reputation developed and magnified a career. As so many more officers joined the fleet, most coming from civilian life, Scott could feel that sense of a close-knit fraternity ebbing out like a tide.

When the small boat hit the rickety pier at Tulagi, Scott grabbed his seabag and headed toward the nearest Quonset hut, one of a row of a dozen or so. As he approached it, he saw that it had the letters *HQ* painted in rough white paint on the door, although from above, it was identical to every other hut in the row. Scott pulled the screen door open and saw that there was evidently at least some electricity at work, as there were three ceiling fans sluggishly moving tropical air around. The desks on either side were a standard Navy battleship gray. After Pearl Harbor and nine *battleships* down, we probably need to come up with a different descriptor for the color gray, Scott thought.

He was snapped out of his color palette reverie by a lieutenant junior grade waving at him from three desks down, and he moved to the front of his desk.

"Morning, Lieutenant," said the JG. "You checking in? Ship, squadron afloat, or staff?"

"I'm headed to *Fletcher*," Scott said, "ship's company. Just got here on her sister ship out there, *Nicholas*."

The JG looked slightly impressed. "*Fletcher*. She's a tight ship. Just got here too. Got a crackerjack skipper, name of Cap'n Bill Cole, but I hear the XO is really the one to watch. Name's J. C. Wylie, and the two of them are on the lead ship of the class for a reason. Big brains on both of them."

Scott wondered how this rear-echelon pogue, someone a safe distance away from the front lines, seemed to have such opinions, but he simply nodded briskly as though he already knew all that.

"They are underway through at least tonight, on a patrol out in the Slot. Should be back at dawn tomorrow. Guess you can join up then. Meantime if you go out the front and down six Quonsets, you'll find an officers' mess tent, and behind it a couple of big transient tents where you can bunk up. Orders? I can endorse 'em here and get your sea-duty clock started today." Shortly after Pearl Harbor, the Navy had instituted "sea pay," which meant that commissioned officers' salaries increased by 10 percent during the time they were permanently assigned to ships. The JG swatted a fly away and held out his hand. Scott thanked him and handed over his orders. Fifteen minutes later, he was walking down the improvised Main Street of the tiny base.

Down near the mess tent, he could see several big charcoal grills set up, and a collection of cooks prepping lunch. They had three big tureens of some kind of soup or stew on one of the grills and were scraping down the tops of the other two. It smelled good. He walked over and asked what was for lunch. "Good timing, sir. We're gonna throw some sliders on the grill today, Lieutenant. Might even have a pallet of beer we can crack open if our suppo says it's okay. Come on back in half an hour, right around eleven thirty, and we'll take good care of you." Scott went into the mess tent and sat at one of the rough wooden tables to wait for lunch, hoping that the supply officer was in a generous mood.

In the distance, Scott heard big guns firing across the strait toward the Marine landing zone near Henderson Field. Probably the cruisers hitting the Jap positions, he thought. Wonder where Kelley is over there. He dismissed the thought from his mind. The images he still had rattling around in his head of Kai with her arms around him at Joe's wetting-down party at the snake ranch were still raw. From what he heard from Joe, Kelley had finally gotten a combat assignment and had been shipped out late in the summer, his request for real action finally fulfilled.

According to Taussig, Kelley was now part of the First Marine Division under Major General Vandegrift, assigned to the Seventh Marine Regiment in the first battalion under someone named Lieutenant Colonel Chesty Puller. Kelley's skipper was a minor legend in the Corps, a little bantam rooster of a guy not much over five feet six inches tall, his nickname owing to his tendency to throw his chest out and charge himself and his Marines at whatever stood in his way. Puller had fought in World War I and in the Caribbean and Central America and been the commander of the Marine detachment on the cruiser *Augusta* under then-Captain Chester Nimitz. Joe said he was a huge character. Given all of that, Scott figured Puller's battalion was probably going to be in the thick of it. Everyone knew the fight for the island of Guadalcanal, especially the airfield there, Henderson Field, might end up being a big turning point. God help that big Mick, even if I want to punch his lights out, Scott thought. The guns boomed their agreement.

On the cruise down, the CO of *Nicholas* had filled him in on the operation, called Watchtower, that had been underway in earnest since September. "Here's the deal, Mr. James. We took big parts of the islands up and down the strait and got control of the airfield. The Marines are dug in, but the Japs are pushing back big time. Seems the key is the airfield, Henderson Field. The Navy's job is to control the waters of the strait so that the Japs can't bring their battleships and cruisers in and pound the Marines and Army ashore. But the problem is that the Navy is throwing everything it has got in the Atlantic at the Germans, and I'm hearing folks on the staff at Pearl aren't calling it Operation Watchtower. They are starting to call it Operation Shoestring. So our job is to do our best to cut off the Jap surface ships when they try and come down the strait, which we are calling the Tokyo Express. Every few days, they seem to mount an operation to test us out."

Scott nodded. When the war is over, this guy ought to teach operations at the Academy, he thought. "What really worries me, Scott, is night operations. The Japs have been thinking and planning on that kind of knife fight in the very tight waters of the strait for a long time. Intelligence thinks they've got better optics, illuminating fires, and torpedoes that actually go straight. We've got a cruiser-destroyer force, and we're adding more destroyers as they come off the ways—including this one and, of course, your ship, *Fletcher.*" Scott was surprised at the commander's candor. "Frankly, a bunch of us, including your skipper and XO, think the brass aren't using destroyers right. They just want us out front, effectively acting like scouts. But we're not back at the Battle of Jutland again. We need to let the destroyers operate more independently to take full advantage of our torpedoes, especially of these new Fletcher class." Scott was beginning to wonder what he had gotten himself into. "Anyway, you're going to be right in the thick of it, alongside us. Up and down that strait, day and night, and it's going to be hell in a very small place. But personally, I'd still rather be at sea than slogging it ashore through those jungles. It's a different kind of hell in there, a green one, and I'd rather take my chances at sea. But we'll do all we can to cover them, whatever the Japs send down the strait."

Remembering the conversation as he listened to the guns sounding across the strait, Scott felt a pang of guilt, made stronger when the messman waved at him from the grills to let him know his cheeseburger was ready. But he got up and headed over for a simple but filling lunch, getting in line with the shore-duty crowd and other transients waiting for their ship or a ride up the coast to the landing zone. He washed the burgers down with a couple of cans of Budweiser beer that the mess boys had tried unsuccessfully to cool by dipping them in salt water and blowing a fan on them. The cans were festooned with patriotic images to make clear the brewer was all-American despite its German-sounding name. The rhythm of the guns pounding on in the distance reminded Scott of the bass drums signifying the start of a parade on Worden Field back at Annapolis. But these drums just kept hammering home the sound of war, over and over.

The Knife Fighters

TULAGI ANCHORAGE, SOLOMON ISLANDS

The next morning, as advertised, Scott saw his ship anchored near the *Nicholas*. The hull number of USS
Fletcher, 445, was illuminated in the early-morning light,
and the ship was slowly swinging around on her hook. She looked
a bit rusty and tired from the voyage over, but to him she was the
most beautiful ship in the world. He skipped breakfast and
bummed a ride out on one of the harbor boats, and by seven thirty
was coming up the accommodation ladder with his seabag over
his shoulder. The OOD, an ensign, threw him a salute. "Hey,
Lieutenant, we heard you were on the beach. Good to see you.
I'm Doug Crowder, the first lieutenant. Sorry the sides don't look
a little better, but we got pounded on the way over. Hopefully, my
deck gang can get after some of the rust. XO said for you to head
to the wardroom and get settled, then go see him in the ship's
office."

Crowder's job as first lieutenant entailed trying to corral the surly deck seamen, running the rigs during replenishment at sea, and fighting the never-ending battle to keep the sides clean and free of corrosion. Scott was glad he had skipped that kind of ensign's job. He wondered exactly how the XO on *Fletcher* would use him. Gunnery officer would be swell, he thought to himself, or maybe navigator. Even though Scott had gotten his assignment when the last gunnery officer was lost overboard, the ship could juggle junior officer billets, so the ultimate nature of his job was not certain. After dropping his seabag in the wardroom and slamming a cup of coffee and a roll, he followed the messenger to the ship's office. Fortunately, having sailed over on a ship of the same class, he knew his way around. He dismissed the messenger as he entered the tiny ship's office.

He saw a handsome man in his early thirties, wearing the gold oak leaves of a lieutenant commander. The XO stood and shook his hand, saying, "Welcome aboard, Mr. James. My name is Wylie. Good to have you here, particularly as our last gunnery officer got washed overboard on the way down here and we're a man short in the wardroom."

Scott's ears perked up at the word *gunnery*. "Sir, great to be aboard. I was part of the gunnery team on my battleship but then got hooked up with the admiral's staff on *Enterprise*. But Admiral Spruance said he'd try to get me to destroyers, which is fine with me. And I do know gunnery, sir."

They stared at each other for a beat. "Nope, we've filled the gunnery slot with another lieutenant who was ready for his step." Scott's heart sank. Wylie continued, "But I've got a big idea for you, Mr. James. The captain and I have been cooking up a totally new way to use the systems on these ships. We want to integrate the fire-control radars, the gunnery systems, and the torpedoes. No one has really figured out how to make them all work together to create a lethal killer out of a destroyer, not just a picket vessel. Our idea is to set up something we are calling a combat information center. It's going to take control of the combat power off the bridge and put it down below, where we can have access to all the information and control the offensive systems. Mr. James, you are going to be the combat information center officer." He smiled slightly. "Believe me, if we do this right, the CICO"—the XO spelled out the letters—"is going to be running this thing in combat with just the captain and me over him."

Scott felt skeptical, but the XO was obviously passionate about the idea. "Got it, sir. CICO sounds great. I rode down here on *Nicholas*, and I've got a pretty good sense of the ship's combat and sensor capabilities. Who do I report to? The weapons officer?"

The XO thought for a minute. "We haven't got quite that far in our thinking, but for the moment, you can report to the operations officer. We'll figure all that out as we go along. Speaking of which, go find him, Lieutenant Bob Moeller, and get yourself on the watch bill. We're getting underway around dusk tonight, and we'll be out in the strait all night and then some. And at midnight it turns into Friday the 13th, by the way. Get ready for a knife fight out there, Mr. James." He paused. "Hopefully we'll be the ones bringing a gun to the knife fight, as the saying goes. And did I say it already? Welcome aboard."

3 2

Twisting on a Hook

TULAGI ANCHORAGE, SAVO SOUND,
ALSO CALLED "THE SLOT"

Since Scott was brand-new to the ship, the captain gave him the conn just as the sun was setting over Guadalcanal on the 12th of November. The naval gunfire had stopped, and Scott felt uncharacteristically nervous as he said the ritual words that would be recorded in the ship's deck log: "This is Lieutenant James. I have the deck and the conn." He was in charge of maneuvering the ship, safely navigating it, and giving the engine and rudder orders to the expectant sailors standing by at the ship's wheel and engine-order telegraph, a shiny brass device that transmitted the engine orders down through the steel decks to the superheated engineering spaces far below the feet of the bridge watch. You only get one chance to make a first impression, he thought to himself. I hope I haven't lost my touch after all that time on the damn aircraft carrier. Don't screw this up, Scott.

ADMIRAL JAMES STAVRIDIS, USN (RET.)

He checked both bridge wings. As the captain sat in his chair on the starboard side and pretended not to watch the new lieutenant closely, Scott gave his first commands as a fleet lieutenant on a destroyer: "Port engine ahead one third, starboard engine back one third, right full rudder." Scott wanted to twist the ship around on its anchor and heavy anchor chain and get the bow pointed fair out toward the Savo Strait, where *Fletcher* was due to fall into formation with the other destroyers and cruisers of Rear Admiral Dan Callaghan's task force. As the ship started to wing toward the open water, he ordered "rudder amidship" to center the bow, and both engines dead slow. This allowed the boatswain's mates on the forecastle to take in the anchor chain. When the bow was just above the anchor, Scott heard them call out, "Anchor is up and down, sir," and a moment later they declared "underway" as the heavy anchor lifted off the sand floor of the lagoon. As soon as the anchor was housed into its slot in the bow, Scott gave the order "All engines ahead two thirds, right standard rudder," and USS *Fletcher* headed cleanly into the fading light of a tropical evening.

Ahead of them were the other ships of the task force. Scott knew from the XO that Rear Admiral Callaghan, a big-gun officer with a strong background in cruisers, had his flag in USS *San Francisco*. He had put four destroyers in the van of the formation, a traditional role as a scout-and-shock element for the cruisers that came behind. On the night of the 12th, Callaghan put his five cruisers—a formidable force, especially in the constrained waters of the Slot—just behind the lead destroyers. Trailing the formation were four more destroyers. As Scott conned *Fletcher* into her appointed spot as the fourth of the destroyers in the rear, at the very end of the formation, he glimpsed the hull number 450, USS *O'Bannon*, sliding by his port side quite close aboard. "Let's get a little more sea room for ourselves, Mr. James," murmured the XO, who had slipped quietly onto the bridge and was standing just behind Scott. "Bring her a bit to starboard." Scott liked the way the XO just gave him a hint of what was desired and let the junior officer make the decisions about exact stations, course, and speed.

Scott had the junior officer of the deck get out a mo board. The good-sized piece of paper with a printed compass rose on it was used to calculate the exact course and speed to drop the destroyer into her station in the formation. Scott had been using them since he was a third-class midshipman on his first cruise. When the JOOD had figured out the course, Scott swung the ship into station smoothly and moved to the bridge wing. From there he could see the stern lights of a couple of the other destroyers ahead of *Fletcher* in the rear of the formation, as well as the darkened forms of the cruisers looming just ahead of them. I guess we're just the new kid on the block, so the flag staff stuck us here in the after part of the formation, Scott thought. What a waste of our new radar and extra ammo. Jesus, I hope we can get into the action at all—there are twelve ships ahead of us. And we're number thirteen, on Friday the 13th. Swell. All the ships were running with darkened external lights, under a very dim moon on a dark night.

"Go ahead and turn over the deck and the conn to the navigator, Scott," said the XO. "I want you to come below and we are going to start synchronizing the sensors." Scott followed the XO below the bridge to the small space they had designated as the combat information center, just aft of the bridge and a deck below.

It was a tiny place with a couple of transparent boards that two sailors, radarmen, were marking up with yellow grease pencils. There was a fairly detailed sketch of the coastlines on both sides of the sound, and the sailors were talking to the bridge and marking the positions of all the ships in the formation. The radar was sweeping round and round, its greenish light casting an eerie glow on everyone's faces. All hands in the CIC were smoking. Scott toyed with the idea of lighting a cigarette himself but decided he was getting plenty of nicotine just standing in the space and inhaling.

The XO was talking on the sound-powered phone line to the fire-control center and relaying information to the plot. "We need to spread the destroyers out more," Wylie said. He rang up the captain on the bridge, who sent a flashing-light signal to the destroyers on either side. "But the admiral isn't going to like it," Wylie said absently to Scott.

"Why not, sir?" Scott asked.

"Because all he thinks about is getting his big guns into play. He doesn't get it that the destroyer's torpedoes could be deadly in these tight waters. And believe me, the Japanese understand that in spades. They come down this slot every few nights to try and shoot up our boys on the ground, especially around Henderson Field. And they're hoping to sink a few of us in the process." He passed a few more fixes to the plotters, and the ship settled into a routine.

Scott was getting a little drowsy. The cigarette smoke, initially energizing as the nicotine kicked in, was starting to have the opposite effect, stinging his eyes and making him feel claustrophobic.

The flag had put all the ships in a single "formation one," the simplest signal in the tactical maneuvering book, meaning they were in one long line, steaming northwest.

"Skunks, bearing three one five," sang out one of the sailors by the radar, Navy code for an unknown surface contact. "And bogies down that bearing too." Unknown air contacts, thought Scott. Can't be good.

He and the XO both grabbed for the dials of the scope, but the XO got there first and was adjusting it swiftly and professionally. "I see another couple of contacts right behind the lead skunk. What do the lookouts see? The contacts should be just visible on the horizon, and the moon is low and behind them." *Fletcher* began to heel over from side to side, rendering the small CIC a difficult place in which to stand upright. The captain maneuvered the ship to minimize targeting by the Japanese force. The XO said to Scott, "Fuse the data. Goddamn it, we've got to get a firing bearing for the forward batteries and get ready to get our torpedoes in the water."

The captain called the XO over the internal voice tube, and the radios in the CIC were all chattering at once. It was a scene of barely controlled chaos, like the complex action on a carrier flight deck that Scott knew so well, but with all of it packed into a little room in the beating heart of this ship. All the destroyers in the van were reporting visual contact of a heavy Japanese force, including initial reports of Japanese battleships, at least two of them, all headed southeast, straight toward the American formation. Scott braced himself between the plot and the radar repeater, trying to calculate a course that could get the ship into optimal launch position for the torpedoes if they got the order to move out toward the Japanese. Above him, he kept hearing the swiveling noises of the five-inch gun mounts, but no firing yet. He hoped to hear the deeper booms of the heavy guns on Rear Admiral Callaghan's cruiser force starting to fire over the small destroyers toward the Japanese main force. *Fletcher* was swerving sickeningly on shorter and shorter rudder cycles. Scott glanced at the luminous clock on the wall—it was approaching 2 a.m.

The XO, Scott, and the sailors in the CIC worked the data flowing in, including the radio reports, lookouts topside, radars, and their own sense of the increasingly populated plot. They were facing a large Japanese force, probably two fast battleships, at least one or two light cruisers, and maybe a dozen destroyers. They were headed straight down the throat of Savo Sound by Savo Island, just off the north coast of Guadalcanal. The XO directed the plotters to get the info from U.S. aircraft—thank God the bogies had turned out to be U.S. planes operating from Henderson Field—onto the picture, and he had the lookouts focused on the five U.S. cruisers just ahead of the destroyers who were the rear guard. Rain squalls swept through the small battle space and diminished the accuracy of both lookout reports and the radars. "I can't understand why the hell he put us in the back of the formation," Wylie said to Scott. "We've got the best radar by far with the new SG. And he didn't put out any preset battle plan, so we're going to have to get permission from the flag staff to do anything." Scott shrugged and concentrated on updating the plot. The lookouts reported the moon was completely obscured and there was little visibility, with the ships on both sides sailing with darkened navigation lights. Looking at the plot, the XO cursed softly. "They're coming down between Savo and Guadalcanal. We're headed square at them. They want to put those guns on our Marines. Goddamn it, what is the admiral waiting for?"

On the radar scope, Scott watched as the orderly naval formation began to fall apart, like kids drifting apart on a playground. There was still no direction from the flag staff. It seemed to Scott that the admiral was somehow paralyzed. And these weren't little kids, Scott thought to himself, but two naval forces heading dead at each other. "The admiral is probably on the bridge of *Atlanta*, looking through a damn pair of binoculars, trying to figure out what's going on. He's not going to get any answers up there," spat out the XO. "Jesus, this isn't the Battle of Trafalgar. What's he thinking he's going to do? Cross their T?" Scott had studied the maneuver at Annapolis in his Sea Power class. It could open up powerful gunnery options if it went just right, but he wasn't looking forward to seeing it go into practice for the first time on a dark, moonless night in the South Pacific with a seemingly confused commander and narrow space to maneuver.

Explosions. Suddenly, big guns fired from the vicinity of the contacts—flashes were reported by the lookouts, along with splashes in the water and whooshing sounds as the shells passed nearby. *Fletcher* heeled over hard, and the engines kicked in at flank speed. Scott heard gunnery along the bearing toward the Japanese but couldn't tell who was shooting. On the radar, the neat columns dissolved, and the ships were suddenly in a melee without any certain means to know who was friend or foe. "Message from the flag, sir," said one sailor. "Odd ships fire to starboard, even ships fire to port."

Scott and the XO looked at each other in total confusion. "Odd? Even? Does he mean our hull number or our position in the original formation?" Scott asked.

The XO shrugged theatrically. "Either way, we're odd numbered. I guess we just point the guns at a Jap ship, if we can figure out which ones they are. This is a damn bar fight with knives, and all the lights got shot out before it really got started."

The XO reached for the line to call the captain and recommend firing bearing based on the plot. He listened quietly for some time. "Jesus," he said, and hung up the phone. Turning to Scott, he said, "*Atlanta* is getting the hell shot out of her. She's lost power and is drifting. And here is the worst part. It looks like some of the hits were friendly fire. *San Francisco*'s guns hit her on the bridge. Then the Japs poured onto *San Francisco*, the admiral's flagship, and it looks bad. Captain says don't expect to hear anything from the flag for a while. And *Cushing* is dead in the water too, with most her crew in the water. At least one other of our destroyers is sinking, maybe *Laffey*." The sailors at the plot were frantically updating the picture, which was changing by the minute. *Fletcher*'s guns and torpedoes had yet to come into action, given her initial position at the back end of the long U.S. battle line. When can we start shooting? was all Scott could think.

"Sir, one of the Jap battleships is going down, according to reports, plus the other one is taking a lot of fire and torpedoes," said a radio talker.

"But here comes trouble," said the XO, looking at the radar. "Five skunks headed inbound, coming from three hundred degrees, moving at twenty-five knots minimum. I'm thinking destroyers. Scott, get our guns and torpedoes pointing down the bearing."

One of the talkers quietly said, "Destroyer *Barton* hit with Jap torpedo, abandoning ship." Scott was sending orders up to the bridge to the conning officer to bring the ship to bear on the Japanese forces, and *Fletcher's* five-inch guns were barking continuously. The ship unloaded salvos of torpedoes against what Scott hoped was a Japanese warship. The fact that *San Francisco* had reportedly struck *Atlanta* scared the hell out of him.

Blips on the radar drifted in and out of focus as ships sank or were masked by other hulls. Finally, *Fletcher*, the thirteenth ship on the thirteenth day, opened up, landing blows on the Japanese destroyers and, incredibly, not getting scratched in return. Scott kept a steady flow of information to the fire-control positions. It felt to him like he was truly alive for the first time in his life. And he was scared too. Get it right, James, he repeated to himself over and over, trying to ignore the obvious fact that at any moment he could be dead or abandoning ship and jumping into the warm tropical sea. His hand drifted to the small cartridge in his pocket and rubbed it hard. The XO raced back and forth between the bridge and the CIC, encouraging both teams and giving the order to release the batteries, and so the killing continued. On and on. The sound of the guns and the smell of cordite and fear filled the dark night air.

The guns and torpedoes spat at each other for what seemed like hours. But when Scott looked again at the big clock, the hands had not even moved a single hour. The battle had lasted around forty minutes when the order came from the captain of *Helena*, where the surviving senior Navy officer was embarked. Rear Admiral Callaghan and most of his staff had been killed in action on the bridge of his flagship, *San Francisco*. "The Japs are withdrawing," said the XO. "The sound is safe—at least for now." He slumped over the radar repeater, his face green in the misty light. After a moment, he said, "I'm going back up to the bridge, Scott. Keep the plot updated." He paused and looked at Scott for a long moment. Then he nodded and said, "You have batteries-release authority if you need it." Another first, thought Scott. First time driving a destroyer on a combat mission. First time under direct fire in one. And now I have the firing keys. War is hell, like General Sherman said. But it's pretty damn exciting.

Scott turned to the senior enlisted sailor in the CIC to establish his authority, sensing everyone looking at him. "Have someone get me a cup of coffee, will ya, Chief? And what do we know about the rest of our force?" The ops chief summarized the situation as the clock moved on toward the morning. "Looks like *Portland* and *San Francisco* are still floating but pretty beat up. Same with *Ward* and *Sterett*. The Japs sank one of our cruisers, *Atlanta*, and four of the destroyers: *Cushing*, *Laffey*, *Barton*, and *Monssen*. We're steaming in company now with the cruisers *Helena*, *San Francisco*, and *Juneau*. *O'Bannon* and *Sterett* still with us. Headed southeast and clearing the sound. Got to be near on a couple of thousand dead, sir, on our side. Including the admiral, who, according to reports, was killed by a direct big-shell hit on his bridge.

Not sure on Jap losses, but intel says we sank at least one of their two light battleships, maybe a light cruiser, probably two or three of the destroyers. But they're pulling back, and the troops ashore are safe for now from Jap reinforcements and shore bombardment. Pretty big butcher's bill on both sides, I'd say, Lieutenant."

An hour. Not even an hour. There had been no order to the fight. For a moment Scott imagined what it might have looked like from above: a smooth black sea like the surface of a polished stone, and all around the center, concentric rings of small, insect-like dark-gray ships, each of them spitting flames toward the center of this microscopic inferno. Star shells going up, searchlights being shot out, no one knowing one ship from another, just shooting at big, dark shapes. It must have looked like a swinging door on the front of a boiler, just going back and forth and all that fire inside lighting up the engine room of hell. Jesus, he thought, I'm living in that poem "Dover Beach." He remembered a snippet of the poem that his mother had quoted to him long ago: "Swept with confused alarms of struggle and flight / Where ignorant armies clash by night." Yeah, except we're navies, thought the newly blooded lieutenant. We're the Navy. But we are pretty ignorant too.

33

The Morning After

L ate the next morning, after taking a four-hour nap in his stateroom, Scott walked up to the bridge. He yawned, accepted a hot mug of coffee from the boatswain, and scanned the horizon. In the distance he saw a group of three large U.S. warships, steaming very slowly. Putting his binoculars around his neck and looking closely, he recognized the silhouettes of the three remaining cruisers—*San Francisco*, *Helena*, and *Juneau*. All had clearly been mauled; smoke and oil were leaking from their hulls. The greatly reduced formation was clearing the area and heading southeast. Scott wondered why *Fletcher* and the other unscathed vessels didn't stay closer to the wounded ships. The destroyers in company that had survived the night in addition to *Fletcher* included sister ship *O'Bannon* and the smaller 1,500-ton *Sterett*. Well, he thought, at least we pushed the Japs back. Can't figure why they backed out, because it seems they still had plenty of combat power—more than us, for sure, looking at what's left this morning.

He took his coffee down to the combat information center and refreshed the plot, updating the images and times on the grease-pencil boards. He wanted to talk to the XO about some ideas to make the flow of information from the CIC to the captain on the bridge a lot smoother. He was standing there jotting some ideas on the back of a used mo board when he heard a radio transmission, in the clear, on an emergency frequency: "ICEHOUSE hit by a torpedo, ICEHOUSE hit by torpedo, I repeat, ICEHOUSE hit by a torpedo." "ICEHOUSE" was the call sign for the cruiser *Juneau*. Jesus, thought Scott, will this never end? He pulled on a set of headphones as the ship went to general quarters, and in a matter of minutes, Lieutenant Commander Wylie was in the CIC, blinking sleep out of his eyes and asking Scott what the hell was going on.

At that moment the lookout said flatly, "*Juneau*'s gone. Off the horizon. She just sank. Bow down."

Scott and the XO looked at each other in horror. The XO rang the captain on the bridge. They spoke for a few moments, and the XO gently put the receiver down. "Captain says the ship went down in minutes, maybe seconds. No time to abandon ship. And the acting flag on *San Francisco* says we can't stay in the area, not with Jap submarines here. Start evasive maneuvers, and we're all to move at best speed to clear the area."

Scott looked at the XO. "Christ, sir, there are, what, six or seven hundred sailors on that cruiser. We can't just cut and run."

The XO said woodenly, "We could lose another thousand if there are a couple of Jap subs out here, Scott. And Captain said she went down too fast for anyone to get out. Let's get moving. Plot a course back toward the Slot, and let's hope we don't join *Juneau* on the bottom. Maybe we will get a couple of days off before we go back up front."

Scott watched the XO's back as he left the CIC. He turned to the chief, who was staring at him in disbelief. He sighed and said softly, "You heard him, Chief. Let's go back to Guadalcanal."

Late that night, on the midwatch, Scott looked moodily out to sea. He knew as well as the CO and XO did that some of the sailors on *Juneau* had to have gotten into the water, no matter how fast the ship went down. There had to be a hundred or more topside in a situation like that, doing repairs and working to hold the ship together. It bothered him like hell, leaving sailors behind, no matter what the calculus of risk might have been. We haven't even been scratched, he thought, and yet we won't make a fast run to look for survivors. It's not right. It's just not right.

That night he dreamed of Caroline for the first time in many months. It was more than three and a half years since she had died. She was waving at him from across a wide sea, not speaking, just waving slowly, her hands moving back and forth in front of her. Like a mermaid, signaling him a warning he couldn't quite understand.

Within another day or so, they were back in Tulagi's harbor, back to swinging on a hook. They settled into a routine, doing repairs around the ship, tweaking the radar, performing maintenance on *Fletcher*'s guns, grooming the engineering plant, all the dull day-to-day things that ships do in port. Routine announcements blared from the 1MC. At the end of the normal workday came the daily reminder: "Sweepers, sweepers, man your brooms.

Give the ship a good clean sweep-down both fore and aft! Sweep down all lower decks, ladder backs, and passageways! Dump all garbage clear of the fantail! Now, sweepers." The announcement seemed unnecessary to Scott, but the Navy was nothing if not hidebound in its traditions. *Too bad we didn't follow our own traditions in picking up those sailors,* he thought bitterly.

After a week, everyone was chattering about when *Fletcher* would get back into it. After the beating the task force had taken under Admiral Callaghan, Scott figured the fleet would want to wait and get another flag to lead it. Some of the sailors were using the phrase "Iron Bottom Sound" to describe all the hulls that once sailed the surface of the sea and were now resting beneath the placid waters. *At least some of the wrecks are flying a rising-sun flag that isn't going to rise anytime soon,* Scott thought. He proposed to the XO that he go ashore to try to gather some intel on what was next, maybe work over that JG in the HQ Quonset hut. But the XO brushed it off, saying they would be underway again soon enough. They didn't need to do anything more than just be ready when the call came.

Scott eventually was sent ashore anyway. His mission was to collect some parts for the SG radar and see if there was mail for *Fletcher.* While he was in, he went down to the officers' mess tent and chatted with some of the cooks, often the best source of accurate information. "Dunno, Lieutenant, not sure of anything," one of the mess cooks said as he tapped a cup of coffee, "but I'm hearing the Japs are gonna make another run down the Slot. All the small boys—excuse me, no offense, destroyers, sir—are being scraped together, and word is they're going back in the next couple of days."

That was fine news to Scott. The cook continued, "Also heard there's a new flag coming in, Rear Admiral Carleton Wright, who is some kind of expert in mining. He's done a bunch of assignments in the world of mining." The business of both dumping mines into the sea and pulling them out to make a safe passage was the most boring thing in the Navy, as far as Scott was concerned. This guy's background sounded about as uninspiring as Scott could imagine.

But there was something else, far worse. According to the mess circuit, well over a hundred sailors had initially survived the sinking of *Juneau*. They had been left in the water for just over a week before a rescue ship had arrived. By then almost all were dead from exposure, dehydration, or shark attacks. "Only ten of those boys were left by then, Lieutenant," said the chief cook. "Can't believe other ships just took off and left 'em there like that." Scott couldn't bear to admit that his was one of the ships that had abandoned them. The cook looked down and stirred a pot of beef stew. "I heard from another cook who had been in the *Juneau* that there were five Irish brothers on that cruiser, all from some little town in Iowa. Sailors named Sullivan. Don't know if any of them made it, but odds are all five are gone. That's a damn bad telegram for their mama to get back home. Makes a sailor sick."

Scott skipped lunch, collected the two bags of mail for *Fletcher*, and caught the lagoon boat back to his ship. *Fletcher* was backlit by the afternoon sun and thus appeared like a black silhouette to the eye. The national ensign at her stern was entirely slack. A listless hull tied up to an anchor at the far end of the sandy lagoon, she looked a lot less exciting to Scott than the first time he'd approached her, just a week or so earlier.

34

Two Letters

SOUTH PACIFIC

S cott leaned back in the metal chair in front of the tiny drop-down desk in his stateroom on USS *Fletcher*. Between learning the ropes on the ship, standing an initial set of watches, and settling into a routine in the new combat information center he and the XO had put together, he'd not had any time for letter writing. But he'd promised Kai's mother he'd write, and the days since he'd left Hawaii were ticking by rapidly. He looked down at what he'd written so far on a flimsy airmail flyer and considered how it would sound to Kai.

November 1942
South Pacific
USS Fletcher, Fleet Post Office San Francisco

Dear "Beatrice,"

Just kidding, Kai. I couldn't resist. Tell your uncle I will always be in his debt for revealing your secret name! At least I put it in quotes, right?

I got here to the South Pacific (not allowed to say any more about location) a while ago, and I apologize for not writing sooner—I'm really sorry, and I will do better. As you can imagine, things are hectic. The CO and XO seem great, and they've given me a special project having to do with the offensive side of things (can't say any more), but it is both challenging and important work. I guess in a war, that's what you want.

We are giving the Japs hell, believe me. My ship has done some patrols, and again I can't say much but we are hitting back at them hard. Every time I get a little tired, I just think to myself about those bombs dropping around Battleship Row, and then going to the Army hospital, at Tripler on Oahu, and seeing Joe with his leg blown off, and all those nurses running around and trying to comfort the wounded, so many men crying and in terrible pain, and the look in the eyes of all the exhausted doctors. We are going to beat these bastards, pardon my French, and I'm proud to be out here and doing my part.

And also, it is important for my career that I do well. I admit it, I like the Navy so far, and anyway I'm planning on staying for a career. Of course, a lot can change at any minute, and it sure does in life, just look at the attack on Pearl Harbor, but that's my plan. I'll need some good breaks, good assignments, a medal or two would be nice, and of course to get through this war in one piece.

But I've learned a lot out here already, and I'm going to learn more, and I want to go as far as I can in the Navy, or at least that's what I think right now.

Kai, we had so many wonderful times together in Hawaii. It seems like a dream to me now, learning to surf (well, sort of), going to all the little restaurants and bars on the North Shore, meeting your folks, and really spending very special time together (I know you know what I mean). All of that means the world to me, and I want it to go on and on when I come back. I know things got a little confused at the end there, but that doesn't matter if we hold onto the idea of us together. It doesn't matter at all. And I know it's not fair for me to say: "Oh, just wait for me," it's not like we ever discussed getting engaged or married, of course, but what I can say is that I think of you all the time. You are always out there in front of me, encouraging me, helping me in little ways that you don't even know but I sure do. I've got that funny picture you gave me of you in the Hawaiian skirt, and I carry it with me in my wallet everywhere I go. I don't mean to be sappy, but you should know that. And the golden cross you gave me is always, always in the pocket of my khakis.

I wish I knew when I will come back. The XO says he thinks we are all out here "for the duration," whatever that means. It could be months or a year or more, I guess. And I know you have options back there, and I respect that. But I hope you'll write me back and tell me what you think about all this. And if I get a chance to come back, maybe if I get a transfer to another bigger ship or back to a flag staff, the first place I will go when I step off the plane or the ship is right to your doorstep. That I promise.

Write me when you can and please know that you mean the world to me.

And give your parents a big ALOHA for me.

Your surfer boy, with love,
Scott

P.S. Remind your parents that I'm no longer "the ensign," not even a JG. Now I'm a real "fleet lieutenant," and I bet I make lieutenant commander real soon, so I'm a pretty good catch.

Scott finished rereading it and liked it. He took the pen and blotted out the words *South Pacific*, since he figured including that might create a problem with the censor. He walked out of the stateroom and headed back to the CIC to conduct a mini class for three radiomen he was grooming for higher positions in the tight combat organization. On the way, he dropped the letter in the basket marked "mail" in the wardroom, feeling he'd gone about as far as he could in telling her how he felt.

Three days later, when he walked into the wardroom and instinctively looked at the piles of sorted letters, he saw one from his mother. Bella wrote to him at least once a week, nice letters that took about a month to arrive on whatever ship he was on. He could almost smell the honeysuckle in the backyard down in Key West from her letters. Next to his mother's letter was another small envelope. It was postmarked three weeks earlier and the franking on the stamp said "Honolulu, Hawaii." The letter was in

Kai's loopy schoolgirl handwriting. He took it in his hand and turned it over and over. He put both letters in his back pocket and went up to the CIC for a six-hour watch. He was dying to read Kai's note but knew that doing so would require more privacy than the CIC offered. His letter must have crossed with hers, and he hoped they would be close in tone and promise. For six hours, all he could think of was a little surfer on the North Shore of Oahu, knees on her board, smiling at him as a wave brought her back to the beach. It's a good thing the Japs aren't running the Tokyo Express tonight, he thought to himself as the hours dragged by.

When he went back to his stateroom after midnight, he was happy to see his roomie, the ship's operations officer, had the midwatch on the bridge. Scott forced himself to read his mother's letter first, which was nice but routine. The charter business was going well for his dad. Hemingway was off doing some war correspondent thing, it seemed, and had asked Robert to keep an eye on the *Pilar* for him. And she made clear that she was not impressed with Papa's latest wife, another journalist, a "skinny, blond-from-a-bottle reporter who thinks she is a war correspondent," according to his mom. As he would have guessed from her tone, it was obvious his mom did not approve of Hemingway's multiple marriages. Scott knew exactly what his mother was talking about. Martha Gellhorn would end up putting Hemingway through hell, Scott thought to himself, but she had some big balls. He skimmed the rest of the note and put it in the top drawer of his desk to reread later.

Then he opened Kai's letter. As he read it, his breathing deepened, and he had to stop in a couple of places and clear his head by shaking it vigorously from side to side. It was not the letter he was hoping for.

Dear Scott,

I've been wanting to write you since you left, but I was waiting to hear from you first. But it's been weeks, and I know mail is very hit-or-miss out where you are, wherever that may be. My mom has told me again and again to wait until I hear from you, but you know me—I'm not so good at waiting. So here goes.

I'm just not sure we are right for each other, Scott. Or maybe we are, but I can't tell for sure. Everything was easy, maybe too easy for us in '41. (Well, at least until December 7th.) All those days riding around on your motorcycle, seeing the island again through your eyes, teaching you to surf (my uncle says you'll never be any good, but he likes you anyway), and especially finding time to be together in very important ways, and that means so much to me. You'll always be the first time for me and part of me will always be with you in that way.

But then you changed. I don't know if it was the war, or something inside you, or if you just got tired of me once we had done everything you wanted. I'd hate to think it was that, but sometimes that's how it is with men, I hear. I know the war is more important than you and me and all of us, but I sensed that even bigger than the war was your ambition. And you were gone, and not helping me understand what had happened, and I think things just started to drift for me. Sometimes I would close my eyes in bed at night and feel like I was floating, like a ghost, above the bed, above the house, up in the sky. I know that sounds crazy and maybe it is. And during that time, I started to get close to Kelley. He's very different than you, but in a lot of ways he's kind of the same. But he cares about me and tells me that constantly. And he was here with me, and we got closer and closer. I was confused and uncertain about where everything was going, and I know you must have heard about us or seen us together and that must have shocked you. I'm sorry for that, truly I am.

Then suddenly you came back, and we were together again just before you left. I'll never be able to explain that night, not to myself, or to you, or to Kelley. He left right after you and is on some island somewhere, he wasn't allowed to say where, but he has written me twice. For all I know you two have met up and may even have talked about this or laughed about me and all my mistakes. I told my mom about this (well, part of it) and she sighed and said really quietly that sometimes the heart wants what the heart wants, whatever that means. She won't tell my dad, I'm sure of that.

Anyway, I know this is a hard letter for you to read. It doesn't really say anything or settle anything, I guess, but I wanted to be honest with you about me and Kelley. I don't know where that leaves us, but maybe over time we'll have a chance to see each other back here in Hawaii. This is a beautiful place, and no matter what, I'm glad we saw it together, and I was kind of a guide for your first time in this magical place. It would have been perfect, I think to myself sometimes, if the war and the bombs hadn't come. It was like the world exploding in fire, and the fires are still burning. I'm not saying this very well, and especially because you're in the middle of this war.

I keep opening and then closing my textbooks. Somehow, someday, I want to be able to put this war in the arc of the Pacific. It is consuming us minute by minute every single day, but there is a long, long sweep to the history of this gorgeous sea. Maybe one day you and I will sit on a beach again, and go in and out of the water, again and again, and when we do we could talk about the war and what it all meant. But for now, we just have to keep going through the fire, I guess.

I do think of you all the time, and when I do, I keep feeling like I'm floating and floating. I hope you still have the cross I gave you on our last night together. I know it will help you find your way, but where that voyage leads is up to you. Part of me thinks about you every day, and hopes you are safe.

There are a few other things I should tell you, but I don't know about them for sure yet. And maybe I'll hear from you soon. I hope so.

Love from your Beatrice,
Kai

35

The End of the Beginning

The Japanese had not stopped the Tokyo Express runs. The shoot-out in the strait in the middle of November in which Rear Admiral Callaghan died was dubbed the Naval Battle of Guadalcanal by the press in the U.S. Scott hated to turn on the radio and hear Tokyo Rose crowing about the sinking of so many U.S. cruisers and destroyers. She too started using the term *Iron Bottom Sound* to describe the strait. When the Japanese sank *Juneau*, their propaganda machine kicked into high gear. Despite having been pushed back, they seemed determined to continue to resupply their troops on Guadalcanal, and the pitched battles ashore continued day and night. Scott pulled together a daily intelligence brief for the skipper and the wardroom. It was clear that the Japanese desperately wanted to shut down

Henderson Field. The rugged airstrip had become the center of gravity in the fight. It was from there that the "Cactus Air Force," named after an Allied code name for the island, was inflicting high casualties on the Japanese forces ashore and preventing Japanese control of the seas, at least by day. Everyone in the destroyer force knew the Japanese would be back for more at sea, and the sailors were betting it would be by the end of November. The wardroom on Scott's ship discussed it endlessly.

On the 30th of the month, Rear Admiral Wright, the Navy's leading mine guy, as Scott called him in the junior officer staterooms, out of earshot of the CO and XO, led his forces to sea. "Intel from aerial recon says they are coming with a pure destroyer force this time," the XO explained as he and Scott manned up the CIC after *Fletcher* joined the other ships of the task force in the strait. "Maybe a dozen, maybe a few less. Their destroyers have damn good long-range torpedoes, better than ours." He sighed.

Scott ventured, "It's gonna come down to how the flag maneuvers us. We gotta get close enough to score hits."

Just then the radio crackled with a short-range burst of tactical signals, and the XO and Scott looked at each other. "They've got us up front, exact opposite of last time," Wylie observed. "But they've put a choke chain on us again. No attack until we have permission from the admiral. Jesus, I wish they would let us take the initiative. But orders are orders."

Scott walked over to the operational plot and started marking the positions of the U.S. warships. In addition to *Fletcher* up front, there were some of the smaller, older destroyers, including *Perkins*, *Maury*, and *Drayton*. There were five cruisers spread out behind the destroyers and a couple more destroyers in the rear of the formation.

Scott began feeding info up to the bridge, including recommendations for course and speed adjustments so that *Fletcher* could maintain her position at the lead of the formation. Scott heard and felt the propellers ramping up as the destroyer increased speed. The captain began ordering the helm thrown back and forth. He was clearly following the recommendations from the CIC to position the ship for a torpedo strike. "Sir, I've got them on radar," shouted one of the sailors.

Scott and the XO both lunged for the repeater. Scott got there first and quickly adjusted the advanced radar settings. "I've got them, XO," he said, "about twenty-two thousand yards and closing fast. They are just south of Savo Island and look like they are closing the beach so they can start getting supplies ashore for the Jap troops there." Scott looked at the clock in the CIC, which registered around half past ten. It was another moonless night, an advantage for the Japs, Scott thought. The XO relayed the positions and recommendations to the captain on the bridge, including guiding the ships of the van into torpedo firing positions. Scott asked Wylie, "Should we get permission to fire torpedoes now, XO?" The XO nodded, and Scott ginned up the signal to the flag staff just as the clock swept past 11 p.m.

Radar contact, which had been going in and out, firmed up as the Japanese destroyer force closed to about seven thousand yards ahead, and *Fletcher* again requested permission to fire. "Range on all skunks excessive at present" came back from the flag staff. "Do not fire. Repeat, do not fire."

Scott and the XO both grimaced. "Goddamn it, we are never going to get a better shot," growled the XO. "Ask 'em again, Scott." After another couple of minutes, *Fletcher* finally got a green light to fire, but it was clear to the CIC team that the Japanese destroyers would now be able to evade. "Fire a spread NOW," shouted the XO, and four of the destroyers did so, almost in unison. But Scott could see that the delay of long minutes had given the Japs a chance to get out ahead of the Mark 15 torpedoes, and as twenty of them were launched from the U.S. destroyer force, Scott thought they weren't going to hit a goddamn thing.

At the same moment, the big guns of the cruiser force lit off and Scott could hear the reports from the lookouts of star shells illuminating the night action. "That's the signal for us to clear out," said the XO. "Give the bridge a clear course and send a tactical signal to the other destroyers. We need to get behind the cruisers to give them a clear field of fire. Any hits from the torpedoes?"

Scott grimaced again. "Nothing I can see, XO. Those fish just aren't running straight, goddamn it. And you can bet the Japs are unloading all their torpedoes at those cruisers. Now that the big guns are firing, their exact positions are easy to figure out. Their torpedoes have longer range and run straight, and I'm betting they'll get at least three dozen fish into the water, looking at the number of Jap destroyers."

At that moment, the radios lit up with reporting from the cruiser force: *Minneapolis* and *New Orleans* were both hit hard, and the turrets on both cruisers were out of action. A few minutes later, another report came in that cruiser *Pensacola* had likewise taken a torpedo in the side and was on fire. One U.S. cruiser,

Honolulu, continued firing, but the final cruiser in the formation, *Northampton,* was also hit by two torpedoes a few minutes before midnight. "Get this destroyer formation on the far side of Savo, then back into the strait," said the XO quietly to Scott. "Maybe we can get behind them and launch another round of torpedoes." The tactical orders went out, and the four high-speed destroyers circumnavigated the small island and reentered the battle space from the north.

Inexplicably, the Japanese warships began to withdraw. Scott wondered why. They were in command of the battle space, the U.S. cruisers had almost all been hit, and the Japanese did not seem to have suffered significant losses. But when the U.S. destroyers came back into the strait between Savo and Guadalcanal, the Japanese ships were heading outbound, back to their base. When Scott and the XO debriefed the battle afterward in the wardroom with the department heads, going over the logbooks and getting a sense of everything the captain had seen on the bridge, three things seemed clear. Captain Cole summarized: "One, the flag tied our hands on the first salvo of torpedoes. That gave away the advantage of surprise that we had over the Japs given our radar range. Four minutes doesn't sound like a long time, but it hurt us badly. Two, we only put down one Jap destroyer, but they knocked out four of our cruisers, and one sank on the spot in Iron Bottom Sound. We'll be lucky if the other three of them can be repaired and brought back into the fight. I'd call that kicking our ass, not to put too fine a point on it. And three, our gear just isn't up to the task right now—the fish don't work right, the radar isn't connecting with the fire-control solutions, our fuses aren't set right. Big Navy has some work to do. This one isn't going to go down well back in Washington." The XO and Scott both nodded in assent, as did the other department heads. Everyone looked gloomy as the meeting broke up.

But over the next couple of days, the story began to sound a lot different. Scott looked in amazement when the "mine guy" admiral touted the great gunnery work of his cruisers and minimized the destroyers in a series of dispatches available on every ship in the task force. Halsey piled on and praised the task force commander, who would be put in for a Navy Cross, to the amazement of the *Fletcher* wardroom. Despite having most of his force shot out from under him and losing hundreds of sailors (the official death toll was over four hundred), Wright was going to come out a hero with a Navy Cross. The press was hailing it as the Battle of Tassafaronga. Captain Cole's concerns about freeing up the destroyers to fire torpedoes at the optimal moment without specific permission from the flag never reached the ears of senior leadership. It burned Scott, and he could tell the XO hated it as well.

The three cruisers were knocked out of the force for a significant repair period, and all the *Fletcher*'s crew could do was go around the lagoon in their motor whaleboat from destroyer to destroyer, briefing their ideas on tactical employment of the fast destroyer forces, and continue to push the idea of combat information centers. Most of the destroyers took them up on the gouge session, and the stock of Lieutenant Commander J. C. Wylie continued to rise. As a sign of it, the new commodore, Captain Robert Briscoe of Destroyer Squadron 5, chose *Fletcher* to embark in as his flagship in early December. They were assigned under Rear

Admiral Kelly Turner's flag. Turner was in charge of the overall amphibious landing force. In addition to *Fletcher*, the destroyer squadron included her sister ships *Nicholas*, *O'Bannon*, *Radford*, and *De Haven*. Other destroyers were joining every day, many sent from combat off North Africa as part of the successful Allied Operation Torch, which freed up the destroyers and other surface combatants. The South Pacific was "Operation Shoestring" no more, evidently.

A couple of months later, by early January 1943, it was clear to Scott based on the dispatches he was seeing in the radio shack that the Japanese high command felt that it was time to pull chocks. They were leaving. "Those bastards never broke through us," said Captain Cole as he toasted his wardroom and the other destroyer officers of the six ships in the squadron. They were gathered at an impromptu beach picnic ashore with warm beer and hamburgers in late January.

After Captain Cole's toast as the senior destroyer skipper, he handed off to Commodore Briscoe. The squadron commodore was the guest of honor, and he nodded approvingly to his wardrooms arrayed on the beach and said, "You watch, by February, the Japs will all be out of here, trying to pull their last troops out." He raised a can of Budweiser. "Here's to the Marines ashore and the destroyers at sea." He didn't mention the cruisers, and certainly not the admirals, and everyone at the squadron-wide barbecue noted his omissions with approval.

The commodore had reason to enjoy his beer. His destroyer squadron had operated with distinction through the end of 1942 and into January of 1943. There had not been another pitched battle to equal the two significant fights in which Scott had found himself, probably thanks to the increased U.S. naval forces and the mettle of the destroyers. As Lieutenant James finished the last of his warm beer and turned his attention to a double-stacked cheeseburger fresh off the grill, he thought to himself, Well, I've been shot at and lived through it a bunch of times now. I've seen an admiral get a medal he doesn't deserve and watched ships get blown apart and sink in front of me. But I still haven't really made my mark. Yet. I hope we get another crack at the Japs soon, now, here in these waters, before we drive them off.

But on the 8th of February, a week later, the Tokyo Express closed forever. As Scott's commodore had predicted, the Japanese evacuated the rest of their garrison from Guadalcanal and effectively turned over the islands to the First Marine Division. Scott heard it reported over the radio in the CIC. He and the XO turned and shook hands over the radar repeater between them, the smoky green light doing little to hide the grins on their faces.

"Now what, sir?" asked Scott.

"God only knows," said the XO, "but I hear we may have another senior officer headed out here. The commodores are going to each divide up the ten ships in the destroyer squadrons into divisions, called destroyer divisions, so there may be some senior commanders or captain selects headed our way. The XO over on the *Waller* told me they are going to embark a DesDiv commander name of Burke, Arleigh Burke." Scott looked quizzically at the XO. "I guess that's a Swedish name or something," Wylie said. They agreed that neither of them had ever heard of anyone named

Arleigh before. "Supposedly he's a big brain," the XO offered. "Always reading, reading, reading. First thing he asked to see were the battle reports from the Battle of Tassafaronga or whatever the press call it. You and I are gonna go over there tomorrow and brief him, Scott."

36

A Random Walk

L ieutenant Commander J. C. Wylie and Lieutenant Scott James were brought to the bridge of USS *Waller* promptly after eight bells rang on the destroyer, which was at anchor in the lagoon and serving as flagship for Destroyer Division 43. As he heard the bells ringing throughout the ship, Scott wondered why the hell the Navy used a system where the *only* time the bells corresponded to the actual hour on the clock was at 8 a.m. Every half hour after that, the bridge watch used the ship's announcing system to ring one more gong of the bell, until they hit another eight full strokes; then they started the cycle over again with a single gong. Thus eight bells occurred every four hours, but only once on the actual hour of eight.

Scott shook his head to clear his thoughts just as a Navy commander in his mid-to-late forties with a shock of blond hair and a thoughtful look on his face stepped onto the bridge. The commander of Destroyer Division 43 shook hands with each of the officers from *Fletcher* and wished them good morning. Scott had heard from the mess-cook circuit that Burke had started the war in the naval gun factory back in D.C. on shore duty. But he had given the Navy hell, day after day, until a senior administrator in some admiral's office took pity on him and cut him a set of orders to the South Pacific and destroyer duty. He looked like a serious commander, and from all Scott could gather he was a workhorse, not a show horse. "Some folks think he plugs himself in at night," one of the mess cooks had said. "Or maybe there are actually two of him." An eighteen-hour day was the norm, according to the scuttlebutt. Boy, I pity the poor bastards working for him, Scott thought.

True to his reputation, Burke didn't engage in any warm-up. "So, what's the gouge on this 'Battle of Tassafaronga,' which I can't even pronounce half the time? Looked to me like a good old-fashioned Navy goat rope where we got our asses kicked." The three Naval Academy graduates all smiled briefly at the shared allusion to the Annapolis mascot.

"Sir, can I show you on a chart?" said the XO, moving to the navigation table. The ship's watch was posted down on the quarterdeck since *Waller* was at anchor, so they had the bridge to themselves. Wylie unfurled a nautical chart that was heavily annotated in thick pencil with the XO's notes and observations. He walked Burke through the basics, and Scott could see a hint of impatience on the commander's face. "Right, got all that from the battle reports, J.C., but what I want is the dope on what *really* happened. The reports talk about the destroyers not accomplishing a damn thing and the cruisers—who basically got themselves shot to hell and half or fully sunk—made out to be the big heroes."

Scott and the XO looked at each other and turned back to Burke. The XO plunged in: "Sir, this was a significant defeat for the U.S. Navy, and I bet in a few years it'll go down just behind Pearl Harbor in terms of real disasters. We had a superior, alerted, and technologically more advanced U.S. Navy force, including *five* cruisers, initially get the drop on a bunch of Jap destroyers. But the Japs win big—they end up trading one destroyer for four of our cruisers. In chess terms, they gave up a pawn and took two bishops and two rooks off the table."

Burke again looked impatient. "Yeah, yeah, I already figured that. And I know how to play chess. But that's why you two are here—not to school me on chess but to help me figure out where we failed and what we should do next time. I'll be damned if I'm going to let my destroyers get shot up like those cruisers, if I have anything to say about it."

The XO laid out the case he and Scott had been building for several weeks. "Okay, sir, here's the gouge on what went wrong. First, we have got to get the choke chains off the destroyers, sir. A big reason the Japs succeeded was we weren't allowed to fire our torpedoes until we got an approval of our 'Mother, may I' from the flag. Second, the destroyers shouldn't be tied up in a mandated tactical position in a formation, basically making some admiral on a flagship feel good about his ring of steel. The destroyer skippers— or at most you as the division commander—need to have complete latitude to maneuver their ships. A third problem is internal.

Too many of the ships are still trying to fight the battle from the bridge. That's just not the best way in this modern technological age. We don't take full advantage of our sensors if we don't fuse the data and react from a combat information center. And I bet you don't even have one set up here on the *Waller* yet, sir, but we can help your team create one if you want. It's a perfect setup for a small embarked command staff like yours, supporting the division commander or the commodore. Finally, sir . . ." Wiley paused for a second. "Permission to speak freely, sir?"

Burke, who was absorbing all this and jotting notes to himself on the back of a mo board he'd picked up off the navigation table, looked up and grunted. "We're not plebes back in Bancroft Hall at Annapolis, J.C. Tell me what I need to know."

The XO took a breath. "Admiral Wright failed us, sir. He was slow and hesitant. He doesn't understand the new technology. His battle plan looked like something Dewey might have used in bombarding Manila in the Spanish-American War. And he lost four cruisers in combat, including his flagship, against a significantly weaker force. But they hung a medal on him—a Navy Cross—for no reason I can see. Sorry to be so blunt, sir."

Burke looked a little annoyed. "I don't give a good goddamn about medals, J.C."

Wylie paused a beat. "Neither do I, sir. But a lot of Navy does, and if they keep giving them out for bad performance—well, they are going to get a lot more of it."

Burke nodded and jotted another note to himself. "Appreciate the honesty, and we'll keep the last part between us, of course. It has always seemed to me the three most random things in the

Navy appear to be early promotion, flag selection, and the award-ing of medals. Tends to be a random walk most times. So let's just focus on the tactical items here, and hopefully the leadership problems will sort themselves out."

Listening to the exchange, Scott also couldn't help thinking: Early promotion, like Joe Taussig. Flag selection eventually. And despite what Wylie said, a big medal right now, preferably a Navy Cross. Sounds good to me. Wonder how I get some of that random-walk stuff the commander is talking about. He was snapped out of his career self-assessment by Burke's voice directed to him. "Lieutenant James, what's your first name? Scott, is that right? How long have you been down here in destroyers? Where did you come from? And what do you think of all this?" The questions were delivered in a staccato fashion and in a tone that was neither friendly nor unfriendly. But the blue eyes of the Swedish Ameri-can commander had a challenging expression to them. Looking at them was like staring down into a light-blue lagoon, like the one surrounding the ship, with no bottom he could see. Scott replied with a basic and quick career sketch from *West Virginia* to the Big E, concluding with his time on *Fletcher*. "That's a pretty good ré-sumé for this early in a war, Scott," said Burke thoughtfully. "You married? Kids?" Scott shook his head.

"So, what's your assessment, Mr. James? Got anything to add to what the XO here laid out? He must have brought you along for a reason." No smile touched Burke's face.

Scott paused for a few seconds that seemed like a minute. "Only thing I'd add, sir, is that we aren't using our best technology very well. Like the XO says, we need to fuse the data in the CIC model. But it's more than that. We aren't operating the new radars in the best modes, the sailors aren't really trained on them, our torpedoes are for shit, begging your pardon, sir. They don't work very well or at all, and even our fire control hasn't adapted to the speed and altitude of the Zeros. I could go on, sir, but you get the idea. We need better tactics, a smooth flow of information, leadership, and technology." He paused, wondering if he'd overstepped himself. He flinched when he heard himself mention bad leadership.

Both the XO and the division commander were nodding. "Good summary, Mr. James. I can see why the XO has snapped you up to work on his CIC idea. And we need one here in *Waller*, yesterday." He paused and looked at the horizon through the bridge windows, over the narrow bow of his flagship.

Burke walked out onto the starboard bridge wing and motioned for the XO to join him. Scott figured they were going over some higher-level issues and remained at the navigation table on the port side of the bridge. When the two officers came back into the bridge, the XO had a troubled look on his face, his lips in a tight line. Burke was grinning slightly. "Mr. James, welcome to DesDiv 43. I'm going to pull you up to my staff. We'll start with temporary duty and sort of see where it goes over the next month or so. If things are working out, I'll fix it with the commodore to make it permanent." Burke turned to the XO, who had managed to reconfigure his features into a more benign visage. "Don't worry, J.C., I suspect you're going to get pulled off the *Fletcher* pretty soon yourself. Best thing we can do at this point is start spreading these ideas more widely. I'll square Scott's TDY with your skipper, and he can report tomorrow morning."

He turned to both of them, gave them a tight smile, and walked off the bridge. Neither Scott nor the XO spoke for a minute. Finally, the tight-lipped XO said, "Well, Scott, I guess congratulations are in order. Let's get back to *Fletcher* and break the news to Cap'n Cole. He won't be happy. And neither am I." Neither spoke on the ride back to their ship.

Scott went down to his tiny stateroom and packed his seabag. Jesus, he thought, now what? Working for a Swede who never sleeps on a temporary basis on my fourth ship in just over a year? And worst of all, right back to staff duty. Seems like a pretty random walk, like the commander said, but I gotta say, I don't particularly like the direction this walk is headed. He flung himself onto the narrow bunk in the small cabin and pulled the pillow over his head.

37

Ten Seconds

For Scott, the next six months were a blur of activity, a kind of medieval perpetual motion machine fueled by the twin demands of combat operations and the intensity of Commander Arleigh Burke. It never stopped, beginning with the early-morning staff meeting, hours before breakfast, reporting the whereabouts of every ship in the formation, the fuel and material condition of the guns, and every other important detail. Then he stood a six-hour watch as the flag tactical duty officer, representing Burke in the tiny CIC. He followed that up with a twenty-minute lunch in the wardroom and then long sessions with Burke and a couple of other officers on the staff, inventing new tactics and techniques to prepare for combat. Then another six-hour watch, either just before or after dinner. Scott tried to find a few free hours to draft messages and lay out tactical plans, but often his hope for rest was overtaken by the gongs of general quarters sounding as the division's operational schedule created pockets of furious combat.

He found working for Arleigh Burke in equal measures exhilarating, inspiring, and exhausting. The commander of Destroyer Division 43 really did not seem to need much sleep; Scott would often come bleary-eyed onto watch in the tiny combat information center in the small hours of the morning and find his leader there. Burke had the habit of reading and annotating every message that came to the staff, and he'd also ask to see all record message traffic coming into the flagship and his other destroyers. It was a staggering amount of information, but Burke seemed to process it easily. He had a measured tone with the staff, as if he knew that he would always be catching small details they would miss. Scott had never met anyone who had the ability to soar to the heights of strategic thinking—"Scott, when are we are going to come up with an entirely new way to use these destroyers in night combat when near enemy shores?"—and in the next moment descend into utter minutiae—"Mr. James, what the hell is *Pringle* doing refueling again? We topped her off twelve hours ago." From the sublime to the ridiculous, it seemed to Scott, given the press of the commander's duties. But Scott found himself gradually settling into the rhythm of Arleigh Burke's brutal work schedule, which typically included snatching a few hours of sleep just before dawn, and maybe a forty-five-minute nooner, hitting his rack after a quick lunch.

There were five destroyers in the division, including *Waller*. The others were *Philip*, *Pringle*, *Renshaw*, and *Saufley*. Under Burke's guidance, they came to operate as a single unit, capable of

creating billowing smoke, charging through it, launching torpedoes, then quickly darting out of the line of fire by the heavier
cruisers in the task force. In battles in Kula Gulf and Kolomban-
gara ("Can't pronounce that either," said Burke), the destroyers
drew real blood, with *Waller* providing the coup de grâce via torpedo to a Japanese destroyer disabled by cruiser gunfire. The battles and skirmishes of the task force piled up, as did the body
count of Japanese warships. With two new fighting admirals, Rear
Admirals Pug Ainsworth and Tip Merrill, the task force grew in
number of warships and striking power. Based on intelligence and
the daily news feeds from back in the States, Scott could see that
the ability of the United States to continuously produce ships by the
dozens every few months was something the Japanese were never
going to be able to match. Bill Halsey's campaign plan—simply
pounding the Japanese emplacements up the Solomon Islands
chain—was bearing ripe fruit.

In March of 1943, after what was later called the Battle of
Blackett Strait, Scott and Burke were debriefing the hot action. As
usual, Burke was critical of his own performance. "We were still
too damn slow in taking our shot, Mr. James. That's my fault, but
you need to push me harder. You're the young guy who's supposed
to want to take chances, and my job is to sort of meter your im-
pulses as we get into it. But I'm finding it's me doing the pushing,
but then not actually pulling the trigger. Push me harder at the
right time, will you?"

Scott swallowed and nodded. His own sense was that Burke
had been tactically correct to hold fire to clarify the target ahead
of his ship in the dark tropical night.

Burke went on. "Look, Scott, let me ask you a question. What would you say is the difference between a good officer and a poor one? What's the dividing line?"

Scott thought for a second and launched into a belabored explanation of knowledge, experience, gumption, guts, on and on. He trotted out every cliché he'd ever heard about heroic warriors from the Spartan king Leonidas at the gates of fire of Thermopylae in ancient Greece to Jimmy Doolittle's heroic raid on Tokyo earlier in the war.

Burke let him drone on for several minutes, until he sensed Scott running out of steam and heroes. He pointed a finger at Scott that felt like that of a director of a fire-control radar homing in on a target it was about to destroy. "I'll tell you the difference between a good officer and a poor one, Mr. James. It's about ten seconds. Try and remember that." Burke turned around and walked out of the CIC.

Scott wondered how he could conjure up those ten extra seconds the next time they were in the middle of a knife fight in the shallow coastal waters. Maybe if I could get a little more goddamn sleep, he thought. He pulled the message board to his chest and started going through the stack of after-action reports.

Scott worked endless hours refining Burke's battle plans. He accompanied him through success after success, the sinking Japanese ships raising Burke's profile and career. By the fall of 1943, Burke had been promoted to captain and become commodore of Destroyer Squadron 23, nicknamed the Little Beavers. Burke had taken to the cartoon character that appeared in the Sunday funnies as a sidekick to cowboy Red Ryder after he saw it painted on the torpedo tubes of his flagship by the sailors. He asked them why beavers and was told, "Because we are as busy as beavers, sir." Being Arleigh Burke, he liked that just fine, and soon it was on the sides of all ten of his destroyers.

Scott hated the nickname and especially despised the cartoon of the Indian chief that served as their logo. He kept his views to himself but looked enviously at their sister organization, Destroyer Squadron 21, which had the more noble-sounding name of the Rampant Lions and the motto "Solomons Onward." Both squadrons had nine or ten destroyers, normally divided into two divisions. Commodore Burke generally kept his flag in USS *Charles Ausburne*, named for a sailor who had been awarded the Navy Cross during World War I. Burke kept both the staff and the ship's company figuratively chopping wood—like little beavers— from the minute he broke his commodore's flag in the new Fletcher-class destroyer.

The Battles of Vella Gulf and Vella Lavella in midsummer demonstrated the sound use of destroyers as independent killers, moving and darting like bees in and out of their own cloudy fog. It reminded Scott of his mother's passion for honey, and all the stings he'd received as a little boy taking one more honeycomb for her out of the hives behind their house in the Keys. He still dreamed of bees, but their buzzing in his sleep was often overtaken by the whining pitch of his destroyer's propellers speeding up to attack speed. Scott helped Burke cook up what the commodore called "the doctrine of faith," which wasn't religious in the least. It meant that the swarm of bees represented by the destroyer force would be allowed to operate independently whenever the opportunity arose. They would circle and circle, their buzzing propellers chopping up the turquoise waters, then flash a cloud of fog, and then the stingers would launch. And finally the gear was starting to work right. By the fall, American torpedoes were running hot, straight, and true.

In the fall, Burke's attention turned to the island of Bougainville, which had a significant Japanese garrison and plenty of Imperial Japanese Navy warships in the vicinity. As Scott surveyed the bogey tote board in the CIC, he was happy to see that a brand-new Destroyer Squadron 45 had joined the task force. As he wrote their names on the side of the grease-pencil plot, Scott considered a prominent land feature, Cape Saint George.

The engagement began inauspiciously when Scott reported to the commodore that one of his destroyers, USS *Spence*, had a casualty to its number-four boiler, which was out of commission for the foreseeable future. Burke swore and said, "Well, ask the skipper, what's their top speed?" although he knew damn well it was going to be significantly under the maximum sprint speed of thirty-six to thirty-seven knots.

Scott said, "They say the cap is thirty-one knots, sir. And the captain knows he's going to slow us down. But he is hoping the commodore will let *Spence* come anyway."

Commodore Burke swore again, softly and under his breath, paused, and looked at the charts. "Tell the flag we are stuck at thirty-one knots. Goddamn it."

In a few minutes, Halsey's staff shot back a message with a small lick of black humor: FOR "31-KNOT BURKE" . . . GET ATHWART THE BUKA-RABAUL EVACUATION LINE . . . IF ENEMY CONTACT YOU KNOW

WHAT TO DO . . . For the third time, Burke swore, as if he somehow knew that thirty-one-knot sobriquet, a new and lousy call sign, was going to park atop his head like a painful crown of thorns for the rest of his life. Scott rolled his eyes at the chief staff officer of the squadron, who returned his look with a wink and a shrug, and they began replotting the speed indicators for the group of ships. It was early morning of Thanksgiving Day.

PT boats first detected the Japanese destroyers departing the waters of Torokina and heading back to their major base at Rabaul. Scott was on the long midwatch, from midnight to 6 a.m., monitoring the attempts by the PT boats to score a hit or two on the Japanese without success. It was like listening to a baseball game on the radio, Scott thought to himself. The long radar of the destroyers had yet to pick up the action, but the radios chattered with misses and no real hits. Scott quickly called to the CIC the chief staff officer, who in turn asked the commodore to step in. Burke immediately walked to the radar repeater, spun a couple of dials, and picked up the Japanese destroyers just a bit before 2 a.m. "This is the one big thing we've really got over on the Japs in these nighttime fights," said the commodore in a satisfied voice. "Let's go get 'em, boys." He turned to Scott with an impish look on his face and simply said, "Good call, watch officer. Glad you didn't wait the extra ten seconds." The American destroyers sped up and, using the preordered battle plan, spread their ships and commenced firing torpedoes.

"Explosions reported ahead," sang out one of the phone talkers. "And bridge reports flames on the horizon."

Burke fiddled with the dials again. "One of them just vanished from radar. Scratch one Jap destroyer. Must be one of its play-mates burning away. Good backlighting for us, I'd say."

Minutes later, the radar saw the rest of the Japanese force just over ten thousand yards ahead. "The Japs are hightailing it out of here, but watch for torpedoes inbound from them firing over the shoulder," said the chief staff officer, calling up to the bridge. Soon the familiar ski-slalom movements of the destroyers had all of them staggering to keep their footing. The five-inch guns were chiming in, firing at the backlit Japanese destroyers.

An explosion or two sounded behind them. Burke called out, "Jap torps going off on our wake, I bet. I see three of their tin cans ahead on radar, but they're splitting up. Go after the one to the starboard side, she's the slowest."

By 3 a.m., the lagging Japanese destroyer was being pounded by the entire American destroyer division, and at 3:30 a.m. Scott—now manning the radar—reported, "She's gone sir. That's the third one."

Burke nodded. "Any casualties or hits on our forces, Scott?"

Scott shook his head. "Congratulations, Commodore. That's got to be five or six hundred Japs, maybe more, floating around or dead, and three of their destroyers on the bottom."

Burke nodded briskly and started studying the charts, focusing on the fuel he had in his destroyers and the location of his other destroyer division. He sighed. "Goddamn, I'd like to keep going, but I don't want to get us way out on a string depending on an oiler getting to us tomorrow. Let's head back."

Weeks later, Arleigh Burke was awarded the Navy Cross for what was truly a perfect destroyer action. As Scott and the chief staff officer stood in ranks watching Rear Admiral Merrill pin it on, they exchanged knowing looks. "The boss really deserves that one," said Scott.

"And so do his destroyers," replied the chief staff officer. Scott thought back to his initial meeting with Burke months before. Nothing random about that, no damn random walk, he thought. The chief of staff continued, "And keep it to yourself, Scott, but the squadron is up for a Presidential Unit Citation, first time ever for a destroyer squadron. And you, Mr. James, have been personally nominated by Commodore Burke for a Bronze Star. Seems to me Cape Saint George was pretty good for you. Best ten seconds of your young life, I'd say."

A Ten-Second Decision

For the next few months, Scott was completely submerged in the routine of war. He sent a few letters to Kai, somehow trying via mail to rekindle what they'd once had, yet feeling it was all hollow. He hadn't had a letter from her since the one he'd received months before. He knew that the only realistic way to reconnect with her would be to return to Pearl and do it in person. How he would be able to do so, in a way that would permit him to remain on Commodore Burke's staff, which he believed was his pathway to success, stymied him.

Then a germ of an idea began to take root. At one of the shoreside beer calls, he brought it up casually with the new chief staff officer, a slender Italian American lieutenant commander named Virgil Purgati. "Sir, I've heard that J. C. Wylie, the XO of *Waller*, where I was assigned before the commodore pulled me up to the staff, is heading back to Pearl for temporary duty to set up a CIC school. Heard anything about that?"

Virge nodded slowly. "Yup, J.C. is pissed as hell, but he knows he's the one that really has the gouge and only he can set up a schoolhouse to sort of get the ideas out there. Feel kind of sorry for him, actually." He looked at the lieutenant. "Why are you asking, Scott?"

Scott looked across the lagoon at the large British brewery ship HMS *Menestheus*. "No reason, Chief Staff. Just wondering." He changed the subject to the brewery ship, an object of near hero worship among the American sailors. "How much beer can that thing make, anyway, I wonder?" They both contemplated this important piece of military intelligence. "I've heard she's an old Blue Funnel liner turned into a minelayer. But the Brits, being the Brits, decided a smarter use would be to turn her into a floating brewery." Scott shaded his eyes. "She's an enormous ship. Looks like six thousand tons at least, three times the size of our destroyers."

Virge licked his lips. "Yup, I think actually seventy-five hundred tons, and word is she can made two hundred fifty barrels of ale every day. And they have a full pub on board, I'm told. Named after a mythical king of Athens, supposedly. Boy, the Brits really have some dumb names for ships. Hard to pronounce. But I bet the beer is really, really good." They both paused respectfully and took a sip from their cans of Schlitz, which suddenly didn't taste quite as good. "Let's go get a hot dog." As they walked toward the crowd of officers, Scott thought, Seed planted.

That afternoon, he returned to the *Fletcher* and headed to his stateroom for a nooner, given that the ship was observing holiday routine. Scott had been looking forward to the crew being allowed to relax, sleep in a bit, and generally stand down. He stopped by the wardroom and found, to his immense surprise, a single letter on the sideboard for him—from Captain of Marines Sean Kelley. He looked at it like it might reach out and burn him, like a smoldering coal on the edge of a firepit, not a paper envelope on the buffet next to the table in the wardroom. He took the letter and went to the bridge, which was deserted. He opened it, spread it out on the navigation table, and read.

Dear Scott Bradley James,

Hey classmate, remember the first time we met on induction day? I sure do, clear as the sky here on . . . well, this island they won't let me mention. The sky is pretty easy to see these days, by the way, because we've blown up most of the fucking jungle at this point. Just black sand, twisted stumps of what were palm trees once, and that big tropical sky. Anyway, that first day at Annapolis, when we were standing by the big black gates of the Academy, you were joking around with a couple of other plebes that we should all "abandon hope" as we entered the Academy. And I introduced myself, asked your name, and when you told me, I said, "Aha, the man with three first names, what for, in case you lose one?" Really goddamn witty, right? God, we had a good four years there, well, three and a half anyway. Some good adventures and some bad ones, losing Caroline, winning boxing matches, skating through that fucking scare (don't worry, your secret and mine is safe with me), but somehow, we made it out, and we did it together.

Then Pearl Harbor and being on Battleship Row together for a few months. You and Joe and that snake ranch. That was a hoot. I actually had more fun there in a few months than I did all through our four years at the Academy. That was pretty much perfect, although I think both of us were itching for action. I know you and Kai were really close then, and I guess I respected that and kind of stayed away. But the attack came, and everything turned sideways, and before she or I could figure out what was going on, you were gone, gone, gone. Off on the Big E, and there for the big fight out at Midway Island. You asked me to watch your motorcycle, and Joe said it would be fine to move into the snake ranch with him, and then things happened I need to tell you about. Well here goes, Scott.

Kai and I fell in love. I know it must hurt you to read that, and I bet you are thinking how can you get over here to this side of the slot and punch me right in my fat Irish mug, and I wouldn't blame you. But it happened, and all I can say is that it was the war and everything that was part of it, kind of exploding and on fire like our battleships on the day of the attack. And she and I, well, it was like we went up in the air, and drifted around, and then fell down and landed next to each other.

And that was it, Scott. No one meant to hurt you, least of all me. You were my Naval Academy classmate, and my roommate, and my best friend. At least until this fucking war came along and burned everything in its path. We had some perfect times together, and you'll laugh, but I even learned to make that goddamn pomegranate cocktail Kai likes, me making a cocktail, Lord in Heaven. Hope none of my cousins in Boston find out.

But here is what I've got to tell you, Scott. I am going to ask her to marry me. We've talked about it, maybe not in a totally serious way, but it's serious on my part, I know that. I couldn't stand the idea that you didn't know and that I didn't tell you, and I hate it that I have to do it in a letter. But there it is, and I don't know what else to tell you. It's funny that you're probably just a few miles away across the Slot, but you might as well be stuck on the far side of the sun with me trapped here in the center of a hot, green hell—two places full of fire, but no good way to talk across the divide between us.

The fight here is brutal. Like I said, it's a green hell, what's left of the foliage, and it stinks of cordite, and latrines, and gasoline, and the dead. I'm a company commander now, and the way things are going I may end up a battalion exec if either of my bosses get killed, which seems a better than even chance cause both of them are lead from the front guys. I know you Navy guys are doing what you can to keep the Japs from getting supplies or rein-forcements, but this has turned into a Marine fight, with some help from the Army, especially their Air Corps planes from Henderson Field. It's kind of hard to imagine you guys on those ships, sort of floating around and popping a few guns or torpedoes or whatever at the Japs, then dining by candlelight in the wardroom while the mess attendants polish your shoes. And you probably get time off for swim call in a lagoon and probably drinking beer and eating lobster. In fact, I bet you can hear the guns from across the sound. Hey, we all pick our service branch, right, and I wouldn't be any-where else in the world besides this hellhole at this minute.

That's about all I have to say, Scott. I figure right about now you must hate me, thinking I snaked you and stole Kai away from you. Maybe I did, although that was never my plan, and if that's how you see it, I'm sorry and I can understand why you feel that way. But at least I have come clean about this, and I hope we can meet somewhere down the line and deal with it, man to man in any way you think we need to.

Until then, classmate,

Sean Kelley
Captain of Marines

Scott looked out the destroyer's bridge window toward the west, in the direction of the Marines on Guadalcanal. Jesus, thought Scott, well, that about sums it up. Just what I thought from the moment I saw Kai with her arm around him at the snake ranch. But then why did she tumble back into bed with me and give me the cross? He patted it instinctively in his shirt pocket, where he always kept it, reassuring himself it was still there. He didn't know what else to do with the letter, so he stuffed it in his back pocket and continued down to his cabin. He got into bed and tried to think of something besides Kai, without success.

He dreamed of the day he and Kelley had given their testimony before the honor committee, when Kelley hadn't given a second thought to his lies and Scott had almost blurted out the truth. In the dream, he saw his new chief staff officer, Virge Purgati, beckoning him to a door. On the other side of the door, he knew, would be Beatrice Kailani Wallace. How he knew that, he couldn't say. The last thing he noticed as the dream dissolved was that the door had a golden cross on it.

The next morning, the ship got underway and headed out into the Slot. The Japanese patrols had more or less stopped, although there was always a danger of a stray submarine, or an air raid launched at long range from their bases to the northwest. Scott was in the CIC monitoring routine traffic when Arleigh Burke opened the hatch and entered. "Commodore is in CIC!" Scott called out.

"Scott, can I have a word?" The two went to Burke's tiny embarked-commander cabin and settled into the only two chairs in the room.

"Virge says you heard about J. C. Wylie going back to Pearl to set up a combat information center school. I wanted to let you know that was my idea. I hate to lose him out here from the squadron, but I think there is greater good having him kind of planting lots of seeds back there in Pearl. It is important to teach the fleet the lessons we have learned out here. It isn't going to take him long to get all the pieces in place, and I'm told that even Admiral Nimitz is on board with the basic idea. Although he may require a little more convincing." He paused and took a sip of coffee. "This is important and has got to succeed. And I'm thinking it might make sense to send you back with him. It'll take you out of the fight for a few months, probably six or so, but we're kind of resetting the theater, and there is going to be plenty of war ahead. You got a Bronze Star that tells the world you are good, and you're going to get selected for lieutenant commander early, I would bet. That'll put you in line for a destroyer XO job. In any case, I'd want you back out here with the Little Beavers." Scott stifled a slight inner cringe at the nickname. Burke continued: "I haven't decided for sure, but I wanted to run it by you. What do you think, Mr. James?"

Scott didn't hesitate. "Commodore, I'm more than willing. I loved my time working for XO Wylie and for you here, and if you and he both think I can best contribute back there, for a little while, anyway, I'm ready, willing, and able, sir."

Arleigh Burke nodded. "Well, that didn't even take you ten seconds to decide, Lieutenant James." He smiled slightly. "Virge will cut the orders. TDY. Not to exceed six months. Off you go."

A Letter and a Funeral

J ust before Scott got on the seaplane, a yeoman ran up and handed him a satchel of paperwork that Commodore Burke was sending back to Pearl with Scott and now-Commander J. C. Wylie. Once the mail was on board, the big plane's propellers started to turn. Scott quickly sorted through the files and envelopes. He was surprised to see among them a letter from Joe Taussig to him, dated a few weeks earlier, postmarked "Pearl Harbor Naval Station." That's odd, he thought. Must have just arrived and someone tossed it into the bag. Nice of them. Scott put it in his breast pocket with Kai's cross and went forward in the aircraft to give a stack of paperwork to Wylie. He got a thumbs-up from the former XO and walked back to his assigned seat, staggering a bit as the float plane bounced across the waters of the lagoon and lifted off.

It amused Scott that the passengers were seated according to their seniority. The more senior you were, the closer you were placed to the overhead escape hatch to be used in the event of a crash landing.

He pulled a warm bottle of Coke out of his flight bag, cracked it open with a church key he borrowed from one of the crewmen, and took a long sip. What does Joe want now? he wondered. Probably feels like he finally ought to tell me about Kelley and Kai. Scott sighed and again contemplated the idea of his former roommate and his lover in bed behind his back. That bastard Taussig better have a good explanation for why he didn't tell me sooner, or I'm going to pull that peg leg off of him and smack him with it. The thought brought a smile to his face. He opened the letter.

Dear Scott,

Hope you guys are doing well out there. From everything I can see here in the intel dungeon (and I can see pretty much everything), you've got a lot to be proud of. Many people are talking about "31-Knot Burke," even some dummies who think that he got the name for going at high speed. I envy you the destroyer-man's life, but I'm still beavering away (pun intended, you little beaver) here on the intel side with my boss Joe Rochefort and a few others. I'm no genius like some of them, but I'm learning and getting my licks in against the Japs in my own way, I guess. My dad is back on active duty now, working on the Naval Clemency and Prison Inspection Board. So, if you ever need clemency, I can fix you up. Believe it or not, for once I actually have more gouge than he does, which is killing him.

Things at the snake ranch are not like they once were. With both you and Kelley deployed, I got another intel guy to move in and split the rent, and we try to have a party from time to time, but no one's much in the mood these days. Your beloved Indian Sport Scout is fine, parked just inside the door where you left it. No one's touched it since that last time, and it's not like I'm going to take it out for a spin with just one pin to wrap around it.

I'm guessing by now you know about Kai and Kelley. I should have told you, but Kelley begged me not to when he was shipping out (to you-know-where), because he wanted to convey the news himself. I had to respect that, and I'm assuming he carried out his plan, probably via mail, even though you two must have been within gunshot range of each other for a lot of time. I haven't seen Kai since you left, although I see her dad from time to time and ask about her. He always seems a little non-committal. Maybe he's not happy about her hanging out with a bunch of junior officers. Hopefully she's fine.

But here's why I'm writing, classmate. It's not about Kai and Kelley, but it is about Kelley. As you know, I'm pretty hooked into our class of 1941 circuit, and I've been working hard to let everyone in the class know what's going on with all of us when I can. I put out a kind of newsletter that I send through channels that keeps up the gouge about the best class in USNA history. Hopefully, you've seen an edition or two. Most of it is rah-rah stuff, and lots of our classmates—like you, Scott, and I'm proud of you—are in the thick of it. I also make sure we know about who's been promoted, wounded, and, sadly for some, killed in action, and the circumstances. Obviously, I have a lot of info here and pretty good formal and informal sources.

Scott, I'm about to push out a new edition, and before I do, I wanted to get word to you personally.

Sean Kelley is dead. He was killed a few weeks before the date of this letter, on that island. The bitch of it is that it happened after all the major fighting was over, and the battle essentially won. Sean was a battalion exec, had been nominated for a Navy Cross, and was doing perimeter scouting with some other HQ elements from the battalion. It was something he didn't have to do personally, but you know that big dumb Irishman, never missed a chance to go right to the source of trouble. From the reports, he was out in front, walking the perimeter, even though basically all the Japs had been killed or captured by that point. He was with a couple of other grunts, and the last contact with his patrol was around 2200. From what the battalion could piece together, they were doing a recon of some Jap emplacements and Sean stepped on a mine. Evidently blew him up in the air, and when he landed, both his legs were gone. They got a corpsman to him and did what they could, but Kelley bled out and died. He never knew what hit him, I hope. Goddamn it, this war keeps chewing us up.

I'm sure you were mad as hell with Kelley for having taken liberties with your motorcycle and with Kai. Like I said before, hopefully he got through to you and explained the best he could. It is too much to expect that you forgave him, but I know it was eating him up thinking he had ruined your friendship.

They got his body back here now, and as you know he wasn't that close to his family. The family sent word from Boston to bury him here at Pearl, so the Marines will do the honors sometime in the next few weeks. I think he'll be buried up on the Windward Side, near Kaneohe Bay, at the Marine base cemetery there. There has been a Marine escorting his body every mile of the journey back, which you may know is their tradition. Once he's buried on the Marine base, he'll be guarded by Marines forever as he sleeps, and my bet is he'll be watching over them right back from heaven or wherever he ends up.

Unfortunately, there's a backlog for the funerals, and I'll try to get you a naval message so that on the day, you can raise a toast to him, or curse him one last time if that is your preference. I'm going to call Kai's dad and have him tell her that Kelley is gone. I'll do that as soon as I post this letter, Scott.

I always thought of Sean as kind of indestructible, maybe not the intellectual in the class (not to speak ill of the dead), but someone who was going to be a big part of the class of 1941 for the long run of our careers. A lot of other classmates have been killed so far, Scott, and more will fall, no doubt. But I hope you and he resolved the situation with Kai, and you'll think of him as a classmate, a shipmate, a roommate, and the closest of friends. I know he respected you, and in his way loved you. As far as the situation with Kai, I'd say that it was just another of the endless unexpected casualties of this war. At least that's how I'll think of it.

Lot of rumors about what's next in this war, and the only thing I know for sure is that there will be plenty of firepower rolling north from where you and your commodore are now. You're doing incredible work, Scott, and I hope we can see each other someday soon. Proud to see you earn that Bronze Star, and at least you

didn't have to have something blown off to get a medal—smart
man.

To quote the Marines: Semper Fi, Scott
Joe

Scott felt his eyes tear up. He looked out the small porthole-style window and saw the horizon of the sea touching the edge of the sky. What am I looking at? he asked himself. It occurred to him suddenly: I'm looking at eternity. And that's where Kelley is now, somewhere floating in eternity. Scott didn't often pray, but he folded his hands at his waist in the tight aircraft jump seat and thought, God, I hope they have cold beer in heaven, and hopefully a good, tight company of Marines guarding the Pearly Gates, with Saint Peter in the chain of command. And maybe, just maybe, they need a good captain of Marines up there. I know one who would be perfect. And then he bowed his head and cried, the tears dropping onto the letter still open on his lap, the blue ink running with his salt tears, like the long, rolling, dark-azure waves below.

Kai, he thought. I've got to get to Kai.

Pearl Redux

PEARL HARBOR, OAHU, HAWAII

When the seaplane landed, Scott and the XO went over to CINCPACFLT headquarters and then lugged their seabags over to check in with the duty officer. It was a hot and tropical Sunday morning. Even with the buzz of war, the HQ had a Sunday routine that allowed many of the officers and enlisted personnel a chance to get home—at least briefly. "Let's go to the long-term bachelor officers' quarters and nail down some rooms for a few months," the XO said to Scott. "We can get started with the staff on the CIC school on Monday."

Scott nodded but said, "Sir, I've got a place just outside the base, a rental with a couple of classmates. If it's okay with you, I'll bunk up there."

The XO raised his eyebrows. "A snake ranch, huh. Fine, just meet me here at the quarterdeck at zero seven hundred Monday.

Khakis are fine, no need for that check-in bullshit in whites. Let's split up here."

Scott walked to the officers' club, found a cab with gas, and headed out to see Joe Taussig.

The door to the snake ranch was, as usual, unlocked. Scott let himself in and patted his motorcycle happily, taking a quick look at his gas tank: three quarters full. He called out for Joe but got no reply. He was wheeling the motorcycle down the short driveway and out to the street when his classmate opened the screen door and called out to him, "Sailor returns from the sea. Hey, Scott." Joe was leaning on the doorframe, a crutch under his arm. Scott turned and they hugged awkwardly. Joe said, "I saw in message traffic that you and that commander—Wylie, right?—were coming to town." That explained why Joe didn't seem surprised to see him. "Word is you guys are going to be setting up a combat information center school or something. Welcome back, classmate." Joe was his usual upbeat and well-informed self. "I also hear you're going to have an in call with Admiral Nimitz—that's a big deal. You're on his calendar for Monday."

Scott shrugged and looked down at his motorcycle. Joe continued, "Look, I just want to say to your face I'm sorry I didn't write and let you know about Kai and Kelley. I started to a couple of times, but Kelley kept asking me not to—he wanted to be the one to tell you. Then he shipped out to Guadalcanal, and I just let things lapse. You were both off in the war, in the fire, and it somehow didn't seem right to distract you, Scott, or to step in for Kelley. Maybe I overthought it all, I don't know. But now he's gone, and I guess it doesn't matter as much. But here's the thing—the

Marines are going to bury him up on the Windward Side, at Kaneohe Bay, on Friday. No memorial, no wake, no family. It's at ten a.m. in the Marine cemetery there. I'm going to go, and I'm trying to get the word to other classmates here on Oahu. And I'm going to let Kai know too, Scott, if I can track her down. I haven't seen her in months."

Scott looked off at the low mountains up behind the bungalow. He started to speak a couple of times and paused to swallow. There were low, dark clouds, threatening a tropical thunderstorm. He shook his head to clear his thoughts and turned back to Joe. Almost formally, like he was reading lines from a play, he said evenly, "Thanks, and I understand about Kai and Kelley. And I guess I understand how you could not let me know what was going on, Joe." He paused and they looked levelly at each other for a long beat. Scott continued, "But now that he's dead, it's a different world, or at least in my head. I'm going to see her." He got on his motorcycle and roared off.

When he got to the Naval Magazine, his heart was pounding. He followed his usual custom of stopping a block away and walking his motorcycle up to the door of the chief's quarters. The grass was overgrown, which seemed very out of character. He went to the door and knocked loudly. There was no answer. He walked around the back and looked at the back porch. The lanai furniture was gone. There was no car in the simple carport on the side of the bungalow. The Wallaces had evidently moved.

He walked back around to the front and saw a tall, slim figure in shorts and a Hawaiian shirt, negotiating a crutch as he approached Scott from the other quarters. Scott figured he must be another chief who lived nearby. "Hi, Chief, I'm Lieutenant Scott James from Destroyer Squadron 23—here for a couple of months of TDY over with Pac Fleet headquarters. I stopped by to see the Wallace family. Have they moved out?"

The chief stuck out his hand. "Oh, I know you, Mr. James. You're the boxer from Annapolis with a pretty fast left hand. I'm Chief Finn, John Finn—we met when I was on shore patrol before all this war started, remember? Kai was there and you were the knight in white armor, so to speak, that night. You and some other ensign. I'm actually an ensign now too, a limited duty officer, they commissioned me in forty-two, but you can still call me Chief— it's a higher calling than ensign." He smiled thinly at the former Ensign James. "Chief Wallace and I have talked about you a couple of times, and maybe you should go find him and ask what's going on. I will say this: They left quarters a few months ago, and I think Kai and her mom went to the Big Island to be away from here, maybe worried about another Jap raid, although that is pretty far-fetched since Midway. Chief Wallace is over in the bachelor quarters at Makalapa, but he's still working at headquarters."

The gaunt figure paused and adjusted his crutch, looking down at his feet, as if to balance himself. Scott followed his gaze and looked at the chief's legs. He could see Chief Finn had been wounded pretty severely. "Yeah," said the chief, anticipating the question, "I got shot up during the attack, bunch of shrapnel, and too many operations to count, but I'm mending up pretty nicely now. Should get back in the fight soon. From what I heard from Chief Wallace, you've been in the middle of it down south. God bless you, we need to kick those Jap asses."

Scott nodded, not sure what else to say. They chatted a few more moments about the Guadalcanal campaign and what was likely to follow. As the conversation wound down, Finn gestured at Scott's shoulders. "I hear you're a fleet lieutenant now, Mr. James. And whatever you're doing over at HQ, I hope you finish it up quick and get back to destroyers. We've got to keep the momentum going. There's another year or two at least in this war, and I know you're like me, you want to be in it."

Scott nodded again. "Well, I'm going to be in the HQ on Monday, and I'll try to run down Chief Wallace." There didn't seem to be anything else to say. He started his motorcycle, shook hands with Finn while straddling it, and headed home. Damn it, he thought, she's not even on the island. I've got to figure out how to find her.

By the time he got back to the snake ranch, Joe Taussig was gone, presumably to the dungeon to stand a watch. Scott pulled a beer from the reefer and popped the top with an opener molded in the shape of a hula dancer. It reminded him of Kai and her swishy skirts working the photo racket down on Hotel Street before the war. It seemed a long time ago and made him smile. It was the first cold beer he'd had in nine months, and it tasted pretty damn good. That made him smile too. Before he could finish the second one, he was asleep.

41

The Serene Admiral

On Monday morning, Scott met with Commander Wylie at the CINCPACFLT quarterdeck. They were ushered up to the flag spaces and parked in a waiting room. It had a plush new navy-blue carpet. Scott realized he hadn't seen a piece of carpet in over a year. He was staring out the window and down at the windy basin, which was thick with destroyers. He started to count all the new Fletcher-class destroyers but lost the tally around thirty-five. Scott kept walking around the suite, looking out different windows, sitting for a moment and standing back up, until J.C. grew irritated. "Sit down and relax, Scott," he growled. "You're making me nervous, and I never get nervous." Scott sat down and picked up *The Honolulu Advertiser*. He noticed an article in the newspaper about the University of Hawaii and wondered if Kai was keeping up with her studies. Knowing her, she was probably way ahead of anyone else in her program. It put a smile on his face. Wylie kept his head down and went over his notes in preparation for the meeting with Admiral Nimitz.

In less than half an hour, they were summoned into the admiral's office and found Nimitz just breaking up a briefing with his various senior staffers. Nimitz came over and shook hands with both Scott and Wylie. Joined by the assistant chief of staff for training, he sat with them at the big teak conference table. "So, J.C., the team has been singing the praises of what you and Arleigh Burke are doing down there. I'm hearing the cruiser-destroyer flags want to make these—what do you call them, combat information rooms?—a standard on all the small boys."

"Yes, sir," said Wylie, "that's the idea. Make a combat information center the standard way to organize a ship for combat and fight the ship from down below the bridge. It is less vulnerable to incoming fire, allows the operators down there to fuse together all the data—radar, sonar, fire control, lookouts, radio reports, all of it—and plot it in one place. Then the commodore or the captain of the ship can make all the decisions."

Nimitz's eyes narrowed. It was clear he was not completely sold. "But who's up on the bridge and driving the ship or the formation?" he asked.

Wylie said smoothly, "I know this is an unconventional way of thinking, sir, but it would actually be the second-in-command. On my ship, for example, we started with the CO up on the bridge and me as XO down in combat. But the more we worked on this, the more it made sense to put the real commander of the ship down belowdecks. That's where all the key decisions are going to be made, and more importantly it's where all the information—the gouge—is going to come together."

Nimitz smiled at the Annapolis slang and nodded. "Well, you and the destroyers are certainly getting some good results down south. I'm real proud of what you've been up to down there working for Bill Halsey." He looked at Scott and asked, "What ship are you on, lieutenant?"

Scott looked directly into the admiral's cool blue eyes. "Sir, I was on the *Fletcher* with Commander Wylie, which is where I got involved in the CIC concept. But then Commodore Burke pulled me over to the destroyer division, then up to the overall destroyer squadron, setting up CICs as we went. We've been on a bunch of the new Fletchers, sir." Nimitz nodded again, seeming to place Scott in a good category.

Wylie and Scott proceeded to brief Nimitz more fully on how well the CIC concept was working in the South Pacific. They gave him data on how the ships so equipped were outperforming those without it. After hearing them out, Nimitz looked out the window over the harbor, seeing the dozens of new Fletcher destroyers. "I'm not a destroyer officer, but they may be one of the real keys to all this before the war is over. And Arleigh Burke is the best we have. So I may not like it personally as much as the idea of being back on the bridge of a ship as a CO and driving the fight from up there, but I understand the reasoning of what you two are suggesting. Let's do it."

The admiral turned to his assistant chief of staff, a senior-looking captain. "So the idea is to set up a sort of schoolhouse here in Pearl, Tom? And run all the wardrooms through it when they show up before we push them forward for combat?" The captain nodded in assent. "Fine," Nimitz said. "Do it. What do you need from me?" The captain gave Nimitz a rundown of the resources—a building, a lot of training equipment, a team of instructors, a captain to run it. Nimitz was nodding vigorously, but Scott could see his mind already turning to the next meeting.

The captain sensed it too. "We'll get right to work on this, sir. I'll back brief the chief of staff on the way out. We'll keep the commander and the lieutenant here for a few months to make sure we're doing it in a way that will have the most impact in combat."

Nimitz stood and grinned broadly. "Sounds about right, Tom. And ask the chief of staff to add the CIC school to his list of key projects on his tracking list. That way I'll get updated as this project goes along." He turned to Wylie and Scott. "And thank you for the briefing, gentlemen. Good luck and let us know what you need."

Outside the door, the captain smiled. "Well, that went perfectly. Come by my office tomorrow at zero eight hundred, before my daily staff meeting, and I'll get you connected with the folks I've got working on this. We've already got a building set aside, over near the flight line, and I've got a message queued up to send to the Bureau of Navigation to assign the first group of instructors. We'll pull them off the front line destroyers, but we'll spread the pain through the various destroyer squadrons, so it doesn't drag any one unit down too much to lose their hotshot tacticians." He looked shrewdly at the two officers. "I suppose it is asking too much for both of you to take two-year orders to set up the schoolhouse?" Both Wylie and Scott physically flinched. Before Wylie could start in, the captain chuckled and said, "Don't worry, Arleigh is a classmate of mine, and he made me promise we'd get both of you back to destroyers within three months. I pushed him for six, and that's what your TDY orders read, but the sooner you get this set up, the sooner I'll get you back with your commodore. And by the way, J.C., we're going to get you to a command ride— you should have been a commanding officer long ago. And Mr. James, when you are done here, our agreement is you will get a pair of gold oak leaves and either an XO shot or back working directly for Commodore Burke. Sound about right?" Both nodded in relief, and they excused themselves after the captain said, "All right, go to it. Clock is starting now."

Scott and Wylie headed over to the officers' club for an early lunch and a strategy session. Wylie wanted to go over a rough draft he'd worked up on the plan of the curriculum, sketch out lesson plans, and discuss drills they would put each of the CIC classes through. He and Scott quickly became absorbed in the work. In the midafternoon, Wylie looked satisfied and pushed the stack of yellow pads at the lieutenant. "Go back to CINCPAC and get someone to type all this up, hopefully by tomorrow morning in time for the meeting back there with the assistant chief of staff and his team. See if they can use a mimeograph and produce a dozen copies so we can hand some of them out right away. I'm going to think through a more detailed list of what we're going to need, and after we get a feel for what the flag staff will be willing to provide, we can go final on all this and get cracking." He got up and stretched. "Get a move on, Scott. Come by the BOQ and collect me tomorrow morning, and we'll go over some final details and head back to the headquarters. The sooner we get this schoolhouse up and running, the sooner you and I can get back to sea. And back to the war."

Scott walked out of the cool, dark officers' club and went around back, where he'd parked his motorcycle. He thought about Nimitz. There was something there, a quality or an attitude that he wanted to understand but that was floating just out of his conscious reach. As he started the motorcycle and headed toward the snake ranch, the word popped into his head: Nimitz was *serene*. Here he was, running the biggest battle fleet ever put to sea, with a thousand decisions hovering just in front of him, subordinates and peers like Douglas MacArthur and Bill Halsey with huge egos, but he just seemed so damn *calm*. Scott's dad had always said to him, "When I was an enlisted man, what I wanted in an officer is someone who can bring order out of chaos. So often, officers start scrambling when they are under pressure, shouting and yelling about this and that, and pretty soon whatever is going wrong is ten times worse. The best officers just know how to calm everyone down and get things moving in an orderly way—even when the bullets are flying." Being around Nimitz had reassured Scott. As he thought more about the tall, gray-haired admiral, who seemed impossibly old, he said to himself, That's the kind of officer I want to be too.

The rest of the week was chaotic but successful. The flag staff seemed very energized and supportive, and soon naval messages were flying to set in motion what would become the first CIC school. Scott spent a lot of time with Wylie refining the plan for the course, which would be somewhere between four and six weeks in length and include plenty of exercises in a couple of tactical simulators they were designing. It was satisfying work, and Scott was deeply absorbed in it.

But always in the back of his mind was Kai and how he could find a way to see her again, to see what—if anything—could be salvaged of their relationship. He had no idea how to get the three or four days he would need to get over to the Big Island of Hawaii, nor how to find her. When he asked about her father in the radio spaces of CINCPAC, he was told that Chief Wallace was on TDY himself, setting up new radar stations and lashing them together on the northern and western sides of Oahu. He'd be back in Pearl in a couple of weeks, according to the communication shack administrators. When Scott asked about the exact whereabouts of the chief's family or any contact information they could share, the yeomen had clammed up and told him he'd have to get that from the chief himself.

42

Taps to Guard the Dead

OAHU, HAWAII

That night at the snake ranch, he saw Joe Taussig again for just the second time since his arrival. After a couple of beers apiece, Joe put on a record, Lena Horne's *Stormy Weather* and they started to have a real conversation. "So, Scott, are you going to come to Kelley's burial? Doubt there are going to be many people there, but the Marines will do a first-class job of it. And they will make sure there are enough folks to make it respectable. I've talked to a couple of classmates who are here on TDY like you or assigned to one of the new ships over at Pearl, and several are going to try to come."

Scott reflexively touched Kai's cross in his shirt pocket. "I don't know, Joe. I've still got a lot of mixed feelings about Kelley at this point." Joe nodded and took another swig of beer, and they both listened to the record for another moment or two.

Scott spoke first, asking Joe if he had managed to contact Kai or her mom. "I tried to get some contact information from the radio gang at CINCPAC, but you know how that works. The chief is off on some goofy TDY up on the northwest coast of Oahu, and no one will give me anything to work with."

Joe looked pensive. "I got a message to the chief just before he headed out on that TDY, or at least I think he got it. But I never heard back. Doesn't she have family on the Big Island?"

Scott nodded. "Yeah, that's what I got out of one of the other chiefs over at the Naval Magazine, where they used to live. He was walking around with a crutch. It's that chief we met before the war started, remember? He was on shore patrol down on Hotel Street when we met Kai and I punched out that snipe."

Joe looked incredulously at Scott. "Finn? You met Chief Finn again? Jesus, was he in uniform? Did you notice anything in particular about his uniform?" The last question was delivered with a slightly sarcastic tone.

Scott finished his beer and reached for another one. "No, he was in civvies, shorts actually. It was Sunday. We had a nice talk for a few minutes. He's actually an ensign now, or so he says. An LDO."

"Yeah, he's an ensign, all right. They commissioned him right after they hung the Medal of Honor around his neck. He's a real hero, Scott. When the attack started on December 7th, he was up at the naval air base on the North Shore, and he organized a bunch of air crew to set up their fifty-cals from the PBYs and started shooting down the Jap Zeros. He's the real deal, classmate. He ended up with a couple of dozen pieces of shrapnel inside him that they are still digging out."

Scott took it all in. He thought about the gaunt figure he had been chattering with about Kai and her family. Here he was drinking beer with a Navy Cross–winning classmate who was missing a leg, discussing a Medal of Honor–wearing former chief petty officer still recovering from multiple wounds. His roommate was dead, with both legs blown off, and his Navy Cross was in the works. All of a sudden, his red-white-and-blue Bronze Star felt a bit lighter on his chest. While he remained proud of it, the conversation was lighting those familiar fires of jealousy and ambition. He knew it wasn't right to feel that way, especially the jealous part. It made him ashamed.

After a moment, he said quietly, "Of course I'll try to be there for Kelley. Can you get us a car? I'll drive us up there together, Joe." He felt tired and sad and empty, and the beer suddenly tasted bitter on the back of his throat. "Guess I'll turn in, classmate. I'll see if Commander Wylie can spare me on Friday." Walking slightly unsteadily down the hallway toward the bedroom, where he'd been entangled so delightfully with Kai on summer and fall nights in 1941, he couldn't help wondering again what she'd been doing in those little bedrooms with another classmate who was far beyond his reach today.

Friday morning was another warm and balmy autumn day in the islands. Joe Taussig had managed to requisition a staff car and enough gas to get them to Kaneohe Bay and back. In honor of their fallen classmate, they both donned their service dress uniforms, the "choker whites" with the high, stiff collars. Joe looked stable on his prosthetic, and the two-and-a-half-stripe shoulder boards of a lieutenant commander gleamed in the morning sun.

He wore a Navy Cross ribbon and a Purple Heart, and his jet-black hair was slicked back. He looked every inch the card-carrying member of the naval aristocracy that he was.

Scott, on the other hand, seemed subdued and diminished. He'd gotten up early and downed two shots of whiskey before Joe had arisen. Then he'd downed a scalding cup of black coffee, trying to erase the smell of alcohol on his breath. Jesus, since when do I have to have Dutch courage to get through a bad day? he thought to himself. He'd pinned his Bronze Star carefully above the left breast pocket of his chokers, alongside the Pacific campaign ribbon. And he had Kai's gold cross in his breast pocket. At least Joe doesn't have either of those, he thought, then caught himself and pushed the thought away. They walked out front and boarded the old sedan, with Scott driving.

As they went up the highway toward Kaneohe Bay, they didn't talk much. Scott was full of reflections on his time on these same roads with Kai, and he could almost feel her arms wrapped around him from behind on his motorcycle, whispering warmly in his ear and pointing out the best little beach bars and places to pull over for the spectacular views. He was so unsettled in his mind about her, but the thought that seemed to strike him with more clarity minute by minute was simple: he had to find her. Scott had begun to see Kai as a kind of guide for him, someone who could help him navigate between the twin poles of his dark ambition and the better angels that he knew were ultimately an equally important part of his heart, or so he hoped.

Without her, he sensed that over time the risk would be of winning his way to a successful career, but one without a moral compass. He wanted desperately to sail true north, a phrase that his father had planted in his mind so long ago in the Florida Keys, but he was afraid he'd turn out hollow and empty, and it would all be meaningless, even with all the success in the world. He didn't know how or why a slender island girl could help him navigate those waters, but his fear was that without her, his voyage was doomed. Kai was the lighthouse that he needed to guide him. But how to find her in the midst of all the fires and darkness of war was beyond him. As he did so often, he patted the cross she had given him in the pocket of his service dress white blouse.

They pulled into the parking lot of the cemetery an hour before the ceremony was scheduled to start. Scott helped Joe out of the car. They stood by the vehicle smoking cigarettes. In the distance they could hear a bugler practicing different calls on his instrument. They heard reveille, followed by general quarters, then a couple of versions of recall, then assembly, then retreat. Scott could hear a couple of different buglers tackling each of the individual calls. There was a pause, and first one, then another and another of the buglers played taps. The notes were haunting and seemed to hang floating in the air, suspended over the distant shoreline. They could hear the surf crashing against the uncaring beach. Scott ground out his cigarette. "It's time, I think, Joe." They walked through the low gate of the cemetery perimeter.

Scott thought of Kelley's letter, and the day they had met at Annapolis, induction day, Scott quoting Dante from his mother's old copy of the *Inferno*, the melancholy power of the simple and foreboding words "Abandon all hope, ye who enter here" above the gates of hell. He thought to himself, What a crowing ass I must have seemed that day. And he realized that Sean Kelley had come over to him and introduced himself, had wanted to lighten that moment and help Scott fit in. And he thought again of his friend, and their long years together at Annapolis, and his death. Again Scott Bradley James found his vision blurred with tears.

He and Joe joined the line of Marine mourners, maybe a dozen or so, all wearing their service dress uniforms as well. Several did not look well, and one of them, like Joe, had lost a limb—in his case a right arm. His sleeve hung down, empty and blowing slightly in the onshore breeze. Scott felt weak in his knees and tried to keep his eyes focused on the waves coming across the beach in the distance. There was also a squad of Marine privates, there to render the final salute with their rifles. A Navy chaplain rounded out the small burial party, and at the top of the hour of 1000, he stepped to the head of the grave and began to intone the words of the Roman Catholic prayers for the dead.

Scott didn't know much about the Catholic faith, and he doubted Sean Kelley had either, but the soaring rhetoric struck him as just right on the edge of the vast Pacific Ocean. Words Scott vaguely understood to be prayers to shorten the soul's time in purgatory and ensure its ultimate ascension to heaven were offered. The chaplain, in a fine baritone, said: "Lord Jesus Christ, by your own three days in the tomb, you hallowed the graves of all who believe in you and so made the grave a sign of hope that promises resurrection even as it claims our mortal bodies. Grant that our brother Sean may sleep here in peace until you awaken him to glory, for you are the resurrection and the life. Then he will see you face-to-face and in your light will see light and know the splendor of God, for you live and reign forever and ever. Amen."

All Scott could think of was Kelley rolling down Main Street in Annapolis as a midshipman, his tall, strong form alight with vitality and energy. He and Scott had spent many a night exploring the taverns of that Navy town. It was so hard for Scott to picture Kelley not being part of the earthly world. But the words "awaken him in glory" also struck him hard, and his breath came raggedly as he contemplated the secrets Kelley had withheld from him, and it all mixed up in his head and his heart, and yet suddenly the service was over.

The chaplain folded his hands in front of him and asked if everyone knew the words to the Navy Hymn, first and fourth verses. Nods from the participants greeted him. In his smooth voice, he led the group of men in the words:

Eternal Father, strong to save,
Whose arm hath bound the restless wave,
Who bidd'st the mighty ocean deep
Its own appointed limits keep,
O hear us when we cry to thee
For those in peril on the sea!
Eternal Father, grant, we pray,
To all Marines, both night and day,
The courage, honor, strength, and skill
Their land to serve, thy law fulfill;
Be thou the shield forevermore
From every peril to the Corps.

No one was openly weeping, but most of the men looked deeply somber, and several wiped their eyes repeatedly, including Scott. Each of them moved to the open grave and, as the casket was lowered, tossed handfuls of Hawaiian black volcanic earth onto the wooden lid. It made a scratchy sound as it hit the top of the casket. Then the seven Marine riflemen stepped in unison and presented arms, then raised them to fire together three times. The military personnel present saluted throughout the volleys, with the one Marine saluting with his left hand, lacking a right. And then came the bugler. Scott hoped the best of the trainees or maybe the teacher had been selected to play taps. His wish for his classmate was granted, because the bugler was first-rate. His rendition was perfect and therefore heartbreaking. Later Scott would say that he could almost see the notes, rising from the shining horn and floating out to sea.

The three-rifle-volley tradition consisted of no less than three and no more than seven rifles firing three volleys together in memory of the fallen. Scott was pleased the Marines had the full seven for Kelley. He remembered that the original history of the tradition came from the Roman era. At the end of the day of battle, when the field of battle was cleared, if the soldier removing the slain soldier knew the name of the soldier, then he would call his name three times into the night as a way to remember his sacrifice. "Kelley, Kelley, Kelley," Scott softly intoned to himself. Crisply, the seven Marine riflemen had pointed their barrels toward the sea, and together, in perfect unison, fired the three volleys. Twenty-one shots were fired, no more, no less.

And then it was over. There was no one from Kelley's family to receive the flag, and so Joe Taussig stepped over to the squad leader and said, "I'll take that, Corporal." Scott stooped to pick up three of the spent cartridges, thinking he'd keep one with the cartridge his dad gave him. He thought Kelley would like that. He had no idea what to do with the other two.

Then he and Joe were walking back to the parking lot. On the way, Scott wordlessly handed one of the three shells to his classmate. Joe took it and put it in his shirt pocket, patting it in place. Scott said softly, "I wonder who I should give the third cartridge to, Joe. Is there anyone from his unit here?"

Joe was looking across the parking lot at a small gray convertible with the top down and two women in the front seat. He nodded slowly. "How about giving it to her, Scott?" He pointed to the car.

Scott stopped and stared. Time seemed to both slow down and speed up. Behind the wheel was Beatrice Kailani Wallace. She was staring at Scott and Joe. She got out of the car and started walking toward them. Scott recognized the stoic form of her mother, still in the front passenger seat, making no move to get out and come over. Kai walked, almost gliding over the rough volcanic soil of the unfinished parking lot, until she stood about ten feet in front of the two Navy officers.

"We missed it, didn't we?" she said. "We were trying so hard to get here, but every little thing is so hard now. Was it a good send-off? He deserved it so much."

Scott tried to speak, swallowed, turned to Joe, and said, "Give us a minute, Joe?" Taussig was already walking toward the convertible, his hat off his head and in his hand, the sunlight reflecting the obsidian black of his hair. Scott took a step or two toward Kai, taking in her dark, beautiful eyes, the uncut heft of her hair, the slim body, the same beautiful girl he had seen again and again in his memories. "I've missed you, Kai" was all he could think to say.

She looked out to sea, the mane of her dark hair waving in the breeze. He noticed she was wearing another cross around her neck, although he couldn't tell if it was soldered like the one in his pocket had been. Her head swung back, and she looked him in the eyes. She still didn't speak, and Scott patted the breast pocket of his white blouse and said, "I have your cross here, right here. You said it would keep me safe and bring me back, and here I am."

She looked out to sea for a moment. "Oh, Scott, I just don't know. I don't know. Everything was so confused when you left, and somehow I turned to Sean, and one thing led to another. I didn't mean for it to ever hurt you, and now he's dead, and we're still here, and I don't know what comes next. I just don't know what comes next."

Scott nodded. "It was a beautiful ceremony for him, Kai. He was surrounded by Marines. There's been a Marine escorting him every moment since he fell—that's their tradition, to guard the dead—and now he'll sleep here forever at Kaneohe Bay, surrounded by Marines. You know 'The Marines' Hymn' says the streets of heaven are guarded by Marines too. He was never close to his family back in Boston, and he hated the cold, always complaining about it—even a Maryland winter at Annapolis was too much for him. From the minute he came here, Hawaii was home for him. And you were part of that, and so was I, Kai.

"At the end of the burial, the Marines fired three volleys over his grave, one, two, three. Seven Marines. All in perfect unison, and then they played taps, and I saw the notes, floating out on the wind, headed out to sea. I saw them and I'll remember them forever. I loved him, Kai, and I hated him for stealing you from me, and somehow, I've got to figure all that out, and I will. But here, this is for you: one of the cartridges from the three-shot volley." He held out the third cartridge, which she took and held in her hand, and she looked out to sea again, as if she was thinking of what to say.

She turned back to Scott and said in a quiet voice: "Thank you. He would like it, I think, that we are here and talking about him." They looked at each other, neither knowing what would come next.

Finally, Kai said, "Come over and say hello to my mom." She nervously added, "And I have something to show you. Something beautiful, something that makes all of this worth it, if anything can." She turned, still holding the cartridge in one small hand, and glided back again, leading Scott toward the convertible, where Joe Taussig was in an animated conversation with Kai's mother.

As Scott approached the car, he saw that Mrs. Wallace was holding something on her lap, a bundle wrapped in a soft white cloth. As Kai got to the driver's-side door, she turned back and said, "Meet my daughter, Scott." At that moment, the bundle shook slightly, and a small pink face appeared and yawned, looking up at the sound of her mother's voice. "Her name is Lani, and she's four months old tomorrow. Her name means 'heaven' in Hawaiian. And she's perfect."

For the first time since coming back to Oahu, Scott saw the

Kai he had loved from the moment he saw her, the smiling face, the light in her eyes. Kai reached for the baby, handing the spent cartridge to her mother. She held the baby close to Scott and said, "We call her Lani because when I hold her, every time I pick her up, I see the stars in heaven. As if they were brand-new and I'd never seen them before. Every time. She is perfect, and she's mine, and now I know, I really know, what love means."

Scott Bradley James, lieutenant, U.S. Navy, reached a hand slowly toward the infant nestled in her mother's arms. He gently touched her forehead, just brushing his hand across her perfect, smooth skin, and she reached up and grasped his finger in her tiny, perfect fist. Back in the cemetery, another burial was in progress, and he heard the three crisp volleys once again. And then the bugler was again playing taps, the notes low and sweet and hanging again on the soft tropical breeze. Scott looked at Kai, holding her baby and smiling at him, and he thought, She looks so calm. She looks so serene.

CODA

Where we came forth, and once more saw the stars.

DANTE ALIGHIERI, *INFERNO*, CANTO 34

OAHU, HAWAII

The next three months were in many ways the best of Scott's life. The CIC schoolhouse project unfolded smoothly, and by February of 1944, the basic outline of the course, most of the lesson plans, and the physical plant were all completed. The first cadre of instructors, most of them coming directly from the South Pacific campaign, were arriving on station. While CINCPAC wasn't quite ready to release Wylie or Scott, they could see their usefulness to the project diminishing as others with even fresher combat experience arrived.

Chief Wallace reclaimed the set of quarters where Scott had first dropped Kai off after the Hotel Street incident. While there was some understandable tension between Lieutenant James and Kai's parents, who seemed well aware of her dalliances with both

Scott and Kelley, the four of them settled into a routine. Scott would come over many evenings for dinner, often bringing a bottle of wine or a six-pack of cold beer from the base liquor store. He and Kai would play with Lani, who was still more interested in sleeping than in entertaining adults, then she would be put back in the bassinet in Kai's room and the four of them would have dinner.

Scott would often walk back to the little bedroom with Kai at bedtime and help put the tiny baby into her sleeping outfit. As he did so, he'd often glance at the bed where he and Kai had made love just before he left for the South Pacific and wonder if Lani had been conceived right there. He'd counted the days a thousand times, and yes, he would think, she *could* be mine. But he knew, or thought he knew, that Kai and Kelley had been together either before or after his abrupt departure, or probably both, and so Lani could as easily be Irish Hawaiian.

The thought depressed him at first, but as time went on, he knew that it didn't matter. He was still here, alive and looking at the miracle of a baby. His mother, Bella, had said once to him that "you are never closer to God than when you hold a baby in your arms." Scott thought wryly, I hope that's right, Mom, and maybe it's especially true if you know for sure it's your own baby. But either way, in his eyes, Lani was truly a tiny slice of the heavens her name carried.

On those evenings, for Scott, the stars over the Hawaiian mountains would shine a bit more brightly. He would also occasionally lapse into thoughts about Caroline, and her baby, who had died with her. Scott hoped that wherever she sailed now, somehow she had a child to comfort her as well.

In late March, Commander J. C. Wylie detached and left to take command of USS *Ault*, a brand-new Fletcher-class destroyer. While he'd briefly held command of USS *Trevor*, an older ship, just before coming to set up the CIC school, his heart and his mind were firmly focused on the newest and best destroyer technologies. He dropped by the CIC school to say goodbye to Scott, wearing a Silver Star that had recently come through channels, reflecting the battles he and Scott had fought together in the far South Pacific. "Well, Scott, I hope something good comes through for you soon in terms of getting back to sea." Scott simply nodded. Then Wylie took a folded message out of his pocket. "But in the meantime, I'm very happy to be the one to hand you this," he said, and thrust the message at Scott.

Scott unfolded it slowly. It was a list of names in alphabetical order. He flipped it over and saw his name circled in pencil. The subject line of the message was "Fiscal Year 1944 Lieutenant Commander Selectees." Scott looked up at Wylie with a slightly disoriented look on his face. "Gosh, I'm deep selected for lieutenant commander." A huge smile spread across his face.

"Yup," Wylie said. "Deep selected and well deserved, Scott. Don't screw it up." With a quick handshake he was gone.

That night over dinner, Scott told the Wallace family he was going to be promoted to lieutenant commander. Former Chief, now Ensign Finn and his wife were over for dinner that night as well, and they were roasting a small pig on the barbecue. John Finn congratulated Scott. "Well, whatever you do, Lieutenant *Commander* James, don't lose sight of your chief's mess. They can save you when you think everything is falling apart in front of you."

Scott nodded in agreement, and Chief Wallace raised a glass of beer and said, "To Lieutenant Commander Scott James. May success follow your flag, sir." The others followed suit with their glasses, and Kai gave Scott's hand a squeeze under the table.

Over the past month, they had become increasingly close, both emotionally and physically, although they had not managed to spend any significant time alone. Kai's hand had a warm and lingering feeling to it. Life felt pretty good that night as he piloted his motorcycle back to the snake ranch after midnight. And his TDY orders from Destroyer Squadron 23 still had at least a few more months to run. Keep your head down, he thought to himself.

But the following evening, after he got back from dinner with Kai, Scott found Joe Taussig in the living room of the snake ranch, nursing a scotch. He looked up at Scott. "Let's sit out back and have a nightcap." When they were settled in chairs on the lanai out back, Joe cleared his throat. "I've got some news. Scott, your boss, Commodore Burke, just got a set of unexpected orders. The scuttlebutt had been that he'd be going stateside for a month, then bringing a brand-new squadron of destroyers from the East Coast building yards. But the Navy Board and Admiral King have cooked up the idea that aviator admirals need a black-shoe chief of staff, and Thirty-One-Knot Burke is getting pulled out of destroyers and headed to be the chief of staff for a two-star aviator, Rear Admiral Marc Mitscher, commander, Carrier Division 3. They're embarked in a brand-new carrier, USS *Lexington* down south. And I just saw the 'Personal For' messages exchanged between the current chief of staff, a Captain Truman Hedding, who's an aviator, and Commodore Burke. Arleigh is mad as hell, says he doesn't know a damn thing about carriers and can't figure out, of all the Navy captains in the Pacific Fleet, why they have to choose him." He took a sip of whiskey.

Joe paused for another moment and drained his drink. "But Burke closes by saying if he's going to do the job, he wants to take two officers along with him from DesRon 23. He wants *his* chief of staff, Commander Virgil Purgati. And he wants Lieutenant Commander (select) Scott Bradley James, currently on TDY to CINCPAC. Looks like you're headed back to the carrier Navy, classmate. Congratulations, I guess."

Scott looked up at the mountain range behind the bungalow and saw that the moon and all the stars were obscured by thick, low clouds, as dark and black as the surface of the sea on a still and unlit night. A growl of thunder punctuated the moment, and the silence that followed grew and grew, until a single bolt of lightning crackled to earth, far off in the dark night sky. Kai, he thought. Kai and Lani. At first, all Scott could think of was that he'd finally found himself happy, had sailed through the rough seas of burying Kelley, returning to Kai, and coming to know the tiny infant daughter he hoped was his own. But he also felt in that first flash of knowledge of his new orders that familiar surge of ambition, the realization that he'd be back in the center of the inferno, where promotion and medals could be won at sea on the flag bridge of a carrier headed into a distant war at sea. It felt good.

Joe Taussig swirled the whiskey in his glass, swallowed the final taste, and wordlessly patted Scott's shoulder. He walked into the bungalow and turned down the hallway to his room at the back.

Lieutenant Commander Scott Bradley James sat on the back

porch for a long time, slowly finishing the bourbon in his glass, watching the thunderstorm crashing on the side of the distant mountain. He'd tell Kai tomorrow that he was headed back to sea, back to the restless waves of the vast, uncaring Pacific Ocean, back to a war that seemed unending.

ACKNOWLEDGMENTS

There are so many people to thank for helping me safely navigate through *The Restless Wave*. I was inspired by writers of the sea—not only those to whom I dedicate the book at the outset but also to so many others who chronicled perilous voyages over millennia. You can see some of the books that helped illuminate my path in the Further Reading section. And, of course, I owe thanks to the members of "The Greatest Generation," whose heroism saved the world and is illustrated in this and in so many other books of nonfiction and fiction—and are at the very heart of this story.

I also owe my deepest thanks to my longtime publisher, editor, and friend, Scott Moyers, who initially suggested and then quickly endorsed my notion of writing a series of books that would follow the exploits of a young man who joins the Navy at the eve of the Second World War and follows him through triumph and tragedy in the Pacific theater through that inferno—and beyond. Scott's guidance has been essential, acting as the Virgil of this story—and I named the hero of this book, and those to come, "Scott" in his honor. In addition to Scott, the crew at Penguin Press, including Liz Calamari, Mia Council, and Helen Rouner, have been wonderful shipmates all.

Another essential sailor helping me navigate the shoals of publishing has been my friend and literary agent, Andrew Wylie. He has kept me from running aground on countless occasions over the many books of mine he has guided into the port of publication. My fearless executive officer, Paulette Folkins, made sure the ships sailed on time.

Kudos as well to retired Rear Admiral Sam Cox, who is the director of naval history at the Naval History and Heritage Command. Sam and his fine crew swiftly and ably answered my questions as I tried to mine the priceless nuggets of history and sea lore. The history of our naval service is surely safe in their diligent custody, and they helped convey authenticity to my recounting of events in a bygone era.

Many thanks to my good friend retired Admiral Harry Harris, whose eagle eye and deep knowledge of Naval Academy history and other subjects in the book greatly helped improve its accuracy.

So many fellow naval officers shaped this narrative, and at the top of the list is my friend and shipmate of well over thirty years, Captain Bill Harlow, USN, Ret., who was central to keeping this project on course. He is the truest of professionals. Other fellow officers are too numerous to name, but certainly my classmates in the proud and unique Bicentennial Class of 1976 have been much on my mind as I've told this mid-twentieth-century story.

My mother and father lived these years, my father as a U.S. Marine and my mother on the home front. My mother's vivid recollections of the Second World War at home were deeply helpful. She is the sharpest observer and writer in the family.

And finally, I must thank, as always, my lovely wife, Laura, and our daughters, Christina and Julia, who sailed with me through so much of the long Navy career that shaped this story. I love you more than I can ever properly express.

AUTHOR'S NOTE

*T*he *Restless Wave* is very much a work of fiction. The prin-
cipal characters, Scott Bradley James and Kailani Wallace, are figments of my imagination. I set out to write
this book as an examination of the voyage of character of talented
but flawed individuals at a critical time in the history of the
United States. Though I was born in another era, my own voyage
of discovery both at the U.S. Naval Academy and during a long
career at sea helped plot the course of those featured in the novel.

But while Scott and Kai were invented out of whole cloth,
many of the other characters and incidents in the book are based
in reality. Though for the most part I invent dialogue and interac-
tion among the players in this book, some of the most incredible
stories and characters contained in it are real. For example, Joe
Taussig Jr. was indeed a member of the USNA class of 1941. His
father, then a Navy rear admiral, was reprimanded and forced to
retire in September 1941, in part because he predicted that war
with Japan was inevitable. Joe Jr.'s first real-world assignment

(just as in the book) was to USS *Nevada*, where on December 7, 1941, he was severely wounded, losing a leg but heroically fighting on and earning a Navy Cross. The scene in the book of Taussig describing the events of December 7 to Scott James is based on an article Taussig wrote for the U.S. Naval Institute's *Proceedings*. Joe remained in uniform until retiring in 1954 and was the youngest captain in the Navy at one time. He continued his service to the Navy and the nation as a civilian for many years. I was privileged to meet him through my long association with the U.S. Naval Institute, and I continue to be friends with his son.

Petty Officer Dorie Miller, whom Scott meets aboard USS *West Virginia*, was another real-life hero. Miller was serving aboard that ship on December 7 and manned an antiaircraft gun and likely shot down several Japanese aircraft despite never having been formally trained on that weapon. He came to the aid of his gravely wounded captain during the attack. He too was awarded a Navy Cross. Tragically Miller later died when the escort carrier USS *Liscome Bay* was sunk by Japanese torpedoes. The Navy has announced that a Gerald R. Ford–class aircraft carrier that will soon be built will carry his name.

Chief John Finn, who meets Ensigns James and Taussig on their first night out in Honolulu, is also based on a real naval hero. Finn was the first Medal of Honor recipient of World War II, recognized for manning a machine gun for two hours on December 7, displaying, according to Admiral Nimitz, "magnificent courage in the face of certain death." He was grievously wounded, but his death was not certain that day and he lived to be one hundred. His name graces the Arleigh Burke–class destroyer USS *John Finn*

(DDG-113). The ship was commissioned on July 15, 2017, and was lucky enough to have as her sponsor Mrs. Laura Stavridis, my wife.

Many other characters in the book are also based on real naval officers—and many, like Admiral Arleigh Burke, are personal heroes of mine. I met Admiral Burke when I was a young commander headed off to take command of USS *Barry* (DDG-52), the second of the class that bore his name. He spent several hours with me, an incredible gift, talking to me about war in the Pacific. Many of the comments from Burke in this book are paraphrases of things he said to me on those occasions, including the idea of the close combat among destroyers in the night missions off Guadalcanal being a knife fight. Fleet Admiral Nimitz, Fleet Admiral Halsey, Admiral (should have been Fleet Admiral, in my book) Spruance, Rear Admiral J. C. Wylie, and many of the ship captains and Marine commanders are all quite real.

Likewise, many of the incidents in the book—ranging from the attack on December 7 to the Battles of Midway, Guadalcanal, and more—are very accurate as depicted in the novel. While the dialogue among the participants is largely my invention, the military action is almost entirely fact based. I have taken a few factual liberties for the purpose of advancing the story or amusing myself and readers—but very few indeed. For example, I mention a British ship, HMS *Menestheus*, that had been converted into a brewery to supply beer for the troops. Surely, you might think, Stavridis is making that one up. Only slightly. There was such a ship, but it did not become operational until late in the war, so for the purpose of storytelling, I sped up its delivery just a bit.

There is no "Dark Forest Key" in the real-world Florida, my native state, but there is in my mind, and the name was inspired by the opening lines of Dante's *Inferno*, which readers will note is a recurring theme in this novel. The opening acts of the Second World War in the Pacific were indeed an inferno; there is a Beatrice who guides and inspires Dante in the journey he undertakes in his masterpiece; pomegranates play a symbolic role; a Virgil character appears and helps guide Dante; and other echoes of one of the greatest works in literature occur here and there.

Ernest Hemingway and Martha Gellhorn did meet in Key West in the late 1930s. And they did take a brief trip to Asia together in the run-up to the start of World War II, visiting Pearl on both ends of the trip in mid-1941. I wrote those sections of this novel while the writer-in-residence at the Hemingway House in Sun Valley, Idaho, in the summer of 2022. I like to think Papa helped me, and I hope he would like the complicated portrait that emerges of him and his third wife in these pages.

I hope you find the characters, events, and locations, both real and invented, interesting and occasionally inspirational, and that you find the journey instructive. You'll note that *The Restless Wave* ends with World War II very much still in progress. Rest assured, I am hard at work on a subsequent volume to bring to closure that war and to continue to explore the career and personal voyage of Scott Bradley James. It is no easy course that he steers.

Sun Valley, Idaho

July 2022

FOR FURTHER READING

While *The Restless Wave* is a novel, readers interested in the period and subject matter covered might wish to explore some books that helped inform me and inspire my imagination while working on the book:

Alighieri, Dante. *The Divine Comedy.* The ultimate story of failure, struggle, and redemption in three volumes: *Inferno, Purgatorio, Paradiso.*

Bassett, James. *Harm's Way.* A post–Pearl Harbor story of a warship in many of the critical engagements of World War II.

Beach, Edward. *Run Silent, Run Deep* and *Dust on the Sea.* The story of the Navy's diesel submarine force in the Pacific.

Beach, Edward. *Salt and Steel: Reflections of a Submariner.* The life and career of a preeminent naval officer and writer.

Beach, Edward. *The United States Navy: 200 Years.* A fine, concise history.

Bruce, George. *Navy Blue and Gold.* A view of life at Annapolis in the pre–World War II years.

Dull, Paul S. *A Battle History of the Imperial Japanese Navy.* An in-depth look at the foe.

Hara, Tameichi. *Japanese Destroyer Captain.* Pearl Harbor, Guadalcanal, Midway, and the final battles of the war, all seen through the eyes of a destroyer captain on the other side.

Hopwood, R. A. *The Old Way and Other Poems* and *The New Navy and Other Poems.* Collections of poetry that illuminate the U.S. Navy.

Horgan, Paul. *Memories of the Future*. A novel depicting the influence of the U.S. Naval Academy on the ethos of naval officers and their families throughout World War II.

Hornfischer, James. *The Fleet at Flood Tide*. The story of the final two years of the war.

Hornfischer, James. *The Last Stand of the Tin Can Sailors*. The story of the Battle of Leyte Gulf.

Hornfischer, James. *Neptune's Inferno*. The story of the naval battles of Guadalcanal.

Howren, Jamie, and Taylor Baldwin Kiland. *A Walk in the Yard: A Self-Guided Tour of the U.S. Naval Academy*.

Kestrel, James. *Five Decembers*. A murder mystery set in 1941–1945 and focused on World War II as the backdrop to a heinous crime in Hawaii.

Jones, James. *From Here to Eternity*. A depiction of garrison life in the "pineapple Army" on Oahu in the days leading up to Pearl Harbor.

Mason, Theodore. *Battleship Sailor*. A portrait of the men of USS *California* in wartime service in Pearl Harbor.

McComb, Dave. *US Destroyers 1942–1945: Wartime Classes* and *US Destroyers 1934–1945: Pre-war Classes*, illustrated by Paul Wright.

Potter, E. B. *Admiral Arleigh Burke*. The story of the finest destroyer officer and longest-serving chief of naval operations in U.S. history.

Potter, E. B., and Chester Nimitz. *Sea Power*. A global history of war at sea, from the ancient Greeks and Persians to the late twentieth century.

Pigott, John T. *Destroyer Man*. A memoir of destroyer service from 1942 to 1945.

Reef Points, 1997–1998. The USNA handbook for entering midshipmen.

Reynolds, Clark G. *The Fast Carriers*. A focused look at the big decks throughout the war.

Riesenberg, Felix. *The Story of the Naval Academy*. A basic history of Annapolis.

Stafford, Edward. *The Big E: The Story of the USS* Enterprise. A gripping account of the life of the most decorated ship in U.S. Navy history.

Symonds, Craig. *Nimitz at War*. An in-depth portrait of the admiral throughout World War II, with a focus on his war leadership.

Webb, James. *A Sense of Honor*. A beautifully realized story of life at Annapolis in the 1960s.

Wouk, Herman. *The Winds of War* and *War and Remembrance*. An epic pair of novels that follow a Navy captain throughout the lead-up to the Second World War and the conflict itself.